SPEAKING MY MIND

BY

Ronald Reagan

SELECTED SPEECHES

SIMON & SCHUSTER PAPERBACKS
NEW YORK LONDON TORONTO SYDNEY

SIMON & SCHUSTER PAPERBACKS
ROCKEFELLER CENTER
1230 AVENUE OF THE AMERICAS
NEW YORK, NEW YORK 10020

FIRST SIMON & SCHUSTER PAPERBACK EDITION 2004

SIMON & SCHUSTER PAPERBACKS AND COLOPHON ARE
REGISTERED TRADEMARKS OF SIMON & SCHUSTER, INC.

FOR INFORMATION ABOUT SPECIAL DISCOUNTS FOR BULK PURCHASES,
PLEASE CONTACT SIMON & SCHUSTER SPECIAL SALES:
1-800-456-6798 OR BUSINESS@SIMONANDSCHUSTER.COM.

DESIGNED BY EVE METZ

MANUFACTURED IN THE UNITED STATES OF AMERICA

1   3   5   7   9   10   8   6   4   2

THE LIBRARY OF CONGRESS HAS CATALOGED THE HARDCOVER EDITION AS FOLLOWS:
REAGAN, RONALD.
SPEAKING MY MIND: SELECTED SPEECHES / RONALD REAGAN.
P.   CM.
INCLUDES INDEX.
1. UNITED STATES—POLITICS AND GOVERNMENT—1981–1989.   2. CALIFORNIA—
POLITICS AND GOVERNMENT—1951–   I. TITLE.
E838.5.R435 1989   89-035533
973.927'092—DC20   CIP
ISBN 0-671-68857-X
0-7432-7111-4 (PBK)

UNLESS OTHERWISE CREDITED, ALL PHOTOS WERE TAKEN BY WHITE HOUSE
PHOTOGRAPHERS AND APPEAR IN THE BOOK COURTESY OF THE
RONALD REAGAN PRESIDENTIAL LIBRARY.

PHOTOS ON PAGES 15 AND 55 BY JOHN LOENGARD,
LIFE MAGAZINE © TIME, INC.

To the American people

ACKNOWLEDGMENTS

There are so many people who have helped to make this book possible. First and foremost, there is Landon Parvin, whose contribution has been immeasurable. I shall be indebted to him forever.

And I'd also like to thank Kathy Osborne, who is as kind and competent an assistant as anyone could wish, and Misty Church, one of my loyal researchers at the White House, who looked over the manuscript to be sure everything was in order. The people at Simon and Schuster have been a terrific group—Michael Korda, Lydia Buechler, Eve Metz. You would be surprised by all the people it takes to put out a book. And, of course, the highly respected literary agent Mort Janklow brought it all together.

I'd also like to thank all those who had anything to do with my speeches over the years—from the individuals who sent me the moving letters that I loved to put in my speeches to my staff who assisted me in getting the ideas together in the first place. One of the people I was most impressed with at the White House was Nancy Roberts, who worked under great pressure typing my speeches, sometimes still typing last-minute changes as I was heading for the helicopter to take off for the event.

And, most of all, I'd like to express my gratitude to the American people, who listened to what I had to say and responded with support and even affection.

I thank you all.

Contents

CONTENTS

CONTENTS

1984

1985

1986

CONTENTS

1987

1988

CONTENTS

Foreword

I CAN'T HELP BUT IMAGINE someone a couple hundred years from now stumbling upon this very book in a forgotten trunk somewhere. By then, these pages will be dry and crumbly—not to mention me, who will be long gone and buried. But I'd like to think that if a future reader sits down to browse through this selection of speeches, he would come to know me both as a president and as a person. I hope that the reader would also come to learn something about the America that I knew and loved.

This is not a book about policies. I've not felt compelled to include a speech on education, another on agriculture, another on social security, and so forth. I've not included a single one of my State of the Union addresses. My purpose has not been to give a definitive history of the Reagan years.

No, what I've done is this. I've selected a group of speeches that will give anyone who's interested some insights into who I am, where I came from, what I believe, and what I tried to do as a result. I hope this collection also tells a certain story; it does in my mind. I'll leave it up to the reader to interpret that story for himself or herself.

The speeches selected from my White House years are verbatim transcripts with no deletions for misstatements I may have made or for hopes I voiced that never came true. I didn't want to edit the texts because I didn't want to edit history. I'll just take my chances.

Speechmaking has played a major role in my life. Some of my critics over the years have said that I became president because I was an actor who knew how to give a good speech. I suppose that's not too far wrong. Because an actor knows two important things—to be honest in what he's doing and to be in touch with the audience. That's not bad advice for a politician either. My actor's instinct simply told me to speak the truth as I saw it and felt it.

I don't believe my speeches took me as far as they did merely because of my rhetoric or delivery, but because there were certain basic truths in them that the average American citizen recognized. When I first began speaking of political things, I could feel that people were as frustrated about the government as I was. What I said simply made sense to the guy on the street, and it's the guy on the street who elects presidents of the United States.

And that's exactly what happened to me.

The
California
Years

Remarks at the
Kiwanis International Convention

ST. LOUIS, MISSOURI
JUNE 21, 1951

Let me begin by telling you how an actor like myself started giving speeches in the first place. If you didn't sing or dance in the Hollywood of my day, you wound up as an after-dinner speaker. Personal appearances were part of a performer's life. People wanted to see and hear the actors and actresses of the screen in the flesh.

As a board member and later president of the Screen Actors Guild, I found myself out on the "mashed potato" circuit fairly regularly. I made Hollywood the subject of my speeches, trying to correct some of the misimpressions about the gaudy, bawdy Hollywood lifestyle created by gossip columnists and fan magazines among others.

Looking back, I realize that even then I was discussing political issues. I remember speaking about a plan that was introduced in the United States Senate to license actors. Congress would do the licensing and only performers who met certain moral standards would be allowed to act in movies. The outrage of this kind of government intrusion became part of my speeches. I pointed out there were two United States senators in prison at the time and no actors. That always got a laugh.

I would also point out ways in which my colleagues in Hollywood were discriminated against by government in terms of taxes and so forth. This was how I learned government had an adversarial relationship with its own business community. Increasingly after my speeches, I would find individuals waiting to tell me what they were putting up with in their own professions or industries. Gradually the Hollywood part of my speech grew shorter and shorter until eventually it was barely an introduction to a speech in which I exposed government's growing unfairness to the citizenry and called for action to make government once again the servant of "we the people."

Ten years after the bare-boned little speech you're about to read, I was speaking fifty solid minutes on the abuses of government. People often found it odd that an actor would be concerned with such things. I guess they forgot I was also a citizen.

But, I'm getting ahead of myself. Let me first give you my basic Hollywood speech. The one you're about to read was to the Kiwanis International Convention in St. Louis in 1951. Of course, I would ad-lib the latest anecdote I'd heard and personalize the remarks for the audience, but it's from this plain little acorn of a speech that my political speechmaking grew.

I WOULD LIKE TO TALK to you as a travel narrator would talk about a very strange and foreign land. But it is a foreign land which has more actual press coverage than any other locality in the world except the capital in Washington, D.C. Some 450 correspondents cover the daily activities of the motion picture industry in Hollywood, California. Yet this remains the least-discovered place on earth.

Probably more misconceptions and misinformation exist about the people I work with, the people in my industry and my town, than any other spot on earth. Part of this is due to the fact that among these 450 newspaper people that are there doing an honest job of gathering and reporting news we have attracted many camp followers. These are people who do not have the journalistic integrity to go through the task of gathering and reporting news honestly. With only a few hundred newsworthy names to deal with every day and a column to fill, they have chosen the easy path of gossip. They have the mistaken idea that the American people want to hear the worst instead of the best. And when they are hardpressed to fill their columns, they invent what does not happen.

The result is that among you and your communities and out through America there exists an idea that the people of motion pictures are crazy, extravagant, immoral, fickle, and are flitting from one husband or wife to the other, with no regard for each other. There exists also the idea that if we are interested in politics at all, it is because we are Communists.

The statements I have just made are not out of my own mind but are the result of a survey to find out what you people do think about those of us in Hollywood. Consequently, you will be a little surprised to learn that the people of motion pictures are not the troubadours, the strolling players who used to come into your town and live out of a trunk for a week and then pass on. Being a part of the community now, and because the mechanical nature of motion pictures is so difficult, they have to go to work in the morning like everyone else, and they come home in the evening like everyone else. They have lawns to mow and they own their own homes. Seventy percent of them are high-school graduates or better, as against the national average of 28 percent. Seventy-nine percent of the people in my industry are married; 70 percent to their first husband or wife; 70 percent of them have children; 61 percent of them are regular members and attendants at the churches of Hollywood.

They constitute 1 percent of the population of Los Angeles. They contribute annually 12 percent of all the money in Los Angeles that is contributed to charity. Twenty-five percent of the personnel in the motion picture business were in the armed forces in the last war.

We are pretty proud of the fact that our government says that in the ideological struggle that is going on on the screens of the world, it is the American motion picture, not with its message picture, just showing our store windows in the street scenes with the things that Americans can buy, our parking lots, our streets with the automobiles, our shots of American working men driving those automobiles, that is holding back the flood of propaganda from the other side of the Iron Curtain. Last, but not least, we are most proud of the great tribute that was paid to us by the Kremlin in Moscow, when recently it said, "The worst enemy of the people, the worst tool of degenerate capitalism that must be destroyed is the motion picture screen of Hollywood, California." We are very proud of that tribute.

Well, these are just a few of the things about our community that make us rather proud. Some of the things we feel a little badly about. We feel badly that the divorce rate in Hollywood is 29.9 percent. We feel worse that the national average is 40 percent. We wish that the rest of the country could catch up with us.

Because the public has a misconception about us and because there is so much apathy about us, certain enemies of ours—enemies of democracy and our way of life—think they have found a leak in the dike. They have found a way to attack some of our American institutions and our American principles by way of the motion picture industry. What we must all learn is that you can't lose a freedom anyplace without losing freedom everyplace.

If you are going to let one segment of society or one area of the country become maligned without insisting that the truth be known, all other segments and areas are subject to similar fates.

You know that the Communists have tried to invade our industry and that we have fought them to the point where we now have them licked. But there are other more insidious and less obvious inroads being made at our democratic institutions by way of the motion picture industry. For example, no industry has been picked for such discriminatory taxes as have the individuals in the industry of motion pictures, and you don't realize that because the average citizen is too prone to say, "They are all overpaid in Hollywood, so let it go at that," but if they can get away with it there, it is aimed at your pocketbook and you are next.

Another one of the insidious infiltrations and the worst on our American freedom is by way of censorship. There isn't an American who wouldn't stand up and strike back at the imposition of controls on our freedom of press and freedom of speech, and yet here, for the last fifteen years, we have been permitting it in spite of a self-imposed production code by the motion picture industry. We have political censorship in eight states and over two hundred cities in the United States.

Do you realize that we are raising an entire generation of Americans in this way to assume that it is all right for someone to tell them what they can see and hear from a motion picture screen? Isn't it a rather short step from there when they have grown up to tell those same people, "Well, we might go just a little further. It is all right for us to tell you what you can read." And from there you don't have very far to go to telling them what they can say and then what they can think.

I wanted to correct the misconceptions about Hollywood so you could take a word or two of it back to your communities because this is your struggle, not alone ours. The reason I want to say all of this to you and ask you to take it back to your communities is because we feel that we are operating in the best manner of free enterprise, because never once has our industry asked for government aid nor any subsidy of any kind. We still stand today as one of the greatest fields of opportunity. We are in the American way. You can come into our field and the heights are unlimited, based only upon your ability and your talent.

We feel that you people should join us now in the struggle to preserve some of these freedoms, some of these American principles that are being nibbled away through our industry. In short, we would like to invite you to be on our side because we feel that we have been on your side for a very long time.

Televised Nationwide Address
on Behalf of
Senator Barry Goldwater

OCTOBER 27, 1964

What happened after a while was that my speeches were no longer personal-appearance gimmicks. I genuinely had a cause —exposing big government and its intrusive, domineering ways. During this period, I was host for a television show called GE Theater. As part of my arrangement, the company would make me available to local Rotary Clubs, Chambers of Commerce, and other organizations in those towns where GE had plants and offices.

My speeches began getting nationwide attention as these organizations would reprint and distribute my remarks. During this time I was told that I was the most popular speaker in the country after President Kennedy. And after a while I noticed something very interesting. I would go into a city and find out at the other end of town, there'd be a member of the Kennedy cabinet. After a while I realized it was deliberate. I guess I was getting too much attention to suit them.

You should know that I had been a lifelong Democrat until the 1960s. My first vote was cast for Franklin Delano Roosevelt. He campaigned on a platform of reducing federal spending, eliminating useless federal boards and commissions, and returning authority to the states, the communities, and the people, which, he said, had been unjustly seized by the federal government.

The theme of my speeches had been along these lines. But one day I came home from a speaking trip and said to Nancy that it had just dawned on me that I'd been making these speeches on what I thought was wrong with government and then every four years I'd campaign for the people who were doing these things.

So finally I changed parties, and in 1964 I became cochairman of Californians for Barry Goldwater. I went up and down the state with a campaign speech I'd written that wasn't too different in tone and message from my GE presentations. The speech seemed to go over very well.

One night a few weeks before the election I addressed a fundraiser at the Coconut Grove in Los Angeles. When the evening was over, a delegation of high-powered Republicans waited for me. They asked whether I would deliver that same speech on nationwide TV if they raised the money to buy the time. I said yes and suggested that, instead of just having me in a studio alone, they bring in an audience to get a little better feel. They readily agreed.

A few days before the speech, Senator Goldwater himself called me and mentioned canceling the address. His people told him that I talked about social security, and he'd been getting kicked all over the place on the issue. I explained to him that I'd been making the speech all over the state and nobody had ever said anything.

His people apparently wanted to repeat some show of former president Eisenhower and him strolling around fields at Ike's farm outside Gettysburg. I said, "Barry, I can't just turn the time over to you, because it's not mine to give. A private group bought this time."

Well, he said, "I haven't seen the speech or heard it, let me call you back." So he got a copy of the sound track and listened to it. I'm told that when he heard it, he said, "Well, what the hell's wrong with that?"

I was getting a little scared, though, thinking that this was pretty big-league stuff for me to be going nationwide for a candidate for president. I started having second thoughts and thinking, "Holy Toledo, here's a man running for president and his people think something else could be better. Maybe they're right."

The night that the tape of the speech was to air on NBC, Nancy and I went over to another couple's home to watch it. Everyone thought I'd done well, but still you don't always know about these things. The phone rang about midnight. It was a call from Washington, D.C., where it was three A.M. One of Barry's staff called to tell me that the switchboard was still lit up from the calls pledging money to his campaign. I then slept peacefully. The speech raised $8 million and soon changed my entire life.

Here's that speech. Although I didn't put a title on it, it later became known as "A Time for Choosing."

Announcer. The following prerecorded political program is sponsored by TV for Goldwater-Miller on behalf of Barry

Goldwater, Republican candidate for president of the United States. Ladies and gentlemen, we take pride in presenting a thoughtful address by Ronald Reagan. Mr. Reagan . . .

Ronald Reagan. Thank you very much. Thank you, and good evening. The sponsor has been identified, but unlike most television programs, the performer hasn't been provided with a script. As a matter of fact, I have been permitted to choose my own words and discuss my own ideas regarding the choice that we face in the next few weeks.

I have spent most of my life as a Democrat. I recently have seen fit to follow another course. I believe that the issues confronting us cross party lines. Now, one side in this campaign has been telling us that the issues of this election are the maintenance of peace and prosperity. The line has been used "We've never had it so good!"

But I have an uncomfortable feeling that this prosperity isn't something upon which we can base our hopes for the future. No nation in history has ever survived a tax burden that reached a third of its national income. Today thirty-seven cents out of every dollar earned in this country is the tax collector's share, and yet our government continues to spend 17 million dollars a day more than the government takes in. We haven't balanced our budget twenty-eight out of the last thirty-four years. We have raised our debt limit three times in the last twelve months, and now our national debt is one and a half times bigger than all the combined debts of all the nations of the world. We have 15 billion dollars in gold in our treasury— we don't own an ounce. Foreign dollar claims are 27.3 billion dollars, and we have just had announced that the dollar of 1939 will now purchase forty-five cents in its total value.

As for the peace that we would preserve, I wonder who among us would like to approach the wife or mother whose husband or son has died in Vietnam and ask them if they think this is a peace that should be maintained indefinitely. Do they mean peace, or do they mean we just want to be left in peace? There can be no real peace while one American is dying someplace in the world for the rest of us. We are at war with the most dangerous enemy that has ever faced mankind in his long climb from the swamp to the stars, and it has been said if we lose that war, and in so doing lose this way of freedom of ours, history will record with the greatest astonishment that those who had the most to lose did the least to prevent its happening. Well, I think it's time we ask ourselves if we still know the freedoms that were intended for us by the Founding Fathers.

Not too long ago two friends of mine were talking to a Cuban refugee, a businessman who had escaped from Castro, and in the midst of his story one of my friends turned to the other and said, "We don't know how lucky we are." And the Cuban stopped and said, "How lucky you are! I had someplace to escape to." In that sentence he told us the entire story. If we lose freedom here, there is no place to escape to. This is the last stand on earth.

And this idea that government is beholden to the people, that it has no other source of power except the sovereign people, is still the newest and most unique idea in all the long history of man's relation to man. This is the issue of this election. Whether we believe in our capacity for self-government or whether we abandon the American Revolution and confess that a little intellectual elite in a far-distant capital can plan our lives for us better than we can plan them ourselves.

You and I are told increasingly that we have to choose between a left or right, but I would like to suggest that there is no such thing as a left or right. There is only an up or down—up to man's age-old dream—the ultimate in individual freedom consistent with law and order—or down to the ant heap of totalitarianism, and regardless of their sincerity, their humanitarian motives, those who would trade our freedom for security have embarked on this downward course.

In this vote-harvesting time they use terms like the "Great Society," or as we were told a few days ago by the President, we must accept a "greater government activity in the affairs of the people." But they have been a little more explicit in the past and among themselves—and all of the things that I now will quote have appeared in print. These are not Republican accusations. For example, they have voices that say "the cold war will end through our acceptance of a not undemocratic socialism." Another voice says that the profit motive has become outmoded, it must be replaced by the incentives of the welfare state; or our traditional system of individual freedom is incapable of solving the complex problems of the twentieth century.

Senator Fulbright has said at Stanford University that the Constitution is outmoded. He referred to the president as our moral teacher and our leader, and he said he is hobbled in his task by the restrictions in power imposed on him by this antiquated document. He must be freed so that he can do for us what he knows is best.

And Senator Clark of Pennsylvania, another articulate spokesman, defines liberalism as "meeting the material needs of the masses through the full power of centralized government." Well, I for one resent it when a representative of the people refers to you and me—the free men and women of this country—as "the masses." This is a term we haven't applied to ourselves in America. But beyond that, "the full power of centralized government"—this was the very thing the Founding Fathers sought to minimize. They knew that governments don't control *things.* A government can't control the economy without controlling people. And they knew when a government sets out to do that, it must use force and coercion to achieve its purpose. They also knew, those Founding Fathers, that outside of its legitimate functions, government does nothing as well or as economically as the private sector of the economy.

Now, we have no better example of this than the government's involvement in the farm economy over the last thirty years. Since 1955 the cost of this program has nearly doubled. One-fourth of farming in America is responsible for 85 percent of the farm surplus. Three-fourths of farming is out on the free market and has known a 21 percent increase in the per capita consumption of all its produce. You see, that one-fourth of farming is regulated and controlled by the federal government. In the last three years we have spent forty-three dollars in the feed grain program for every dollar bushel of corn we don't grow.

Senator Humphrey last week charged that Barry Goldwater as president would seek to eliminate farmers. He should do his homework a little better, because he will find out that we have had a decline of 5 million in the farm population under these government programs. He will also find that the Democratic administration has sought to get from Congress an extension of the farm program to include that three-fourths that is now free. He will find that they have also asked for the right to imprison farmers who wouldn't keep books as prescribed by the federal government. The secretary of agriculture asked for the right to seize farms through condemnation and resell them to other individuals. And contained in that same program was a provision that would have allowed the federal government to remove 2 million farmers from the soil.

At the same time there has been an increase in the Department of Agriculture employees. There is now one for every thirty farms in the United States, and still they can't tell us how sixty-six shiploads of grain headed for Austria disappeared without a trace, and Billie Sol Estes never left shore!

Every responsible farmer and farm organization has repeatedly asked the government to free the farm economy, but who are farmers to know what is best for them? The wheat farmers voted against a wheat program. The government passed it anyway. Now the price of bread goes up; the price of wheat to the farmers goes down.

Meanwhile, back in the city, under urban renewal the assault on freedom carries on. Private property rights are so diluted that public interest is almost anything that a few government planners decide it should be. In a program that takes from the needy and gives to the greedy, we see such spectacles as in Cleveland, Ohio, a million-and-a-half-dollar building completed only three years ago must be destroyed to make way for what government officials call a "more compatible use of the land." The President tells us he is now going to start building public housing units in the thousands where heretofore we have only built them in the hundreds. But FHA and the Veterans Administration tell us that they have 120,000 housing units they've taken back through mortgage foreclosures.

For three decades we have sought to solve the problems of unemployment through government planning, and the more the plans fail, the more the planners plan. The latest is the Area Redevelopment Agency. They have just declared Rice County, Kansas, a depressed area. Rice County, Kansas, has two hundred oil wells, and the 14,000 people there have over thirty million dollars on deposit in personal savings in their banks. When the government tells you you are depressed, lie down and be depressed!

We have so many people who can't see a fat man standing beside a thin one without coming to the conclusion that the fat man got that way by taking advantage of the thin one! So they are going to solve all the problems of human misery through government and government planning. Well, now if government planning and welfare had the answer, and they've had almost thirty years of it, shouldn't we expect government to read the score to us once in a while? Shouldn't they be telling us about the decline each year in the number of people needing help? . . . the reduction in the need for public housing?

But the reverse is true. Each year the need grows greater, the program grows greater. We were told four years ago that seventeen million people went to bed hungry each night. Well, that was probably true. They were all on a diet! But now we are told that 9.3 million families in this country are poverty-stricken on the basis of earning less than $3,000 a year. Welfare spending is ten times greater than in the dark depths of the Depression. We are spending 45 billion dollars on welfare. Now do a little arithmetic, and you will find that if we divided the 45 billion dollars up equally among those 9 million poor families, we would be able to give each family $4,600 a year, and this added to their present income should eliminate poverty! Direct aid to the poor, however, is running only about $600 per family. It seems that someplace there must be some overhead.

So now we declare "war on poverty," or "you, too, can be a Bobby Baker!" How do they honestly expect us to believe that if we add 1 billion dollars to the 45 billion we are spending . . . one more program to the thirty-odd we have—and remember, this new program doesn't replace any, it just duplicates existing programs . . . do they believe that poverty is suddenly going to disappear by magic? Well, in all fairness I should explain that there is one part of the new program that isn't duplicated. This is the youth feature. We are now going to solve the dropout problem, juvenile delinquency, by reinstituting something like the old CCC camps, and we are going to put our young people in camps, but again we do some arithmetic, and we find that we are going to spend each year just on room and board for each young person that we help $4,700 a year! We can send them to Harvard for $2,700! Don't get me wrong. I'm not suggesting that Harvard is the answer to juvenile delinquency!

But seriously, what are we doing to those we seek to help? Not too long ago, a judge called me here in Los Angeles. He told me of a young woman who had come before him for a divorce. She had six children, was pregnant with her seventh. Under his questioning, she revealed her husband was a laborer earning $250 a month. She wanted a divorce so that she could get an $80 raise. She is eligible for $330 a month in the Aid to Dependent Children Program. She got the idea from two women in her neighborhood who had already done that very thing.

Yet anytime you and I question the schemes of the do-gooders, we are denounced as being against their humanitarian goals. They say we are always "against" things, never "for" anything. Well, the trouble with our liberal friends is not that they are ignorant, but that they know so much that isn't so! We are for a provision that destitution should not follow unemployment by reason of old age, and to that end we have accepted social security as a step toward meeting the problem.

But we are against those entrusted with this program when they practice deception regarding its fiscal shortcomings, when they charge that any criticism of the program means that we want to end payments to those people who depend on them for a livelihood. They have called it insurance to us in a hundred million pieces of literature. But then they appeared before the Supreme Court and they testified that it was a welfare program. They only use the term "insurance" to sell it to the people. And they said social security dues are a tax for the general use of the government, and the government has used that tax. There is no fund, because Robert Byers, the actuarial head, appeared before a congressional committee and admitted that social security as of this moment is $298 billion in the hole! But he said there should be no cause for worry because as long as they have the power to tax, they could always take away from the people whatever they needed to bail them out of trouble! And they are doing just that.

A young man, twenty-one years of age, working at an average salary . . . his social security contribution would, in the open market, buy him an insurance policy that would guarantee $220 a month at age sixty-five. The government promises 127! He could live it up until he is thirty-one and then take out a policy that would pay more than social security. Now, are we so lacking in business sense that we can't put this program on a sound basis so that people who do require those payments will find that they can get them when they are due . . . that the cupboard isn't bare? Barry Goldwater thinks we can.

At the same time, can't we introduce voluntary features that would permit a citizen to do better on his own, to be excused upon presentation of evidence that he had made provisions for the nonearning years? Should we not allow a widow with children to work, and not lose the benefits supposedly paid for by her deceased husband? Shouldn't you and I be allowed to declare who our beneficiaries will be under these programs, which we cannot do? I think we are for telling our senior citizens that no one in this country should be denied medical care because of a lack of funds. But I think we are against forcing all citizens, regardless of need, into a compulsory government program, especially when we have such examples, as announced last week,

31

when France admitted that their medicare program was now bankrupt. They've come to the end of the road.

In addition, was Barry Goldwater so irresponsible when he suggested that our government give up its program of deliberate planned inflation so that when you do get your social security pension, a dollar will buy a dollar's worth, and not forty-five cents' worth?

I think we are for the international organization, where the nations of the world can seek peace. But I think we are against subordinating American interests to an organization that has become so structurally unsound that today you can muster a two-thirds vote on the floor of the General Assembly among nations that represent less than 10 percent of the world's population. I think we are against the hypocrisy of assailing our allies because here and there they cling to a colony, while we engage in a conspiracy of silence and never open our mouths about the millions of people enslaved in Soviet colonies in the satellite nations.

I think we are for aiding our allies by sharing of our material blessings with those nations which share in our fundamental beliefs, but we are against doling out money government to government, creating bureaucracy, if not socialism, all over the world. We set out to help 19 countries. We are helping 107. We spent $146 billion. With that money, we bought a 2-million-dollar yacht for Haile Selassie. We bought dress suits for Greek undertakers, extra wives for Kenya government officials. We bought a thousand TV sets for a place where they have no electricity. In the last six years, fifty-two nations have bought $7 billion of our gold, and all fifty-two are receiving foreign aid from us. No government ever voluntarily reduces itself in size. Government programs, once launched, never disappear. Actually, a government bureau is the nearest thing to eternal life we'll ever see on this earth!

Federal employees number 2.5 million, and federal, state, and local, one out of six of the nation's work force is employed by government. These proliferating bureaus with their thousands of regulations have cost us many of our constitutional safeguards. How many of us realize that today federal agents can invade a man's property without a warrant? They can impose a fine without a formal hearing, let alone a trial by jury, and they can seize and sell his property in auction to enforce the payment of that fine. In Chicot County, Arkansas, James Wier overplanted his rice allotment. The government obtained a $17,000 judgment, and a U.S. marshal sold his 950-acre farm at auction. The government said it was necessary as a warning to others to make the system work! Last February 19th, at the University of Minnesota, Norman Thomas, six times candidate for president on the Socialist Party ticket, said, "If Barry Goldwater became president, he would stop the advance of socialism in the United States." I think that's exactly what he will do!

As a former Democrat, I can tell you Norman Thomas isn't the only man who has drawn this parallel to socialism with the present administration. Back in 1936, Mr. Democrat himself, Al Smith, the great American, came before the American people and charged that the leadership of his party was taking the party of Jefferson, Jackson, and Cleveland down the road under the banners of Marx, Lenin, and Stalin. And he walked away from his party, and he never returned to the day he died, because to this day, the leadership of that party has been taking that party, that honorable party, down the road in the image of the labor socialist party of England. Now it doesn't require expropriation or confiscation of private property or business to impose socialism upon a people. What does it mean whether you hold the deed or the title to your business or property if the government holds the power of life and death over that business or property? Such machinery already exists. The government can find some charge to bring against any concern it chooses to prosecute. Every businessman has his own tale of harassment. Somewhere a perversion has taken place. Our natural, inalienable rights are now considered to be a dispensation from government, and freedom has never been so fragile, so close to slipping from our grasp as it is at this moment. Our Democratic opponents seem unwilling to debate these issues. They want to make you and I think that this is a contest between two men

. . . that we are to choose just between two personalities. Well, what of this man they would destroy . . . and in destroying, they would destroy that which he represents, the ideas that you and I hold dear.

Is he the brash and shallow and trigger-happy man they say he is? Well, I have been privileged to know him "when." I knew him long before he ever dreamed of trying for high office, and I can tell you personally I have never known a man in my life I believe so incapable of doing a dishonest or dishonorable thing.

This is a man who in his own business, before he entered politics, instituted a profit-sharing plan, before unions had ever thought of it. He put in health and medical insurance for all his employees. He took 50 percent of the profits before taxes and set up a retirement plan, and a pension plan for all his employees. He sent monthly checks for life to an employee who was ill and couldn't work. He provided nursing care for the children of mothers who work in the stores. When Mexico was ravaged by the floods from the Rio Grande, he climbed in his airplane and flew medicine and supplies down there.

An ex-GI told me how he met him. It was the week before Christmas during the Korean War, and he was at the Los Angeles airport trying to get a ride home to Arizona, and he said that there were a lot of servicemen there and no seats available on the planes. Then a voice came over the loudspeaker and said, "Any men in uniform wanting a ride to Arizona, go to runway such-and-such," and they went down there, and there was a fellow named Barry Goldwater sitting in his plane. Every day in the weeks before Christmas, all day long, he would load up the plane, fly to Arizona, fly them to their homes, then fly back over to get another load.

During the hectic split-second timing of a campaign, this is a man who took time out to sit beside an old friend who was dying of cancer. His campaign managers were understandably impatient, but he said, "There aren't many left who care what happens to her. I'd like her to know that I care." This is a man who said to his nineteen-year-old son, "There is no foundation like the rock of honesty and fairness, and when you begin to build your life upon that rock, with the cement of the faith in God that you have, then you have a real start!" This is not a man who could carelessly send other people's sons to war. And that is the issue of this campaign that makes all of the other problems I have discussed academic, unless we realize that we are in a war that must be won.

Those who would trade our freedom for the soup kitchen of the welfare state have told us that they have a utopian solution of peace without victory. They call their policy "accommodation." And they say if we only avoid any direct confrontation with the enemy, he will forget his evil ways and learn to love us. All who oppose them are indicted as warmongers. They say we offer simple answers to complex problems. Well, perhaps there is a simple answer . . . not an easy one . . . but a simple one, if you and I have the courage to tell our elected officials that we want our *national* policy based upon what we know in our hearts is morally right.

We cannot buy our security, our freedom from the threat of the bomb by committing an immorality so great as saying to a billion human beings now in slavery behind the Iron Curtain, "Give up your dreams of freedom because to save our own skin, we are willing to make a deal with your slave-masters." Alexander Hamilton said, "A nation which can prefer disgrace to danger is prepared for a master, and deserves one!" Let's set the record straight. There is no argument over the choice between peace and war, but there is only one guaranteed way you can have peace . . . and you can have it in the next second . . . surrender!

Admittedly there is a risk in any course we follow other than this, but every lesson in history tells us that the greater risk lies in appeasement, and this is the specter our well-meaning liberal friends refuse to face . . . that their policy of accommodation is appeasement, and it gives no choice between peace and war, only between fight or surrender. If we continue to accommodate, continue to back and retreat, eventually we have to face the final demand—the ultimatum. And what then? When Nikita Khrushchev has told his people he knows what our answer

35

will be? He has told them that we are retreating under the pressure of the cold war, and someday when the time comes to deliver the ultimatum, our surrender will be voluntary because by that time we will have been weakened from within spiritually, morally, and economically. He believes this because from our side he has heard voices pleading for "peace at any price" or "better Red than dead," or as one commentator put it, he would rather "live on his knees than die on his feet." And therein lies the road to war, because those voices don't speak for the rest of us. You and I know and do not believe that life is so dear and peace so sweet as to be purchased at the price of chains and slavery. If nothing in life is worth dying for, when did this begin—just in the face of this enemy?—or should Moses have told the children of Israel to live in slavery under the pharaohs? Should Christ have refused the cross? Should the patriots at Concord Bridge have thrown down their guns and refused to fire the shot heard round the world? The martyrs of history were not fools, and our honored dead who gave their lives to stop the advance of the Nazis didn't die in vain! Where, then, is the road to peace? Well, it's a simple answer after all.

You and I have the courage to say to our enemies, "There is a price we will not pay." There is a point beyond which they must not advance! This is the meaning in the phrase of Barry Goldwater's "peace through strength!" Winston Churchill said that "the destiny of man is not measured by material computation. When great forces are on the move in the world, we learn we are spirits—not animals." And he said, "There is something going on in time and space, and beyond time and space, which, whether we like it or not, spells duty." You and I have a rendezvous with destiny. We will preserve for our children this, the last best hope of man on earth, or we will sentence them to take the last step into a thousand years of darkness.

We will keep in mind and remember that Barry Goldwater has faith in us. He has faith that you and I have the ability and the dignity and the right to make our own decisions and determine our own destiny.

Thank you.

Eisenhower College Fund-Raiser

WASHINGTON, D.C.
OCTOBER 14, 1969

Little did I know then how my life was going to change. Now, although I had always believed in people participating in elections—after all, I'd been elected president of my union—never for a minute did I want to change my line of work. I hadn't the slightest interest in public office. Indeed, in my mind, it was completely unexciting and unattractive compared to show business.

There was no evidence of any change for the next year after the Goldwater speech, but then one evening as the 1966 gubernatorial race in California began to appear on the horizon, I had callers.

Some of them were the same ones who had financed my speech for Goldwater. They waded right in. They told me the California Republican party was split right down the middle by the previous campaign, and I was the only one who could unite the party and defeat the incumbent governor. They never told me I'd make a good governor; they just told me I could win.

I said that I had no intention of seeking public office. I told them to pick a candidate and I'd work for him as I did for Goldwater, and that was final.

Well, they didn't take it as final. They kept coming back and with reinforcements. Finally, I told them if they would make it possible for me to go up and down the state accepting speaking engagements for six months, I'd come back and tell them if they were right or wrong about me being a candidate. I felt sure that the people would accept me as a campaigner for someone else, but not as a candidate myself. After all, I was "just an actor."

But again the people seemed to respond to the message that I was bringing them. They, too, had the idea I should be a candidate. Pretty soon Nancy and I were having trouble sleeping —what if those people were right?

So I gave in and said I'd be a candidate, although in my heart I really believed I'd be back in show business come election day. The people had a different idea. They elected me governor of California. I began applying the conservative principles I'd simply been talking about to running a state government. This isn't the place to run down how we did this. But one issue does stand out during my years in the statehouse in Sacramento— the turmoil on the campuses.

You know, the odd thing is that when I was campaigning for governor, I went on campuses quite a lot and was well received. I think it was because I was running against the establishment, which was represented by the then governor, Pat Brown. When I became governor, I then became the establishment, and there was a time I would've caused a riot by just stepping onto the campus at Berkeley for example.

Thinking back, I'm amazed how intimidated the educational system was by the student rebellion. Free speech was accorded only to the rowdies who had the bullhorn. I regret to say this attitude still is prevalent on many of our campuses. But to show you how tense the campuses were back in the sixties, while I was governor the chancellor at UCLA once canceled the playing of the national anthem at commencement exercises because it might be provocative. I know, I was there.

The following speech focused on the turmoil on our campuses. I'm quite proud I never lost faith in our young people even though I was burned in effigy so regularly I must have helped gasoline sales. In retrospect, it's clear that my faith in them was not misplaced. They became my strongest supporters as president. And my affection and respect for them grows daily.

Y OU HAVE DONE ME an honor for which I will ever be grateful in allowing me to be here and to share this occasion with you.

In this day when image-making occupies the time and energy of so many, I am quite cognizant of the effort to portray me as an anti-intellectual holding little regard for higher education. It is frustrating, to say the least.

We have been brought together here tonight remembering a man we held in high esteem and for whom we felt a great personal warmth and affection. At the ground-breaking for Eisenhower College, my good friend Bob Hope commented that the school is a monument, "a living monument to a monumental man." Bob said, "The general believed that education was something more than one of freedom's blessings, education was freedom—freedom of the mind to search for and find a better way of life for all mankind."

The general's great and good friend Winston Churchill said, "The destiny of man is not measured by material computation. When great forces are on the move in the world, we learn we are spirits—not animals. There is something going on in time and space, and beyond time and space, which, whether we like it or not, spells duty."

How appropriate to this man we could refer to as President, or as General, but who is enshrined in so many hearts as "Ike."

His was a lifetime devoted to duty. He said, in expressing his pride in the college which he wanted to be "of benefit to the young people of the nation" that "we must, all of us, have a sharper understanding of how we are to exercise the rights of citizenship—and to discharge its duties." He spent his life preserving the American tradition. He was trained in the science of war, but he called it "man's greatest stupidity," and his dream for all of us was a world at peace.

Still, he knew that his craft—his profession—was an absolute necessity in this world, for there is a price on peace and sometimes the price is more than free men can pay.

There is one with us here tonight who knows the weight of duty and knows, too, that the price of immediate peace could be a thousand years of darkness for generations yet unborn.

Parades are held in the name of peace, but some of those who march carry the flag of a nation that has killed almost 40,000 of our young men. We have a right to suspect that at least some of those who arrange the parades are less concerned with peace than with lending comfort and aid to the enemy.

Many of our universities, which should be committed to learning and free inquiry, will close down their classes in what is called a Vietnam Moratorium Day—which, probably, is correctly named, for there will be a moratorium on free discussion. A decision has been reached by the national Vietnam Day committee—but those responsible for the safety and security of this nation and its people, those with access to all the facts and information on the situation, will simply be told by the self-anointed.

And some young Americans living today will die tomorrow as the enemy frames his strategy to add fuel to the demonstrations in our streets.

I know it is something of a cliché to draw a parallel between the rise and fall of Rome and our own republic. Certainly, in academic circles, this is so, and yet the parallel is there in such detail as to be almost eerie.

Dr. Robert Strausz-Hupé recently published a series of articles based on the observations of historians such as Spengler, De Reincourt, Ferrero, and Gibbon. The history of the Roman Empire has been better recorded and documented than almost all of the great civilizations of the past.

We know it started with a kind of pioneer heritage not unlike our own. Then it entered into its two centuries of greatness, reaching its height in the second of those two centuries, going into its decline and collapse in the third. However, the signs of decay were becoming apparent in the latter years of that second century.

We are approaching the end of our second century. It has been pointed out that the days of democracy are numbered once the belly takes command of the head. When the less afflu-ent feel the urge to break a commandment and begin to covet that which their more affluent neighbors possess, they are tempted to use their votes to obtain instant satisfaction. Then equal opportunity at the starting line becomes an extended guarantee of at least a tie at the finish of the race. Under the euphemism "the greatest good for the greatest number," we destroy a system which has accomplished just that and move toward the managed economy which strangles freedom and mortgages generations yet to come.

We've known rioting in our streets. The abuse of drugs and narcotics soars, particularly among our young people. We have campus demonstrations to force the college to divorce itself from participating in the defense of the nation. We no longer walk in the countryside or on our city streets after dark without fear. The jungle seems to be closing in on this little plot we've been trying to civilize for 6,000 years. Half of those who commit crime have not yet reached the age of eighteen, and half of all the crimes are committed in a desperate frenzy to finance addiction to narcotics.

All of us are disturbed at the virus that has infected the campus, and no doubt we could top each other with frightening and unbelievable stories. Hardly a day passes without the mail bringing new evidence of the campus revolt—a leaflet entitled "The Need to Fight the Cops," a pamphlet explaining how to make and throw firebombs.

One day I listened to a tape recording of a so-called student meeting where plans for campus disruption were being dis-cussed. Explicit directions were given on how to start fires, and subsequently there were fifty fires started in the buildings of the campus in one day. Continuing to listen to the tape, we hear a voice say, "If in the process it becomes necessary to kill, you will kill."

One is gripped by an overwhelming sense of unreality—un-reality that it's happening at all, but even more frightening at how close we've come to accepting this as normal. Dr. Spock's babies have grown up—which is probably more than we can say for him. Certainly he served us better when his concern was pabulum and potty training.

Last year, on our California campuses, one million dollars' worth of damage was done by arson and vandalism and there were three murders. Two young people live with mangled hands and sightless eyes. One, a twenty-year-old girl, was picking up the mail delivery in a college administration office when the bomb went off. The other, a nineteen-year-old boy, in the dark hours of the morning was planting a bomb—a symbol of his rage and hatred.

How and when did all this begin? It began the first time someone old enough to know better declared it was no crime to break the law in the name of social protest. It started with those who proclaimed, in the name of academic freedom, that the campus was a sanctuary immune to the laws and rules that govern the rest of us. It began with those who, in the name of change and progress, decided they could scrap all the time-tested wisdom man has accumulated in his climb from the swamp to the stars. Simply call its constricting tradition and morality the dead hand of the past and wipe it out as a discipline no longer binding on us.

St. Thomas Aquinas warned teachers they must never dig a ditch in front of a student that they failed to fill in. To clearly raise doubts and to ever seek and never find is to be in opposition to education and progress. To discuss freely all sides of all questions without values is to ensure the creation of a generation of uninformed and talkative minds. Our obligation is to help our young people find truth and purpose, to find identity and goal.

I've talked of those already in rebellion—club and torch in hand. Admittedly only a few. But there is a ferment involving the great majority of our young men and women. They have complaints and their complaints are legitimate. They want to invest their energy and their idealism in causes they believe in. They refuse to become numbers in a computer in some kind of diploma factory where they lose their identity and are spewed from the assembly line in four years stamped "educated" . . . but no one really knows who they are or where they were during all those four years. These young people want a reordering of the priorities—let "publish or perish" and research come along behind teaching in the order of importance.

Is it possible that all of the ferment and rebellion is in reality a cry for help? All the more poignant because it has gone unheeded?

I stood one day in the giant field house of one of our Midwestern universities. There were about 4,000 townspeople and 10,000 students in the tiers of seats extending around the oval and all the way to the ceiling. The program called for a question-and-answer period, and one question from an adult had to do with the rebellion of youth against all the principles and standards we had known and tried to pass on to them.

I almost answered the question with a question because frankly I wasn't sure I had the answer. But then I suggested that perhaps young people aren't rebelling against our standards— they are rebelling because they don't think we *ourselves* are living by the standards we've tried to teach them. There was a second of silence and then the 10,000 young people came to their feet with a roar I'll never forget.

Have they lost faith in our standards or have they lost faith in us? Do they doubt our willingness to practice what we preach? Where were we when God was expelled from the classroom?

Last year the banks and financial institutions of this country lost $117 million—not to masked bandits, but to petty pilfering by employees. Retail establishments lose $4 billion a year to a kind of self-declared fringe benefit on the part of employees who take home samples.

What about us when that youngster comes home from the practice field telling how he learned to get away with holding illegally on a block? How many times have they seen us look over our shoulder and fudge on the stop sign if no policeman was in sight? As the country pastor said, "The fellow who left the gate open is only slightly more guilty than the one who saw it open and didn't close it."

Is is possible that much of what frightens and disturbs us actually started with us? With a gradual and silent erosion of our own moral code? Are *we* the lost generation?

No government at any level and for any price can afford the police necessary to assure our safety and our freedom unless the overwhelming majority of us are guided by an inner personal code of morality.

On the deck of the tiny *Arabella* off the coast of Massachusetts in 1630, John Winthrop gathered the little band of pilgrims together and spoke of the life they would have in that land they had never seen.

"We shall be as a city upon a hill. The eyes of all the people are upon us, so that if we shall deal falsely with our God in this work we have undertaken and so cause Him to withdraw His present help from us, we shall be made a story and a byword through all the world."

To you who are considering what you can do to support Eisenhower College, I tell you that without such schools, this shining dream of John Winthrop's may well become the taste of ashes in our mouths.

They are an educational whetstone, serving to hone the educational process, helping to improve the public, tax-supported system, keeping it competitive in the drive for excellence. By that very competition they help preserve the public institutions from political interference, guaranteeing a measure of academic freedom they could never attain by themselves.

General Eisenhower commended those who give of their time and their sustenance to bring this college into being and to keep it alive. He knew that institutions such as Eisenhower College are essential to America. They provide leadership out of all proportion to their size. America will be needing them more and more in the days ahead.

You—ladies and gentlemen of the world of commerce and the professions—you can make no greater investment in freedom than your contributions to independent schools and colleges in this country.

Having a captive audience of the makeup of this one, I go even farther. I dare to hope that one day the federal government will grant tax credits—not deductions but tax credits—for at least a portion of the tuition fees paid by parents sending their sons and daughters to such colleges. I even dare to hope that we will explore the possibility of extending federal aid, not through more bureaucracy, but by creating tax credits for contributions to schools and colleges—within a prescribed limit, of course, as to the overall amount.

If we are to win the battle where it is being fought today, in the minds and hearts of our young people, I pray that you will keep alive this dream of a man named Ike—this viable force that will help ensure the preservation of our American culture and our heritage.

Robert Taylor Eulogy

LOS ANGELES, CALIFORNIA
JUNE 11, 1969

Now, you might wonder why I put this eulogy to Robert Taylor in here. It obviously has nothing to do with my being governor or the development of my political thought.

I placed this among the collection because I honestly believe eulogies have significance, and I included many eulogies in this book because I believe they are some of the most important speeches I've ever given. I don't mean because they changed the face of the nation in any way, but because it's a very great responsibility to capture the spirit of an individual and what he or she meant to the world.

You can give comfort. You can give perspective. To be asked to give a eulogy is a great honor because you have the power to sum up a human life. I've always taken this power quite seriously.

I liked Bob Taylor a lot. We were good friends; and since I still think about him now and then, I guess you could say I miss him.

How TO SAY FAREWELL to a friend named Bob. He'd probably say, "Don't make any fuss. I wouldn't want to cause any trouble."

How to speak of Robert Taylor—one of the truly great and most enduring stars in the golden era of Hollywood. What can we say about a boy named—well, a boy from Nebraska with an un-Nebraska-like name of Spangler Arlington Brugh.

Perhaps that's as good a starting point as any. A young man, son of a Nebraska doctor, coming to California—to Pomona —for his last years in college, and from there the story reads like a script from one of those early musicals. And it happens to the last person in the world who would have thought that great fame was in store for him.

There was the college play, the talent scout, and most improbable of all, the coincidence of timing that found him in an MGM casting office on the day that had been picked for the testing of a prospective actress. Who can we get to do the scene with her? What about that kid in the outer office? When the test was over, they didn't hire her, they hired him. And I suppose that would be first-act curtain.

And the second act followed the same pattern—was almost a repeat. A newly signed contract player getting a minor role in a picture. No one remembers who had the principal roles— most have forgotten even the title of the picture. But when it was previewed, everyone wanted to know who was Robert Taylor—a young man with the name that sounded like one the studio would think up and become instead Robert Taylor, a name with a kind of honest Midwest sound.

MGM was a giant and the home of giants. It had the greatest stars in an era when Hollywood was a Mount Olympus peopled with godlike stars—Gable, Tracy, Grant, Montgomery, Colman, Cooper, the Barrymores. And there were goddesses to match—Garbo, Shearer, Crawford, Irene Dunne. Bob Taylor became one of the all-time greats of motion picture stardom. Twenty-four years at that one studio, MGM, alone. Thirty-five years before the public. His face, instantly recognizable in every corner of the world. His name a new one—a household word.

And all of this came to be in one sudden, dazzling burst. To simply appear in public caused a traffic jam. There has never been anything like it before or since—possibly the only thing that can compare to it—Rudolph Valentino, and why not? Because on all of Mount Olympus, he was the most handsome.

Now there were those in our midst who worked very hard to bring him down with the label "pretty boy." And of course, there's that standard Hollywood rule that true talent must never be admitted as playing a part in success if the individual is too handsome or too beautiful.

It's only in the recent years of our friendship that I've been able to understand how painful all of this must have been to him—to a truly modest man—because he was modest to the point of being painfully shy. In all of the years of stardom, he never got quite over being genuinely embarrassed at the furor that his appearance created. He went a long way to avoid putting himself in a position where he could become the center of attention.

And in these later years I have learned . . . and not by any complaints from him—complaining wasn't a part of him . . . but I have learned of something else that must have been hard for him to bear: that idea that just a handsome face was responsible for his success—that he wasn't truly an actor. Because Bob had one intolerance—he had no patience with those who came into the business with the idea that they could shortcut hard work and substitute gimmicks for craftsmanship.

He respected his profession and he was a superb master of it. He took a quiet pride in his work. He was a pro, and the "pretty boy" tag couldn't begin to survive roles like *Magnificent Obsession, Camille, Waterloo Bridge, Johnny Eager, Quo Vadis.*

It takes a rare and unique actor to be believable, as he was believable, in costume epics like *Ivanhoe, Knights of the Round Table,* and also, at the same time, as a fighter in *The Crowd Roars* and the almost psychopathic *Billy the Kid.* Some of his pictures live on as true classics, and generally, the standard is so high that in retrospect it would appear his modesty caused this industry to underrate the caliber of this man who was truly a star among stars.

And yet, none of this is what brought us together here today.

Perhaps each one of us has his own different memory, but I'll bet that somehow they all add up to "nice man." Mervyn Le Roy, who directed so many of his great pictures, speaks of his always showing consideration for everyone who worked with him. Artie Deutsch said he never worked in a company where he wasn't well-loved, well-liked, even beloved, by cast and crew.

His quiet and disciplined manner had a steadying effect on every company he was ever in, and at the same time, throughout this country, there are hundreds of men who remember him because he taught them to fly. He sought combat duty in World War II as a Navy flier, and he wound up teaching others—and I'll bet he taught 'em good. There was no caste system in his love of humanity.

Today I am sure there is sorrow among the rugged men in the Northwest who run the swift water of the Rogue River and who knew him as one of them. There are cowpokes up in a valley in Wyoming who remember him and mourn—mourn a man who rode and hunted with them. And millions and millions of people who only knew him by way of the silver screen, and they remember with gratitude that in the darkened theater he never embarrassed them in front of their children.

I know that some night on the late, late show I'm going to see him resplendent in white tie and tails dining at Delmonico's, and I am sure I'll smile—smile at Robert Spangler Arlington Brugh Taylor, because I'll remember how a fellow named Bob really preferred blue jeans and boots. And I'll see him squinting through the smoke of a barbecue as I have seen him a hundred times.

He loved his home and everything that it meant. Above all, he loved his family and his beautiful Ursula—lovely Manuela, all grown up; little Tessa; Terry, his son, a young man in whom he had such great pride.

(To the family) In a little while the hurt will be gone. Time will do that for you. Then you will find you can bring out your memories. You can look at them—take comfort from their warmth. As the years go by you will be very proud. Not so much of the things that we have talked about here—you are going to be proud of simple things. Things not so stylish in certain circles today, but that just makes them a little more rare and of greater value. Simple things he had, like honor and honesty, responsibility to those he worked for and who worked for him, standing up for what he believed, and yes, even a simple old-fashioned love for his country, and above all, an inner humility.

(To the children) I think, too, that he'd want me to tell you how very much he loved your mother. What happiness she brought him and how wonderful she is. The papers say he was in the hospital seven times; actually he was out of the hospital seven times. He needed the strength that he could only get from being in that home so filled with her presence.

He spoke to me of this just a few days ago. It was uppermost in his mind, and I am sure he meant for me to tell you something that he wanted above all else. Ursula, there is just one last thing that only you can do for him—be happy. This was his last thought to me.

I don't pretend to know God's plan for each one of us, but I have faith in His infinite mercy. Bob had great success in the work he loved, and he returned each day from that work with the knowledge there were those who waited affectionately for the sound of his footsteps.

Syndicated Radio Shows

I've always loved radio. My first job out of college was as a radio sportscaster, and it was one of the happiest times of my life. I had a fun job, a new car, a certain amount of fame and recognition there in the Midwest. I was having a good time. Eventually I got a crack at working in motion pictures, and I left radio, but it always had a certain hold on my heart.

After I left the governorship, I got into radio again—this time doing syndicated commentaries. Writing these pieces was a lot harder than sportscasting. In fact, it was something of a grind turning these things out. But I'll tell you what these commentaries did. They kept my name before the public while I was out of office, and they did something else that was probably more important. The commentaries forced me to have a broader, more national outlook on issues than perhaps I had when I was governor. They forced me to articulate my opinions on a whole range of matters, which I think in turn helped prepare me for my run for the presidency.

The following two commentaries embody beliefs that became central to my political philosophy.

An UNBORN CHILD's property rights are protected by law—its right to life is not. I'll be right back.

Eight years ago when I became governor, I found myself involved almost immediately in a controversy over abortion. It was a subject I'd never given much thought to and one for which I didn't really have an opinion. But now I was governor, and abortion turned out to be something I couldn't walk away from.

A bill had been introduced in the California legislature to make abortion available upon demand. The pro and anti forces were already marshaling their troops, and emotions were running high. Then the author of the bill sent word down that he'd amend his bill to anything I felt I could sign. The ball—to coin a cliché—was in my court. Suddenly I had to have a position on abortion.

I did more studying and soul-searching than on anything that was to face me as governor. I discovered that neither medicine, law, or theology had really found a common ground on the subject. Some believed an unborn child was no more than a growth on the body female and she should be able to remove it as she would her appendix. Others felt a human life existed from the moment the fertilized egg was implanted in the womb. Strangely enough, the same legislature that couldn't agree on abortion had unanimously passed a law making it murder to abuse a pregnant woman so as to cause the death of her unborn child.

Another inconsistency—the unborn have property rights protected by law. A man can will his estate to his wife and children and any children yet to be born of his marriage. Yet the proposed abortion law would deny the unborn the protection of the law in preserving its life.

I went to the lawyers on my staff and posed a hypothetical question. What if a pregnant woman became a widow during her pregnancy and found her husband had left his fortune to her and the unborn child. Under the proposed abortion law, she could take the life of her child and inherit all of her husband's estate. Wouldn't that be murder for financial gain? The only answer I got was that they were glad I wasn't asking the questions on the bar exam.

There is a quite common acceptance in medical circles that the cell—let's call it the egg—once it has been fertilized is on its way as a human being with individual physical traits and personality characteristics already determined.

My answer as to what kind of abortion bill I could sign was one that recognized an abortion is the taking of a human life. In our Judeo-Christian religion we recognize the right to take life in defense of our own. Therefore an abortion is justified when done in self-defense. My belief is that a woman has the right to protect her own life and health against even her own unborn child. I believe also that just as she has the right to defend herself against rape, she should not be made to bear a child resulting from the violation of her person and therefore abortion is an act of self-defense.

I know there will be disagreements with this view, but I can find no evidence whatsoever that a fetus is not a living human being with human rights. This is Ronald Reagan. Thanks for listening.

Anyone who has been plagued by bureaucratic nonsense, forms to fill out, regulations to comply with even though they make little sense, has to be a fan of a mayor in Texas. I'll be right back.

The mayor of Midland, Texas, Ernest Angelo, will see that Midland never suffers the problems of New York City. As a matter of fact, New York City would never have suffered the problems of New York City if it had had a few Ernie Angelos in City Hall these past twenty years.

As a former governor, I can testify as to the ridiculous demands inflicted on state and local government by the paper pushers of the Potomac. And I know any of you listening who are in business or farming can reel off personal horror stories of the hours spent filling out government-required paperwork and bowing to the demands of senseless regulations. Well, give a listen. You'll enjoy the mayor of Midland's revenge.

Mayor Angelo struggled through a bureaucratic jungle of red tape in the U.S. Department of Housing and Urban Development to obtain for his city some federal funds that were due. It took him eight long, frustrating months of paperwork, questionnaires in duplicate, triplicate, and quadruplicate before he broke through into daylight.

Then one day the regional office of HUD (that's bureaucratese for the Housing and Urban Development agency) requested a reserved parking space at the Midland Municipal Airport. Mayor Angelo was delighted to comply with the request—if HUD would do a little complying.

He sent a letter to the Dallas regional office of HUD with copies to the President, Secretary Carla Hills, and a few others in Washington. His letter requested three executed and fourteen confirmed copies of their application. It further said, "Submit the make and model of the proposed vehicle to be parked in the space together with certified assurance that everyone connected with the manufacture, servicing, and operating of same was paid according to wage scale in compliance with requirements of the Davis-Bacon Act.

"Submit a genealogical table for everyone who will operate said vehicle so that we can ascertain that there will be a precisely exact equal percentage of whites, blacks, and other minorities, as well as women and elderly.

"Submit certified assurances that all operators of said vehicle and any filling station personnel that service same will be equipped with steel-toed boots, safety goggles, and crash helmets, and that the vehicle will be equipped with at least safety belts and an air bag in compliance with the Occupational Safety and Health Act.

"Submit environmental impact statements"—well, you get the idea. His letter went on for quite a few additional paragraphs citing all the red-tape requirements (so dear to the hearts of those who toil on the banks of the Potomac) that would have to be complied with before favorable consideration could be given to their request for a parking space.

Then Mayor Angelo added a postscript. He told them they could have their parking space without complying with all the aforementioned red tape.

I hope he made his point because the General Accounting Office in Washington estimates the yearly cost of regulations at $60 billion. The Federal Trade Commission puts it at $80 billion—all waste due to regulatory overkill. Probably the correct figure is nearer the $130 billion the Council of Economic Advisers estimate is prorated out at $2,000 per family.

Maybe we'll talk some more about this tomorrow. This is Ronald Reagan. Thanks for listening.

1981

Inaugural Address

WEST FRONT OF THE U.S. CAPITOL
JANUARY 20, 1981

I know, the last thing you read I was an ex-governor doing radio commentaries, and now I'm about to be sworn in as president of the United States. Well, yes, a lot happened in between, but it really didn't have much to do with any particular speech. The speeches I gave in 1976 when I ran against President Ford for the Republican nomination and the speeches I gave in the 1980 race against President Carter were simply refinements of the basic ideas I'd been talking about sixteen years earlier in the Goldwater speech.

In fact, that's one of my theories about political speechmaking. You have to keep pounding away with your message, year after year, because that's the only way it will sink into the collective consciousness. I'm a big believer in stump speeches— speeches you can give over and over again with slight variations. Because if you have something you believe in deeply, it's worth repeating time and again until you achieve it. You also get better at delivering it.

I do think, however, that my faith in the American people and in what they could do had a special resonance in 1980. The Democratic party's leaders would never admit this, but the simple fact is that they had lost faith in the citizens and the future of our country. They couldn't see this, but the American people did, and they elected me the fortieth president of the United States.

The year 1981 was one of applying the conservative principles that I had so long espoused to national government. The great exercise was almost cut short by Mr. Hinckley's bullet, which got within an inch of my heart. That slowed me down for a couple of months, but in a way it allowed the pressure for change to build, so that when I was back in the fray I had momentum on my side. I had an agenda. I had things that I wanted to accomplish. I began outlining all that with my inaugural address.

Senator hatfield, Mr. Chief Justice, Mr. President, Vice President Bush, Vice President Mondale, Senator Baker, Speaker O'Neill, Reverend Moomaw, and my fellow citizens.

To a few of us here today this is a solemn and most momentous occasion, and yet in the history of our nation it is a commonplace occurrence. The orderly transfer of authority as called for in the Constitution routinely takes place, as it has for almost two centuries, and few of us stop to think how unique we really are. In the eyes of many in the world, this every-four-year ceremony we accept as normal is nothing less than a miracle.

Mr. President, I want our fellow citizens to know how much you did to carry on this tradition. By your gracious cooperation in the transition process, you have shown a watching world that we are a united people pledged to maintaining a political system which guarantees individual liberty to a greater degree than any other, and I thank you and your people for all your help in maintaining the continuity which is the bulwark of our republic.

The business of our nation goes forward. These United States are confronted with an economic affliction of great proportions. We suffer from the longest and one of the worst sustained inflations in our national history. It distorts our economic decisions, penalizes thrift, and crushes the struggling young and the fixed-income elderly alike. It threatens to shatter the lives of millions of our people.

Idle industries have cast workers into unemployment, human misery, and personal indignity. Those who do work are denied a fair return for their labor by a tax system which penalizes successful achievement and keeps us from maintaining full productivity.

But great as our tax burden is, it has not kept pace with public spending. For decades we have piled deficit upon deficit, mortgaging our future and our children's future for the temporary convenience of the present. To continue this long trend is to guarantee tremendous social, cultural, political, and economic upheavals.

You and I, as individuals, can, by borrowing, live beyond our means, but for only a limited period of time. Why, then, should we think that collectively, as a nation, we're not bound by that same limitation? We must act today in order to preserve tomorrow. And let there be no misunderstanding: We are going to begin to act, beginning today.

The economic ills we suffer have come upon us over several decades. They will not go away in days, weeks, or months, but they will go away. They will go away because we as Americans have the capacity now, as we've had in the past, to do whatever needs to be done to preserve this last and greatest bastion of freedom.

In this present crisis, government is not the solution to our problem; government is the problem. From time to time we've been tempted to believe that society has become too complex to be managed by self-rule, that government by an elite group is superior to government for, by, and of the people. Well, if no one among us is capable of governing himself, then who among us has the capacity to govern someone else? All of us together, in and out of government, must bear the burden. The solutions we seek must be equitable, with no one group singled out to pay a higher price.

We hear much of special interest groups. Well, our concern

61

must be for a special interest group that has been too long neglected. It knows no sectional boundaries or ethnic and racial divisions, and it crosses political party lines. It is made up of men and women who raise our food, patrol our streets, man our mines and factories, teach our children, keep our homes, and heal us when we're sick—professionals, industrialists, shopkeepers, clerks, cabbies, and truck drivers. They are, in short, "we the people," this breed called Americans.

Well, this administration's objective will be a healthy, vigorous, growing economy that provides equal opportunities for all Americans, with no barriers born of bigotry or discrimination. Putting America back to work means putting all Americans back to work. Ending inflation means freeing all Americans from the terror of runaway living costs. All must share in the productive work of this "new beginning," and all must share in the bounty of a revived economy. With the idealism and fair play which are the core of our system and our strength, we can have a strong and prosperous America, at peace with itself and the world.

So, as we begin, let us take inventory. We are a nation that has a government—not the other way around. And this makes us special among the nations of the earth. Our government has no power except that granted it by the people. It is time to check and reverse the growth of government, which shows signs of having grown beyond the consent of the governed.

It is my intention to curb the size and influence of the federal establishment and to demand recognition of the distinction between the powers granted to the federal government and those reserved to the states or to the people. All of us need to be reminded that the federal government did not create the states; the states created the federal government.

Now, so there will be no misunderstanding, it's not my intention to do away with government. It is rather to make it work —work with us, not over us; to stand by our side, not ride on our back. Government can and must provide opportunity, not smother it; foster productivity, not stifle it.

If we look to the answer as to why for so many years we

achieved so much, prospered as no other people on earth, it was because here in this land we unleashed the energy and individual genius of man to a greater extent than has ever been done before. Freedom and the dignity of the individual have been more available and assured here than in any other place on earth. The price for this freedom at times has been high, but we have never been unwilling to pay that price.

It is no coincidence that our present troubles parallel and are proportionate to the intervention and intrusion in our lives that result from unnecessary and excessive growth of government. It is time for us to realize that we're too great a nation to limit ourselves to small dreams. We're not, as some would have us believe, doomed to an inevitable decline. I do not believe in a fate that will fall on us no matter what we do. I do believe in a fate that will fall on us if we do nothing. So, with all the creative energy at our command, let us begin an era of national renewal. Let us renew our determination, our courage, and our strength. And let us renew our faith and our hope.

We have every right to dream heroic dreams. Those who say that we're in a time when there are no heroes, they just don't know where to look. You can see heroes every day going in and out of factory gates. Others, a handful in number, produce enough food to feed all of us and then the world beyond. You meet heroes across a counter, and they're on both sides of that counter. There are entrepreneurs with faith in themselves and faith in an idea who create new jobs, new wealth and opportunity. They're individuals and families whose taxes support the government and whose voluntary gifts support church, charity, culture, art, and education. Their patriotism is quiet, but deep. Their values sustain our national life.

Now, I have used the words "they" and "their" in speaking of these heroes. I could say "you" and "your," because I'm addressing the heroes of whom I speak—you, the citizens of this blessed land. Your dreams, your hopes, your goals are going to be the dreams, the hopes, and the goals of this administration, so help me God.

We shall reflect the compassion that is so much a part of

your makeup. How can we love our country and not love our countrymen; and loving them, reach out a hand when they fall, heal them when they're sick, and provide opportunity to make them self-sufficient so they will be equal in fact and not just in theory?

Can we solve the problems confronting us? Well, the answer is an unequivocal and emphatic "yes." To paraphrase Winston Churchill, I did not take the oath I've just taken with the intention of presiding over the dissolution of the world's strongest economy.

In the days ahead I will propose removing the roadblocks that have slowed our economy and reduced productivity. Steps will be taken aimed at restoring the balance between the various levels of government. Progress may be slow, measured in inches and feet, not miles, but we will progress. It is time to reawaken this industrial giant, to get government back within its means, and to lighten our punitive tax burden. And these will be our first priorities, and on these principles there will be no compromise.

On the eve of our struggle for independence a man who might have been one of the greatest among the Founding Fathers, Dr. Joseph Warren, president of the Massachusetts Congress, said to his fellow Americans, "Our country is in danger, but not to be despaired of. . . . On you depend the fortunes of America. You are to decide the important questions upon which rests the happiness and the liberty of millions yet unborn. Act worthy of yourselves."

Well, I believe we, the Americans of today, are ready to act worthy of ourselves, ready to do what must be done to ensure happiness and liberty for ourselves, our children, and our children's children. And as we renew ourselves here in our own land, we will be seen as having greater strength throughout the world. We will again be the exemplar of freedom and a beacon of hope for those who do not now have freedom.

To those neighbors and allies who share our freedom, we will strengthen our historic ties and assure them of our support and firm commitment. We will match loyalty with loyalty. We will strive for mutually beneficial relations. We will not use our friendship to impose on their sovereignty, for our own sovereignty is not for sale.

As for the enemies of freedom, those who are potential adversaries, they will be reminded that peace is the highest aspiration of the American people. We will negotiate for it, sacrifice for it; we will not surrender for it, now or ever.

Our forbearance should never be misunderstood. Our reluctance for conflict should not be misjudged as a failure of will. When action is required to preserve our national security, we will act. We will maintain sufficient strength to prevail if need be, knowing that if we do so we have the best chance of never having to use that strength.

Above all, we must realize that no arsenal or no weapon in the arsenals of the world is so formidable as the will and moral courage of free men and women. It is a weapon our adversaries in today's world do not have. It is a weapon that we as Americans do have. Let that be understood by those who practice terrorism and prey upon their neighbors.

I'm told that tens of thousands of prayer meetings are being held on this day, and for that I'm deeply grateful. We are a nation under God, and I believe God intended for us to be free. It would be fitting and good, I think, if on each Inaugural Day in future years it should be declared a day of prayer.

This is the first time in our history that this ceremony has been held, as you've been told, on this West Front of the Capitol. Standing here, one faces a magnificent vista, opening up on this city's special beauty and history. At the end of this open mall are those shrines to the giants on whose shoulders we stand.

Directly in front of me, the monument to a monumental man, George Washington, father of our country. A man of humility who came to greatness reluctantly. He led America out of revolutionary victory into infant nationhood. Off to one side, the stately memorial to Thomas Jefferson. The Declaration of Independence flames with his eloquence. And then, beyond the Reflecting Pool, the dignified columns of the Lincoln Memorial.

Whoever would understand in his heart the meaning of America will find it in the life of Abraham Lincoln.

Beyond those monuments to heroism is the Potomac River, and on the far shore the sloping hills of Arlington National Cemetery, with its row upon row of simple white markers bearing crosses or Stars of David. They add up to only a tiny fraction of the price that has been paid for our freedom.

Each one of those markers is a monument to the kind of hero I spoke of earlier. Their lives ended in places called Belleau Wood, the Argonne, Omaha Beach, Salerno, and halfway around the world on Guadalcanal, Tarawa, Pork Chop Hill, the Chosin Reservoir, and in a hundred rice paddies and jungles of a place called Vietnam.

Under one such marker lies a young man, Martin Treptow, who left his job in a small town barbershop in 1917 to go to France with the famed Rainbow Division. There, on the western front, he was killed trying to carry a message between battalions under heavy artillery fire.

We're told that on his body was found a diary. On the flyleaf under the heading "My Pledge," he had written these words: "America must win this war. Therefore I will work, I will save, I will sacrifice, I will endure, I will fight cheerfully and do my utmost, as if the issue of the whole struggle depended on me alone."

The crisis we are facing today does not require of us the kind of sacrifice that Martin Treptow and so many thousands of others were called upon to make. It does require, however, our best effort and our willingness to believe in ourselves and to believe in our capacity to perform great deeds, to believe that together with God's help we can and will resolve the problems which now confront us.

And after all, why shouldn't we believe that? We are Americans.

God bless you, and thank you.

Remarks at a Luncheon for Members of the Baseball Hall of Fame

STATE DINING ROOM

MARCH 27, 1981

One of the great things about being president is that you can invite anyone you want to lunch or dinner, and chances are they'll come. I don't remember exactly how this event got on the schedule, but it's representative of the kind of fun you can have even living in a museum called the White House.

As you may know, I love to tell stories, and boy, did I get to tell my share to these guys. There's something very therapeutic about hearing laughter and about laughing yourself. I believe there is some basis to this business about laughter being able to heal. So can friendship, which is what I considered this gathering to be all about.

The President. Gentlemen, go ahead with your coffee and all, but I know that time is getting by and we have a few remarks.

I'm delighted—well, I can't tell you how thrilled to have you all here. And over there at the other table is a ballplayer who is delighted to be here, Vice President George Bush, and he did play. But I want to tell you, you span the years for me, and all these young gentlemen here that are growing up as ballplayers. It's a delight to have all of you here.

The nostalgia is bubbling within me, and I may have to be dragged out of here because of all the stories that are coming up in my mind. Baseball—I had to finally confess over here, no, I didn't play when I was young. I went down the football path. But I did play in a way, as Bob Lemon well knows, I was old Grover Cleveland Alexander, and I've been very proud of that. It was a wonderful experience.

There were quite a few ballplayers, including Bob Lemon, who were on the set for that picture. And I remember one day when they wanted some shots of me pitching, but kind of close up—so, they wanted me to throw past the camera, and they had a fellow back there—well, Al Lyons, one of the ballplayers that was there, was going to catch the ball back there and then toss it back over the camera to me. And the cam was getting these close shots for use wherever they could use them. And he was on one side of the camera, and my control wasn't all that it should be at one point, and I threw it on the other side of the camera. And he speared it with his left hand with no glove on. He was a left-hander, and after he brought the ball to me, and he said, "Alex, I'm sorry I had to catch your blazer bare-handed." [*Laughter*] He didn't suffer any pain, I am sure of it.

But I remember we had a fellow that I'm sure some of you know and remember, Metkovitch. And Metkovitch, during the day's shooting, would memorize everyone's lines. And then if we were on location and got in the bus to go back in from location, he would now play all the scenes for us on the bus. [*Laughter*] So, thinking about this, one day, on the process screen, an umpire behind him, he was at the plate, and they wanted a shot of a ballplayer at the plate. And the director said, "There are no lines, but you'll know what to say." He said, "The umpire's going to call it a strike," and he said, "You don't think it's a strike. So, do what you do in a ball game when you think it's a bad call." And extroverted Metkovitch, who was so happy to play all the scenes, was standing up at the plate, and if you looked closely, you could see that the bat was beginning to shake a little bit—[*Laughter*]—and the ball came by on an after play and the umpire bellowed out, "Strike one!" and Metkovitch lowered the bat and he says, "Gee, that was no strike." [*Laughter*] The picture wasn't a comedy, so we couldn't leave it in.

But you know, I've always been sorry about one thing. Alex is in the Hall of Fame and deservedly so. Everyone knows that great 1926 World Series, when he had won two games, received the greatest ovation anyone's ever received, and then was called on in the seventh inning with the bases loaded, no one out, and one of the most dangerous hitters in baseball at the plate. And he came in and saved the game. The tragedy that I've always regretted is that the studio was unwilling to reveal in the picture, was afraid to reveal what I think was the best-kept secret in sports.

A bad habit of Alex's was widely heralded and took something away from his luster. But they wouldn't let us use the actual word of what was behind, maybe, his bad habit. Alex was an epileptic. And when he was arrested and picked up for being drunk in a gutter, as he once was, he wasn't at all. But he would rather take that than admit to the disease that plagued him all his life.

But he also, early in his baseball career, was hit in the head going from first base down to second on a throw from second; they caught him right in the head. And he was out of baseball for a while, and they didn't know whether forever, because he had double vision. And he kept experimenting, trying to find out if there wasn't some way that he could pitch. And he went to a minor league club and asked for a tryout, and the manager got up at the plate and said, "Well, go on out on the mound and throw me a few." Alex broke three of his ribs on the first pitch. [*Laughter*] His experiment had been that he thought that if he closed one eye and threw, he'd only—[*Laughter*]—and the friend that was with him when they were thrown out of the ball park said, "What happened?" And he said, "I closed the wrong eye." [*Laughter*]

But there are men in this room that were playing when I was

broadcasting, and I promised to say something here to a great Cub fan that we have at the table that would make him feel good. I was broadcasting the Cubs when the only mathematical possibility—and Billy Herman will remember this very well—that the Cubs had of winning the pennant was to win the last twenty-one games of the season. And they did. And I was so imbued with baseball by that time that I know you're not supposed to talk about a no-hitter while it's going on because you'll jinx them. So, there I was, a broadcaster, and never mentioned once in the twenty-one games—and I was getting as uptight as they were—and never mentioned the fact that they were at sixteen, they were at seventeen, and that they hadn't lost a game, because I was afraid I'd jinx them. But anyway, they did it and it's still in the record books.

What isn't in the record books is Billy Jurges staying at the plate, I think, the longest of any ballplayer in the history of the game. I was doing the games by telegraphic report, and the fellow on the other side of a window with a little slit underneath, the headphones on, getting the dot-and-dash Morse code from the ball park, would type out the play. And the paper would come through to me—it would say, "S1C." Well you're not going to sell any Wheaties yelling "S1C!" [Laughter] So, I'd say, "And so-and-so comes out of the windup, here's the pitch, and it's a called strike, breaking over the outside corner to so-and-so, who'd rather have a ball someplace else and so forth and backed out there."

Well, I saw him start to type, and I started—Dizzy Dean was on the mound—and I started the ball on the way to the plate —or him in the windup and he, Curly, the fellow on the other side, was shaking his head, and I thought he just—maybe it was a miraculous play or something. But when the slip came through it said, "The wire's gone dead." Well, I had the ball on the way to the plate. [Laughter] And I figured real quick, I could say we'll tell them what had happened and then play transcribed music. But in those days there were at least seven or eight other fellows that were doing the same ball game. I didn't want to lose the audience.

70

So, I thought real quick, "There's one thing that doesn't get in the score book," so I had Billy foul one off. And I looked at Curly, and Curly just went like this; so I had him foul another one. And I had him foul one back at third base and described the fight between the two kids that were trying to get the ball. [*Laughter*] Then I had him foul one that just missed being a home run, about a foot and a half. And I did set a world record for successive fouls or for someone standing there, except that no one keeps records of that kind. And I was beginning to sweat, when Curly sat up straight and started typing, and he was nodding his head, "Yes." And the slip came through the window, and I could hardly talk for laughing, because it said, "Jurges popped out on the first ball pitch." [*Laughter*]

But those were wonderful days, not only playing the part, but some of you here, I think, will—I'm going to tell another story here that has been confirmed for me by Waite Hoyt. Those of you who played when the Dodgers were in Brooklyn know that Brooklynese have a tendency to refer to someone by the name of Earl as "oil." But if they want a quart of oil in the car, they say, "Give me a quart of earl." And Waite was sliding into second. And he twisted his ankle. And instead of getting up, he was lying there, and there was a deep hush over the whole ball park. And then a Brooklyn voice was heard above all that silence and said, "Gee, Hurt is hoyt." [*Laughter*]

But, I can't take any more time doing this or we'd be here all day. They tell me that I'm supposed to go out there in front of the door to the Blue Room, and because I haven't been able to say hello to all of you in here and, as I say, there are many of you that were playing when I broadcast in those telegraphic report games, and not only re-created but—as I just told you—now and then created some of the ball game. But I understand that we're going to have a chance outside here—kind of a line where I can say hello and good-bye at the same time to each one of you.

And now I'm going to present—the commissioner has something here that I think should be said. Commissioner, come on up here.

Mr. Kuhn.* Okay, fine. I just wanted to take a moment on behalf of all of us gathered here together to thank the President for his great kindness in having us all here today.

I'm going to borrow a line from the man I talked to yesterday who's sitting here in the room, Mr. President, Bob Howsam. When Bob and I were talking, I said, "I'll see you there tomorrow, won't I?" And Bob's a member of our executive council from the Cincinnati Reds sitting over here, and he said, "Commissioner, I will never be so proud or so old that I won't be thrilled to set foot in the White House and say hello to the President of the United States." And I think on behalf of us all, I can say we're very thrilled to be here, to be with you, to share with you some anecdotes about the game of baseball.

I want to just do one little thing that I found. I want to say to the President on behalf of baseball that I think we have contributed mightily to the President's situation here in Washington, because he was a Cubs fan, as you can tell. And I've got an article I found in the *Chicago Tribune* which plainly indicates that baseball has prepared him for his career here. It says, "For four years, Ronald Reagan broadcast games of the Cubs and in the process became that rarest of nature's noblemen," Dave Broder, "a Cub fan. Nothing before or since those four years has prepared him more fully to face with fortitude the travails of the Oval Office. As a Cub fan, he learned that virtue will not necessarily prevail over chicanery, that swift failure follows closely on the heels of even the most modest success, that the world mocks those who are pure in heart, but slow of foot. But"—and here's the good news, Mr. President—"but that the bitterest disappointment will soon yield to the hope and promise of a new season."

We thank you from the bottoms of our heart for your kindness and generosity here today.

Mr. Stack. I'm Ed Stack, the president of the Baseball Hall of Fame, and I have a couple presentations I'd like to make.

* Bowie Kuhn, Commissioner of the American Baseball Association.

Before the luncheon, the President greeted the commissioner and myself in the Oval Office and was very gracious to sign our historic presidential baseball, which we have on display at the Baseball Hall of Fame in Cooperstown. He added his signature to the baseballs that have been signed by all the presidents since William Howard Taft. And tomorrow morning, it'll be on display in Cooperstown for the millions of visitors to see when they come through the shrine.

Also, we presented the President with a lifetime gold pass to the Baseball Hall of Fame, and we hope that he will use it many times in the future.

I'd like to ask the President to accept from us a couple of gifts. The first gift that we have to present is something that Billy Martin sent from Oakland. Bill heard about the luncheon and asked that I present this to the President. And if he could open it and show the audience, I think he'll enjoy it.

[*The President was presented with an Oakland A's team jacket.*]

The President. Hey, look, Ma, I made the team! [*Laughter*] I hope he hasn't got this too big. [*Laughter*] A little big.

Well, I thank him very much. I thank all of you.

Address to the Nation on the Economy

OVAL OFFICE
FEBRUARY 5, 1981

A major reason I was elected president was because the American economy had become a basket case. Here we were, a country bursting with economic promise, and yet our political leadership had gone out of its way to frustrate America's natu-

ral economic strength. It made no sense. My attitude had always been—let the people flourish.

With the help of some Democratic "boll weevils" in Congress, we enacted the largest tax and budget cuts in history. Later we would enact the most extensive reform ever of the tax code. In the process, we cut inflation, interest rates, and unemployment. The consequence is that we have enjoyed the longest peacetime economic expansion in our nation's history.

The following speech was my first appeal to the American people about the economic crisis we were facing. There would be many more appeals over the years. Some I would win, some I would lose, such as my continual fights with Congress to get control of the budget deficit. The Congress of the United States today is a captive of the special interest groups and totally unable to balance the budget. I am convinced we'll never have a balanced budget unless we have a constitutional amendment requiring one.

To make clear the erosion of our nation's economy, I used some coins in this speech to show how inflation had eaten into the value of a dollar. The commentators all noted how effective this was. I guess my acting background did pay off now and then.

GOOD EVENING.

I'm speaking to you tonight to give you a report on the state of our nation's economy. I regret to say that we're in the worst economic mess since the Great Depression.

A few days ago I was presented with a report I'd asked for, a comprehensive audit, if you will, of our economic condition. You won't like it. I didn't like it. But we have to face the truth and then go to work to turn things around. And make no mistake about it, we can turn them around.

I'm not going to subject you to the jumble of charts, figures, and economic jargon of that audit, but rather will try to explain

75

where we are, how we got there, and how we can get back. First, however, let me just give a few "attention getters" from the audit.

The federal budget is out of control, and we face runaway deficits of almost $80 billion for this budget year that ends September 30th. That deficit is larger than the entire federal budget in 1957, and so is the almost $80 billion we will pay in interest this year on the national debt.

Twenty years ago, in 1960, our federal government payroll was less than $13 billion. Today it is 75 billion. During these twenty years our population has only increased by 23.3 percent. The federal budget has gone up 528 percent.

Now, we've just had two years of back-to-back double-digit inflation—13.3 percent in 1979. 12.4 percent last year. The last time this happened was in World War I.

In 1960 mortgage interest rates averaged about 6 percent. They're two and a half times as high now, 15.4 percent.

The percentage of your earnings the federal government took in taxes in 1960 has almost doubled.

And finally there are 7 million Americans caught up in the personal indignity and human tragedy of unemployment. If they stood in a line, allowing three feet for each person, the line would reach from the coast of Maine to California.

Well, so much for the audit itself. Let me try to put this in personal terms. Here is a dollar such as you earned, spent, or saved in 1960. And here is a quarter, a dime, and a penny— thirty-six cents. That's what this 1960 dollar is worth today. And if the present world inflation rate should continue three more years, that dollar of 1960 will be worth a quarter. What initiative is there to save? And if we don't save we're short of the investment capital needed for business and industry expansion. Workers in Japan and West Germany save several times the percentage of their income that Americans do.

What's happened to that American dream of owning a home? Only ten years ago a family could buy a home, and the monthly payment averaged little more than a quarter—twenty-seven cents out of each dollar earned. Today, it takes forty-two cents out of every dollar of income. So, fewer than one out of eleven families can afford to buy their first new home.

Regulations adopted by government with the best of intentions have added $666 to the cost of an automobile. It is estimated that altogether regulations of every kind, on shopkeepers, farmers, and major industries, add $100 billion or more to the cost of the goods and services we buy. And then another 20 billion is spent by government handling the paperwork created by those regulations.

I'm sure you're getting the idea that the audit presented to me found government policies of the last few decades responsible for our economic troubles. We forgot or just overlooked the fact that government—any government—has a built-in tendency to grow. Now, we all had a hand in looking to government for benefits as if government had some source of revenue other than our earnings. Many if not most of the things we thought of or that government offered to us seemed attractive.

In the years following the Second World War it was easy, for a while at least, to overlook the price tag. Our income more than doubled in the twenty-five years after the war. We increased our take-home pay in those twenty-five years by more than we had amassed in all the preceding one hundred and fifty years put together. Yes, there was some inflation, 1 or 1½ percent a year. That didn't bother us. But if we look back at those golden years, we recall that even then voices had been raised, warning that inflation, like radioactivity, was cumulative and that once started it could get out of control.

Some government programs seemed so worthwhile that borrowing to fund them didn't bother us. By 1960 our national debt stood at $284 billion. Congress in 1971 decided to put a ceiling of 400 billion on our ability to borrow. Today the debt is 934 billion. So-called temporary increases or extensions in the debt ceiling have been allowed twenty-one times in these ten years, and now I've been forced to ask for another increase in the debt ceiling or the government will be unable to function past the middle of February—and I've only been here sixteen days. Before we reach the day when we can reduce the debt ceiling, we may in spite of our best efforts see a national debt in excess of a trillion dollars. Now, this is a figure that's literally beyond our comprehension.

We know now that inflation results from all that deficit spending. Government has only two ways of getting money other than raising taxes. It can go into the money market and borrow, competing with its own citizens and driving up interest rates, which it has done, or it can print money, and it's done that. Both methods are inflationary.

We're victims of language. The very word "inflation" leads us to think of it as just high prices. Then, of course, we resent the person who puts on the price tags, forgetting that he or she is also a victim of inflation. Inflation is not just high prices; it's a reduction in the value of our money. When the money supply is increased but the goods and services available for buying are not, we have too much money chasing too few goods. Wars are usually accompanied by inflation. Everyone is working or fighting, but production is of weapons and munitions, not things we can buy and use.

Now, one way out would be to raise taxes so that government need not borrow or print money. But in all these years of government growth, we've reached, indeed surpassed, the limit of our people's tolerance or ability to bear an increase in the tax burden. Prior to World War II, taxes were such that on the average we only had to work just a little over one month each year to pay our total federal, state, and local tax bill. Today we have to work four months to pay that bill.

Some say shift the tax burden to business and industry, but business doesn't pay taxes. Oh, don't get the wrong idea. Business is being taxed, so much so that we're being priced out of the world market. But business must pass its costs of operations —and that includes taxes—on to the customer in the price of the product. Only people pay taxes, all the taxes. Government just uses business in a kind of sneaky way to help collect the taxes. They're hidden in the price; we aren't aware of how much tax we actually pay.

Today this once great industrial giant of ours has the lowest rate of gain in productivity of virtually all the industrial nations with whom we must compete in the world market. We can't even hold our own market here in America against foreign automobiles, steel, and a number of other products. Japanese production of automobiles is almost twice as great per worker as it is in America. Japanese steelworkers outproduce their American counterparts by about 25 percent.

Now, this isn't because they're better workers. I'll match the American working man or woman against anyone in the world. But we have to give them the tools and equipment that workers in the other industrial nations have.

We invented the assembly line and mass production, but punitive tax policies and excessive and unnecessary regulations plus government borrowing have stifled our ability to update plant and equipment. When capital investment is made, it's too often for some unproductive alterations demanded by government to meet various of its regulations. Excessive taxation of individuals has robbed us of incentive and made overtime unprofitable.

We once produced about 40 percent of the world's steel. We now produce 19 percent. We were once the greatest producer of automobiles, producing more than all the rest of the world combined. That is no longer true, and in addition, the "Big Three," the major auto companies in our land, have sustained tremendous losses in the past year and have been forced to lay off thousands of workers.

All of you who are working know that even with cost-of-living pay raises, you can't keep up with inflation. In our progressive tax system, as you increase the number of dollars you earn, you find yourself moved up into higher tax brackets, paying a higher tax rate just for trying to hold your own. The result? Your standard of living is going down.

Over the past decades we've talked of curtailing government spending so that we can then lower the tax burden. Sometimes we've even taken a run at doing that. But there were always those who told us that taxes couldn't be cut until spending was reduced. Well, you know, we can lecture our children about extravagance until we run out of voice and breath. Or we can cure their extravagance by simply reducing their allowance.

It's time to recognize that we've come to a turning point. We're threatened with an economic calamity of tremendous proportions, and the old business-as-usual treatment can't save us. Together, we must chart a different course.

We must increase productivity. That means making it possible for industry to modernize and make use of the technology which we ourselves invented. That means putting Americans back to work. And that means above all bringing government spending back within government revenues, which is the only way, together with increased productivity, that we can reduce and, yes, eliminate inflation.

In the past we've tried to fight inflation one year and then, with unemployment increased, turn the next year to fighting unemployment with more deficit spending as a pump primer. So, again, up goes inflation. It hasn't worked. We don't have to choose between inflation and unemployment—they go hand in hand. It's time to try something different, and that's what we're going to do.

I've already placed a freeze on hiring replacements for those who retire or leave government service. I've ordered a cut in government travel, the number of consultants to the government, and the buying of office equipment and other items. I've put a freeze on pending regulations and set up a task force under Vice President Bush to review regulations with an eye toward getting rid of as many as possible. I have decontrolled oil, which should result in more domestic production and less dependence on foreign oil. And I'm eliminating that ineffective Council on Wage and Price Stability.

But it will take more, much more. And we must realize there is no quick fix. At the same time, however, we cannot delay in implementing an economic program aimed at both reducing tax rates to stimulate productivity and reducing the growth in government spending to reduce unemployment and inflation.

On February 18th, I will present in detail an economic program to Congress embodying the features I've just stated. It will propose budget cuts in virtually every department of government. It is my belief that these actual budget cuts will only be part of the savings. As our cabinet secretaries take charge of their departments, they will search out areas of waste, extravagance, and costly overhead which could yield additional and substantial reductions.

Now, at the same time we're doing this, we must go forward with a tax relief package. I shall ask for a 10-percent reduction across the board in personal income tax rates for each of the next three years. Proposals will also be submitted for accelerated depreciation allowances for business to provide necessary capital so as to create jobs.

Now, here again, in saying this, I know that language, as I said earlier, can get in the way of a clear understanding of what our program is intended to do. Budget cuts can sound as if we're going to reduce total government spending to a lower level than was spent the year before. Well, this is not the case. The budgets will increase as our population increases, and each year we'll see spending increases to match that growth. Government revenues will increase as the economy grows, but the burden will be lighter for each individual, because the economic base will have been expanded by reason of the reduced rates.

Now, let me show you a chart that I've had drawn to illustrate how this can be.

Here you see two trend lines. The bottom line shows the increase in tax revenues. The red line on top is the increase in government spending. Both lines turn upward, reflecting the giant tax increase already built into the system for this year 1981, and the increases in spending built into the '81 and '82 budgets and on into the future. As you can see, the spending line rises at a steeper slant than the revenue line. And that gap between those lines illustrates the increasing deficits we've been running, including this year's $80-billion deficit.

Now, in the second chart, the lines represent the positive effects when Congress accepts our economic program. Both lines continue to rise, allowing for necessary growth, but the gap narrows as spending cuts continue over the next few years until finally the two lines come together, meaning a balanced budget.

I am confident that my administration can achieve that. At that point tax revenues, in spite of rate reductions, will be increasing faster than spending, which means we can look forward to further reductions in the tax rates.

Now, in all of this we will, of course, work closely with the Federal Reserve System toward the objective of a stable monetary policy.

Our spending cuts will not be at the expense of the truly needy. We will, however, seek to eliminate benefits to those who are not really qualified by reason of need.

As I've said before, on February 18th I will present this economic package of budget reductions and tax reform to a joint session of Congress and to you in full detail.

Our basic system is sound. We can, with compassion, continue to meet our responsibility to those who, through no fault of their own, need our help. We can meet fully the other legitimate responsibilities of government. We cannot continue any longer our wasteful ways at the expense of the workers of this land or of our children.

Since 1960 our government has spent $5.1 trillion. Our debt has grown by 648 billion. Prices have exploded by 178 percent. How much better off are we for all that? Well, we all know we're very much worse off. When we measure how harshly these years of inflation, lower productivity, and uncontrolled government growth have affected our lives, we know we must act and act now. We must not be timid. We will restore the freedom of all men and women to excel and to create. We will unleash the energy and genius of the American people, traits which have never failed us.

To the Congress of the United States, I extend my hand in cooperation, and I believe we can go forward in a bipartisan manner. I've found a real willingness to cooperate on the part of Democrats and members of my own party.

To my colleagues in the executive branch of government and

to all federal employees, I ask that we work in the spirit of service.

I urge those great institutions in America, business and labor, to be guided by the national interest, and I'm confident they will. The only special interest that we will serve is the interest of all the people.

We can create the incentives which take advantage of the genius of our economic system—a system, as Walter Lippmann observed more than forty years ago, which for the first time in history gave men "a way of producing wealth in which the good fortune of others multiplied their own."

Our aim is to increase our national wealth so all will have more, not just redistribute what we already have, which is just a sharing of scarcity. We can begin to reward hard work and risk-taking, by forcing this government to live within its means.

Over the years we've let negative economic forces run out of control. We stalled the judgment day, but we no longer have that luxury. We're out of time.

And to you, my fellow citizens, let us join in a new determination to rebuild the foundation of our society, to work together, to act responsibly. Let us do so with the most profound respect for that which must be preserved as well as with sensitive understanding and compassion for those who must be protected.

We can leave our children with an unrepayable massive debt and a shattered economy, or we can leave them liberty in a land where every individual has the opportunity to be whatever God intended us to be. All it takes is a little common sense and recognition of our own ability. Together we can forge a new beginning for America.

Thank you, and good night.

Statement on the Air Traffic Controllers' Strike

WHITE HOUSE ROSE GARDEN
AUGUST 3, 1981

I'm not very good at firing people; maybe it goes back to the fact that as a child I can remember my father being out of work. I know the hardship and dislocation it can cause a family. But I also believe that people should keep their word when they make a promise. This is why I fired the air controllers.

As a former union president myself, I couldn't go along with the controllers violating not only the law, but their own pledges, not to strike. I also don't believe government employees have the right to strike, because the strike is against their fellow citizens, not some moneyed employer.

This episode was an early test of my administration's resolve. We had the choice of caving in to unreasonable demands while keeping our air traffic system operating without incident, or of taking a stand for what we thought was right with the risk of throwing the system into possible chaos. I felt we had to do what was right. This decision forced us to train almost an entirely new crop of air traffic controllers. It took years for our air traffic system to return to normal. I think the principle was worth the price.

Most often it's not how handsomely or eloquently you say something, but the fact that your words mean something. That's the case here.

THIS MORNING AT SEVEN A.M. the union representing those who man America's air traffic control facilities called a strike. This was the culmination of seven months of negotiations between the Federal Aviation Administration and the union. At one point in these negotiations agreement was reached and signed by both sides, granting a $40 million increase in salaries and benefits. This is twice what other government employees can expect. It was granted in recognition of the difficulties inherent in the work these people perform. Now, however, the union demands are seventeen times what had been agreed to—$681 million. This would impose a tax burden on their fellow citizens which is unacceptable.

I would like to thank the supervisors and controllers who are on the job today, helping to get the nation's air system operating safely. In the New York area, for example, four supervisors were scheduled to report for work, and seventeen additionally volunteered. At National Airport a traffic controller told a newsperson he had resigned from the union and reported to work because, "How can I ask my kids to obey the law if I don't?" This is a great tribute to America.

85

Let me make one thing plain. I respect the right of workers in the private sector to strike. Indeed, as president of my own union, I led the first strike ever called by that union. I guess I'm maybe the first one to ever hold this office who is a lifetime member of an AFL-CIO union. But we cannot compare labor-management relations in the private sector with government. Government cannot close down the assembly line. It has to provide without interruption the protective services which are government's reason for being.

It was in recognition of this that the Congress passed a law forbidding strikes by government employees against the public safety. Let me read the solemn oath taken by each of these employees, a sworn affidavit, when they accepted their jobs: "I am not participating in any strike against the Government of the United States or any agency thereof, and I will not so participate while an employee of the Government of the United States or any agency thereof."

It is for this reason that I must tell those who fail to report for duty this morning they are in violation of the law, and if they do not report for work within forty-eight hours, they have forfeited their jobs and will be terminated.

Remarks at the Eighty-fourth Annual Dinner of the Irish American Historical Society

NEW YORK CITY
NOVEMBER 6, 1981

On more than one occasion I got into scraps in the schoolyard because of some Protestant kid saying that the Catholic church basement was filled with rifles in preparation for the Pope's takeover of the United States. My father went to that church. I knew the story wasn't true; he had told me so. But there was a prejudice against Catholics in those days. At one time there was also a prejudice against the Irish in this country.

My father was both—Irish and Catholic. My mother was of English and Scottish descent and took my brother and me to the Protestant church. But I think anyone who's the least bit Irish, however, likes to consider himself so and wear a bit of the green. In any event, I've always considered myself an Irishman, and I love Irish events, such as this dinner I attended in New York.

D<small>R.</small> C<small>AHILL,</small>* I thank you and all those who are responsible for this great honor. And I want to say that I happen to know that there is one among us here who has known, also, today,

* Dr. Kevin Cahill, president of the Society.

the same joy and even greater, if possible, than I could feel. And that is Dr. Cahill himself, who this morning was presented by Cardinal Cooke, on behalf of the Pope, the Grand Cross Pro Merito Melitensi. He is the first American to ever receive this award.

Your Eminence, the other clergy here at the head table, the other distinguished guests, and one in particular that I might pick out and mention, Teddy Gleason of the International Longshoremen's Association. And I mention him because on Sunday he is going to celebrate the forty-second anniversary of his thirty-ninth birthday. Teddy, I've found that for some time, that makes it much easier to greet each one of these annual occasions.

But I do thank you very much. You know, there is the legend in Ireland of the happy colleen of Ballisodare who lived gaily among the wee people, the tiny people, for seven years, and then when she came home discovered that she had no toes. She had danced them off. I feel happy enough—when I get home tonight I'm going to count mine. [*Laughter*]

Nancy is sorry that she couldn't be here, and so am I. She sent her warm regards and her regrets. Unfortunately, on the last trip into town she picked up the bug.

Now, I'm happy to say that's not a situation for me, like the two sons of Ireland who were in the pub one evening and one asked the other about his wife. And he said, "Oh, she's terribly sick." He said, "She's terribly ill." And the other one says, "Oh, I'm sorry to hear that." But he said, "Is there any danger?" "Oh," he said, "no. She's too weak to be dangerous anymore." [*Laughter*]

A writer for the Irish press who was based in Washington, a correspondent for the press there, stated to me the other day— or stated the other day about me—that I have only recently developed a pride in my Irish heritage or background, and that up till now I have had an apathy about it. Well, let me correct the record. That is not so. I have been troubled until fairly recently about a lack of knowledge about my father's history.

My father was orphaned at age six. He knew very little about

88

his family history. And so I grew up knowing nothing more beyond him than an old photograph, a single photo that he had of his mother and father, and no knowledge of that family history. But somehow, a funny thing happened to me on the way to Washington. [*Laughter*] When I changed my line of work about a year ago, it seemed that I became of a certain interest to people in Ireland, who very kindly began to fill me in. And so I have learned that my great-grandfather took off from the village of Ballyporeen in County Tipperary to come to America. And that isn't the limit to all that I have learned about that.

Some years ago, when I was just beginning in Hollywood in the motion picture business, I had been sentenced for the few years I'd been there to movies that the studio didn't want good, it wanted them Thursday. [*Laughter*]

And then came that opportunity that every actor asks for or hopes for, and that was a picture that was going to be made and the biography of the late Knute Rockne, the great immortal coach of Notre Dame. Pat O'Brien was to play Rockne. And there was a part in there that from my own experience as a sports announcer I had long dreamed of, the part of George Gipp. And generously, Pat O'Brien, who was then a star at the studio, held out his hand to a young aspiring actor, and I played Gipp. Pat playing Rockne, he himself will say, was the high point of his theatrical career. My playing "The Gipp" opened the door to stardom and a better kind of picture.

I've been asked at times, "What's it like to see yourself in the old movies, the reruns on TV?" It's like looking at a son you never knew you had. [*Laughter*] But I found out—in learning about my own heritage, going back to Ballyporeen—that, believe it or not, what a small world it is, Pat O'Brien's family came from Ballyporeen.

But I've been filled-in much more since. An historian has informed me that our family was one of the four tribes of Tara, and that from the year 200 until about 900 A.D., they defended the only pass through the Slieve Bloom Mountains. They held it for all those centuries and adopted the motto, "The Hills

Forever." And that, too, is strange, because for the better part of nine months now, I've been saying much the same thing, only in the singular: "The Hill Forever." Capitol Hill, that is. [*Laughter*]

I do remember my father telling me once when I was a boy, and with great pride he said to me, "The Irish are the only people in the country, in America, that built the jails and then filled them." [*Laughter*] I was a little perturbed even then, at that tender age, because at the sound of pride in his voice and from the way I'd been raised, I couldn't quite understand why that was something to be proud of, until I then later learned, which he had never explained to me, that he was referring to the fact that the overwhelming majority of men wearing the blue of the police department in America were of Irish descent.

You know, those weren't the only jobs that were open to the Irish. Back in the high day of vaudeville, long before sound pictures drove it out, there were, very popular in this country, comedians who would reach great stardom in vaudeville with a broad German accent. German comedians coming on *"Ach und Himmel Sie der."* What is little known in show business is that almost without exception, they were Irish. Their wit and humor that made them comedians, they came by naturally and honestly.

I was on a mission to England for our government some ten years ago. I should say to Europe, to several countries, and finally wound up and the last country was Ireland.

On the last day in Ireland, I was taken to Cashel Rock. I didn't know at that time that it's only twenty-five miles from Ballyporeen. But I do know that the young Irish guide who was showing us around the ruins of the ancient cathedral, there on the rock, finally took us to the little cemetery. We walked with great interest and looked at those ancient tombstones and the inscriptions.

And then we came to one and the inscription said: "Remember me as you pass by, for as you are, so once was I. But as I am, you too will be, so be content to follow me." And that was too much for the Irish wit and humor of someone who came after, because underneath was scratched: "To follow you I am content, I wish I knew which way you went." [*Laughter*]

But the Irish, like many, a great many of the people and like my grandfather, great-grandfather, were driven to the New World by famine and by tragedies of other kinds. The Irish—they built the railroads, they opened the West wearing the blue and gold of the United States Cavalry. There was John L. Sullivan, the heavyweight champion of the world, writers like Eugene O'Neill, clergy like Cardinal Cooke, and even physicians to the Pope like Dr. Cahill.

And it goes all the way back in our history. George Washington said, "When our friendless standard was first unfurled, who were the strangers who first mustered around our staff? And when it reeled in the fight, who more brilliantly sustained it than Erin's generous sons?" And a century and a half later, who else than George M. Cohan would write of the Grand Old Flag, the Stars and Stripes, and Yankee Doodle Dandy with the line, "I'm a real live nephew of my Uncle Sam."

There must have been a divine plan that brought to this blessed land people from every corner of the earth. And here, those people kept their love for the land of their origin at the same time that they pledged their love and loyalty to this new land, this great melting pot. They worked for it, they fought for it, and yes, they died for it—and none more bravely than Erin's generous sons.

Tragedy, as I've said, very often was the impetus that sent many to America. Today, as has been said here already tonight, there is tragedy again in the Emerald Isle. The cardinal prayed and His Holiness, the Pope, pleaded for peace when he visited Ireland. I think we all should pray that responsible leaders on both sides and the governments of the United Kingdom and the Republic of Ireland can bring peace to that beautiful isle once again. And once again, we can join John Locke in saying, "O Ireland, isn't it grand you look—like a bride in her rich adornment? And with all the pent-up love in [of] my heart, I bid you top o' the mornin'!"

No, I have no apathy, no feeling at all, I am just so grateful that among the other things that happened when I was allowed to move into public housing—[*Laughter*]—I had a chance, finally, to learn of the very rich heritage that my father had left me.

And I can only say once again, with heartfelt thanks, I wear this * and take it home with a feeling of great honor, and say something that I know to all of you is as familiar as "top o' the mornin' " or anything else. That is: "May the road rise beneath your feet, the sun shine warm upon your face, and the wind be always at your back, and may God, until we meet again, hold you in the hollow of His hand."

Thank you.

* The President was presented with a medal representing the Society's highest award.

Remarks at the
Conservative Political Action Conference

WASHINGTON, D.C.
MARCH 20, 1981

I went to these Conservative Political Action Conference events almost every year I was president. I attended before I was president, too. These were my people, the people who had labored for the conservative cause when it seemed like a hopeless endeavor. These were the people who fought the cause for individual liberty and freedom when the government seemed to be getting more powerful by the day. They were the people who persevered, and I can't tell you how much I admire them for their tenacity and their hope.

I also can't tell you how embattled we felt over the years. The pundits and the intelligentsia often treated us as if we were some kind of Neanderthals, our brains developed barely enough to come into our caves out of the rain. We were often ridiculed and usually dismissed. Such treatment only strengthened our ideals and our resolve.

The speech you're about to read is special because it marked a coming home. The evening was a celebration of what we'd worked so long for—a conservative president in the White House.

Mr. chairman* and Congressman Mickey Edwards, thank you very much. My goodness, I can't realize how much time has gone by, because I remember when I first knew Mickey, he was just a clean-shaven boy. [*Laughter*] But thank you for inviting me here once again. And as Mickey told you, with the exception of those two years, it is true about how often I've been here. So, let me say now that I hope we'll be able to keep this tradition going forward and that you'll invite me again next year.

And in the rough days ahead, and I know there will be such days, I hope that you'll be like the mother of the young lad in camp when the camp director told her that he was going to have to discipline her son. And she said, "Well, don't be too hard on him. He's very sensitive. Slap the boy next to him, and that will scare Irving." [*Laughter*] But let us also, tonight, salute those with vision who labored to found this group—the American Conservative Union, the Young Americans for Freedom, *National Review* and *Human Events.*

It's been said that anyone who seeks success or greatness should first forget about both and seek only the truth, and the rest will follow. Well, fellow truth seekers, none of us here tonight—contemplating the seal on this podium and a balanced budget in 1984—can argue with that kind of logic. For whatever history does finally say about our cause, it must say: The conservative movement in twentieth-century America held fast through hard and difficult years to its vision of the truth. And history must also say that our victory, when it was achieved, was not so much a victory of politics as it was a victory of ideas, not so much a victory for any one man or party as it was a victory for a set of principles—principles that were protected and nourished by a few unselfish Americans through many grim and heartbreaking defeats.

Now, you are those Americans that I'm talking about. I

* James Lacey, national chairman of the Young Americans for Freedom.

wanted to be here not just to acknowledge your efforts on my behalf, not just to remark that last November's victory was singularly your victory, not just to mention that the new administration in Washington is a testimony to your perseverance and devotion to principle, but to say simply, "Thank you," and to say those words not as a president, or even as a conservative; thank you as an American. I say this knowing that there are many in this room whose talents might have entitled them to a life of affluence but who chose another career out of a higher sense of duty to country. And I know, too, that the story of their selflessness will never be written up in *Time* or *Newsweek* or go down in the history books.

You know, on an occasion like this it's a little hard not to reminisce, not to think back and just realize how far we've come. The Portuguese have a word for such recollection—*saudade*—a poetic term rich with the dreams of yesterday. And surely in our past there was many a dream that went aglimmering and many a field littered with broken lances.

Who can forget that July night in San Francisco when Barry Goldwater told us that we must set the tides running again in the cause of freedom, and he said, "until our cause has won the day, inspired the world, and shown the way to a tomorrow worthy of all our yesteryears"? And had there not been a Barry Goldwater willing to take that lonely walk, we wouldn't be here talking of a celebration tonight.

But our memories are not just political ones. I like to think back about a small artfully written magazine named *National Review,* founded in 1955 and ridiculed by the intellectual establishment because it published an editorial that said it would stand athwart the course of history yelling, "Stop!" And then there was a sprightly written newsweekly coming out of Washington named *Human Events* that many said would never be taken seriously, but it would become later "must reading" not only for Capitol Hill insiders but for all of those in public life.

How many of us were there who used to go home from meetings like this with no thought of giving up, but still find ourselves wondering in the dark of night whether this much-loved land might go the way of other great nations that lost a sense of mission and a passion for freedom?

There are so many people and institutions who come to mind for their role in the success we celebrate tonight. Intellectual leaders like Russell Kirk, Friedrich Hayek, Henry Hazlitt, Milton Friedman, James Burnham, Ludwig von Mises—they shaped so much of our thoughts.

It's especially hard to believe that it was only a decade ago, on a cold April day on a small hill in upstate New York, that another of these great thinkers, Frank Meyer, was buried. He'd made the awful journey that so many others had: He pulled himself from the clutches of "The God That Failed," and then in his writing fashioned a vigorous new synthesis of traditional and libertarian thought—a synthesis that is today recognized by many as modern conservatism.

It was Frank Meyer who reminded us that the robust individualism of the American experience was part of the deeper current of Western learning and culture. He pointed out that a respect for law, an appreciation for tradition, and regard for the social consensus that gives stability to our public and private institutions, these civilized ideas must still motivate us even as we seek a new economic prosperity based on reducing government interference in the marketplace.

Our goals complement each other. We're not cutting the budget simply for the sake of sounder financial management. This is only a first step toward returning power to the states and communities, only a first step toward reordering the relationship between citizen and government. We can make government again responsive to people not only by cutting its size and scope and thereby ensuring that its legitimate functions are performed efficiently and justly.

Because ours is a consistent philosophy of government, we can be very clear: We do not have a social agenda, separate, separate economic agenda, and a separate foreign agenda. We have one agenda. Just as surely as we seek to put our financial house in order and rebuild our nation's defenses, so too we seek to protect the unborn, to end the manipulation of schoolchildren by utopian planners, and permit the acknowledgment of a Supreme Being in our classrooms just as we allow such acknowledgments in other public institutions.

Now, obviously we're not going to be able to accomplish all this at once. The American people are patient. I think they realize that the wrongs done over several decades cannot be corrected instantly. You know, I had the pleasure in appearing before a Senate committee once while I was still governor, and I was challenged because there was a Republican president in the White House who'd been there for several months—why we hadn't then corrected everything that had been done. And the only way I could think to answer him is I told him about a ranch many years ago that Nancy and I acquired. It had a barn with eight stalls in it in which they had kept cattle, and we wanted to keep horses. And I was in there day after day with a pick and a shovel, lowering the level of those stalls, which had accumulated over the years. [*Laughter*] And I told this senator who'd asked that question that I discovered that you did not undo in weeks or months what it had taken some fifteen years to accumulate.

I also believe that we conservatives, if we mean to continue governing, must realize that it will not always be so easy to place the blame on the past for our national difficulties. You know, one day the great baseball manager Frankie Frisch sent a rookie out to play center field. The rookie promptly dropped the first fly ball that was hit to him. On the next play he let a grounder go between his feet and then threw the ball to the wrong base. Frankie stormed out of the dugout, took his glove away from him, and said, "I'll show you how to play this position." And the next batter slammed a line drive right over second base. Frankie came in on it, missed it completely, fell down when he tried to chase it, threw down his glove, and yelled at the rookie, "You've got center field so screwed up nobody can play it." [*Laughter*]

The point is we must lead a nation, and that means more than criticizing the past. Indeed, as T. S. Eliot once said, "Only by acceptance of the past will you alter its meaning."

Now, during our political efforts, we were the subject of much indifference and oftentimes intolerance, and that's why I hope our political victory will be remembered as a generous one and our time in power will be recalled for the tolerance we showed for those with whom we disagree.

But beyond this, beyond this we have to offer America and the world a larger vision. We must remove government's smothering hand from where it does harm; we must seek to revitalize the proper functions of government. But we do these things to set loose again the energy and the ingenuity of the American people. We do these things to reinvigorate those social and economic institutions which serve as a buffer and a bridge between the individual and the state—and which remain the real source of our progress as a people.

And we must hold out this exciting prospect of an orderly, compassionate, pluralistic society—an archipelago of prospering communities and divergent institutions—a place where a free and energetic people can work out their own destiny under God.

I know that some will think about the perilous world we live in and the dangerous decade before us and ask what practical effect this conservative vision can have today. When Prime Minister Thatcher was here recently we both remarked on the sudden, overwhelming changes that had come recently to politics in both our countries.

At our last official function, I told the Prime Minister that everywhere we look in the world the cult of the state is dying. And I held out hope that it wouldn't be long before those of our adversaries who preach the supremacy of the state were remembered only for their role in a sad, rather bizarre chapter in human history. The largest planned economy in the world has to buy food elsewhere or its people would starve.

We've heard in our century far too much of the sounds of anguish from those who live under totalitarian rule. We've seen too many monuments made not out of marble or stone but out of barbed wire and terror. But from these terrible places have come survivors, witnesses to the triumph of the human spirit over the mystique of state power, prisoners whose spiritual values made them the rulers of their guards. With their survival, they brought us "the secret of the camps," a lesson for our time and for any age: Evil is powerless if the good are unafraid.

That's why the Marxist vision of man without God must eventually be seen as an empty and a false faith—the second-oldest in the world—first proclaimed in the Garden of Eden with whispered words of temptation: "Ye shall be as gods." The crisis of the Western World, Whittaker Chambers reminded us, exists to the degree in which it is indifferent to God. "The Western World does not know it," he said about our struggle, "but it already possesses the answer to this problem —but only provided that its faith in God and the freedom He enjoins is as great as communism's faith in man."

This is the real task before us: to reassert our commitment as a nation to a law higher than our own, to renew our spiritual strength. Only by building a wall of such spiritual resolve can we, as a free people, hope to protect our own heritage and make it someday the birthright of all men.

There is, in America, a greatness and a tremendous heritage of idealism which is a reservoir of strength and goodness. It is ours if we will but tap it. And, because of this—because that greatness is there—there is need in America today for a reaffirmation of that goodness and a reformation of our greatness.

The dialog and the deeds of the past few decades are not sufficient to the day in which we live. They cannot keep the promise of tomorrow. The encrusted bureaucracies and the ingrained procedures which have developed of late respond neither to the minority nor the majority. We've come to a turning point. We have a decision to make. Will we continue with yesterday's agenda and yesterday's failures, or will we reassert our ideals and our standards, will we reaffirm our faith, and renew our purpose? This is a time for choosing.

I made a speech by that title in 1964. I said, "We've been

told increasingly that we must choose between left or right." But we're still using those terms—left or right. And I'll repeat what I said then in '64. "There is no left or right. There's only an up or down": up to the ultimate in individual freedom, man's age-old dream, the ultimate in individual freedom consistent with an orderly society—or down to the totalitarianism of the ant heap. And those today who, however good their intentions, tell us that we should trade freedom for security are on that downward path.

Those of us who call ourselves conservative have pointed out what's wrong with government policy for more than a quarter of a century. Now we have an opportunity to make policy and to change our national direction. All of us in government—in the House, in the Senate, in the executive branch—and in private life can now stand together. We can stop the drain on the economy by the public sector. We can restore our national prosperity. We can replace the overregulated society with the creative society. We can appoint to the bench distinguished judges who understand the first responsibility of any legal system is to punish the guilty and protect the innocent. We can restore to their rightful place in our national consciousness the values of family, work, neighborhood, and religion. And finally, we can see to it that the nations of the world clearly understand America's intentions and respect our resolve.

Now we have the opportunity—yes, and the necessity—to prove that the American promise is equal to the task of redressing our grievances and equal to the challenge of inventing a great tomorrow.

This reformation, this renaissance, will not be achieved or will it be served by those who engage in political claptrap or false promises. It will not be achieved by those who set people against people, class against class, or institution against institution. So, while we celebrate our recent political victory we must understand there's much work before us: to gain control again of government, to reward personal initiative and risk-taking in the marketplace, to revitalize our system of federalism, to strengthen the private institutions that make up the independent sector of our society, and to make our own spiritual affirmation in the face of those who would deny man has a place before God. Not easy tasks perhaps. But I would remind you as I did on January 20th, they're not impossible, because, after all, we're Americans.

This year we will celebrate a victory won two centuries ago at Yorktown, the victory of a small, fledgling nation over a mighty world power. How many people are aware—I've been told that a British band played the music at that surrender ceremony because we didn't have a band. [*Laughter*] And they played a tune that was very popular in England at the time. Its title was "The World Turned Upside Down." I'm sure it was far more appropriate than they realized at that moment. The heritage from that long, difficult struggle is before our eyes today in this city, in the great halls of our government and in the monuments to the memory of our great men.

It is this heritage that evokes the images of a much-loved land, a land of struggling settlers and lonely immigrants, of giant cities and great frontiers, images of all that our country is and all that we want her to be. That's the America entrusted to us, to stand by, to protect, and yes, to lead her wisely.

Fellow citizens, fellow conservatives, our time is now. Our moment has arrived. We stand together shoulder to shoulder in the thickest of the fight. If we carry the day and turn the tide, we can hope that as long as men speak of freedom and those who have protected it, they will remember us, and they will say, "Here were the brave and here their place of honor."

Thank you.

Remarks on the Departure of the U.S. Delegation to Funeral Services
for President Anwar Sadat

WHITE HOUSE SOUTH LAWN

OCTOBER 8, 1981

When news of President Sadat's assassination came, both Nancy and I had the same feeling—this is personal with us. He had crossed the line from that of simply another head of state with whom we did business to something more. Our sense of loss was personal with him, and we still keep in contact with Mrs. Sadat, whom we also greatly admire.

Just two months before, he had made an official state visit to the U.S. There were welcoming ceremonies with twenty-one–gun salutes, substantive meetings, and a state dinner with toasts to each other's health and friendship. And then it seemed he no sooner returned home than he was gone.

Anwar was a warm human being who didn't hold back from personalizing things. He had a wonderful laugh and a remarkable courage. He was one of a kind, and it's a damn shame we lost him.

Former presidents Nixon, Ford, and Carter led our official delegation to his funeral. I delivered the following remarks on the South Lawn of the White House on a cold, rainy evening before they departed.

ON BEHALF OF THE COUNTRY, I want to express a heartfelt thanks to Presidents Nixon, Ford, and Carter, and Mrs. Carter, for undertaking this sad mission. Their presence in Cairo will express to the Egyptian people the depth of America's grief and sorrow at the loss of a great leader and a beloved friend.

Today the American people stand beside the Egyptian people —the people of a new nation with the people of an ancient land; people of the West with the people of the East. We stand together in mourning the loss of Anwar Sadat and rededicating ourselves to the cause for which he so willingly gave his life.

There are times, there are moments in history, when the martyrdom of a single life can symbolize all that's wrong with an age and all that is right about humanity. The noble remnants of such lives—the spoken words of an Illinois lawyer who lived in this house, the diary of a young Dutch schoolgirl, the final moments of a soldier-statesman from Mit Abu el-Qum—can gain the force and power that endures and inspires and wins the ultimate triumph over the forces of violence, madness, and hatred.

Anwar Sadat, a man of peace in a time of violence, understood his age. In his final moments, as he had during all his days, he stood in defiance of the enemies of peace, the enemies of humanity. Today, those of us who follow him can do no less. And so to those who rejoice in the death of Anwar Sadat, to those who seek to set class against class, nation against nation, people against people, those who would choose violence over brotherhood and who prefer war over peace, let us stand in defiance and let our words of warning to them be clear: In life you feared Anwar Sadat, but in death you must fear him more. For the memory of this good and brave man will vanquish you. The meaning of his life and the cause for which he stood will endure and triumph. Not too long ago, he was asked in an interview if he didn't fear the possibility of the kind of violence that has now just taken his life. And he said, "I will not die one hour before God decides it is time for me to go."

Again, a heartfelt thank you to these men here, these three who are making this mission on behalf of our country. I thank you, and if I may, in the language of my own ancestry, say: Until we meet again, may God hold you in the hollow of His hand.

1982

Address to Members of the British Parliament

PALACE OF WESTMINSTER

JUNE 8, 1982

We had a rough year economically and politically in 1982. The recession, which began under my predecessor, hit full force in 1982. My Democratic opponents in the Congress began blaming our economic program, which they called Reaganomics, for the recession even before our tax and budget cuts had gone into effect. That really burned me up. Of course, after our program took effect and began turning the economy around, they didn't call it Reaganomics anymore. Unfortunately, that was too late for the congressional elections, in which the Republicans lost a number of seats.

But I think the real story of 1982 is that we began applying conservatism to foreign affairs. When I came into office, I believed there had been mistakes in our policy toward the Soviets in particular. I wanted to do some things differently, like speaking the truth about them for a change, rather than hiding reality behind the niceties of diplomacy. In the section for next year, for example, you'll see that I even called them an evil empire. That woke everybody up.

This speech before the British Parliament examined the West's concepts of democracy and its attitude toward communism and is probably one of the most important speeches I gave as president. What eventually flowed from it became known as the Reagan Doctrine, which was our often controversial policy of supporting those fighting for freedom and against communism wherever we found them. And we found them in such places as Afghanistan, Nicaragua, and Angola.

This address also fit into my plan of speaking my mind about communism. In retrospect, I am amazed that our national leaders had not philosophically and intellectually taken on the principles of Marxist-Leninism. We were always too worried we would offend the Soviets if we struck at anything so basic. Well, so what? Marxist-Leninist thought is an empty cupboard. Everyone knew it by the 1980s, but no one was saying it. I decided to articulate a few of these things.

I think our honesty helped the Soviets face up to their own weaknesses and uncertain future. General Secretary Gorbachev has had the foresight to see things previous Soviet leaders had been unwilling to see. We'll talk about my friend Gorbachev later. This speech is before his time.

M Y LORD CHANCELLOR, Mr. Speaker:
The journey of which this visit forms a part is a long one. Already it has taken me to two great cities of the West, Rome and Paris, and to the economic summit at Versailles. And there, once again, our sister democracies have proved that even in a time of severe economic strain, free peoples can work together freely and voluntarily to address problems as serious as inflation, unemployment, trade, and economic development in a spirit of cooperation and solidarity.

Other milestones lie ahead. Later this week, in Germany, we and our NATO allies will discuss measures for our joint defense and America's latest initiatives for a more peaceful, secure world through arms reductions.

Each stop of this trip is important, but among them all, this moment occupies a special place in my heart and in the hearts of my countrymen—a moment of kinship and homecoming in these hallowed halls.

Speaking for all Americans, I want to say how very much at home we feel in your house. Every American would, because this is, as we have been so eloquently told, one of democracy's shrines. Here the rights of free people and the processes of representation have been debated and refined.

It has been said that an institution is the lengthening shadow of a man. This institution is the lengthening shadow of all the men and women who have sat here and all those who have voted to send representatives here.

This is my second visit to Great Britain as president of the United States. My first opportunity to stand on British soil occurred almost a year and a half ago when your prime minister graciously hosted a diplomatic dinner at the British Embassy in Washington. Mrs. Thatcher said then that she hoped I was not distressed to find staring down at me from the grand staircase a portrait of His Royal Majesty King George III. She suggested it was best to let bygones be bygones, and in view of our two countries' remarkable friendship in succeeding years, she added that most Englishmen today would agree with Thomas Jefferson that "a little rebellion now and then is a very good thing." [*Laughter*]

Well, from here I will go to Bonn and then Berlin, where there stands a grim symbol of power untamed. The Berlin Wall, that dreadful gray gash across the city, is in its third decade. It is the fitting signature of the regime that built it.

And a few hundred kilometers behind the Berlin Wall, there is another symbol. In the center of Warsaw, there is a sign that notes the distances to two capitals. In one direction it points toward Moscow. In the other it points toward Brussels, headquarters of Western Europe's tangible unity. The marker says that the distances from Warsaw to Moscow and Warsaw to Brussels are equal. The sign makes this point: Poland is not East or West. Poland is at the center of European civilization. It has contributed mightily to that civilization. It is doing so today by being magnificently unreconciled to oppression.

Poland's struggle to be Poland and to secure the basic rights we often take for granted demonstrates why we dare not take those rights for granted. Gladstone, defending the Reform Bill of 1866, declared, "You cannot fight against the future. Time is on our side." It was easier to believe in the march of democracy in Gladstone's day—in that high noon of Victorian optimism.

We're approaching the end of a bloody century plagued by a terrible political invention—totalitarianism. Optimism comes less easily today, not because democracy is less vigorous, but because democracy's enemies have refined their instruments of repression. Yet optimism is in order, because day by day democracy is proving itself to be a not-at-all-fragile flower. From Stettin on the Baltic to Varna on the Black Sea, the regimes planted by totalitarianism have had more than thirty years to establish their legitimacy. But none—not one regime—has yet been able to risk free elections. Regimes planted by bayonets do not take root.

The strength of the Solidarity movement in Poland demonstrates the truth told in an underground joke in the Soviet Union. It is that the Soviet Union would remain a one-party nation even if an opposition party were permitted, because everyone would join the opposition party. [*Laughter*]

America's time as a player on the stage of world history has been brief. I think understanding this fact has always made you patient with your younger cousins—well, not always patient. I do recall that on one occasion, Sir Winston Churchill said in exasperation about one of our most distinguished diplomats: "He is the only case I know of a bull who carries his china shop with him." [*Laughter*]

But witty as Sir Winston was, he also had that special attribute of great statesmen—the gift of vision, the willingness to see the future based on the experience of the past. It is this sense of history, this understanding of the past that I want to talk with you about today, for it is in remembering what we share of the past that our two nations can make common cause for the future.

We have not inherited an easy world. If developments like the Industrial Revolution, which began here in England, and the gifts of science and technology have made life much easier for us, they have also made it more dangerous. There are threats now to our freedom, indeed to our very existence, that other generations could never even have imagined.

There is first the threat of global war. No president, no congress, no prime minister, no parliament can spend a day entirely free of this threat. And I don't have to tell you that in today's world the existence of nuclear weapons could mean, if not the extinction of mankind, then surely the end of civilization as we know it. That's why negotiations on intermediate-range nuclear forces now under way in Europe and the START talks—Strategic Arms Reduction Talks—which will begin later this month, are not just critical to American or Western policy; they are critical to mankind. Our commitment to early success in these negotiations is firm and unshakable, and our purpose is clear: reducing the risk of war by reducing the means of waging war on both sides.

At the same time there is a threat posed to human freedom by the enormous power of the modern state. History teaches the dangers of government that overreaches—political control taking precedence over free economic growth, secret police, mindless bureaucracy, all combining to stifle individual excellence and personal freedom.

Now, I'm aware that among us here and throughout Europe there is legitimate disagreement over the extent to which the public sector should play a role in a nation's economy and life. But on one point all of us are united—our abhorrence of dictatorship in all its forms, but most particularly totalitarianism and the terrible inhumanities it has caused in our time—the great purge, Auschwitz and Dachau, the gulag, and Cambodia.

Historians looking back at our time will note the consistent restraint and peaceful intentions of the West. They will note that it was the democracies who refused to use the threat of their nuclear monopoly in the forties and early fifties for territorial or imperial gain. Had that nuclear monopoly been in the hands of the Communist world, the map of Europe—indeed, the world—would look very different today. And certainly they will note it was not the democracies that invaded Afghanistan or suppressed Polish Solidarity or used chemical and toxic warfare in Afghanistan and Southeast Asia.

If history teaches anything, it teaches self-delusion in the face of unpleasant facts is folly. We see around us today the marks of our terrible dilemma—predictions of doomsday, antinuclear demonstrations, an arms race in which the West must, for its own protection, be an unwilling participant. At the same time we see totalitarian forces in the world who seek subversion and conflict around the globe to further their barbarous assault on the human spirit. What, then, is our course? Must civilization perish in a hail of fiery atoms? Must freedom wither in a quiet, deadening accommodation with totalitarian evil?

Sir Winston Churchill refused to accept the inevitability of war or even that it was imminent. He said, "I do not believe that Soviet Russia desires war. What they desire is the fruits of war and the indefinite expansion of their power and doctrines. But what we have to consider here today while time remains is the permanent prevention of war and the establishment of conditions of freedom and democracy as rapidly as possible in all countries."

Well, this is precisely our mission today: to preserve freedom as well as peace. It may not be easy to see; but I believe we live now at a turning point.

In an ironic sense Karl Marx was right. We are witnessing today a great revolutionary crisis, a crisis where the demands of the economic order are conflicting directly with those of the political order. But the crisis is happening not in the free, non-Marxist West, but in the home of Marxist-Leninism, the Soviet Union. It is the Soviet Union that runs against the tide of history by denying human freedom and human dignity to its citizens. It also is in deep economic difficulty. The rate of growth in the national product has been steadily declining since the fifties and is less than half of what it was then.

The dimensions of this failure are astounding: A country

which employs one-fifth of its population in agriculture is unable to feed its own people. Were it not for the private sector, the tiny private sector tolerated in Soviet agriculture, the country might be on the brink of famine. These private plots occupy a bare 3 percent of the arable land but account for nearly one-quarter of Soviet farm output and nearly one-third of meat products and vegetables. Overcentralized, with little or no incentives, year after year the Soviet system pours its best resources into the making of instruments of destruction. The constant shrinkage of economic growth combined with the growth of military production is putting a heavy strain on the Soviet people. What we see here is a political structure that no longer corresponds to its economic base, a society where productive forces are hampered by political ones.

The decay of the Soviet experiment should come as no surprise to us. Wherever the comparisons have been made between free and closed societies—West Germany and East Germany, Austria and Czechoslovakia, Malaysia and Vietnam—it is the democratic countries that are prosperous and responsive to the needs of their people. And one of the simple but overwhelming facts of our time is this: Of all the millions of refugees we've seen in the modern world, their flight is always away from, not toward the Communist world. Today on the NATO line, our military forces face east to prevent a possible invasion. On the other side of the line, the Soviet forces also face east to prevent their people from leaving.

The hard evidence of totalitarian rule has caused in mankind an uprising of the intellect and will. Whether it is the growth of the new schools of economics in America or England or the appearance of the so-called new philosophers in France, there is one unifying thread running through the intellectual work of these groups—rejection of the arbitrary power of the state, the refusal to subordinate the rights of the individual to the superstate, the realization that collectivism stifles all the best human impulses.

Since the exodus from Egypt, historians have written of those who sacrificed and struggled for freedom—the stand at Thermopylae, the revolt of Spartacus, the storming of the Bastille, the Warsaw uprising in World War II. More recently we've seen evidence of this same human impulse in one of the developing nations in Central America. For months and months the world news media covered the fighting in El Salvador. Day after day we were treated to stories and film slanted toward the brave freedom fighters battling oppressive government forces in behalf of the silent, suffering people of that tortured country.

And then one day those silent, suffering people were offered a chance to vote, to choose the kind of government they wanted. Suddenly the freedom fighters in the hills were exposed for what they really are—Cuban-backed guerrillas who want power for themselves, and their backers, not democracy for the people. They threatened death to any who voted, and destroyed hundreds of buses and trucks to keep the people from getting to the polling places. But on election day, the people of El Salvador, an unprecedented 1.4 million of them, braved ambush and gunfire, and trudged for miles to vote for freedom.

They stood for hours in the hot sun waiting for their turn to vote. Members of our Congress who went there as observers told me of a woman who was wounded by rifle fire on the way to the polls, who refused to leave the line to have her wound treated until after she had voted. A grandmother, who had been told by the guerrillas she would be killed when she returned from the polls, and she told the guerrillas, "You can kill me, you can kill my family, kill my neighbors, but you can't kill us all." The real freedom fighters of El Salvador turned out to be the people of that country—the young, the old, the in-between.

Strange, but in my own country there's been little if any news coverage of that war since the election. Now, perhaps they'll say it's—well, because there are newer struggles now.

On distant islands in the South Atlantic young men are fighting for Britain. And yes, voices have been raised protesting their sacrifice for lumps of rock and earth so far away. But those young men aren't fighting for mere real estate. They fight for a cause—for the belief that armed aggression must not be allowed to succeed, and the people must participate in the decisions of government—[*Applause*]—the decisions of government under the rule of law. If there had been firmer support for that principle some forty-five years ago, perhaps our generation wouldn't have suffered the bloodletting of World War II.

In the Middle East now the guns sound once more, this time in Lebanon, a country that for too long has had to endure the tragedy of civil war, terrorism, and foreign intervention and occupation. The fighting in Lebanon on the part of all parties must stop, and Israel should bring its forces home. But this is not enough. We must all work to stamp out the scourge of terrorism that in the Middle East makes war an ever-present threat.

But beyond the trouble spots lies a deeper, more positive pattern. Around the world today, the democratic revolution is gathering new strength. In India a critical test has been passed with the peaceful change of governing political parties. In Africa, Nigeria is moving in remarkable and unmistakable ways to build and strengthen its democratic institutions. In the Caribbean and Central America, sixteen of twenty-four countries have freely elected governments. And in the United Nations, eight of the ten developing nations which have joined that body in the past five years are democracies.

In the Communist world as well, man's instinctive desire for freedom and self-determination surfaces again and again. To be sure, there are grim reminders of how brutally the police state attempts to snuff out this quest for self-rule—1953 in East Germany, 1956 in Hungary, 1968 in Czechoslovakia, 1981 in Poland. But the struggle continues in Poland. And we know that there are even those who strive and suffer for freedom within the confines of the Soviet Union itself. How we conduct ourselves here in the Western democracies will determine whether this trend continues.

No, democracy is not a fragile flower. Still it needs cultivating. If the rest of this century is to witness the gradual growth of freedom and democratic ideals, we must take actions to assist the campaign for democracy.

Some argue that we should encourage democratic change in

right-wing dictatorships, but not in Communist regimes. Well, to accept this preposterous notion—as some well-meaning people have—is to invite the argument that once countries achieve a nuclear capability, they should be allowed an undisturbed reign of terror over their own citizens. We reject this course.

As for the Soviet view, Chairman Brezhnev repeatedly has stressed that the competition of ideas and systems must continue and that this is entirely consistent with relaxation of tensions and peace.

Well, we ask only that these systems begin by living up to their own constitutions, abiding by their own laws, and complying with the international obligations they have undertaken. We ask only for a process, a direction, a basic code of decency, not for an instant transformation.

We cannot ignore the fact that even without our encouragement there has been and will continue to be repeated explosions against repression and dictatorships. The Soviet Union itself is not immune to this reality. Any system is inherently unstable that has no peaceful means to legitimize its leaders. In such cases, the very repressiveness of the state ultimately drives people to resist it, if necessary, by force.

While we must be cautious about forcing the pace of change, we must not hesitate to declare our ultimate objectives and to take concrete actions to move toward them. We must be staunch in our conviction that freedom is not the sole prerogative of a lucky few, but the inalienable and universal right of all human beings. So states the United Nations Universal Declaration of Human Rights, which, among other things, guarantees free elections.

The objective I propose is quite simple to state: to foster the infrastructure of democracy, the system of a free press, unions, political parties, universities, which allows a people to choose their own way to develop their own culture, to reconcile their own differences through peaceful means.

This is not cultural imperialism, it is providing the means for genuine self-determination and protection for diversity. Democracy already flourishes in countries with very different cultures and historical experiences. It would be cultural condescension, or worse, to say that any people prefer dictatorship to democracy. Who would voluntarily choose not to have the right to vote, decide to purchase government propaganda handouts instead of independent newspapers, prefer government- to worker-controlled unions, opt for land to be owned by the state instead of those who till it, want government repression of religious liberty, a single political party instead of a free choice, a rigid cultural orthodoxy instead of democratic tolerance and diversity?

Since 1917 the Soviet Union has given covert political training and assistance to Marxist-Leninists in many countries. Of course, it also has promoted the use of violence and subversion by these same forces. Over the past several decades, West European and other Social Democrats, Christian Democrats, and leaders have offered open assistance to fraternal, political, and social institutions to bring about peaceful and democratic progress. Appropriately, for a vigorous new democracy, the Federal Republic of Germany's political foundations have become a major force in this effort.

We in America now intend to take additional steps, as many of our allies have already done, toward realizing this same goal. The chairmen and other leaders of the national Republican and Democratic party organizations are initiating a study with the bipartisan American Political Foundation to determine how the United States can best contribute as a nation to the global campaign for democracy now gathering force. They will have the cooperation of congressional leaders of both parties, along with representatives of business, labor, and other major institutions in our society. I look forward to receiving their recommendations and to working with these institutions and the Congress in the common task of strengthening democracy throughout the world.

It is time that we committed ourselves as a nation—in both the public and private sectors—to assisting democratic development.

We plan to consult with leaders of other nations as well.

There is a proposal before the Council of Europe to invite parliamentarians from democratic countries to a meeting next year in Strasbourg. That prestigious gathering could consider ways to help democratic political movements.

This November in Washington there will take place an international meeting on free elections. And next spring there will be a conference of world authorities on constitutionalism and self-government hosted by the Chief Justice of the United States. Authorities from a number of developing and developed countries—judges, philosophers, and politicians with practical experience—have agreed to explore how to turn principle into practice and further the rule of law.

At the same time, we invite the Soviet Union to consider with us how the competition of ideas and values—which it is committed to support—can be conducted on a peaceful and reciprocal basis. For example, I am prepared to offer President Brezhnev an opportunity to speak to the American people on our television if he will allow me the same opportunity with the Soviet people. We also suggest that panels of our newsmen periodically appear on each other's television to discuss major events.

Now, I don't wish to sound overly optimistic, yet the Soviet Union is not immune from the reality of what is going on in the world. It has happened in the past—a small ruling elite either mistakenly attempts to ease domestic unrest through greater repression and foreign adventure, or it chooses a wiser course. It begins to allow its people a voice in their own destiny. Even if this latter process is not realized soon, I believe the renewed strength of the democratic movement, complemented by a global campaign for freedom, will strengthen the prospects for arms control and a world at peace.

I have discussed on other occasions, including my address on May 9th, the elements of Western policies toward the Soviet Union to safeguard our interests and protect the peace. What I am describing now is a plan and a hope for the long term—the march of freedom and democracy which will leave Marxism-Leninism on the ash heap of history as it has left other tyrannies which stifle the freedom and muzzle the self-expression of the people. And that's why we must continue our efforts to strengthen NATO even as we move forward with our Zero-Option initiative in the negotiations on intermediate-range forces and our proposal for a one-third reduction in strategic ballistic missile warheads.

Our military strength is a prerequisite to peace, but let it be clear we maintain this strength in the hope it will never be used, for the ultimate determinant in the struggle that's now going on in the world will not be bombs and rockets, but a test of wills and ideas, a trial of spiritual resolve, the values we hold, the beliefs we cherish, the ideals to which we are dedicated.

The British people know that, given strong leadership, time, and a little bit of hope, the forces of good ultimately rally and triumph over evil. Here among you is the cradle of self-government, the mother of parliaments. Here is the enduring greatness of the British contribution to mankind, the great civilized ideas: individual liberty, representative government, and the rule of law under God.

I've often wondered about the shyness of some of us in the West about standing for these ideals that have done so much to ease the plight of man and the hardships of our imperfect world. This reluctance to use those vast resources at our command reminds me of the elderly lady whose home was bombed in the Blitz. As the rescuers moved about, they found a bottle of brandy she'd stored behind the staircase, which was all that was left standing. And since she was barely conscious, one of the workers pulled the cork to give her a taste of it. She came around immediately and said, "Here now—there now, put it back. That's for emergencies." [*Laughter*]

Well, the emergency is upon us. Let us be shy no longer. Let us go to our strength. Let us offer hope. Let us tell the world that a new age is not only possible but probable.

During the dark days of the Second World War, when this island was incandescent with courage, Winston Churchill exclaimed about Britain's adversaries, "What kind of a people do they think we are?" Well, Britain's adversaries found out what extraordinary people the British are. But all the democracies paid a terrible price for allowing the dictators to underestimate us. We dare not make that mistake again. So, let us ask ourselves, "What kind of people do we think we are?" And let us answer, "Free people, worthy of freedom and determined not only to remain so but to help others gain their freedom as well."

Sir Winston led his people to great victory in war and then lost an election just as the fruits of victory were about to be enjoyed. But he left office honorably, and as it turned out, temporarily, knowing that the liberty of his people was more important than the fate of any single leader. History recalls his greatness in ways no dictator will ever know. And he left us a message of hope for the future, as timely now as when he first uttered it, as opposition leader in the Commons nearly twenty-seven years ago, when he said, "When we look back on all the perils through which we have passed and at the mighty foes that we have laid low and all the dark and deadly designs that we have frustrated, why should we fear for our future? We have," he said, "come safely through the worst."

Well, the task I've set forth will long outlive our own generation. But together, we too have come through the worst. Let us now begin a major effort to secure the best—a crusade for freedom that will engage the faith and fortitude of the next generation. For the sake of peace and justice, let us move toward a world in which all people are at last free to determine their own destiny.

Thank you.

--   Thank you. Boy, I cleaned up -- a Golden E pin, a bust in

my honor, and induction into the Eureka Athletic Hall of

Fame. I~~'ve been lucky enough to receive a couple other~~

I thought I'd reached the pinnacle when ~~commendations from our alma mater. listen to what~~ the 1931

Prism ~~had to say,~~ *said that as →* "~~Dutch~~ Reagan, president of the Booster

Club, received commendation for ~~his~~ *my* part in managing the

committees in charge of the homecoming festivities." . . .

I Wish I could ~~manage the committees in the Congress with as much success~~. *remember first what I said. There are a few congressional committees I'd like to manage.*

--

I've stopped telling anyone about receiving Eureka's Centennial ~~I was telling some people the other day that in 1955 I~~ *Citation in 1955. People thought it referred to my centennial.* ~~received Eureka's Centennial Citation. They thought that~~

was wonderful because I didn't look that old. And you know

there's a Reagan Memorabilia Collection on campus. Ed Meese

is scared to death that after we leave office, he's going to

be in it.

-

I've spent the day in a warm flood of ~~But, honestly, today genuinely has caused a flood of~~ *nostalgia.* *you must be feeling the same way.* ~~memories for me.~~ And ~~I know you're feeling the very same emotions.~~ Eureka is ~~something that's~~ *is* in all our hearts.

Eureka College Alumni Dinner

PEORIA, ILLINOIS
MAY 9, 1982

While I was back in Illinois giving a commencement address at my alma mater, I also attended an alumni dinner. This was pure heaven for me. I love Eureka College. It's a very small school without a national Ivy League reputation, but if I had it to do all over again, I'd go right back there for my education.

The advantage of a smaller school is that you can't be anonymous. On these megacampuses with tens of thousands of students, you can get lost. You can escape being part of campus life. In small schools, everybody is part of college life. You're asked to do things because they always need people on this committee or that one.

Also in small schools, the faculty has personal knowledge of you. In my day, the professors would know who your steady girl was or whom you were dating. Sometimes a professor would ask you to watch his house for him while he and his wife went out for the evening. Now, there's no reason in Eureka, Illinois, for someone to watch your house. But the professor knew full well this would give you a chance to sit in front of the fire with a girl.

I genuinely enjoy reminiscing and I did my share of it that evening.

W ELL, I THANK JUST EVERYBODY. I've cleaned up—a Golden E pin, a plaque, a bust in my honor, being in the Eureka Athletic Hall of Fame. I thought I had reached the pinnacle when the 1931 *Prism* said that as president of the Booster Club I received commendation for my part in managing the committees in charge of the homecoming festivities. [*Laughter*] You don't know how much I wish I could remember what I did. [*Laughter*] There are a few committees on Capitol Hill that need some managing right now. [*Laughter*]

But, Mac,* this—if we could have gotten this many people to a football game on a Saturday afternoon, we wouldn't have had to wear the same pants two or three years. [*Laughter*] We could have had you new uniforms. But I'm not quite sure whether I got this for three years as guard or for making some touchdowns for Notre Dame at Warner Brothers. [*Laughter*]

I was interviewed just the other day before I came out here by a reporter from the *Bloomington Pantagraph*, who came up and wanted to talk all about memories, Illinois here and Eureka

---

* William McNett, president of the Eureka College Alumni Association.

College and all. And then he said, "Well now, there's a story going around about you scoring a touchdown against Normal in the last minutes of play." And that just goes to show you how stories can get stretched. [*Laughter*] I can tell you about that touchdown.

We were one point ahead, as I remember. And there was just seconds to go. I'd been in the entire game, and Normal was passing, throwing bombs all over. And I finally decided because —you remember that no one in our backfield was over about five nine or ten in those days, so our pass defense wasn't all it should be if anyone on the other side was taller than they were. So, I used to charge against my man and then when I felt it was going to be a pass, duck back into the secondary and see if I could help cover for passes.

And I saw everyone sucked over to one side of the field, and this Normal fellow—never forget that bright red jersey—going down the field all by himself. And I took out after him. And pretty soon, as he was looking back, I knew the ball must be coming. And I turned around and here it came, and I went up in the air, I got it, but by this time, as I say, having been in the entire game, I knew that there wasn't anything left in me. There was a lineman's dream, a guard way over on the sideline, about seventy-five yards from the goal line but a clear field down that sideline. But coming down with the ball, I thought if I just juggle it for a second or two, he'll tackle me. We still win the ball game, and I won't have to run. [*Laughter*]

Well, I juggled it and I bent over, and I juggled it some more and nothing happened. [*Laughter*] And just as I started to raise my head, he put his arms around me and said, "Tag, you're it." [*Laughter*]

At the same moment, I saw a substitute coming in for me, I knew. And I started for the sideline, and one Ralph McKenzie, very serious of face—indeed, angry of face—said, "What happened to you?" And all I could say was, "I'm tired." [*Laughter*] But that—I told the reporter—that was my touchdown that was never made, my lineman's dream.

You know, one thing I've stopped talking about is that—

receiving Eureka's centennial citation in 1955. Too many people began to think it was *my* centennial. [*Laughter*]

But I've spent the day in a warm flood of nostalgia, as I'm sure a great many of you have. You must be feeling the same way. Eureka is in all our hearts. And it gave me the greatest happiness today to be on the campus and to see today's students and to see that that same spirit and that same love is there among them every bit as great as it has been among us. They'll carry the memory of days at Eureka as abundantly and warm as we have carried them.

I got a letter a few months ago from Mrs. Lee Putnam, class of '50. Lee, are you here someplace? There. Hey, you don't mind if I let them in on your letter. Lee is the daughter of Professor Tom Wiggins, our English professor that so many of us remember so well. And she wrote me this letter about some of the memories that she had of her recollections of the 1930s at Eureka. Well, if she was the class of '50, she had to be pretty young in the 1930s. But she said they're vivid—"faculty teas before the fireplace; Daddy reading; Mother playing the piano; bluebooks being graded; having Carl Sandburg as an overnight guest; and eating canned salmon, spinach, and baked beans night after night. [*Laughter*] The college had an arrangement with the Happy Hour Canning Factory in Bloomington which allowed us to order canned goods, since no salaries were paid during that time." And that's right.

"We also received dairy products from the college farm run by Frank Felter. I was too young to be aware then, but the entire community must have pitched in to save Eureka College." And that is what happened.

Day after day in those classrooms, those professors just as if they were getting paid on time—I've thought about that sometimes when I see some teachers' strikes lately. But I believe that that spirit is still at Eureka—in the town, the faculty, and the students.

And Lee, I have to tell you a memory that I have of your father—God bless him. It seems that the late Bud Cole—God rest his soul—and I were declared ineligible if we did not take a makeup exam, and it was the day before the homecoming game. So, we went over to the gym that afternoon, and we got into our football uniforms. And then we went up in the Burgess Hall to the classroom where your father was there. And he gave us each two questions and said, "Take your choice of one." And he said, "I'll be in the Administration Building if you need me." And we finished the exam in quick time and went out to the field, convinced that we had passed the exam—and we had —and were able to play the next day in the game. That spirit of Eureka lasts not only four years but a lifetime, and that's why there are so many of you gathered here this evening.

And by the way, I want to thank Lee for writing. I don't know quite what to make of this, but later in the letter she writes, "My sister Barbara Cooper is a sergeant in Burbank, California, Police Department and has met you." [*Laughter*] Wait till the press gets hold of that. [*Laughter*]

But I can't tell you how wonderful it has been. The only fly in the ointment—the thing that's really wrong is that today is over, and now we turn back into pumpkins again because we can't even stay for dinner. This is the first time I've been a before-dinner speaker been an after-dinner speaker many times. But we have to go out and get in that airplane and be on our way. So, we have to leave. But to be here among you again —everyone in Washington that's in government should have to, at regular intervals, have this kind of an experience, because there is a real difference between the real world and what's on the other side of the Potomac.

So, from one Red Devil to all the others—[*Laughter*]—hail to maroon and gold, and hail to our alma mater, and I think all of us should pledge in our hearts that it will be there long after we're gone doing for young people what it did for all of us.

God bless you, and I wish we could stay and say hello to every one of you. It's been a very thrilling and exciting time for us. And I leave greatly rewarded.

I have one little story I just want to tell before I go. [*Laughter*] I'm having a hard time getting away from here. For my graduation speech, we had decided in Washington that I should make a speech on the world situation and our plans for attempting disarmament, reduction of nuclear weapons, and so forth. And they were talking about what would be a proper forum in which to make this speech before I go to Europe at the end of this month to meet with our allies and all. And I said, "I have the perfect forum: I am making a speech in Illinois." And I reminded them of Winnie Churchill making a speech at a little college in Missouri some years ago in which he coined the term "Iron Curtain."

So, I said, we'll make the speech there. But to those who were there today, I told them of a little story that illustrates the humor of the Russian people and their cynicism about their way of life and their government. And I had to choose between two. So, I won't repeat the one that I told there today—[*Laughter*]—but the one I wanted to tell and didn't—and this is truly—the jokes—I've come to be a collector of these that the Russian people tell among themselves that reveals their feeling about their government.

And it has to do with when Brezhnev first became president. And he invited his elderly mother to come up and see his suite of offices in the Kremlin and then put her in his limousine and drove her to his fabulous apartment there in Moscow. And in both places, not a word. She looked; she said nothing. Then he put her in his helicopter and took her out to the country home outside Moscow in a forest. And again, not a word. Finally, he put her in his private jet and down to the shores of the Black Sea to see that marble palace which is known as his beach

home. And finally she spoke. She said, "Leonid, what if the Communists find out?" [*Laughter*]

We love you. We envy you for being able to stay, and God bless all of you.

Thank you.

Remarks at the Recommissioning
of the USS *New Jersey*

LONG BEACH, CALIFORNIA
DECEMBER 28, 1982

I believe another reason the American people voted me in was to rebuild our nation's military, which was in a state of disrepair and neglect. For too long, our leaders had thought we could have a strong military on the cheap, and so it was the military budget that was always cut. Eventually the American people no longer felt secure, and I hope they elected me to do something about it. We had our work cut out for us. As I often said during the campaign of 1980, we had planes that couldn't fly and ships that couldn't leave port. Really, that was no exaggeration.

Military hardware and readiness were only part of the problem. We had a serious morale problem in the military as well. The self-esteem of our people in uniform had been going down since Vietnam. Maybe I had seen too many war movies, the heroics of which I sometimes confused with real life, but common sense told me something very essential—you can't have a fighting force without an esprit de corps.

So one of my first priorities was to rebuild our military and, just as important, our military's morale. The recommissioning of the New Jersey *is representative of what we had to do.*

SECRETARY LEHMAN,* I thank you. Captain Fogarty, the officers and members of the crew, the other distinguished guests:

Secretary of Defense Weinberger would be here, but with all of us here he felt that someone had to stay in Washington and mind the store.

Surrounded by all this Navy blue and gold, I've had the strange feeling that I'm back on the set filming *Hellcats of the Navy*. [*Laughter*] That was a picture that was based on a great, victorious operation of the Navy in World War II in the Sea of Japan called Operation Hellcat. I remember at the time I was in love with my leading lady. She is Nancy, my wife, and I'm still in love with her, but I have to confess that today I find myself developing a great respect for the leading lady in these ceremonies. She's gray, she's had her face lifted, but she's still in the prime of life, a gallant lady: the *New Jersey*.

I'm honored to be here for the recommissioning of this mighty force for peace and freedom. Putting this great ship back to work protecting our country represents a major step toward fulfilling our pledge to rebuild America's military capabilities. It marks the resurgence of our nation's strength. It's a strength we can afford. We cannot afford to lose it.

Since the founding of our armed forces during the Revolutionary War, our country has always done without large standing armies and navies. Our great success story—unique in history—has been based on peaceful achievements in every sphere of human experience. In our two centuries of continuous democracy, we've been the envy of the world in technology, commerce, agriculture, and economic potential.

Our status as a free society and world power is not based on brute strength. When we've taken up arms, it has been for the defense of freedom for ourselves and for other peaceful nations

* Secretary of the Navy John Lehman.

who needed our help. But now, faced with the development of weapons with immense destructive power, we've no choice but to maintain ready defense forces that are second to none. Yes, the cost is high, but the price of neglect would be infinitely higher.

Another great power in the world sees its military forces in a different light. The Soviet Union has achieved sheer power status only by—or I should say superpower status—only by virtue of its military might. It has done so by sacrificing and ignoring achievement in virtually any and every other field.

In contrast, America's strength is the bedrock of the free world's security, for the freedom we guard is not just our own. But over the past years we began to drift dangerously away from what was so clearly our responsibility. From 1970 to 1979, our defense spending, in constant dollars, decreased by 22 percent. The Navy, so vital to protecting our interests in faraway trouble spots, shrank—as you've been told by the secretary—from more than 1,000 ships to 453.

Potential adversaries saw this unilateral disarmament, which was matched in all the other services, as a sign of weakness and a lack of will necessary to protect our way of life. While we talked of détente, the lessening of tensions in the world, the Soviet Union embarked on a massive program of militarization. Since around 1965, they have increased their military spending, nearly doubling it over the past fifteen years.

In a free society such as ours, where differing viewpoints are permitted, there will be people who oppose defense spending of any kind at any level. There are others who believe in defense, but who mistakenly feel that the Department of Defense is inherently wasteful and unconcerned about cost-cutting. Well, they're dead wrong.

Waste in government spending of any kind is an ever-present threat. But I can assure our fellow citizens there is no room for waste in our national defense. A dollar wasted is a dollar lost in the crucial effort to build a safer future for our people. Secretary Weinberger and the members of this administration are committed to spending what is necessary for defense to secure the peace and not a penny more. As the recommissioning of this ship demonstrates, we are rearming with prudence, using existing assets to the fullest.

To those who've been led to believe that we've gone overboard on national security needs and are spending a disproportionate share on the military, let me state: This is not true.

In spite of all the sound and fury that we hear and read, defense spending as a percentage of gross national product is well below what it was in the Eisenhower and Kennedy years. The simple fact is that, by reforming defense procurement, by stressing efficiencies and economies in weapons system production, we have been able to structure and fund a defense program our nation can afford. It meets the threat, and it provides wages and benefits that are more akin to what our men and women in uniform deserve.

Already, we're realizing tremendous dividends from our defense program. The readiness of our forces is dramatically improved. As you've just been told, we're more than meeting our recruitment goals. And we've had congressional support for such key initiatives as the purchase of two aircraft carriers, the B-1 bomber, and the C-5 transport plane.

As a nation, we're committed to take every step to reduce substantially the possibility of nuclear war, while providing an unshakable deterrent to such a war for ourselves and our allies. To this end, we're closing the window of vulnerability by instituting a comprehensive strategic force modernization program.

But while we do this, we're advancing vigorous arms control proposals aimed at deep and verifiable reductions in strategic nuclear missiles. We have proposed that intermediate-range nuclear missiles in Europe be reduced to zero on both sides at the same time we cut conventional forces in Europe to balanced levels. And I may say, the news is encouraging. The Soviet Union has met us halfway on the zero option. They've agreed to zero on our part. [*Laughter*]

We can't shut our eyes to the fact that, as the Soviet military power increased, so did their willingness to embark on military adventures. The scars are plainly evident in a number of Third

World countries. We're also aware that, though the Soviet Union is historically a land power—virtually self-sufficient in mineral and energy resources and land-linked to Europe and the vast stretches of Asia—it has created a powerful, blue-ocean navy that cannot be justified by any legitimate defense need. It is a navy built for offensive action, to cut the free world's supply lines and render impossible the support, by sea, of free world allies.

By contrast, the United States is a naval power by necessity, critically dependent on the transoceanic import of vital strategic materials. Over 90 percent of our commerce between the continents moves in ships. Freedom to use the seas is our nation's lifeblood. For that reason, our Navy is designed to keep the sea-lanes open worldwide, a far greater task than closing those sea-lanes at strategic choke points.

Maritime superiority for us is a necessity. We must be able in time of emergency to venture in harm's way, controlling air, surface, and subsurface areas to assure access to all the oceans of the world. Failure to do so will leave the credibility of our conventional defense forces in doubt.

We are, as I said, building a 600-ship fleet, including 15 carrier battle groups. But numbers are not the final test. Those ships must be highly capable.

The *New Jersey* and her sister ships can outgun and outclass any rival platform. This 58,000-ton ship, whose armor alone weighs more than our largest cruiser, is being recommissioned at no more than the cost of a new 4,000-ton frigate. The "Big J" is being reactivated with the latest in missile electronic warfare and communications technology. She's more than the best means of quickly adding real firepower to our Navy; she's a shining example of how this administration will rebuild America's armed forces on budget and on schedule and with the maximum cost-effective application of high technology to existing assets.

The *New Jersey*'s mission is to conduct prompt and sustained operations worldwide, in support of our national interests. In some cases, deployment of the *New Jersey* will free up our overstressed aircraft carriers for other uses. While the aircraft carrier remains the foundation of American naval power, the battleship will today be the sovereign of the seas. In support of amphibious operations, the *New Jersey*'s 16-inch guns can deliver shells as heavy as an automobile with pinpoint accuracy. And with a speed of thirty-five knots, the *New Jersey* will be among the fastest ships afloat.

History tells us that a delegate to the Continental Congress called the creation of our Navy "the maddest idea in the world." Well, we've been questioned for bringing back this battleship. Yet, I would challenge anyone who's been aboard or even seen the *New Jersey* to argue its value. It seems odd and a little ironic to me that some of the same critics who accuse us of chasing technology and gold-plating our weapons systems have led the charge against the superbly cost-effective and maintainable *New Jersey*. I doubt if there's a better example of the cost-consciousness of this administration than the magnificent ship that we're recommissioning today.

However, even with maximum efficiency and an eye toward making every dollar count, we must not fool ourselves. Providing an adequate defense is not cheap. The price of peace is always high, but considering the alternative, it's worth it.

Teddy Roosevelt said it well. "We Americans have many grave problems to solve, many threatening evils to fight, and many deeds to do if, as we hope and believe, we have the wisdom, the strength, the courage, and the virtue to do them. But we must face facts as they are. Our nation is that one among all nations of the earth which holds in its hands the fate of the coming years."

Today, I'd like to take this opportunity to thank all of those who worked on the *New Jersey*. You're a great team, and you did an outstanding job in putting her back into fighting trim. You represent a new spirit, a new sense of responsibility that we must have in all our shipyards and defense-related industries if public support for our vital task is to be maintained.

This ship, as the secretary told us, was brought in on time and on budget. And from all reports, the craftsmanship and professionalism of those involved in the project were superior, and I'm pleased to have the opportunity to extend the thanks of a grateful nation.

The *New Jersey,* like any ship in our fleet, will depend on the ability, dedication, and yes, patriotism of you here who are her crew. You're the elite. Six thousand applied for 1,500 crew spaces on the *New Jersey.* I have no doubt, too, that from among your ranks will come the Spruances and the Halseys and the Thompsons of tomorrow.

A few moments ago I quoted Teddy Roosevelt. Most people remember him as a man of strength and vitality, and yes, some have an image of a warlike man always spoiling for a fight. Well, let us remember, he won the Nobel Peace Prize, an honor bestowed upon him for his courageous and energetic efforts to end the Russo-Japanese war. He knew the relationship between peace and strength. And he knew the importance of a strong navy.

"The Navy of the United States," he said, "is the right arm of the United States and is emphatically the peacemaker. Woe to our country if we permit that right arm to become palsied or even to become flabby and inefficient."

Well, the *New Jersey* today becomes our 514th ship and represents our determination to rebuild the strength of America's right arm so that we can preserve the peace.

After valiant service in Vietnam and after saving the lives of countless marines, the *New Jersey* was decommissioned in 1969. During that solemn ceremony, her last commanding officer, Captain Robert Penniston, spoke prophetically when he suggested that this mighty ship "rest well, yet sleep lightly, and hear the call, if again sounded, to provide firepower for freedom."

Well, the call has been sounded. America needs the battleship once again to provide firepower for the defense of freedom and above all, to maintain the peace. She will truly fulfill her mission if her firepower never has to be used.

Captain Fogarty, I hereby place the United States Ship *New Jersey* in commission.

God bless, and Godspeed.

PRESIDENT'S REMARKS: NATIONAL PRAYER BREAKFAST
                      FEBRUARY 4, 1982

     Thank you, John. Nancy and I are delighted to be with you
this morning and honored to be in such distinguished company.

     General Dozier, I

you only consider doin

going to pull rank on

     We want to give t

want to salute the Ita

rescue, and, Jim, we

your gallantry, and say

said that a hero is no

brave five minutes lor

longer.

     Now we know why I

celebration. Last yea

something else -- my

don't worry because I

commissioned him for

Abraham was 100 and h

truly amazing. He liv

put $2,000 a year inte

     Many of you

that has particular

who dreamt he walked

walked, above him in

Page 2

experience of his life. Reaching the end of the beach, and as

his life, he looked back and saw two sets of footprints

places   only one.

would walk with

hand. Why did Y

of greatest need

leave you. When

there that I ca

          Just year

And now we've s

God carried him

We need only th

" . . . weeping

morning." [Ps

     Speaking

for all your p

are put here i

     There

and a will

People hav

they do i

does.

     Well

Good Sama

law, with fa

wounds o

there's

needs w

Ou

involve

Page 3

     Sometimes, we seem to have strayed from that noble

beginning -- strayed from our conviction that standards of right

and wrong do exist and must be lived up to. God, the source of

our knowledge   public schools. He

gives us His

condone the t

     We cann

turn away fr

     I wonde

waiting for

Him and eac

meaning to

Page 4

               churches and synagogues to take the lead i

restoring our spirit of neighbor caring for neighbor.

     We know what you are already doing, and, believe me, we'

grateful. If all of you worked for the Federal Government, y

would be classified "essential." We need you, now more than

ever.

                      we want the private sector

for dollar -- every Federal program being reduced.

                                                We're not asking you to replace what hasn't worked. Nor

is it

     We want you to raise our spirits and reach into our pockets

spark the conviction in us all that we should be doing God's wor

on Earth.

     We will never find every answer, solve every problem, heal

every wound, or live all our dreams. But we can do a lot, if we

walk together down that one path we know provides real hope. We

have His promise that what we give in love will be given back

many times over. Love will never fail.

     So, let us rekindle the fire of our faith.

     Let our wisdom be vindicated by our deeds.

     and when our work is done, we can say -- we have fought the

good fight, we have finished the race, we have kept the faith.

     Thank you. God bless you.

Annual National Prayer Breakfast

WASHINGTON, D.C.
FEBRUARY 4, 1982

I went to the national prayer breakfasts almost every year. It's a gathering of people who come together because of their belief in prayer. I never came away from one of these sessions without feeling stronger for it. It's a remarkable feeling to know that people are praying for you and for your strength. I know first-hand. I felt those prayers when I was recovering from that bullet.

I find this sort of interesting. When I played football in college, I always said a prayer while waiting for the kickoff. I never asked to win. I prayed to do my best. I prayed that no one got hurt. And I prayed I would have no regrets when the game was over because I had done my utmost. Years later, I realized that this was almost the identical prayer I was saying as president. I find that prayer does sustain and guide.

By the way, the General Dozier I mention in the following remarks is the U.S. general who was kidnapped by terrorists and then dramatically rescued by Italian police.

THANK YOU VERY MUCH, John*, all our friends and distinguished guests here at the head table, and all of you very distinguished people. Nancy and I are delighted to be with you this morning, and are honored to be here.

* Senator John Stennis of Mississippi.

General Dozier, I know you don't like being praised for what you only consider was doing your duty. Forgive me, I'm going to pull rank on you. [*Laughter*] We want to give thanks to God for answering our prayers. We want to salute the Italian authorities for their brilliant rescue, and Jim, we just want to thank both you and Judith for your gallantry. Welcome home, soldier.

Someone once said that a hero is no braver than any other man. He's just brave five minutes longer. Well, General, you were brave forty-two days longer. And now we know why prayer breakfasts are a time for praise and celebration.

Last year, you all helped me begin celebrating the thirty-first anniversary of my thirty-ninth birthday. [*Laughter*] And I must say that all of those pile up, an increase of numbers, don't bother me at all, because I recall that Moses was 80 when God commissioned him for public service, and he lived to be 120. [*Laughter*] And Abraham was 100 and his wife Sarah 90 when they did something truly amazing—[*Laughter*]—and he lived to be 175. Just imagine if he had put $2,000 a year into his IRA account. [*Laughter*]

Those of you who were here last year might remember that I shared a story by an unknown author, a story of a dream he had had. He had dreamt, as you recall, that he walked down the beach beside the Lord. And as they walked, above him in the sky was reflected each experience of his life. And then reaching the end of the beach, he looked back and saw the two sets of footprints extending down the way, but suddenly noticed that every once in a while there was only one set of footprints. And each time, they were opposite a reflection in the sky of a time of great trial and suffering in his life. And he turned to the Lord in surprise and said, "You promised that if I walked with You, You would always be by my side. Why did You desert me in my times of need?" And the Lord said, "My beloved child, I wouldn't desert you when you needed Me. When you see only one set of footprints, it was then that I carried you."

Well, when I told that story last year, I said I knew, having only been here in this position for a few weeks, that there would be many times for me in the days ahead when there would be only one set of footprints and I would need to be carried, and if I didn't believe that I would be, I wouldn't have the courage to do what I was doing.

Shortly thereafter, there came a moment when, without doubt, I was carried. And now, we've seen in General Dozier's life such a moment. Well, God is with us. We need only to believe. The psalmist says, "Weeping may endure for a night, but joy cometh in the morning."

Speaking for Nancy and myself, we thank you for your faith and for all your prayers on our behalf. And it is true that you can sense and feel that power.

I've always believed that we were, each of us, put here for a reason, that there is a plan, somehow a divine plan for all of us. I know now that whatever days are left to me belong to Him.

I also believe this blessed land was set apart in a very special way, a country created by men and women who came here not in search of gold, but in search of God. They would be free people, living under the law with faith in their Maker and their future.

Sometimes, it seems we've strayed from that noble beginning, from our conviction that standards of right and wrong do exist and must be lived up to. God, the source of our knowledge, has been expelled from the classroom. He gives us His greatest blessing, life, and yet many would condone the taking of innocent life. We expect Him to protect us in a crisis, but turn away from Him too often in our day-to-day living. I wonder if He isn't waiting for us to wake up.

There is, as Pete* so eloquently said, in the American heart a spirit of love, of caring, and a willingness to work together. If we remember the parable of the Good Samaritan, he crossed the road, knelt down, and bound up the wounds of the beaten traveler, the Pilgrim, and then carried him into the nearest town. He didn't just hurry on by into town and then look up a

* Senator Pete V. Domenici of New Mexico.

caseworker and tell him there was a fellow back out on the road that looked like he might need help.

Isn't it time for us to get personally involved, for our churches and synagogues to restore our spirit of neighbor caring for neighbor? But talking to this particular gathering, I realize I'm preaching to the choir. If all of you worked for the federal government, you would be classified as essential. We need you now more than ever to remind us that we should be doing God's work on earth. We'll never find every answer, solve every problem, or heal every wound, but we can do a lot if we walk together down that one path that we know provides real hope.

You know, in one of the conflicts that was going on throughout the past year when views were held deeply on both sides of the debate, I recall talking to one senator who came into my office. We both deeply believed what it was we were espousing, but we were on opposite sides. And when we finished talking, as he rose, he said, "I'm going out of here and do some praying." And I said, "Well, if you get a busy signal, it's me there ahead of you." [*Laughter*]

We have God's promise that what we give will be given back many times over, so let us go forth from here and rekindle the fire of our faith. Let our wisdom be vindicated by our deeds.

We are told in II Timothy that when our work is done, we can say, "We have fought the good fight. We have finished the race. We have kept the faith." This is an evidence of it.

I hope that on down through the centuries not only is this great land preserved but this great tradition is preserved and that all over the land there will always be this one day in the year when we remind ourselves of what our real task is.

God bless you. Thank you.

Christmas Day Radio Address
to the Nation

DECEMBER 25, 1982

When I became president, I got back in the radio business again. I gave a five-minute radio address every Saturday at noon eastern standard time. The first one was in April of 1982, and by the time I finished at the end of my two terms, I'd done 331 of these weekly broadcasts, almost a year of Saturdays.

The shows gave me a chance to talk about what was current in the news that week and to get things off my chest. It also gave me a chance to share items that came across my desk, like letters and newspaper clippings and such, with the American people. The following radio piece fits in the latter category.

MERRY CHRISTMAS from the White House. Nancy and I wish we could personally thank the thousands of you who've sent us holiday cards, greetings, and messages. Each one is moving and tells a story of its own—a story of love, hope, prayer, and patriotism. And each one has helped to brighten our Christmas.

Some of the most moving have come from fellow citizens who, unlike most of us, are not spending Christmas day at the family hearth, surrounded by friends and loved ones. I'm thinking of the twelve U.S. marines who sent us a card from Beirut, Lebanon, where they'll spend their Christmas helping to rebuild the shattered hopes for peace in a suffering land. And I'm thinking of the petty officer serving aboard the USS *Enterprise* who asked that we remember him and his shipmates this holiday season. "Christmas in the Indian Ocean is *no* fun," he writes, "but it's for a very good cause."

Well, that's right, sailor. You're serving a very good cause, indeed. On this, the birthday of the Prince of Peace, you and your comrades serve to protect the peace He taught us. You may be thousands of miles away, but to us here at home, you've never been closer.

One of my favorite pieces of Christmas mail came early this year, a sort of modern American Christmas story that took place not in our country's heartland, but on the troubled waters of the South China Sea last October. To me, it sums up so much of what is best about the Christmas spirit, the American character, and what this beloved land of ours stands for—not only to ourselves but to millions of less fortunate people around the globe.

I want to thank Mr. Gary Kemp of Neenah, Wisconsin, for bringing it to my attention. It's a letter from Ordnance Man, First Class, John Mooney, written to his parents from aboard the aircraft carrier *Midway* on October 15th. But it's a true Christmas story in the best sense.

"Dear Mom and Dad," he wrote, "today we spotted a boat in the water, and we rendered assistance. We picked up sixty-five Vietnamese refugees. It was about a two-hour job getting everyone aboard, and then they had to get screened by intelligence and checked out by medical and fed and clothed and all that.

"But now they're resting on the hangar deck, and the kids—most of them seem to be kids . . . are sitting in front of probably the first television set they've ever seen, watching *Star Wars.* Their boat was sinking as we came alongside. They'd been at sea five days and had run out of water. All in all, a couple of more days and the kids would have been in pretty bad shape.

"I guess once in a while," he writes, "we need a jolt like that for us to realize why we do what we do and how important, really, it can be. I mean, it took a lot of guts for those parents to make a choice like that to go to sea in a leaky boat in hope of finding someone to take them from the sea. So much risk! But apparently they felt it was worth it rather than live in a Communist country.

"For all of our problems, with the price of gas, and not being able to afford a new car or other creature comforts this year . . . I really don't see a lot of leaky boats heading out of San Diego looking for the Russian ships out there. . . .

"After the refugees were brought aboard, I took some pictures, but as usual I didn't have my camera with me for the REAL picture—the one blazed in my mind. . . .

"As they approached the ship, they were all waving and trying as best they could to say, 'Hello, America sailor! Hello, freedom man!' It's hard to see a boat full of people like that and not get a lump somewhere between chin and belly button. And it really makes one proud and glad to be an American. People were waving and shouting and choking down lumps and trying not to let other brave men see their wet eyes. A lieutenant next to me said, 'Yeah, I guess it's payday in more ways than one.' (We got paid today.) And I guess no one could say it better than that.

"It reminds us all of what America has always been—a place a man or woman can come to for freedom. I know we're crowded and we have unemployment and we have a real burden with refugees, but I honestly hope and pray we can always find room. We have a unique society, made up of castoffs of all the world's wars and oppressions, and yet we're strong and free. We have one thing in common—no matter where our forefathers came from, we believe in that freedom.

"I hope we always have room for one more person, maybe an Afghan or a Pole or someone else looking for a place . . . where he doesn't have to worry about his family's starving or a knock on the door in the night . . . and where all men who truly seek freedom and honor and respect and dignity for themselves and their posterity can find a place where they can . . . finally see their dreams come true and their kids educated and become the next generation of doctors and lawyers and builders and soldiers and sailors.

"Love, John."

Well, I think that letter just about says it all. In spite of everything, we Americans are still uniquely blessed, not only with the rich bounty of our land but by a bounty of the spirit —a kind of year-round Christmas spirit that still makes our country a beacon of hope in a troubled world and that makes this Christmas and every Christmas even more special for all of us who number among our gifts the birthright of being an American.

Until next week, thanks for listening. Merry Christmas, and God bless you.

1983

Address on Central America
Before a Joint Session of the Congress

APRIL 27, 1983

In my mind, 1983 is the year of regional conflicts—the horrible bombing of our Marine barracks in Beirut, the rescue of Grenada, and the solidifying of the Marxist-Leninist regime in Nicaragua. The situation in Lebanon would return to haunt me in the form of an increasing number of American hostages over there. The situation in Nicaragua would continue to defy resolution because of the weakness of Congress in supporting peoples willing to fight for their freedom.

This address before the Congress deals with the struggle for democracy in Central America and was the first major speech I gave on the subject. I was to give many, many more in my attempts to bring pressure on Nicaragua's Sandinista government. Our best hope for democracy in Nicaragua was and remains the contras, the freedom fighters whom the Democratic Congress kept pulling the rug out from under. History will judge the Congress's grudging and constantly changing policy toward the contras as a disgrace.

I could never seem to convince the Congress what was going on down there. The Nicaraguans had a very sophisticated disinformation campaign that completely bamboozled many on Capitol Hill. Congressional delegations would go to Nicaragua and simply be shown what the Sandinistas wanted them to see. I also honestly believe the Sandinistas hoodwinked many in the American press.

One day I saw an article in the paper about a Catholic bishop

*from Iowa who had led some Nicaraguan refugees out of Nic-
aragua and across the border into Honduras. The story said
they had been attacked by the contras and rescued by the Sandinistas. Well, I found this disturbing if true, so I tracked him
down and called him. He said, yes, he did lead some of his
people out, but that the story was exactly backward—they
were attacked by the Sandinistas and rescued by the contras.*

*On two different occasions I met with Nicaraguan clergymen
who'd had their ears cut off with bayonets by the Sandinistas
for preaching. I remember one man's story in particular. The
Sandinistas had tied this one young Nicaraguan preacher to a
tree and cut off his ears. They then cut his throat and ruthlessly
said, "Now call upon your God. Maybe He can help you." The
clergyman's congregation got to him before he bled to death.
He himself told me that story in the Oval Office of the White
House. Both ministers were available to the press, and yet their
stories never appeared in the major papers or on the evening
news.*

M R. SPEAKER, MR. PRESIDENT, distinguished members of
the Congress, honored guests, and my fellow Americans:

A number of times in past years, members of Congress and a
president have come together in meetings like this to resolve a
crisis. I have asked for this meeting in the hope that we can
prevent one.

It would be hard to find many Americans who aren't aware
of our stake in the Middle East, the Persian Gulf, or the NATO
line dividing the free world from the Communist bloc. And the
same could be said for Asia.

But in spite of, or maybe because of, a flurry of stories about
places like Nicaragua and El Salvador and yes, some concerted
propaganda, many of us find it hard to believe we have a stake
in problems involving those countries. Too many have thought
of Central America as just that place way down below Mexico

that can't possibly constitute a threat to our well-being. And that's why I've asked for this session. Central America's problems do directly affect the security and the well-being of our own people. And Central America is much closer to the United States than many of the world trouble spots that concern us. So, we work to restore our own economy; we cannot afford to lose sight of our neighbors to the south.

El Salvador is nearer to Texas than Texas is to Massachusetts. Nicaragua is just as close to Miami, San Antonio, San Diego, and Tucson as those cities are to Washington, where we're gathered tonight.

But nearness on the map doesn't even begin to tell the strategic importance of Central America, bordering as it does on the Caribbean—our lifeline to the outside world. Two-thirds of all our foreign trade and petroleum pass through the Panama Canal and the Caribbean. In a European crisis at least half of our supplies for NATO would go through these areas by sea. It's well to remember that in early 1942, a handful of Hitler's submarines sank more tonnage there than in all of the Atlantic Ocean. And they did this without a single naval base anywhere in the area. And today, the situation is different. Cuba is host to a Soviet combat brigade, a submarine base capable of servicing Soviet submarines, and military air bases visited regularly by Soviet military aircraft.

Because of its importance, the Caribbean Basin is a magnet for adventurism. We're all aware of the Libyan cargo planes refueling in Brazil a few days ago on their way to deliver "medical supplies" to Nicaragua. Brazilian authorities discovered the so-called medical supplies were actually munitions and prevented their delivery.

You may remember that last month, speaking on national television, I showed an aerial photo of an airfield being built on the island of Grenada. Well, if that airfield had been completed, those planes could have refueled there and completed their journey.

If the Nazis during World War II and the Soviets today could recognize the Caribbean and Central America as vital to our

147

interests, shouldn't we, also? For several years now, under two administrations, the United States has been increasing its defense of freedom in the Caribbean Basin. And I can tell you tonight, democracy is beginning to take root in El Salvador, which, until a short time ago, knew only dictatorship.

The new government is now delivering on its promises of democracy, reforms, and free elections. It wasn't easy, and there was resistance to many of the attempted reforms, with assassinations of some of the reformers. Guerrilla bands and urban terrorists were portrayed in a worldwide propaganda campaign as freedom fighters, representative of the people. Ten days before I came into office, the guerrillas launched what they called "a final offensive" to overthrow the government. And their radio boasted that our new administration would be too late to prevent their victory.

Well, they learned that democracy cannot be so easily defeated. President Carter did not hesitate. He authorized arms and munitions to El Salvador. The guerrilla offensive failed, but not America's will. Every president since this country assumed global responsibilities has known that those responsibilities could only be met if we pursued a bipartisan foreign policy.

As I said a moment ago, the government of El Salvador has been keeping its promises, like the land reform program which is making thousands of farm tenants, farm owners. In a little over three years, 20 percent of the arable land in El Salvador has been redistributed to more than 450,000 people. That's one in ten Salvadorans who have benefited directly from this program.

El Salvador has continued to strive toward an orderly and democratic society. The government promised free elections. On March 28th, a little more than a year ago, after months of campaigning by a variety of candidates, the suffering people of El Salvador were offered a chance to vote, to choose the kind of government they wanted. And suddenly, the so-called freedom fighters in the hills were exposed for what they really are —a small minority who want power for themselves and their backers, not democracy for the people. The guerrillas threatened death to anyone who voted. They destroyed hundreds of buses and trucks to keep the people from getting to the polling places. Their slogan was brutal: "Vote today, die tonight." But on election day, an unprecedented 80 percent of the electorate braved ambush and gunfire and trudged for miles, many of them, to vote for freedom. Now, that's truly fighting for freedom. We can never turn our backs on that.

Members of this Congress who went there as observers told me of a woman who was wounded by rifle fire on the way to the polls, who refused to leave the line to have her wound treated until after she had voted. Another woman had been told by the guerrillas that she would be killed when she returned from the polls, and she told the guerrillas, "You can kill me, you can kill my family, you can kill my neighbors. You can't kill us all." The real freedom fighters of El Salvador turned out to be the people of that country—the young, the old, the in-between—more than a million of them out of a population of less than 5 million. The world should respect this courage and not allow it to be belittled or forgotten. And again I say, in good conscience, we can never turn our backs on that.

The democratic political parties and factions in El Salvador are coming together around the common goal of seeking a political solution to their country's problems. New national elections will be held this year, and they will be open to all political parties. The government has invited the guerrillas to participate in the election and is preparing an amnesty law. The people of El Salvador are earning their freedom, and they deserve our moral and material support to protect it.

Yes, there are still major problems regarding human rights, the criminal justice system, and violence against noncombatants. And like the rest of Central America, El Salvador also faces severe economic problems. But in addition to recession-depressed prices for major agricultural exports, El Salvador's economy is being deliberately sabotaged.

Tonight in El Salvador—because of ruthless guerrilla attacks —much of the fertile land cannot be cultivated; less than half the rolling stock of the railways remains operational; bridges, water facilities, telephone and electric systems have been destroyed and damaged. In one twenty-two-month period, there were five thousand interruptions of electrical power. One region was without electricity for a third of the year.

I think Secretary of State Shultz put it very well the other day: "Unable to win the free loyalty of El Salvador's people, the guerrillas," he said, "are deliberately and systematically depriving them of food, water, transportation, light, sanitation, and jobs. And these are the people who claim they want to help the common people." They don't want elections because they know they'd be defeated. But as the previous election showed, the Salvadoran people's desire for democracy will not be defeated.

The guerrillas are not embattled peasants, armed with muskets. They're professionals, sometimes with better training and weaponry than the government's soldiers. The Salvadoran battalions that have received U.S. training have been conducting themselves well on the battlefield and with the civilian population. But so far, we've only provided enough money to train one Salvadoran soldier out of ten, fewer than the number of guerrillas that are trained by Nicaragua and Cuba.

And let me set the record straight on Nicaragua, a country next to El Salvador. In 1979 when the new government took over in Nicaragua, after a revolution which overthrew the authoritarian rule of Somoza, everyone hoped for the growth of democracy. We in the United States did, too. By January of 1981, our emergency relief and recovery aid to Nicaragua totaled $118 million—more than provided by any other developed country. In fact, in the first two years of Sandinista rule, the United States directly or indirectly sent five times more aid to Nicaragua than it had in the two years prior to the revolution. Can anyone doubt the generosity and the good faith of the American people?

These were hardly the actions of a nation implacably hostile to Nicaragua. Yet, the government of Nicaragua has treated us as an enemy. It has rejected our repeated peace efforts. It has broken its promises to us, to the Organization of American States, and most important of all, to the people of Nicaragua.

No sooner was victory achieved than a small clique ousted others who had been part of the revolution from having any voice in the government. Humberto Ortega, the minister of defense, declared Marxism-Leninism would be their guide, and so it is.

The government of Nicaragua has imposed a new dictatorship. It has refused to hold the elections it promised. It has seized control of most media and subjects all media to heavy prior censorship. It denied the bishops and priests of the Roman Catholic Church the right to say Mass on radio during Holy Week. It insulted and mocked the Pope. It has driven the Miskito Indians from their homelands, burning their villages, destroying their crops, and forcing them into involuntary internment camps far from home. It has moved against the private sector and free labor unions. It condoned mob action against Nicaragua's independent human rights commission and drove the director of that commission into exile.

In short, after all these acts of repression by the government, is it any wonder that opposition has formed? Contrary to propaganda, the opponents of the Sandinistas are not diehard supporters of the previous Somoza regime. In fact, many are anti-Somoza heroes and fought beside the Sandinistas to bring down the Somoza government. Now they've been denied any part in the new government because they truly wanted democracy for Nicaragua and they still do. Others are Miskito Indians fighting for their homes, their lands, and their lives.

The Sandinista revolution in Nicaragua turned out to be just an exchange of one set of autocratic rulers for another, and the people still have no freedom, no democratic rights, and more poverty. Even worse than its predecessor, it is helping Cuba and the Soviets to destabilize our hemisphere.

Meanwhile, the government of El Salvador, making every effort to guarantee democracy, free labor unions, freedom of religion, and a free press, is under attack by guerrillas dedicated to the same philosophy that prevails in Nicaragua, Cuba, and yes, the Soviet Union. Violence has been Nicaragua's most important export to the world. It is the ultimate in hypocrisy for the unelected Nicaraguan government to charge that we seek their overthrow, when they're doing everything they can to bring down the elected government of El Salvador. [*Applause*] Thank you. The guerrilla attacks are directed from a headquarters in Managua, the capital of Nicaragua.

But let us be clear as to the American attitude toward the government of Nicaragua. We do not seek its overthrow. Our interest is to ensure that it does not infect its neighbors through the export of subversion and violence. Our purpose, in conformity with American and international law, is to prevent the flow of arms to El Salvador, Honduras, Guatemala, and Costa Rica. We have attempted to have a dialog with the government of Nicaragua, but it persists in its efforts to spread violence.

We should not, and we will not, protect the Nicaraguan government from the anger of its own people. But we should, through diplomacy, offer an alternative. And as Nicaragua ponders its options, we can and will—with all the resources of diplomacy—protect each country of Central America from the danger of war.

Even Costa Rica, Central America's oldest and strongest democracy—a government so peaceful it doesn't even have an army—is the object of bullying and threats from Nicaragua's dictators.

Nicaragua's neighbors know that Sandinista promises of peace, nonalliance, and nonintervention have not been kept. Some thirty-six new military bases have been built. There were only thirteen during the Somoza years. Nicaragua's new army numbers 25,000 men, supported by a militia of 50,000. It is the largest army in Central America, supplemented by 2,000 Cuban military and security advisers. It is equipped with the most modern weapons—dozens of Soviet-made tanks, 800 Soviet-bloc trucks, Soviet 152-millimeter howitzers, 100 antiaircraft guns, plus planes and helicopters. There are additional thousands of civilian advisers from Cuba, the Soviet Union, East Germany, Libya, and the PLO. And we're attacked because we have 55 military trainers in El Salvador.

The goal of the professional guerrilla movements in Central

America is as simple as it is sinister: to destabilize the entire region from the Panama Canal to Mexico. And if you doubt beyond this point, just consider what Cayetano Cárpio, the now-deceased Salvadoran guerrilla leader, said earlier this month. Cárpio said that after El Salvador falls, El Salvador and Nicaragua would be "arm-in-arm and struggling for the total liberation of Central America."

Nicaragua's dictatorial junta, who themselves made war and won power operating from bases in Honduras and Costa Rica, like to pretend that they are today being attacked by forces based in Honduras. The fact is, it is Nicaragua's government that threatens Honduras, not the reverse. It is Nicaragua who has moved heavy tanks close to the border, and Nicaragua who speaks of war. It was Nicaraguan radio that announced on April 8th the creation of a new, unified, revolutionary coordinating board to push forward the Marxist struggle in Honduras.

Nicaragua, supported by weapons and military resources provided by the Communist bloc, represses its own people, refuses to make peace, and sponsors a guerrilla war against El Salvador.

President Truman's words are as apt today as they were in 1947 when he, too, spoke before a joint session of the Congress:

"At the present moment in world history, nearly every nation must choose between alternate ways of life. The choice is not too often a free one. One way of life is based upon the will of the majority and is distinguished by free institutions, representative government, free elections, guarantees of individual liberty, freedom of speech and religion, and freedom from political oppression. The second way of life is based upon the will of a minority forcibly imposed upon the majority. It relies upon terror and oppression, a controlled press and radio, fixed elections, and the suppression of personal freedoms.

"I believe that it must be the policy of the United States to support free peoples who are resisting attempted subjugation by armed minorities or by outside pressures. I believe that we must assist free peoples to work out their own destinies in their own way. I believe that our help should be primarily through economic and financial aid which is essential to economic stability and orderly political processes.

"Collapse of free institutions and loss of independence would be disastrous not only for them but for the world. Discouragement and possibly failure would quickly be the lot of neighboring peoples striving to maintain their freedom and independence."

The countries of Central America are smaller than the nations that prompted President Truman's message. But the political and strategic stakes are the same. Will our response—economic, social, military—be as appropriate and successful as Mr. Truman's bold solutions to the problems of postwar Europe?

Some people have forgotten the successes of those years and the decades of peace, prosperity, and freedom they secured. Some people talk as though the United States were incapable of acting effectively in international affairs without risking war or damaging those we seek to help.

Are democracies required to remain passive while threats to their security and prosperity accumulate? Must we just accept the destabilization of an entire region from the Panama Canal to Mexico on our southern border? Must we sit by while independent nations of this hemisphere are integrated into the most aggressive empire the modern world has seen? Must we wait while Central Americans are driven from their homes like the more than a million who've sought refuge out of Afghanistan, or the one and a half million who have fled Indochina, or the more than a million Cubans who have fled Castro's Caribbean utopia? Must we, by default, leave the people of El Salvador no choice but to flee their homes, creating another tragic human exodus?

I don't believe there's a majority in the Congress or the country that counsels passivity, resignation, defeatism, in the face of this challenge to freedom and security in our own hemisphere. [*Applause*] Thank you. Thank you.

I do not believe that a majority of the Congress or the country is prepared to stand by passively while the people of Central America are delivered to totalitarianism and we ourselves are left vulnerable to new dangers.

Only last week, an official of the Soviet Union reiterated Brezhnev's threat to station nuclear missiles in this hemisphere, five minutes from the United States. Like an echo, Nicaragua's Comandante Daniel Ortega confirmed that, if asked, his country would consider accepting those missiles. I understand that today they may be having second thoughts.

Now, before I go any further, let me say to those who invoke the memory of Vietnam, there is no thought of sending American combat troops to Central America. They are not needed— [Applause]

Thank you. And, as I say, they are not needed, and indeed, they have not been requested there. All our neighbors ask of us is assistance in training and arms to protect themselves while they build a better, freer life.

We must continue to encourage peace among the nations of Central America. We must support the regional efforts now under way to promote solutions to regional problems.

We cannot be certain that the Marxist-Leninist bands who believe war is an instrument of politics will be readily discouraged. It's crucial that we not become discouraged before they do. Otherwise, the region's freedom will be lost and our security damaged in ways that can hardly be calculated.

If Central America were to fall, what would the consequences be for our position in Asia, Europe, and for alliances such as NATO? If the United States cannot respond to a threat near our own borders, why should Europeans or Asians believe that we're seriously concerned about threats to them? If the Soviets can assume that nothing short of an actual attack on the United States will provoke an American response, which ally, which friend will trust us then?

The Congress shares both the power and the responsibility for our foreign policy. Tonight, I ask you, the Congress, to join me in a bold, generous approach to the problems of peace and poverty, democracy and dictatorship in the region. Join me in a program that prevents Communist victory in the short run, but goes beyond, to produce for the deprived people of the area the reality of present progress and the promise of more to come.

Let us lay the foundation for a bipartisan approach to sustain the independence and freedom of the countries of Central America. We in the administration reach out to you in this spirit.

We will pursue four basic goals in Central America:

First, in response to decades of inequity and indifference, we will support democracy, reform, and human freedom. This means using our assistance, our powers of persuasion, and our legitimate leverage to bolster humane democratic systems where they already exist and to help countries on their way to that goal complete the process as quickly as human institutions can be changed. Elections in El Salvador and also in Nicaragua must be open to all, fair and safe. The international community must help. We will work at human rights problems, not walk away from them.

Second, in response to the challenge of world recession and, in the case of El Salvador, to the unrelenting campaign of economic sabotage by the guerrillas, we will support economic development. And by a margin of two to one our aid is economic now, not military. Seventy-seven cents out of every dollar we will spend in the area this year goes for food, fertilizers, and other essentials for economic growth and development. And our economic program goes beyond traditional aid. The Caribbean Initiative introduced in the House earlier today will provide powerful trade and investment incentives to help these countries achieve self-sustaining economic growth without exporting U.S. jobs. Our goal must be to focus our immense and growing technology to enhance health care, agriculture, industry, and to ensure that we who inhabit this interdependent region come to know and understand each other better, retaining our diverse identities, respecting our diverse traditions and institutions.

And *third,* in response to the military challenge from Cuba and Nicaragua—to their deliberate use of force to spread tyranny—we will support the security of the region's threatened nations. We do not view security assistance as an end in itself, but as a shield for democratization, economic development, and diplomacy. No amount of reform will bring peace so long as guerrillas believe they will win by force. No amount of economic help will suffice if guerrilla units can destroy roads and bridges and power stations and crops, again and again, with impunity. But with better training and material help, our neighbors can hold off the guerrillas and give democratic reform time to take root.

And *fourth,* we will support dialog and negotiations both among the countries of the region and within each country. The terms and conditions of participation in elections are negotiable. Costa Rica is a shining example of democracy. Honduras has made the move from military rule to democratic government. Guatemala is pledged to the same course. The United States will work toward a political solution in Central America which will serve the interests of the democratic process.

To support these diplomatic goals, I offer these assurances: The United States will support any agreement among Central American countries for the withdrawal, under fully verifiable and reciprocal conditions, of all foreign military and security advisers and troops. We want to help opposition groups join the political process in all countries and compete by ballots instead of bullets. We will support any verifiable, reciprocal agreement among Central American countries on the renunciation of support for insurgencies on neighbors' territory. And finally, we desire to help Central America end its costly arms race and will support any verifiable, reciprocal agreements on the nonimportation of offensive weapons.

To move us toward these goals more rapidly, I am tonight announcing my intention to name an ambassador at large as my special envoy to Central America. He or she will report to me through the secretary of state. The ambassador's responsibilities will be to lend U.S. support to the efforts of regional governments to bring peace to this troubled area and to work

Mr. Speaker, Mr. President, distinguished members of Congress honored guests & my fellow Americans.

A number of times in past years members of Congress + a Pres. have come together in meetings like this to resolve a crisis. I have asked for this meeting in the hope that we can prevent one.

It would be hard to find many Americans who aren't aware of our stake in the Middle East, the Persian gulf or the Nato line dividing the free world from the Communist block. The same . . . . . be said for Asia.

But in spite of our magn . . . of stories about places like . . . . and yes some concerted, prop . . . find it hard to believe we . . . problems involving these countr . . . a place, way down below M . . . constitutes a threat to our wel . . .

That is why I have aske . . . Central American problems do . . . security & well being of our . . . America is much closer to the . . . the world trouble spots that . . .

El Salvador is clo . . . . to Te . . . Mass., Nicaragua is closer to Mia . . . San Antonio, Los Angeles & Denver . . . are to Wash. where we are gat . . .

But just nearness on the map . . . strategic importance of Central Amer . . . on the Caribbean — our lifeline to th . . . almost half of all our foreign tra . . . oil pass through the Panama Can . . . In a European crisis ⅔ of our sup . . . would go through these areas by . . . to Europe. It is well to reme . . . 1942 a handful of Hitlers subma . . . tonnage there than in all of the . . . And they did this without a su . . . anywhere in the area.

Central America is much closer to the b . . . trouble spots that concern us. El Salv . . . than Texas is to Massachusetts. Nicara . . . New Orleans, Houston, Los Angeles, and . . . are to Washington where we are gathered . . .

But nearness on the map doesn't tel . . . importance of Central America, bordering . . . Caribbean -- our lifeline to the outside . . . all our foreign trade tonnage and crude o . . . Panama Canal and the Caribbean. In a Eur . . . of our mobilization requirements would go . . . sea. It is well to remember that in earl . . . Hitler's submarines sank more tonnage the . . . Atlantic Ocean. And they did this without . . . anywhere in the area.

Today, the situation is different . . . the soviets are diligently ply . . . host to a Soviet combat brigade, a submari . . . servicing Soviet nuclear submarines, and m . . . visited regularly by Soviet aircraft.

Because of its importance, the Caribb . . . of adventurism. We're all aware of the Lib . . . refueling in Brazil on their way to deliver . . . Nicaragua. Brazilian authorities discovered . . . . prevented their delivery.

If the Nazis during World War II and . . . consider the Caribbean and Central America . . . interests, shouldn't we also?

For several years now, under two adm . . . States has been increasing its defense of . . . Caribbean Basin. And I can tell you toni . . . which would be blossom in El Salvador. The . . . beginning to blossom in El Salvador, . . . delivering on its promises of democracy, . . . elections. It wasn't easy and there was . . . the attempted reforms with assassination . . . Guerrilla bands and urban terrorists we . . . worldwide propaganda campaign as freedo . . . of the people. Ten days before I came . . . guerrillas launched what they called a . . . overthrow the government. Their radio . . . Administration would be too late to pr . . . learned democracy cannot be so easily . . .

President Carter had not hesitat . . . ammunition, and military trainers to . . . offensive failed, but not America's w . . .

As I said a moment ago, the gov . . . promises, like the land reform progr . . . of farm tenants, farm owners. In a . . . 20 percent of the arable land in El . . . . to more than 450,000 . . . . directly benefitted fro . . .

El Salvador . . . democratic socie . . . March 28th, litt . . . campaigning by a . . . El Salvador were . . . of government th . . . fighters in the . . . small minority . . . not democracy . . . anyone who vot . . . to keep the pu . . . slogan was br . . . day, an unpre . . . and gunfire, . . . truly fightin . . .

Members . . . of a woman w . . . who refused . . . after she ha . . . guerrillas . . . and she to . . . family, ki . . . freedom fi . . . that count . . . 1 million . . . The world . . . belittled . . .

---

we seek their overthrow when they are doing everything they c . . . to bring down the elected government of El Salvador. The gu . . . . . . clear as to the American attitude toward . . . But let us be clear as to the American attitude toward . . . government of Nicaragua. We do not seek its overthrow. Our . . . interest is to insure that it does not infect its neighbors . . . through the export of subversion and violence. Our purpos . . . conformity with American and international law, is to pre . . . flow of arms to El Salvador, Guatemala, and Costa Rica. . . . . effective dialogue, however, the government of . . . persists in its efforts to spread violence.

It is Nicaragua's government that has moved heavy . . . It is Nicaragua that speaks of war . . . not the reverse. It is Nicaragua that has moved heavy . . . close to the border; Nicaragua puts forward . . . stockpiles weapons inside Honduras. And it is Radio . . . announced a new revolutionary board to push forward . . . Marxist-Leninist struggle in Honduras.

Even Costa Rica, Central America's oldest and . . . democracy, a government so peaceful it does not ev . . . army, is the object of bullying and threats from . . . military dictators.

Nicaragua's neighbors know that Sandinista . . . peace, non-alliance, and non-intervention have . . . Some 37 new military bases have been built -- . . . during the Somoza years.

Nicaragua's new army numbers 25,000 men . . . militia of 50,000. It is the largest army i . . . supplemented by 2,000 quote, unquote Cuban . . .

---

equipped with the most modern weapons, Soviet tank . . . 50 more . . . Soviet 152 mm Howitzers, 100 Anti Aircraft guns plus planes . . . armored artillery, and helicopters. There are a . . . thousands of advisors from the Soviet Union, East . . . Our mil. advisors between . . . and the P.L.O. By comparison, we have 55 milita . . . El Salvador.

The goal of the professional guerrilla moven . . . America is as simple as it is sinister -- to des . . . entire region from the Panama Canal to Mexico. . . . on this point, let me read you what a leader of . . . guerrillas told the Mexican magazine Proceso: . . . process of Central America is a single process, . . . one are the triumphs of the other . . . Guatem . . . hour. Honduras its. Costa Rica, too, will hav . . . glory. The first note was heard in Nicaragua . . .

. . . . that go fa . . . hemisp . . . conseq . . . allian . . . with a . . . or Asi . . . conce . . . balanc . . . time t . . . unequ . . . Centr . . .

From the desk of President Ronald Reagan

Nicaraguas mil. junta who . . . themselves made war & won fr . . . from operating from bases in . . . & Costa Rica, like to pretend . . . are today being attacked from . . . press based in Honduras. Th . . . fact is it is Nicaragua's go . . . that threatens Honduras n . . . the reverse.

It is Nicaragua who h . . . moved heavy tanks close to t . . . border; Nicaragua who speak . . . and announced on radio - An . . . the creation of a new unif . . . Revolutionary Coord — . . . board to push forward t . . . marxist struggle in Hond . . .

Nicaragua supported by . . . weapons & mil. resources provided by the . . . Communist bloc represses it's own people, . . . refuses to make peace & sponsors a . . . guerrilla war against El Salvador.

I believe that our help shoul . . . through economic and financial . . . to economic stability and orderl . . . processes."

". . . Collapse of free institut . . . of independence would be disast . . . them but for the world. Discour . . . failure would quickly be the lot . . . peoples striving to maintain the . . . independence."

The size and the power of the co . . . America are smaller than Greece and Turk . . . and strategic stakes are similar. Will o . . . social, military -- be as appropriate and . . . Truman's bold solutions to the problems o . . .

Some people have forgotten the w . . . years -- and the decades of peace, prosper . . . secured.

Some people talk as though the U . . . incapable of acting effectively in intern . . . without risking war or damaging those we . . .

Some people think we cannot enga . . . without producing "another Vietnam". Bu . . . how often and how successfully American . . . help others defend themselves.

The political parties and factions in El Salvador are coming
together — they now share the common goal of seeking a political
solution to their country's problems. New national elections
will be held this year and they will be open to all political
parties. ~~The~~ people of El Salvador are earning their freedom
they deserve our moral and material support to protect it.

Yes, there are still major problems regarding human ri[ghts]
the criminal justice system, and violence against non-com[batants]
And like the rest of Central America, El Salvador also f[aces]
severe economic problems. But, in addition to
recession-depressed prices for major agricultural expo[rts]
El Salvador's economy is being deliberately sabotaged

Tonight in El Salvador — because of guerrilla
much of the fertile land cannot be cultivated; les[s]
rolling stock of the railways remains operational
facilities, telephone and electrical systems hav[e]
and damaged.

I think Secretary of State Shultz put it
day: "Unable to win the free loyalty of El S[alvador]
the guerrillas are deliberately and systemat[ically]
of food, water, transportation, light, san[itation]
these are the people who claim they want [to help the]
people."

They don't want elections because
defeated. But as the previous electio[ns]
people's desire for democracy will n[ot]

The government of Nicaragua has imposed a new dictatorship;
it has refused to hold the elections it promised; it has seized
control of all media except a lone newspaper that it subjects to
heavy prior censorship; it denied the bishops and priests of the
Roman Catholic Church the right to say Mass on television during
Holy Week; it insulted and mocked the Pope; it has driven the
Miskito Indians from their homelands — burning their villages,
destroying their crops, and forcing them into involuntary
internment in camps far from home; it has moved against the
private sector and free labor unions; it condoned mob action
against Nicaragua's independent human rights commission and drove
the director of that commission into exile.

In short, after all these acts of repression by the
government, is it any wonder opposition has formed? Contrary to
propaganda, the opponents of the Sandinistas are not die-hard
been denied any part in democracy for Nicaragua in
fighting for their homes, lands, and lives.

Meanwhile, the government of El Salvador, making every
effort to guarantee democracy, free labor unions, freedom of
religion, and a free press, is under attack by guerrillas
dedicated to the same philosophy that prevails in Nicaragua,
Cuba, and, yes, the Soviet Union. Violence has been Nicaragua's
most important export to the world. It is the ultimate in
hypocrisy for the unelected Nicaraguan government to charge that

freedom and security in our hemisphe[re]
I believe that a majori[ty]
is prepared to stand by passively [while]
government to stand by while the p[eople of Central]
America are delivered to
are left vulnerable to ne[w]
dangers.

Only last week an official
Office reiterated Brezhnev's th[reat]
missiles in this hemisphere —
United States.
Daniel Ortega confirmed that,
consider accepting those mis[siles]

present courof [all]
encourage peace among the nations of Central America. We
must continue to support the regional efforts to promote solutions to
regional problems.

The Congress shares the responsibility for our foreign
policy.

Tonight, I
join me in a new, bolder, more generous approach to the
problems of peace and poverty, democracy and dictatorship in
the region.
Program that includes preventing Communist victory in the
short run, but goes beyond it to produce for the chronically
deprived people of the area the reality of present progress
and the promise of more to come.

Tonight, I
developing, in a bipartisan spirit, a new plan for Central
America and the Caribbean as appropriate to our problems as
the Truman Doctrine and Marshall Plans were to those of
the post-World-War II epoch.

The problems are not identical. Neither are the
tools we can bring to bear. But the stakes are both of
great importance.
can be the same. The spirit of determination and generosity
is similar — and so is the

closely with the Congress to assure the fullest possible, bipartisan coordination of our policies toward the region.

What I'm asking for is prompt congressional approval for the full reprogramming of funds for key current economic and security programs so that the people of Central America can hold the line against externally supported aggression. In addition, I am asking for prompt action on the supplemental request in these same areas to carry us through the current fiscal year and for early and favorable congressional action on my requests for fiscal year 1984.

And finally, I am asking that the bipartisan consensus, which last year acted on the trade and tax provisions of the Caribbean Basin Initiative in the House, again take the lead to move this vital proposal to the floor of both chambers. And as I said before, the greatest share of these requests is targeted toward economic and humanitarian aid, not military.

What the administration is asking for on behalf of freedom in Central America is so small, so minimal, considering what is at stake. The total amount requested for aid to all of Central America in 1984 is about $600 million. That's less than one-tenth of what Americans will spend this year on coin-operated video games.

In summation, I say to you that tonight there can be no question: The national security of all the Americas is at stake in Central America. If we cannot defend ourselves there, we cannot expect to prevail elsewhere. Our credibility would collapse, our alliances would crumble, and the safety of our homeland would be put in jeopardy.

We have a vital interest, a moral duty, and a solemn responsibility. This is not a partisan issue. It is a question of our meeting our moral responsibility to ourselves, our friends, and our posterity. It is a duty that falls on all of us—the President, the Congress, and the people. We must perform it together. Who among us would wish to bear responsibility for failing to meet our shared obligation?

Thank you, God bless you, and good night.

Remarks on Greeting the Finalists of the National Spelling Bee

WHITE HOUSE ROSE GARDEN
JUNE 6, 1983

I put this little thing in because I wanted to give you a feel for the small things that presidents do. You meet with spelling bee finalists; you meet with championship sports teams; you receive a live turkey every year before Thanksgiving, although I don't think we ever ended up eating one of those birds. It would be like eating an acquaintance. Anyway, if you add all these things up, they say something about our culture and our people and the American identity.

Hello THERE. Well, first let me welcome all of you spellers to the White House and let me compliment you—and that's compliment with an "i," not complement with an "e." I want to compliment you with an "i" on your accomplishments. You're the 137 finalists out of 8 to 9 million students who participated in this National Spelling Bee. That's quite an honor, and you should be very proud.

You know, because of this event, I learned that the study of spelling is called orthography. Orthography—that's o-r-t-h-o-g-r-a-...uh...p...ummm...[*Laughter*]...ummm....

h-y. [*Laughter*] No, I'm sure you already knew that, and you were just proving it, but I thought I'd give you that just in case they asked for it on Wednesday.

But all of us are proud not only of your spelling ability but of your determination to increase your knowledge. I wish all American students were as interested in their studies as you evidently are and have been. And I wish all teachers and parents took an interest in their children's educational development as your parents and teachers have taken in yours.

Now, on Wednesday, you're going to be feeling the pressure of the competition. But I want you to know that you're already —all of you—winners in my book and in the hearts of your hometowns. So, enjoy the competition and enjoy your trip to Washington. I hope you've been having some fun and seeing some of the sights here.

I'm told you're on your way to a barbecue. That sounds like fun, so I don't want to hold you up. But again, let me wish you all the best of luck on Wednesday. And remember, "i" before "e" except after "c." [*Laughter*] That ought to help a little.

You know, I have to tell you one story. People can get so sure of themselves. I know you must have heard, or read in your studies, about the author of many years ago, Mark Twain. Mark Twain was on a ship going across to Europe. And in the dining salon that night at dinner, someone wanting to impress him at the table asked him to pass the sugar and then said, "Mr. Twain, don't you think it's unusual that sugar is the only word in our language in which 's-u' has the 'shu' sound?" And Mark Twain said: "Are you sure?" [*Laughter*]

Well, good luck to all of you, and as I say, you're all winners, and you all have every reason to be proud. So win, lose, or tie, we're proud of all of you. And I maybe have time to just come down and say hello to a few of you here, and I'm going to do that.

Remarks on the Anniversary of Martin Luther King, Jr.'s, Birth

EAST ROOM OF THE WHITE HOUSE
JANUARY 15, 1983

For all of my so-called powers of communication, I was never able to convince many black citizens of my commitment to their needs. They often mistook my belief in keeping the government out of the average American's life as a cover for doing nothing about racial injustice.

I think of all things that were said about me during my presidency, this charge bothers me the most personally. I abhor racism. These skinheads and white supremacist groups have no place in this country. They are not what we are about, and I wish they would just vaporize.

Now, there's no denying that during my presidency I had a cool relationship with most national black leaders. They fault me for many things, and I fault them for making the plight of poor black people even worse. I know that statement will raise a ruckus, but it's what I think. Many of these leaders over the past twenty years have been so wed to the big-government, status-quo thinking that they have done a terrible disservice to the independence and aspirations of many black Americans. Fortunately, some wonderfully gifted conservative black thinkers have emerged during the 1980s. I hope their influence grows in proportion to their independent brilliance.

I don't know whether Martin Luther King, Jr., would have

*fallen into the trap of the status quo or not, but he certainly
was a great leader at a time when this country needed him. I
didn't appreciate what a remarkable man he was while he was
living. But I suppose that's the way it is with prophets. You
sometimes don't know their impact and importance until
they're gone.*

T HANK YOU ALL FOR BEING HERE. And let me especially
thank the Harlem Boys' Choir. From what we've just heard, I
think that you fellows could show the famous Vienna Boys'
Choir a thing or two.

But welcome, all of you, to the White House on this special
day. Earlier today on my radio broadcast I spoke of Dr. King's
character and contributions. Now let me speak a little more
personally about the man who tumbled the wall of racism in
our country. Though Dr. King and I may not have exactly had
identical political philosophies, we did share a deep belief in
freedom and justice under God.

Freedom is not something to be secured in any one moment
of time. We must struggle to preserve it every day. And freedom
is never more than one generation away from extinction.

History shows that Dr. King's approach achieved great results in a comparatively short time, which was exactly what
America needed. Let me read you part of what he wrote from
a jail cell:

"When you suddenly find your tongue twisted as you seek to
explain to your six-year-old daughter why she can't go to a
public amusement park that's just been advertised on television; when you take a cross-country drive and find it necessary
to sleep night after night in the uncomfortable corners of your
automobile because no motel will accept you; when you're hu-
miliated day in and day out by nagging signs reading 'white'
and 'colored,' then you can understand why we find it difficult
to wait."

Thank you all for being here, and

the Harlem Boys Choir. From what we ju

fellows could show the Vienna Boys Cho

Welcome, all of you, to the White Hous

Earlier today in my radio speech

character and contributions. Now, I

more personally about this man who t

our country.

Though Dr. King and I may not

philosophies, we ~~shered~~ DID SHARE a deep bel

under God. Freedom is not someth ~~it is more more than I gave~~

moment in time. We must struggle

History shows that Dr. King's ap

a comparatively short time -- w

needed. Let me read you part o

~~Birmingham jail.~~ He wrote, ".

tongue twisted as you seek to

daughter why she can't go to

just been advertised on television

cross-

night

motel

by nag

will un

THNK U ALL ... BEING HR. & LET ME LL
ESPCLY THNK ... HARLEM BOYS CHOIR.
FRM. WHT. ... JUST HRD. ... THINK U
FELLOWS CLD. SHO ... FAMOUS VIENNA
BOYS CHOIR ... TH
... U ... WH ... T
EARLIER TODAY ...
... SPOKE ... DR. K
NOW ... LK. ... M
PERSNLY ABT. ...
... RACISM ... C
& I MAY N
POL. PHILS ...
BLF. ... FR
FROM ... N
... ANY I
STRUGGL
WHN. U ...
OUT ... N
EXTIP
Colord
... FND
JR. G
W

APPROACH. ACHVD. GRT. RESULTS IN C2
... COMPRTIVLY SHORT TM. ... WCH.
WS. EXACTLY WHT. AM. NDD. SLET
ME RD. U PRT. ... WHT. ... WROTE ... JAIL
CELL ... WHN. U SUDDNLY FND. YR.
TONGUE TWISTD ...
YR. 6 YR. ... L
GO ... PUB. AHU
ADVRTSD ... TV
CO. DRV. ...
AFR. NITE ...
AUTO. RC
WHN. U ...
... SEEK ... XPLAIN
... NT. ...

HE LIFTD. HVY. BURDN FRM. THS.
CO. ... AS SURELY ... BLCK. AMs. ...
SCARRD ... YOKE ... SLAVRY - AM. ... SCARD
INDULGE 4 ... BE HONEST & ... SO. THS
BFR. ... MNY. AMs. DID NOT FULLY
REALIZE ... HVY. AMs. BURDN WS.
US. ... ALL. US. ... DR. KING ...
GN. LIFTD.
... IN MNY. AMs. ARE
... W

& ESPCLY ... POL. LF. ... SPOKN ... C4
GRT. DEAL. ABT. ... NATURE & SPIRIT.
AM. S ... BLV. ... VAST MAJORITY ... AMs.
SHR. ... SPIRIT WTH. DR. K. SHE SD.
"... GOAL ... AM. ... FRDM." SD. ... AM.
P. ... INFECTD ... DEM. IDEALS 4 & THI
... FOUND HOPE S ... SD. ... BLVD. ...
GRT VAULTS ... OPP. ... THS. NAT.
... GENUNELY BLVD. ... POTENTL ... A
SM. ONE REMRKD ... COMFORT ... HV
... FRND MAY ... TKN. AWY - BUT NOT
... HVNG HD ONE S WL. AM. MAY
LOST ... COMFORT & COURAGE ... DR. I
PERSNL PRSENC BUT ... NOT REALLY
EVRY TTY. ... BLCK W. CASTs ... BA
DR. K. ... THR. S EVRY TM. ... BLCK
... HIRED ... GOOD JOB - DR. K.
EVRY TM. ... BLCK. CHLD. RCVS.
DR. K. ... THR. S EVRY TTY. ... BLCK

... ELECTD ... PUB. OFFICE ... DR. K ... THR. S
& EVRY TM. B. & W. AMs. WRK. SD. ... SD.
... BETTR FUTURE. DR. K. THR. S ... WTH
US & ... VRY MUCH TODAY. S M.L.K.
USED ... SPK. ... HS. ABIDNG FAITH ...
AM. & ... FUT. ... MNKND. S ... REJECTD
WHT. IS ... WHT. OUGHT. BE S ...
DEDICATED ... LF. ... THT. DRM. S NUCH ...
HS. DRM. ... BCM. ... REALITY S BUT MUCH
STILL ... BE ACHVD. S DR. Ks. FAITH
... CONTINU ... BEACN ... HOPE ... US ALGAS
CONTINU ... STRV TOGETHR ... MK. AM.
... NAT. ... KNEW ... CLD. BCM. SO THNK
U ... SHARING ... VRY SPCL. DAY ... US AS
... GATHR. HR. ... REMEMBR ... GRT. AM -
... MN. ... VISION & ... MN. ... PC. S THNK
U. & GOD BLESS U.

Martin Luther King, Jr., burned with the gospel of freedom, and that flame in his heart lit the way for millions. What he accomplished—not just for black Americans, but for all Americans—he lifted a heavy burden from this country. As surely as black Americans were scarred by the yoke of slavery, America was scarred by injustice. Many Americans didn't fully realize how heavy America's burden was until it was lifted. Dr. King did that for us, all of us.

Abraham Lincoln freed the black man. In many ways, Dr. King freed the white man. How did he accomplish this tremendous feat? Where others—white and black—preached hatred, he taught the principles of love and nonviolence. We can be so thankful that Dr. King raised his mighty eloquence for love and hope rather than for hostility and bitterness. He took the tension he found in our nation, a tension of injustice, and channeled it for the good of America and all her people.

Throughout my life, and especially my political life, I've spoken a great deal about the nature and spirit of America. I believe the vast majority of Americans share that spirit with Dr. King. He said, "The goal of America is freedom." He said, "The American people are infected with democratic ideals." And there he found hope. He said he believed there were great vaults of opportunity in this nation. He genuinely believed in the potential of America.

Someone has remarked, the comfort of having a friend may be taken away but not that of having had a friend. Well, America may have lost the comfort and courage of Dr. King's presence, but we've not really lost him. Every time a black woman casts a ballot, Martin King is there. Every time a black man is hired for a good job, Dr. King is there. Every time a black child receives a sound education, Dr. King is there. Every time a black person is elected to public office, Dr. King is there. Every time black and white Americans work side by side for a better future, Dr. King is there. He's with us, and with us very much today.

Martin Luther King used to speak of his abiding faith in America and the future of mankind. He rejected what is for what ought to be, and he dedicated his life to that dream. Much of his dream has become reality, but much is still to be achieved. Dr. King's faith will continue to be a beacon of hope for us all as we continue to serve together to make America the nation that we knew it could become.

So, thank you for this very special day, for being with us as we gather here to remember a great American—a man of vision, a man of peace. Thank you, and God bless you.

Remarks at the
Annual Convention of the
National Association of Evangelicals

ORLANDO, FLORIDA
MARCH 8, 1983

This is the "evil empire" speech that was so often quoted as defining my attitude toward the Soviets. At the time it was portrayed as some kind of know-nothing, archconservative statement that could only drive the Soviets to further heights of paranoia and insecurity.

For too long our leaders were unable to describe the Soviet Union as it actually was. The keepers of our foreign-policy knowledge—in other words, most liberal foreign-affairs scholars, the State Department, and various columnists—found it illiberal and provocative to be so honest. I've always believed, however, that it's important to define differences, because there are choices and decisions to be made in life and history.

The Soviet system over the years has purposely starved, murdered, and brutalized its own people. Millions were killed; it's all right there in the history books. It put other citizens it dis-

agreed with into psychiatric hospitals, sometimes drugging them into oblivion. Is the system that allowed this not evil? Then why shouldn't we say so? Even the Soviets themselves are now admitting to annihilating their own people during Stalin's era.

I could not in good conscience today call the Soviet Union an evil empire. As I write this, the Soviets have just conducted the most democratic elections since their revolution. Remarkable things are happening under Mikhail Gorbachev.

In addition to taking a hard line on the morality of the Soviet Union, this speech also outlines my opinions on a number of other moral issues.

REVEREND CLERGY ALL, Senator Hawkins, distinguished members of the Florida congressional delegation, and all of you:

I can't tell you how you have warmed my heart with your welcome. I'm delighted to be here today.

Those of you in the National Association of Evangelicals are known for your spiritual and humanitarian work. And I would be especially remiss if I didn't discharge right now one personal debt of gratitude. Thank you for your prayers. Nancy and I have felt their presence many times in many ways. And believe me, for us they've made all the difference.

The other day in the East Room of the White House at a meeting there, someone asked me whether I was aware of all the people out there who were praying for the President. And I had to say, "Yes, I am. I've felt it. I believe in intercessionary prayer." But I couldn't help but say to that questioner after he'd asked the question that—or at least say to them that if sometimes when he was praying he got a busy signal, it was just me in there ahead of him. [*Laughter*] I think I understand how Abraham Lincoln felt when he said, "I have been driven many times to my knees by the overwhelming conviction that I had nowhere else to go."

From the joy and the good feeling of this conference, I go to a political reception. [*Laughter*] Now, I don't know why, but that bit of scheduling reminds me of a story—[*Laughter*]—which I'll share with you.

An evangelical minister and a politician arrived at Heaven's gate one day together. And St. Peter, after doing all the necessary formalities, took them in hand to show them where their quarters would be. And he took them to a small, single room with a bed, a chair, and a table and said this was for the clergyman. And the politician was a little worried about what might be in store for him. And he couldn't believe it then when St. Peter stopped in front of a beautiful mansion with lovely grounds, many servants, and told him that these would be his quarters.

And he couldn't help but ask, he said, "But wait, how—there's something wrong—how do I get this mansion while that good and holy man only gets a single room?" And St. Peter said, "You have to understand how things are up here. We've got thousands and thousands of clergy. You're the first politician who ever made it." [*Laughter*]

But I don't want to contribute to a stereotype. [*Laughter*] So I tell you there are a great many God-fearing, dedicated, noble men and women in public life, present company included. And yes, we need your help to keep us ever mindful of the ideas and the principles that brought us into the public arena in the first place. The basis of those ideals and principles is a commitment to freedom and personal liberty that, itself, is grounded in the much deeper realization that freedom prospers only where the blessings of God are avidly sought and humbly accepted.

The American experiment in democracy rests on this insight. Its discovery was the great triumph of our Founding Fathers, voiced by William Penn when he said: "If we will not be governed by God, we must be governed by tyrants." Explaining the inalienable rights of men, Jefferson said, "The God who gave us life, gave us liberty at the same time." And it was George Washington who said that "of all the dispositions and habits which lead to political prosperity, religion and morality are indispensable supports."

And finally, that shrewdest of all observers of American democracy, Alexis de Tocqueville, put it eloquently after he had gone on a search for the secret of America's greatness and genius—and he said: "Not until I went into the churches of America and heard her pulpits aflame with righteousness did I understand the greatness and the genius of America. . . . America is good. And if America ever ceases to be good, America will cease to be great."

Well, I'm pleased to be here today with you who are keeping America great by keeping her good. Only through your work and prayers and those of millions of others can we hope to survive this perilous century and keep alive this experiment in liberty, this last, best hope of man.

I want you to know that this administration is motivated by a political philosophy that sees the greatness of America in you, her people, and in your families, churches, neighborhoods, communities—the institutions that foster and nourish values like concern for others and respect for the rule of law under God.

Now, I don't have to tell you that this puts us in opposition to, or at least out of step with, a prevailing attitude of many who have turned to a modern-day secularism, discarding the tried and time-tested values upon which our very civilization is based. No matter how well intentioned, their value system is radically different from that of most Americans. And while they proclaim that they're freeing us from superstitions of the past, they've taken upon themselves the job of superintending us by government rule and regulation. Sometimes their voices are louder than ours, but they are not yet a majority.

An example of that vocal superiority is evident in a controversy now going on in Washington. And since I'm involved, I've been waiting to hear from the parents of young America. How far are they willing to go in giving to government their prerogatives as parents?

Let me state the case as briefly and simply as I can. An organization of citizens, sincerely motivated and deeply concerned about the increase in illegitimate births and abortions involving girls well below the age of consent, some time ago established a nationwide network of clinics to offer help to these girls and, hopefully, alleviate this situation. Now, again, let me say, I do not fault their intent. However, in their well-intentioned effort, these clinics have decided to provide advice and birth control drugs and devices to underage girls without the knowledge of their parents.

For some years now, the federal government has helped with funds to subsidize these clinics. In providing for this, the Congress decreed that every effort would be made to maximize parental participation. Nevertheless, the drugs and devices are prescribed without getting parental consent or giving notification after they've done so. Girls termed "sexually active"—and that has replaced the word "promiscuous"—are given this help in order to prevent illegitimate birth or abortion.

Well, we have ordered clinics receiving federal funds to notify the parents such help has been given. One of the nation's leading newspapers has created the term "squeal rule" in editorializing against us for doing this, and we're being criticized for violating the privacy of young people. A judge has recently granted an injunction against an enforcement of our rule. I've watched TV panel shows discuss this issue, seen columnists pontificating on our error, but no one seems to mention morality as playing a part in the subject of sex.

Is all of Judeo-Christian tradition wrong? Are we to believe that something so sacred can be looked upon as a purely physical thing with no potential for emotional and psychological harm? And isn't it the parents' right to give counsel and advice to keep their children from making mistakes that may affect their entire lives?

Many of us in government would like to know what parents think about this intrusion in their family by government. We're going to fight in the courts. The right of parents and the rights

of family take precedence over those of Washington-based bu-
reaucrats and social engineers.

But the fight against parental notification is really only one
example of many attempts to water down traditional values
and even abrogate the original terms of American democracy.
Freedom prospers when religion is vibrant and the rule of law
under God is acknowledged. When our Founding Fathers
passed the First Amendment, they sought to protect churches
from government interference. They never intended to con-
struct a wall of hostility between government and the concept
of religious belief itself.

The evidence of this permeates our history and our government. The Declaration of Independence mentions the Supreme
Being no less than four times. "In God We Trust" is engraved
on our coinage. The Supreme Court opens its proceedings with
a religious invocation. And the members of Congress open their
sessions with a prayer. I just happen to believe the schoolchildren of the United States are entitled to the same privileges as
Supreme Court justices and congressmen.

Last year, I sent the Congress a constitutional amendment to
restore prayer to public schools. Already this session, there's
growing bipartisan support for the amendment, and I am calling on the Congress to act speedily to pass it and to let our
children pray.

Perhaps some of you read recently about the Lubbock school
case, where a judge actually ruled that it was unconstitutional
for a school district to give equal treatment to religious and
nonreligious student groups, even when the group meetings
were being held during the students' own time. The First
Amendment never intended to require government to discrimi-
nate against religious speech.

Senators Denton and Hatfield have proposed legislation in
the Congress on the whole question of prohibiting discrimination against religious forms of student speech. Such legislation
could go far to restore freedom of religious speech for public
school students. And I hope the Congress considers these bills

quickly. And with your help, I think it's possible we could also get the constitutional amendment through the Congress this year.

More than a decade ago, a Supreme Court decision literally wiped off the books of fifty states statutes protecting the rights of unborn children. Abortion on demand now takes the lives of up to one and a half million unborn children a year. Human life legislation ending this tragedy will someday pass the Congress, and you and I must never rest until it does. Unless and until it can be proven that the unborn child is not a living entity, then its right to life, liberty, and the pursuit of happiness must be protected.

You may remember that when abortion on demand began, many, and indeed, I'm sure many of you, warned that the practice would lead to a decline in respect for human life, that the philosophical premises used to justify abortion on demand would ultimately be used to justify other attacks on the sacredness of human life—infanticide or mercy killing. Tragically enough, those warnings proved all too true. Only last year a court permitted the death by starvation of a handicapped infant.

I have directed the Health and Human Services Department to make clear to every health care facility in the United States that the Rehabilitation Act of 1973 protects all handicapped persons against discrimination based on handicaps, including infants. And we have taken the further step of requiring that each and every recipient of federal funds who provides health care services to infants must post and keep posted in a conspicuous place a notice stating that "discriminatory failure to feed and care for handicapped infants in this facility is prohibited by federal law." It also lists a twenty-four-hour, toll-free number so that nurses and others may report violations in time to save the infant's life.

In addition, recent legislation introduced in the Congress by Representative Henry Hyde of Illinois not only increases restrictions on publicly financed abortions, it also addresses this whole problem of infanticide. I urge the Congress to begin hearings and to adopt legislation that will protect the right of life to all children, including the disabled or handicapped.

Now, I'm sure that you must get discouraged at times, but you've done better than you know, perhaps. There's a great spiritual awakening in America, a renewal of the traditional values that have been the bedrock of America's goodness and greatness.

One recent survey by a Washington-based research council concluded that Americans were far more religious than the people of other nations; 95 percent of those surveyed expressed a belief in God and a huge majority believed the Ten Commandments had real meaning in their lives. And another study has found that an overwhelming majority of Americans disapprove of adultery, teenage sex, pornography, abortion, and hard drugs. And this same study showed a deep reverence for the importance of family ties and religious belief.

I think the items that we've discussed here today must be a key part of the nation's political agenda. For the first time the Congress is openly and seriously debating and dealing with the prayer and abortion issues—and that's enormous progress right there. I repeat: America is in the midst of a spiritual awakening and a moral renewal. And with your biblical keynote, I say today, "Yes, let justice roll on like a river, righteousness like a never-failing stream."

Now, obviously, much of this new political and social consensus I've talked about is based on a positive view of American history, one that takes pride in our country's accomplishments and record. But we must never forget that no government schemes are going to perfect man. We know that living in this world means dealing with what philosophers would call the phenomenology of evil or, as theologians would put it, the doctrine of sin.

There is sin and evil in the world, and we're enjoined by Scripture and the Lord Jesus to oppose it with all our might. Our nation, too, has a legacy of evil with which it must deal. The glory of this land has been its capacity for transcending the moral evils of our past. For example, the long struggle of minority citizens for equal rights, once a source of disunity and civil war, is now a point of pride for all Americans. We must never go back. There is no room for racism, anti-Semitism, or other forms of ethnic and racial hatred in this country.

I know that you've been horrified, as have I, by the resurgence of some hate groups preaching bigotry and prejudice. Use the mighty voice of your pulpits and the powerful standing of your churches to denounce and isolate these hate groups in our midst. The commandment given us is clear and simple: "Thou shalt love thy neighbor as thyself."

But whatever sad episodes exist in our past, any objective observer must hold a positive view of American history, a history that has been the story of hopes fulfilled and dreams made into reality. Especially in this century, America has kept alight the torch of freedom, but not just for ourselves but for millions of others around the world.

And this brings me to my final point today. During my first press conference as president, in answer to a direct question, I pointed out that, as good Marxist-Leninists, the Soviet leaders have openly and publicly declared that the only morality they recognize is that which will further their cause, which is world revolution. I think I should point out I was only quoting Lenin, their guiding spirit, who said in 1920 that they repudiate all morality that proceeds from supernatural ideas—that's their name for religion—or ideas that are outside class conceptions. Morality is entirely subordinate to the interests of class war. And everything is moral that is necessary for the annihilation of the old, exploiting social order and for uniting the proletariat.

Well, I think the refusal of many influential people to accept this elementary fact of Soviet doctrine illustrates a historical reluctance to see totalitarian powers for what they are. We saw this phenomenon in the 1930s. We see it too often today.

This doesn't mean we should isolate ourselves and refuse to seek an understanding with them. I intend to do everything I can to persuade them of our peaceful intent, to remind them that it was the West that refused to use its nuclear monopoly in the forties and fifties for territorial gain and which now proposes a 50-percent cut in strategic ballistic missiles and the elimination of an entire class of land-based, intermediate-range nuclear missiles.

At the same time, however, they must be made to understand we will never compromise our principles and standards. We will never give away our freedom. We will never abandon our belief in God. And we will never stop searching for a genuine peace. But we can assure none of these things America stands for through the so-called nuclear freeze solutions proposed by some.

The truth is that a freeze now would be a very dangerous fraud, for that is merely the illusion of peace. The reality is that we must find peace through strength.

I would agree to a freeze if only we could freeze the Soviets' global desires. A freeze at current levels of weapons would remove any incentive for the Soviets to negotiate seriously in Geneva and virtually end our chances to achieve the major arms reductions which we have proposed. Instead, they would achieve their objectives through the freeze.

A freeze would reward the Soviet Union for its enormous and unparalleled military buildup. It would prevent the essential and long overdue modernization of United States and allied defenses and would leave our aging forces increasingly vulnerable. And an honest freeze would require extensive prior negotiations on the systems and numbers to be limited and on the measures to ensure effective verification and compliance. And the kind of a freeze that has been suggested would be virtually impossible to verify. Such a major effort would divert us completely from our current negotiations on achieving substantial reductions.

A number of years ago, I heard a young father, a very prominent young man in the entertainment world, addressing a tremendous gathering in California. It was during the time of the cold war, and communism and our own way of life were very much on people's minds. And he was speaking to that subject. And suddenly, though, I heard him saying, "I love my little girls more than anything—" And I said to myself, "Oh, no, don't. You can't—don't say that." But I had underestimated him. He went on: "I would rather see my little girls die now, still believing in God, than have them grow up under communism and one day die no longer believing in God."

There were thousands of young people in that audience. They came to their feet with shouts of joy. They had instantly recognized the profound truth in what he had said, with regard to the physical and the soul and what was truly important.

Yes, let us pray for the salvation of all of those who live in that totalitarian darkness—pray they will discover the joy of knowing God. But until they do, let us be aware that while they preach the supremacy of the state, declare its omnipotence over individual man, and predict its eventual domination of all peoples on the earth, they are the focus of evil in the modern world.

It was C. S. Lewis who, in his unforgettable *Screwtape Letters,* wrote: "The greatest evil is not done now in those sordid 'dens of crime' that Dickens loved to paint. It is not even done in concentration camps and labor camps. In those we see its final result. But it is conceived and ordered (moved, seconded, carried and minuted) in clean, carpeted, warmed, and well-lighted offices, by quiet men with white collars and cut fingernails and smooth-shaven cheeks who do not need to raise their voice."

Well, because these "quiet men" do not "raise their voices," because they sometimes speak in soothing tones of brotherhood and peace, because, like other dictators before them, they're always making "their final territorial demand," some would have us accept them at their word and accommodate ourselves to their aggressive impulses. But if history teaches anything, it teaches that simpleminded appeasement or wishful thinking about our adversaries is folly. It means the betrayal of our past, the squandering of our freedom.

So, I urge you to speak out against those who would place the United States in a position of military and moral inferiority. You know, I've always believed that old Screwtape reserved his best efforts for those of you in the church. So, in your discus-

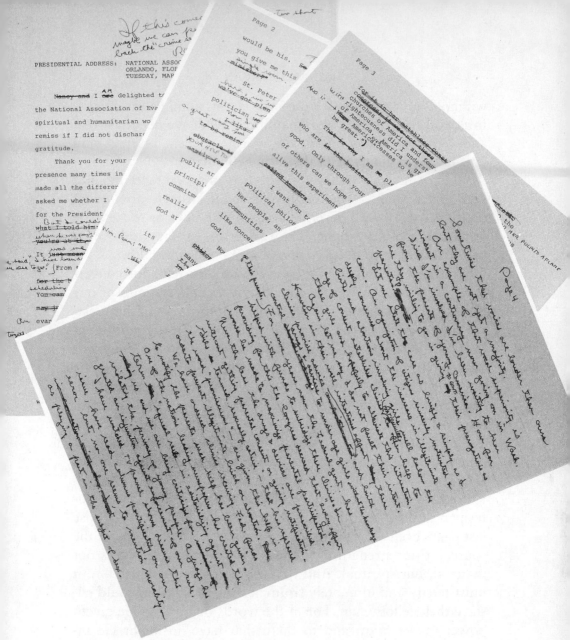

sions of the nuclear freeze proposals, I urge you to beware the temptation of pride—the temptation of blithely declaring yourselves above it all and label both sides equally at fault, to ignore the facts of history and the aggressive impulses of an evil empire, to simply call the arms race a giant misunderstanding and thereby remove yourself from the struggle between right and wrong and good and evil.

I ask you to resist the attempts of those who would have you withhold your support for our efforts, this administration's efforts, to keep America strong and free, while we negotiate real and verifiable reductions in the world's nuclear arsenals and one day, with God's help, their total elimination.

While America's military strength is important, let me add here that I've always maintained that the struggle now going on for the world will never be decided by bombs or rockets, by armies or military might. The real crisis we face today is a spiritual one; at root, it is a test of moral will and faith.

Whittaker Chambers, the man whose own religious conversion made him a witness to one of the terrible traumas of our time, the Hiss-Chambers case, wrote that the crisis of the Western world exists to the degree in which the West is indifferent to God, the degree to which it collaborates in communism's attempt to make man stand alone without God. And then he said, for Marxism-Leninism is actually the second-oldest faith, first proclaimed in the Garden of Eden with the words of temptation, "Ye shall be as gods."

The Western world can answer this challenge, he wrote, "but only provided that its faith in God and the freedom He enjoins is as great as communism's faith in Man."

I believe we shall rise to the challenge. I believe that communism is another sad, bizarre chapter in human history whose last pages even now are being written. I believe this because the source of our strength in the quest for human freedom is not material, but spiritual. And because it knows no limitation, it must terrify and ultimately triumph over those who would enslave their fellow man. For in the words of Isaiah: "He giveth power to the faint; and to them that have no might He increased strength. . . . But they that wait upon the Lord shall renew their strength; they shall mount up with wings as eagles; they shall run, and not be weary. . . ."

Yes, change your world. One of our Founding Fathers, Thomas Paine, said, "We have it within our power to begin the world over again." We can do it, doing together what no one church could do by itself.

God bless you, and thank you very much.

Remarks on Awarding the
U.S. Coast Guard Medal
Posthumously to Arland D. Williams, Jr.

OVAL OFFICE
JUNE 6, 1983

I've always felt that heroes were very important to our nation. They bind us together; they give us strength that we can do great things. I felt that part of my job as president was to let our people know how many heroes we had in this country. Arland Williams, Jr., was one of the best. I wish I had known him.

The President. We're here to honor Arland Williams, Jr. Virtually everyone in the United States knows of his heroism and knows of his deed, but very few, if any, knew his name. Those of us who do know of his bravery have remembered him only as the "unknown hero." And that was in the terrible tragedy that took place down here on January 13th, 1982, when the plane crashed into the bridge and into the ice-covered Potomac. And for a long, long time we have known of the one man who repeatedly handed the line from the helicopter to others that he thought were in a worse situation than he was, saving five people in all. And then when the helicopter went back for him, he was no longer there.

And now an investigation by the Coast Guard and a thorough study has made it known that Arland Williams, Jr., was the hero who gave his life that others might live. And we have here his family—Arland and Virginia Williams; his son and daughter, Arland and Leslie—and the Vice Commander of the Coast Guard. And we are awarding to him this medal—some 607, I think it is, have been given in the one hundred years' history of the medal. There is a gold and silver medal. Two gold were given to other heroes in this same tragedy, two silver, and now this one.

And *Time* magazine said, "If the man in the water gave a lifeline to the people gasping for survival, he was likewise giving a lifeline to those who observed him." And I think that is true, because all of us had to stand a little taller witnessing this heroic deed and knowing now the man who gets the credit.

And now would you read the citation?

Vice Admiral Stabile. Mr. President, I'd be happy to.

"The secretary of transportation takes pleasure in presenting the Gold Lifesaving Medal posthumously to Arland D. Williams, Jr., for acts as set forth in the following citation:

"For extreme and heroic daring on the afternoon of 13 January 1982, following the crash of an airplane in the Potomac River in Washington, D.C. Mr. Williams was a passenger on an Air Florida 737 that crashed in a blinding snowstorm into the Fourteenth Street Bridge that crosses the Potomac River and connects Washington, D.C., and Northern Virginia. After hitting the bridge, the plane plunged into the frozen waters of the Potomac River. Mr. Williams was seated in the rear section of the plane, which was partially above the water. When a U.S. Park Police helicopter arrived to commence rescue efforts, Mr. Williams, although injured, quickly realized that he was trapped in his seat by a jammed seat belt. As the helicopter lowered a line to the survivors for towing them to shore, Mr. Williams, acknowledging the fact that he was trapped, refused to grab the line and passed it on to the other injured persons. The helicopter crew rescued five other survivors and then returned to Mr. Williams. He could not be found as he had sunk beneath the icy waters. By not grabbing the rescue line and occupying valuable time in what would probably have been a futile attempt to pull himself free, other survivors, who might have perished if they had been in the frigid waters much longer, were saved. Mr. Williams sacrificed his own life so that others may live. Mr. Williams's unselfish actions and valiant service reflect the highest credit upon himself and were in keeping with the highest traditions of humanitarian service."

Signed, Elizabeth Hanford Dole, Secretary of Transportation.

The President. Mrs. Williams, I hope that you'll receive this medal for your son. And to his son and daughter, let me just say you can live with tremendous pride in your father.

Address to the Nation
on Events in Lebanon and Grenada

OVAL OFFICE
OCTOBER 27, 1983

*George Shultz invited us down to Augusta one October week-
end to golf. It was a weekend that I will never forget. Nancy
and I were put up in the cottage Ike used when he frequented
the links there. The weekend would have been eventful enough
by the fact that a gunman took over the pro shop and held two
of my staff hostage. Fortunately, the matter ended peacefully.*

*I can't say the same for the other events of that weekend. I
guess it was three or four in the morning when the telephone rang.
We had received a request for help from half a dozen countries
in the Caribbean telling us they knew they were next in line to
fall because of what was happening on their sister island of
Grenada, where armed thugs backed by Cubans had taken over.
The other islands said they didn't have the power to do anything by themselves and that they needed our help in addition.*

I immediately called a meeting in the cottage. I knew if we turned them down, we might as well forget any relationship with other countries in the Americas. I gave the go-ahead. Grenada was so close to Cuba that I said this deal has to be the best-kept secret in town until it's under way. Only a very few outside the Pentagon knew what we were planning. Even though I'd given the go-ahead on the operation, we decided to stay in Augusta so as not to tip anyone off about what we were up to.

Then something happened that caused us to leave immediately for Washington. We received word on the bombing of our Marine barracks in Lebanon. Our boys got hit with two thousand pounds of TNT loaded onto a truck piloted by a suicide driver.

That was our hope—to bring some relief to the people of that suffering, violent place. Those boys gave their lives because of our ideal that life should have some peace to it. We can't abandon our hopes, but my how it still hurts to have lost those young men. Sending our boys to that place is the most anguishing regret of my years as president.

The following is the speech I gave to the American people on the events of that week.

M Y FELLOW AMERICANS:

Some two months ago we were shocked by the brutal massacre of 269 men, women, and children, more than 60 of them Americans, in the shooting down of a Korean airliner. Now, in these past several days, violence has erupted again, in Lebanon and Grenada.

In Lebanon, we have some 1,600 marines, part of a multinational force that's trying to help the people of Lebanon restore order and stability to that troubled land. Our marines are assigned to the south of the city of Beirut, near the only airport operating in Lebanon. Just a mile or so to the north is the Italian contingent and not far from them, the French and a company of British soldiers.

This past Sunday, at twenty-two minutes after six Beirut time, with dawn just breaking, a truck, looking like a lot of other vehicles in the city, approached the airport on a busy main road. There was nothing in its appearance to suggest it was any different than the trucks or cars that were normally seen on and around the airport. But this one was different. At the wheel was a young man on a suicide mission.

The truck carried some 2,000 pounds of explosives, but there was no way our marine guards could know this. Their first warning that something was wrong came when the truck crashed through a series of barriers, including a chain-link fence and barbed wire entanglements. The guards opened fire, but it was too late. The truck smashed through the doors of the headquarters building in which our marines were sleeping and instantly exploded. The four-story concrete building collapsed in a pile of rubble.

More than two hundred of the sleeping men were killed in that one hideous, insane attack. Many others suffered injury and are hospitalized here or in Europe.

This was not the end of the horror. At almost the same instant, another vehicle on a suicide and murder mission crashed into the headquarters of the French peacekeeping force, an eight-story building, destroying it and killing more than fifty French soldiers.

Prior to this day of horror, there had been several tragedies for our men in the multinational force. Attacks by snipers and mortar fire had taken their toll.

I called bereaved parents and/or widows of the victims to express on behalf of all of us our sorrow and sympathy. Sometimes there were questions. And now many of you are asking: Why should our young men be dying in Lebanon? Why is Lebanon important to us?

Well, it's true, Lebanon is a small country, more than five and a half thousand miles from our shores on the edge of what we call the Middle East. But every president who has occupied this office in recent years has recognized that peace in the Middle East is of vital concern to our nation and, indeed, to our allies in Western Europe and Japan. We've been concerned because the Middle East is a powder keg; four times in the last thirty years, the Arabs and Israelis have gone to war. And each time, the world has teetered near the edge of catastrophe.

The area is key to the economic and political life of the West. Its strategic importance, its energy resources, the Suez Canal, and the well-being of the nearly 200 million people living there —all are vital to us and to world peace. If that key should fall into the hands of a power or powers hostile to the free world, there would be a direct threat to the United States and to our allies.

We have another reason to be involved. Since 1948 our nation has recognized and accepted a moral obligation to assure the continued existence of Israel as a nation. Israel shares our democratic values and is a formidable force an invader of the Middle East would have to reckon with.

For several years, Lebanon has been torn by internal strife. Once a prosperous, peaceful nation, its government had become ineffective in controlling the militias that warred on each other. Sixteen months ago, we were watching on our TV screens the shelling and bombing of Beirut, which was being used as a fortress by PLO bands. Hundreds and hundreds of civilians were being killed and wounded in the daily battles.

Syria, which makes no secret of its claim that Lebanon should be a part of a Greater Syria, was occupying a large part of Lebanon. Today, Syria has become a home for 7,000 Soviet advisers and technicians who man a massive amount of Soviet weaponry, including SS-21 ground-to-ground missiles capable of reaching vital areas of Israel.

A little over a year ago, hoping to build on the Camp David accords, which had led to peace between Israel and Egypt, I proposed a peace plan for the Middle East to end the wars between the Arab states and Israel. It was based on U.N. resolutions 242 and 338 and called for a fair and just solution to the Palestinian problem, as well as a fair and just settlement of issues between the Arab states and Israel.

Before the necessary negotiations could begin, it was essential to get all foreign forces out of Lebanon and to end the fighting there. So, why are we there? Well, the answer is straightforward: to help bring peace to Lebanon and stability to the vital Middle East. To that end, the multinational force was created to help stabilize the situation in Lebanon until a government could be established and a Lebanese army mobilized to restore Lebanese sovereignty over its own soil as the foreign forces withdrew. Israel agreed to withdraw as did Syria, but Syria then reneged on its promise. Over 10,000 Palestinians who had been bringing ruin down on Beirut, however, did leave the country.

Lebanon has formed a government under the leadership of President Gemayel, and that government, with our assistance and training, has set up its own army. In only a year's time, that army has been rebuilt. It's a good army, composed of Lebanese of all factions.

A few weeks ago, the Israeli army pulled back to the Awali River in southern Lebanon. Despite fierce resistance by Syrian-backed forces, the Lebanese army was able to hold the line and maintain the defensive perimeter around Beirut.

In the year that our marines have been there, Lebanon has made important steps toward stability and order. The physical presence of the marines lends support to both the Lebanese government and its army. It allows the hard work of diplomacy to go forward. Indeed, without the peacekeepers from the U.S., France, Italy, and Britain, the efforts to find a peaceful solution in Lebanon would collapse.

As to that narrower question—what exactly is the operational mission of the marines—the answer is, to secure a piece of Beirut, to keep order in their sector, and to prevent the area from becoming a battlefield. Our marines are not just sitting in an airport. Part of their task is to guard that airport. Because of their presence, the airport has remained operational. In addition, they patrol the surrounding area. This is their part—a limited, but essential part—in the larger effort that I've described.

If our marines must be there, I'm asked, why can't we make them safer? Who committed this latest atrocity against them and why?

Well, we'll do everything we can to ensure that our men are as safe as possible. We ordered the battleship *New Jersey* to join our naval forces offshore. Without even firing them, the threat of its 16-inch guns silenced those who once fired down on our marines from the hills, and they're a good part of the reason we suddenly had a cease-fire. We're doing our best to make our forces less vulnerable to those who want to snipe at them or send in future suicide missions.

Secretary Shultz called me today from Europe, where he was meeting with the foreign ministers of our allies in the multinational force. They remain committed to our task. And plans were made to share information as to how we can improve security for all our men.

We have strong circumstantial evidence that the attack on the marines was directed by terrorists who used the same method to destroy our embassy in Beirut. Those who directed this atrocity must be dealt justice, and they will be. The obvious purpose behind the sniping and, now, this attack was to weaken American will and force the withdrawal of U.S. and French forces from Lebanon. The clear intent of the terrorists was to eliminate our support of the Lebanese government and to destroy the ability of the Lebanese people to determine their own destiny.

To answer those who ask if we're serving any purpose in being there, let me answer a question with a question. Would the terrorists have launched their suicide attacks against the multinational force if it were not doing its job? The multinational force was attacked precisely because it is doing the job it was sent to do in Beirut. It is accomplishing its mission.

Now then, where do we go from here? What can we do now to help Lebanon gain greater stability so that our marines can come home? Well, I believe we can take three steps now that will make a difference.

First, we will accelerate the search for peace and stability in that region. Little attention has been paid to the fact that we've had special envoys there working, literally, around the clock to bring the warring factions together. This coming Monday in

Geneva, President Gemayel of Lebanon will sit down with other factions from his country to see if national reconciliation can be achieved. He has our firm support. I will soon be announcing a replacement for Bud McFarlane, who was preceded by Phil Habib. Both worked tirelessly and must be credited for much if not most of the progress we've made.

Second, we'll work even more closely with our allies in providing support for the government of Lebanon and for the rebuilding of a national consensus.

Third, we will ensure that the multinational peacekeeping forces, our marines, are given the greatest possible protection. Our commandant of the Marine Corps, General Kelley, returned from Lebanon today and will be advising us on steps we can take to improve security. Vice President Bush returned just last night from Beirut and gave me a full report of his brief visit.

Beyond our progress in Lebanon, let us remember that our main goal and purpose is to achieve a broader peace in all of the Middle East. The factions and bitterness that we see in Lebanon are just a microcosm of the difficulties that are spread across much of that region. A peace initiative for the entire Middle East, consistent with the Camp David accords and U.N. resolutions 242 and 338, still offers the best hope for bringing peace to the region.

Let me ask those who say we should get out of Lebanon: If we were to leave Lebanon now, what message would that send to those who foment instability and terrorism? If America were to walk away from Lebanon, what chance would there be for a negotiated settlement, producing a unified democratic Lebanon?

If we turned our backs on Lebanon now, what would be the future of Israel? At stake is the fate of only the second Arab country to negotiate a major agreement with Israel. That's another accomplishment of this past year, the May 17th accord signed by Lebanon and Israel.

If terrorism and intimidation succeed, it'll be a devastating blow to the peace process and to Israel's search for genuine security. It won't just be Lebanon sentenced to a future of chaos. Can the United States, or the free world, for that matter, stand by and see the Middle East incorporated into the Soviet bloc? What of Western Europe's and Japan's dependence on Middle East oil for the energy to fuel their industries? The Middle East is, as I've said, vital to our national security and economic well-being.

Brave young men have been taken from us. Many others have been grievously wounded. Are we to tell them their sacrifice was wasted? They gave their lives in defense of our national security every bit as much as any man who ever died fighting in a war. We must not strip every ounce of meaning and purpose from their courageous sacrifice.

We're a nation with global responsibilities. We're not somewhere else in the world protecting someone else's interests; we're there protecting our own.

I received a message from the father of a marine in Lebanon. He told me, "In a world where we speak of human rights, there is a sad lack of acceptance of responsibility. My son has chosen the acceptance of responsibility for the privilege of living in this country. Certainly in this country one does not inherently have rights unless the responsibility for these rights is accepted." Dr. Kenneth Morrison said that while he was waiting to learn if his son was one of the dead. I was thrilled for him to learn today that his son Ross is alive and well and carrying on his duties in Lebanon.

Let us meet our responsibilities. For longer than any of us can remember, the people of the Middle East have lived from war to war with no prospect for any other future. That dreadful cycle must be broken. Why are we there? Well, a Lebanese mother told one of our ambassadors that her little girl had only attended school two of the last eight years. Now, because of our presence there, she said her daughter could live a normal life.

With patience and firmness, we can help bring peace to that strife-torn region—and make our own lives more secure. Our role is to help the Lebanese put their country together, not to do it for them.

Now, I know another part of the world is very much on our minds, a place much closer to our shores: Grenada. The island is only twice the size of the District of Columbia, with a total population of about 110,000 people.

Grenada and a half dozen other Caribbean islands here were, until recently, British colonies. They're now independent states and members of the British Commonwealth. While they respect each other's independence, they also feel a kinship with each other and think of themselves as one people.

In 1979 trouble came to Grenada. Maurice Bishop, a protégé of Fidel Castro, staged a military coup and overthrew the government which had been elected under the constitution left to the people by the British. He sought the help of Cuba in building an airport, which he claimed was for tourist trade, but which looked suspiciously suitable for military aircraft, including Soviet-built long-range bombers.

The six sovereign countries and one remaining colony are joined together in what they call the Organization of Eastern Caribbean States. The six became increasingly alarmed as Bishop built an army greater than all of theirs combined. Obviously, it was not purely for defense.

In this last year or so, Prime Minister Bishop gave indications that he might like better relations with the United States. He even made a trip to our country and met with senior officials of the White House and the State Department. Whether he was serious or not, we'll never know. On October 12th, a small group in his militia seized him and put him under arrest. They were, if anything, more radical and more devoted to Castro's Cuba than he had been.

Several days later, a crowd of citizens appeared before Bishop's home, freed him, and escorted him toward the headquarters of the military council. They were fired upon. A number, including some children, were killed, and Bishop was seized. He and several members of his cabinet were subsequently executed, and a twenty-four-hour shoot-to-kill curfew was put in effect. Grenada was without a government, its only authority exercised by a self-proclaimed band of military men.

There were then about one thousand of our citizens on Grenada, eight hundred of them students in St. George's University Medical School. Concerned that they'd be harmed or held as hostages, I ordered a flotilla of ships, then on its way to Lebanon with marines, part of our regular rotation program, to circle south on a course that would put them somewhere in the vicinity of Grenada in case there should be a need to evacuate our people.

Last weekend, I was awakened in the early morning hours and told that six members of the Organization of Eastern Caribbean States, joined by Jamaica and Barbados, had sent an urgent request that we join them in a military operation to restore order and democracy to Grenada. They were proposing this action under the terms of a treaty, a mutual assistance pact that existed among them.

These small, peaceful nations needed our help. Three of them don't have armies at all, and the others have very limited forces. The legitimacy of their request, plus my own concern for our citizens, dictated my decision. I believe our government has a responsibility to go to the aid of its citizens, if their right to life and liberty is threatened. The nightmare of our hostages in Iran must never be repeated.

We knew we had little time and that complete secrecy was vital to ensure both the safety of the young men who would undertake this mission and the Americans they were about to rescue. The Joint Chiefs worked around the clock to come up with a plan. They had little intelligence information about conditions on the island.

We had to assume that several hundred Cubans working on the airport could be military reserves. Well, as it turned out, the number was much larger, and they were a military force. Six hundred of them have been taken prisoner, and we have discovered a complete base with weapons and communications equipment, which makes it clear a Cuban occupation of the island had been planned.

Two hours ago we released the first photos from Grenada. They included pictures of a warehouse of military equipment—

one of three we've uncovered so far. This warehouse contained weapons and ammunition stacked almost to the ceiling, enough to supply thousands of terrorists. Grenada, we were told, was a friendly island paradise for tourism. Well, it wasn't. It was a Soviet-Cuban colony, being readied as a major military bastion to export terror and undermine democracy. We got there just in time.

I can't say enough in praise of our military—Army rangers and paratroopers, Navy, Marine, and Air Force personnel—those who planned a brilliant campaign and those who carried it out. Almost instantly, our military seized the two airports, secured the campus where most of our students were, and are now in the mopping-up phase.

It should be noted that in all the planning, a top priority was to minimize risk, to avoid casualties to our own men and also the Grenadian forces as much as humanly possible. But there were casualties, and we all owe a debt to those who lost their lives or were wounded. They were few in number, but even one is a tragic price to pay.

It's our intention to get our men out as soon as possible. Prime Minister Eugenia Charles of Dominica—I called that wrong; she pronounces it Dominica—she is chairman of OECS. She's calling for help from Commonwealth nations in giving the people their right to establish a constitutional government on Grenada. We anticipate that the governor general, a Grenadian, will participate in setting up a provisional government in the interim.

The events in Lebanon and Grenada, though oceans apart, are closely related. Not only has Moscow assisted and encouraged the violence in both countries, but it provides direct support through a network of surrogates and terrorists. It is no coincidence that when the thugs tried to wrest control over Grenada, there were thirty Soviet advisers and hundreds of Cuban military and paramilitary forces on the island. At the moment of our landing, we communicated with the governments of Cuba and the Soviet Union and told them we would offer shelter and security to their people on Grenada. Regrettably, Castro ordered his men to fight to the death, and some did. The others will be sent to their homelands.

You know, there was a time when our national security was based on a standing army here within our own borders and shore batteries of artillery along our coasts, and of course, a navy to keep the sea-lanes open for the shipping of things necessary to our well-being. The world has changed. Today, our national security can be threatened in faraway places. It's up to all of us to be aware of the strategic importance of such places and to be able to identify them.

Sam Rayburn once said that freedom is not something a nation can work for once and win forever. He said it's like an insurance policy; its premiums must be kept up to date. In order to keep it, we have to keep working for it and sacrificing for it just as long as we live. If we do not, our children may not know the pleasure of working to keep it, for it may not be theirs to keep.

In these last few days, I've been more sure than I've ever been that we Americans of today will keep freedom and maintain peace. I've been made to feel that by the magnificent spirit of our young men and women in uniform and by something here in our nation's capital. In this city, where political strife is so much a part of our lives, I've seen Democratic leaders in the Congress join their Republican colleagues, send a message to the world that we're all Americans before we're anything else, and when our country is threatened, we stand shoulder to shoulder in support of our men and women in the armed forces.

May I share something with you I think you'd like to know? It's something that happened to the commandant of our Marine Corps, General Paul Kelley, while he was visiting our critically injured marines in an Air Force hospital. It says more than any of us could ever hope to say about the gallantry and heroism of these young men, young men who serve so willingly so that others might have a chance at peace and freedom in their own lives and in the life of their country.

I'll let General Kelley's words describe the incident. He spoke of a "young marine with more tubes going in and out of his body than I have ever seen in one body.

"He couldn't see very well. He reached up and grabbed my four stars, just to make sure I was who I said I was. He held my hand with a firm grip. He was making signals, and we realized he wanted to tell me something. We put a pad of paper in his hand—and he wrote 'Semper Fi.' "

Well, if you've been a marine or if, like myself, you're an admirer of the marines, you know those words are a battle cry, a greeting, and a legend in the Marine Corps. They're marine shorthand for the motto of the Corps—"Semper Fidelis"—"always faithful."

General Kelley has a reputation for being a very sophisticated general and a very tough marine. But he cried when he saw those words, and who can blame him?

That marine and all those others like him, living and dead, have been faithful to their ideals. They've given willingly of themselves so that a nearly defenseless people in a region of great strategic importance to the free world will have a chance someday to live lives free of murder and mayhem and terrorism. I think that young marine and all of his comrades have given every one of us something to live up to.

They were not afraid to stand up for their country or, no matter how difficult and slow the journey might be, to give to others that last, best hope of a better future. We cannot and will not dishonor them now and the sacrifices they've made by failing to remain as faithful to the cause of freedom and the pursuit of peace as they have been.

I will not ask you to pray for the dead, because they're safe in God's loving arms and beyond need of our prayers. I would like to ask you all—wherever you may be in this blessed land —to pray for these wounded young men and to pray for the bereaved families of those who gave their lives for our freedom.

God bless you, and God bless America.

Remarks on Accepting the GOP Presidential Nomination

DALLAS, TEXAS
AUGUST 23, 1984

The story of 1984 is the election. The economy was humming, the world was fairly quiet, the wheels of government were turning, so the nation and the media focused on politics.

Even though campaigning can become a grind with so many stops you don't know where you are, it can also be invigorating. It really does get your adrenaline pumping when people respond so warmly and enthusiastically toward you.

The 1984 campaign was nothing if not enthusiastic. A member of my staff who's been reviewing some of the videotapes of the campaign asked me the other day if you can feel an audience's adulation. I said that, yes, you could. (In fact, I bet I have a better idea of what it feels like to be a rock star than most twenty-year-olds.) So then he said, "Well, how do you handle it?" I said, "I pray that I will be deserving." I always tried to remember that; otherwise the power goes to your head, and the history books are littered with such unsavory people.

Now the other thing that I always tried to remember was to campaign as if I was one vote behind. Because if you think you're going to win, you won't do what you need to do. In the '84 convention speech, I think it shows I was running pretty hard and taking nothing for granted. I went after my opponent and his fellow Democrats. You have to draw the line so people will know who you are and what you value.

The President. Mr. Chairman, Mr. Vice President, delegates to this convention, and fellow citizens:

In seventy-five days, I hope we enjoy a victory that is the size of the heart of Texas. Nancy and I extend our deep thanks to the Lone Star State and the "Big D"—the city of Dallas—for all their warmth and hospitality.

Four years ago I didn't know precisely every duty of this office, and not too long ago, I learned about some new ones from the first graders of Corpus Christi School in Chambersburg, Pennsylvania. Little Leah Kline was asked by her teacher to describe my duties. She said: "The President goes to meetings. He helps the animals. The President gets frustrated. He talks to other Presidents." How does wisdom begin at such an early age?

Tonight, with a full heart and deep gratitude for your trust, I accept your nomination for the presidency of the United States. I will campaign on behalf of the principles of our party which lift America confidently into the future.

America is presented with the clearest political choice of half a century. The distinction between our two parties and the different philosophy of our political opponents are at the heart of this campaign and America's future.

I've been campaigning long enough to know that a political party and its leadership can't change their colors in four days. We won't, and no matter how hard they tried, our opponents didn't in San Francisco. We didn't discover our values in a poll taken a week before the convention. And we didn't set a weathervane on top of the Golden Gate Bridge before we started talking about the American family.

The choices this year are not just between two different personalities or between two political parties. They're between two different visions of the future, two fundamentally different ways of governing—their government of pessimism, fear, and limits, or ours of hope, confidence, and growth.

Their government sees people only as members of groups; ours serves all the people of America as individuals. Theirs lives in the past, seeking to apply the old and failed policies to an era that has passed them by. Ours learns from the past and strives to change by boldly charting a new course for the future. Theirs lives by promises, the bigger, the better. We offer proven, workable answers.

Our opponents began this campaign hoping that America has a poor memory. Well, let's take them on a little stroll down memory lane. Let's remind them of how a 4.8-percent inflation rate in 1976 became back-to-back years of double-digit inflation—the worst since World War I—punishing the poor and the elderly, young couples striving to start their new lives, and working people struggling to make ends meet.

Inflation was not some plague borne on the wind; it was a deliberate part of their official economic policy, needed, they said, to maintain prosperity. They didn't tell us that with it would come the highest interest rates since the Civil War. As average monthly mortgage payments more than doubled, home building nearly ground to a halt; tens of thousands of carpenters and others were thrown out of work. And who controlled both houses of the Congress and the executive branch at that time? Not us, not us.

Campaigning across America in 1980, we saw evidence everywhere of industrial decline. And in rural America, farmers' costs were driven up by inflation. They were devastated by a wrongheaded grain embargo and were forced to borrow money at exorbitant interest rates just to get by. And many of them didn't get by. Farmers have to fight insects, weather, and the marketplace; they shouldn't have to fight their own government.

The high interest rates of 1980 were not talked about in San Francisco. But how about taxes? They were talked about in San Francisco. Will Rogers once said he never met a man he didn't like. Well, if I could paraphrase Will, our friends in the other party have never met a tax they didn't like or hike.

Under their policies, tax rates have gone up three times as

much for families with children as they have for everyone else over these past three decades. In just the five years before we came into office, taxes roughly doubled.

Some who spoke so loudly in San Francisco of fairness were among those who brought about the biggest single, individual tax increase in our history in 1977, calling for a series of increases in the social security payroll tax and in the amount of pay subject to that tax. The bill they passed called for two additional increases between now and 1990, increases that bear down hardest on those at the lower income levels.

The Census Bureau confirms that, because of the tax laws we inherited, the number of households at or below the poverty level paying federal income tax more than doubled between 1980 and 1982. Well, they received some relief in 1983, when our across-the-board tax cut was fully in place. And they'll get more help when indexing goes into effect this January.

Our opponents have repeatedly advocated eliminating indexing. Would that really hurt the rich? No, because the rich are already in the top brackets. But those working men and women who depend on a cost-of-living adjustment just to keep abreast of inflation would find themselves pushed into higher tax brackets and wouldn't even be able to keep even with inflation because they'd be paying a higher income tax. That's bracket creep; and our opponents are for it, and we're against it.

It's up to us to see that all our fellow citizens understand that confiscatory taxes, costly social experiments, and economic tinkering were not just the policies of a single administration. For the twenty-six years prior to January of 1981, the opposition party controlled both houses of Congress. Every spending bill and every tax for more than a quarter of a century has been of their doing.

About a decade ago, they said federal spending was out of control, so they passed a budget control act and, in the next five years, ran up deficits of $260 billion. Some control.

In 1981 we gained control of the Senate and the executive branch. With the help of some concerned Democrats in the

House we started a policy of tightening the federal budget instead of the family budget.

A task force chaired by Vice President George Bush—the finest vice president this country has ever had—it eliminated unnecessary regulations that had been strangling business and industry.

And while we have our friends down memory lane, maybe they'd like to recall a gimmick they designed for their 1976 campaign. As President Ford told us the night before last, adding the unemployment and inflation rates, they got what they called a misery index. In '76 it came to 12½ percent. They declared the incumbent had no right to seek reelection with that kind of a misery index. Well, four years ago, in the 1980 election, they didn't mention the misery index, possibly because it was then over 20 percent. And do you know something? They won't mention it in this election either. It's down to 11.6 and dropping.

By nearly every measure, the position of poor Americans worsened under the leadership of our opponents. Teenage drug use, out-of-wedlock births, and crime increased dramatically. Urban neighborhoods and schools deteriorated. Those whom government intended to help discovered a cycle of dependency that could not be broken. Government became a drug, providing temporary relief, but addiction as well.

And let's get some facts on the table that our opponents don't want to hear. The biggest annual increase in poverty took place between 1978 and 1981—over 9 percent each year, in the first two years of our administration. Well, I should—pardon me—I didn't put a period in there. In the first two years of our administration, that annual increase fell to 5.3 percent. And 1983 was the first year since 1978 that there was no appreciable increase in poverty at all.

Pouring hundreds of billions of dollars into programs in order to make people worse off was irrational and unfair. It was time we ended this reliance on the government process and renewed our faith in the human process.

In 1980 the people decided with us that the economic crisis was not caused by the fact that they lived too well. Government lived too well. It was time for tax increases to be an act of last resort, not of first resort.

The people told the liberal leadership in Washington, "Try shrinking the size of government before you shrink the size of our paychecks."

Our government was also in serious trouble abroad. We had aircraft that couldn't fly and ships that couldn't leave port. Many of our military were on food stamps because of meager earnings, and reenlistments were down. Ammunition was low, and spare parts were in short supply.

Many of our allies mistrusted us. In the four years before we took office, country after country fell under the Soviet yoke. Since January 20th, 1981, not one inch of soil has fallen to the Communists.

The Audience. Four more years! Four more years! Four more years!

The President. All right.

The Audience. Four more years! Four more years! Four more years!

The President. But worst of all, Americans were losing the confidence and optimism about the future that has made us unique in the world. Parents were beginning to doubt that their children would have the better life that has been the dream of every American generation.

We can all be proud that pessimism is ended. America is coming back and is more confident than ever about the future. Tonight, we thank the citizens of the United States whose faith and unwillingness to give up on themselves or this country saved us all.

Together, we began the task of controlling the size and activities of the government by reducing the growth of its spending while passing a tax program to provide incentives to increase productivity for both workers and industry. Today, a working family earning $25,000 has about $2,900 more in purchasing power than if tax and inflation rates were still at the 1980 level.

Today, of all the major industrial nations of the world, America has the strongest economic growth; one of the lowest inflation rates; the fastest rate of job creation—6½ million jobs in the last year and a half—a record 600,000 business incorporations in 1983; and the largest increase in real, aftertax personal income since World War II. We're enjoying the highest level of business investment in history, and America has renewed its leadership in developing the vast new opportunities in science and high technology. America is on the move again and expanding toward new eras of opportunity for everyone.

Now, we're accused of having a secret. Well, if we have, it is that we're going to keep the mighty engine of this nation revved up. And that means a future of sustained economic growth without inflation that's going to create for our children and grandchildren a prosperity that finally will last.

Today our troops have newer and better equipment; their morale is higher. The better armed they are, the less likely it is they will have to use that equipment. But if, heaven forbid, they're ever called upon to defend this nation, nothing would be more immoral than asking them to do so with weapons inferior to those of any possible opponent.

We have also begun to repair our valuable alliances, especially our historic NATO alliance. Extensive discussions in Asia have enabled us to start a new round of diplomatic progress there.

In the Middle East, it remains difficult to bring an end to historic conflicts, but we're not discouraged. And we shall always maintain our pledge never to sell out one of our closest friends, the State of Israel.

Closer to home, there remains a struggle for survival for free Latin American states, allies of ours. They valiantly struggle to prevent Communist takeovers fueled massively by the Soviet Union and Cuba. Our policy is simple: We are not going to betray our friends, reward the enemies of freedom, or permit fear and retreat to become American policies—especially in this hemisphere.

None of the four wars in my lifetime came about because we were too strong. It's weakness that invites adventurous adversaries to make mistaken judgments. America is the most peaceful, least warlike nation in modern history. We are not the cause of all the ills of the world. We're a patient and generous people. But for the sake of our freedom and that of others, we cannot permit our reserve to be confused with a lack of resolve.

Ten months ago, we displayed this resolve in a mission to rescue American students on the imprisoned island of Grenada. Democratic candidates have suggested that this could be likened to the Soviet invasion of Afghanistan—

The Audience. Boo-o-o!

The President. —the crushing of human rights in Poland or the genocide in Cambodia.

The Audience. Boo-o-o!

The President. Could you imagine Harry Truman, John Kennedy, Hubert Humphrey, or Scoop Jackson making such a shocking comparison?

The Audience. No!

The President. Nineteen of our fine young men lost their lives on Grenada, and to even remotely compare their sacrifice to the murderous actions taking place in Afghanistan is unconscionable.

There are some obvious and important differences. First, we were invited in by six East Caribbean states. Does anyone seriously believe the people of Eastern Europe or Afghanistan invited the Russians?

The Audience. No!

The President. Second, there are hundreds of thousands of Soviets occupying captive nations across the world. Today, our combat troops have come home. Our students are safe, and freedom is what we left behind in Grenada.

There are some who've forgotten why we have a military. It's not to promote war; it's to be prepared for peace. There's a sign over the entrance to Fairchild Air Force Base in Washington State, and that sign says it all: "Peace is our profession."

Our next administration—

The Audience. Four more years! Four more years! Four more years!

The President. All right.

The Audience. Four more years! Four more years! Four more years!

The President. I heard you. And that administration will be committed to completing the unfinished agenda that we've placed before the Congress and the nation. It is an agenda which calls upon the national Democratic leadership to cease its obstructionist ways.

We've heard a lot about deficits this year from those on the other side of the aisle. Well, they should be experts on budget deficits. They've spent most of their political careers creating deficits. For forty-two of the last fifty years, they have controlled both houses of the Congress.

The Audience. Boo-o-o!

The President. And for almost all of those fifty years, deficit spending has been their deliberate policy. Now, however, they call for an end to deficits. They call them ours. Yet, at the same time, the leadership of their party resists our every effort to bring federal spending under control. For three years straight, they have prevented us from adopting a balanced budget amendment to the Constitution. We will continue to fight for that amendment, mandating that government spend no more than government takes in.

And we will fight, as the vice president told you, for the right of a president to veto items in appropriations bills without having to veto the entire bill. There is no better way than the line-item veto, now used by governors in forty-three states to cut out waste in government. I know. As governor of California, I successfully made such vetos over nine hundred times.

Now, their candidate, it would appear, has only recently found deficits alarming. Nearly ten years ago he insisted that a $52-billion deficit should be allowed to get much bigger in order to lower unemployment, and he said that sometimes "we need a deficit in order to stimulate the economy."

The Audience. Boo-o-o!

The President. As a senator, he voted to override President Ford's veto of billions of dollars in spending bills and then voted no on a proposal to cut the 1976 deficit in half.

The Audience. Boo-o-o!

The President. Was anyone surprised by his pledge to raise your taxes next year if given the chance?

The Audience. No!

The President. In the Senate, he voted time and again for new taxes, including a 10-percent income tax surcharge, higher taxes on certain consumer items. He also voted against cutting the excise tax on automobiles. And he was part and parcel of that biggest single, individual tax increase in history—the social security payroll tax of 1977. It tripled the maximum tax and still didn't make the system solvent.

The Audience. Boo-o-o!

The President. If our opponents were as vigorous in supporting our voluntary prayer amendment as they are in raising taxes, maybe we could get the Lord back in the schoolrooms and drugs and violence out.

Something else illustrates the nature of the choice Americans must make. While we've been hearing a lot of tough talk on crime from our opponents, the House Democratic leadership continues to block a critical anticrime bill that passed the Republican Senate by a 91-to-1 vote. Their burial of this bill means that you and your families will have to wait for even safer homes and streets.

There's no longer any good reason to hold back passage of tuition tax credit legislation. Millions of average parents pay their full share of taxes to support public schools while choosing to send their children to parochial or other independent schools. Doesn't fairness dictate that they should have some help in carrying a double burden?

When we talk of the plight of our cities, what would help more than our enterprise zones bill, which provides tax incentives for private industry to help rebuild and restore decayed areas in seventy-five sites all across America? If they really wanted a future of boundless new opportunities for our citizens, why have they buried enterprise zones over the years in committee?

Our opponents are openly committed to increasing our tax burden.

The Audience. Boo-o-o!

The President. We are committed to stopping them, and we will.

They call their policy the new realism, but their new realism is just the old liberalism. They will place higher and higher taxes on small businesses, on family farms, and on other working families so that government may once again grow at the people's expense. You know, we could say they spend money like drunken sailors, but that would be unfair to drunken sailors [*Laughter*]—

The Audience. Four more years! Four more years! Four more years!

The President. All right. I agree.

The Audience. Four more years! Four more years! Four more years!

The President. I was going to say, it would be unfair, because the sailors are spending their own money. [*Laughter*]

Our tax policies are and will remain prowork, progrowth, and profamily. We intend to simplify the entire tax system—to make taxes more fair, easier to understand, and most important, to bring the tax rates of every American further down, not up. Now, if we bring them down far enough, growth will continue strong; the underground economy will shrink; the world will beat a path to our door; and no one will be able to hold America back; and the future will be ours.

The Audience. U.S.A.! U.S.A.! U.S.A.!

The President. All right. Another part of our future, the greatest challenge of all, is to reduce the risk of nuclear war by reducing the levels of nuclear arms. I have addressed parliaments, have spoken to parliaments in Europe and Asia during these last three and a half years, declaring that a nuclear war cannot be won and must never be fought. And those words, in those assemblies, were greeted with spontaneous applause.

There are only two nations who by their agreement can rid the world of those doomsday weapons—the United States of America and the Soviet Union. For the sake of our children and the safety of this earth, we ask the Soviets—who have walked out of our negotiations—to join us in reducing and yes, ridding the earth of this awful threat.

When we leave this hall tonight, we begin to place those clear choices before our fellow citizens. We must not let them be confused by those who still think that GNP stands for gross national promises. [*Laughter*] But after the debates, the position papers, the speeches, the conventions, the television commercials, primaries, caucuses, and slogans—after all this, is there really any doubt at all about what will happen if we let them win this November?

The Audience. No!

The President. Is there any doubt that they will raise our taxes?

The Audience. No!

The President. That they will send inflation into orbit again?

The Audience. No!

The President. That they will make government bigger than ever?

The Audience. No!

The President. And deficits even worse?

The Audience. No!

The President. Raise unemployment?

The Audience. No!

The President. Cut back our defense preparedness?

The Audience. No!

The President. Raise interest rates?

The Audience. No!

The President. Make unilateral and unwise concessions to the Soviet Union?

The Audience. No!

The President. And they'll do all that in the name of compassion.

The Audience. Boo-o-o!

The President. It's what they've done to America in the past. But if we do our job right, they won't be able to do it again.

The Audience. Reagan! Reagan! Reagan!

The President. It's getting late.

The Audience. Reagan! Reagan! Reagan!

The President. All right. In 1980 we asked the people of America, "Are you better off than you were four years ago?" Well, the people answered then by choosing us to bring about a change. We have every reason now, four years later, to ask that same question again, for we have made a change.

The American people joined us and helped us. Let us ask for their help again to renew the mandate of 1980, to move us further forward on the road we presently travel, the road of common sense, of people in control of their own destiny; the road leading to prosperity and economic expansion in a world at peace.

As we ask for their help, we should also answer the central question of public service: Why are we here? What do we believe in? Well for one thing, we're here to see that government continues to serve the people and not the other way around. Yes, government should do all that is necessary, but only that which is necessary.

We don't lump people by groups or special interests. And let me add, in the party of Lincoln, there is no room for intolerance and not even a small corner for anti-Semitism or bigotry of any kind. Many people are welcome in our house, but not the bigots.

We believe in the uniqueness of each individual. We believe in the sacredness of human life. For some time now we've all fallen into a pattern of describing our choice as left or right. It's become standard rhetoric in discussions of political philosophy. But is that really an accurate description of the choice before us?

Go back a few years to the origin of the terms and see where left or right would take us if we continued far enough in either direction. Stalin. Hitler. One would take us to Communist totalitarianism; the other to the totalitarianism of Hitler.

Isn't our choice really not one of left or right, but of up or down? Down through the welfare state to statism, to more and more government largesse accompanied always by more government authority, less individual liberty, and ultimately, totalitarianism, always advanced as for our own good. The alternative is the dream conceived by our Founding Fathers, up to the ultimate in individual freedom consistent with an orderly society.

We don't celebrate dependence day on the Fourth of July. We celebrate Independence Day.

The Audience. U.S.A.! U.S.A.! U.S.A.!

The President. We celebrate the right of each individual to be recognized as unique, possessed of dignity and the sacred right to life, liberty, and the pursuit of happiness. At the same time, with our independence goes a generosity of spirit more evident here than in almost any other part of the world. Recognizing the equality of all men and women, we're willing and able to lift the weak, cradle those who hurt, and nurture the bonds that tie us together as one nation under God.

Finally, we're here to shield our liberties, not just for now or for a few years but forever.

Could I share a personal thought with you tonight, because tonight's kind of special to me. It's the last time, of course, that I will address you under these same circumstances. I hope you'll invite me back to future conventions. Nancy and I will be forever grateful for the honor you've done us, for the opportunity to serve, and for your friendship and trust.

I began political life as a Democrat, casting my first vote in 1932 for Franklin Delano Roosevelt. That year, the Democrats called for a 25-percent reduction in the cost of government by abolishing useless commissions and offices and consolidating departments and bureaus, and giving more authority to state governments. As the years went by and those promises were forgotten, did I leave the Democratic Party, or did the leadership of that party leave not just me but millions of patriotic Democrats who believed in the principles and philosophy of that platform?

One of the first to declare this was a former Democratic nominee for president—Al Smith, the Happy Warrior, who went before the nation in 1936 to say, on television—or on radio—that he could no longer follow his party's leadership and that he was "taking a walk." As Democratic leaders have taken their party further and further away from its first principles, it's no surprise that so many responsible Democrats feel that our platform is closer to their views, and we welcome them to our side.

Four years ago we raised a banner of bold colors—no pale pastels. We proclaimed a dream of an America that would be "a shining city on a hill."

We promised that we'd reduce the growth of the federal government, and we have. We said we intended to reduce interest rates and inflation, and we have. We said we would reduce taxes to provide incentives for individuals and business to get our economy moving again, and we have. We said there must be jobs with a future for our people, not government make-work programs, and, in the last nineteen months, as I've said, six and a half million new jobs in the private sector have been created. We said we would once again be respected throughout the world, and we are. We said we would restore our ability to protect our freedom on land, sea, and in the air, and we have.

We bring to the American citizens in this election year a record of accomplishment and the promise of continuation.

We came together in a national crusade to make America great again, and to make a new beginning. Well, now it's all coming together. With our beloved nation at peace, we're in the midst of a springtime of hope for America. Greatness lies ahead of us.

Holding the Olympic games here in the United States began defining the promise of this season.

The Audience. U.S.A.! U.S.A.! U.S.A.!

The President. All through the spring and summer, we marveled at the journey of the Olympic torch as it made its passage east to west. Over nine thousand miles, by some four thousand runners, that flame crossed a portrait of our nation.

From our Gotham City, New York, to the Cradle of Liberty, Boston, across the Appalachian springtime, to the City of the

Big Shoulders, Chicago. Moving south toward Atlanta, over to St. Louis, past its Gateway Arch, across wheatfields into the stark beauty of the Southwest and then up into the still, snow-capped Rockies. And after circling the greening Northwest, it came down to California, across the Golden Gate and finally into Los Angeles. And all along the way, that torch became a celebration of America. And we all became participants in the celebration.

Each new story was typical of this land of ours. There was Ansel Stubbs, a youngster of ninety-nine, who passed the torch in Kansas to four-year-old Katie Johnson. In Pineville, Kentucky, it came at one A.M., so hundreds of people lined the streets with candles. At Tupelo, Mississippi, at seven A.M. on a Sunday morning, a robed church choir sang "God Bless America" as the torch went by.

That torch went through the Cumberland Gap, past the Martin Luther King, Jr., Memorial, down the Santa Fe Trail, and alongside Billy the Kid's grave.

In Richardson, Texas, it was carried by a fourteen-year-old boy in a special wheelchair. In West Virginia the runner came across a line of deaf children and let each one pass the torch for a few feet, and at the end these youngsters' hands talked excitedly in their sign language. Crowds spontaneously began singing "America the Beautiful" or "The Battle Hymn of the Republic."

And then, in San Francisco a Vietnamese immigrant, his little son held on his shoulders, dodged photographers and policemen to cheer a nineteen-year-old black man pushing an eighty-eight-year-old white woman in a wheelchair as she carried the torch.

My friends, that's America.

The Audience. U.S.A.! U.S.A.! U.S.A.!

The President. We cheered in Los Angeles as the flame was carried in and the giant Olympic torch burst into a billowing fire in front of the teams, the youth of 140 nations assembled on the floor of the Coliseum. And in that moment, maybe you were struck as I was with the uniqueness of what was taking place before a hundred thousand people in the stadium, most of them citizens of our country, and over a billion worldwide watching on television. There were athletes representing 140 countries here to compete in the one country in all the world whose people carry the bloodlines of all those 140 countries and more. Only in the United States is there such a rich mixture of races, creeds, and nationalities—only in our melting pot.

And that brings to mind another torch, the one that greeted so many of our parents and grandparents. Just this past Fourth of July, the torch atop the Statue of Liberty was hoisted down for replacement. We can be forgiven for thinking that maybe it was just worn out from lighting the way to freedom for 17 million new Americans. So, now we'll put up a new one.

The poet called Miss Liberty's torch the "lamp beside the golden door." Well, that was the entrance to America, and it still is. And now you really know why we're here tonight.

The glistening hope of that lamp is still ours. Every promise, every opportunity is still golden in this land. And through that golden door our children can walk into tomorrow with the knowledge that no one can be denied the promise that is America.

Her heart is full; her door is still golden, her future bright. She has arms big enough to comfort and strong enough to support, for the strength in her arms is the strength of her people. She will carry on in the eighties unafraid, unashamed, and unsurpassed.

In this springtime of hope, some lights seem eternal; America's is.

Thank you, God bless you, and God bless America.

Remarks at the U.S. Ranger Monument

POINTE DU HOC, FRANCE
JUNE 6, 1984

*This was an emotional day. The ceremonies honoring the for-
tieth anniversary of D day became more than commemorations.
They became celebrations of heroism and sacrifice. This place,
Pointe du Hoc, in itself was moving and majestic. I stood there
on that windswept point with the ocean behind me. Before me
were the boys who forty years before had fought their way up
from the ocean. Some rested under the white crosses and Stars*

of David that stretched out across the landscape. Others sat right in front of me. They looked like elderly businessmen, yet these were the kids who climbed the cliffs.

W E'RE HERE TO MARK that day in history when the Allied armies joined in battle to reclaim this continent to liberty. For four long years, much of Europe had been under a terrible shadow. Free nations had fallen, Jews cried out in the camps, millions cried out for liberation. Europe was enslaved, and the world prayed for its rescue. Here in Normandy the rescue began. Here the Allies stood and fought against tyranny in a giant undertaking unparalleled in human history.

We stand on a lonely, windswept point on the northern shore of France. The air is soft, but forty years ago at this moment, the air was dense with smoke and the cries of men, and the air was filled with the crack of rifle fire and the roar of cannon. At dawn, on the morning of the 6th of June, 1944, 225 Rangers jumped off the British landing craft and ran to the bottom of these cliffs. Their mission was one of the most difficult and daring of the invasion: to climb these sheer and desolate cliffs and take out the enemy guns. The Allies had been told that some of the mightiest of these guns were here and they would be trained on the beaches to stop the Allied advance.

The Rangers looked up and saw the enemy soldiers—at the edge of the cliffs shooting down at them with machine guns and throwing grenades. And the American Rangers began to climb. They shot rope ladders over the face of these cliffs and began to pull themselves up. When one Ranger fell, another would take his place. When one rope was cut, a Ranger would grab another and begin his climb again. They climbed, shot back, and held their footing. Soon, one by one, the Rangers pulled themselves over the top, and in seizing the firm land at the top of these cliffs, they began to seize back the continent of

Europe. Two hundred and twenty-five came here. After two days of fighting, only ninety could still bear arms.

Behind me is a memorial that symbolizes the Ranger daggers that were thrust into the top of these cliffs. And before me are the men who put them there.

These are the boys of Pointe du Hoc. These are the men who took the cliffs. These are the champions who helped free a continent. These are the heroes who helped end a war.

Gentlemen, I look at you and I think of the words of Stephen Spender's poem. You are men who in your "lives fought for life . . . and left the vivid air signed with your honor."

I think I know what you may be thinking right now—thinking "we were just part of a bigger effort; everyone was brave that day." Well, everyone was. Do you remember the story of Bill Millin of the 51st Highlanders? Forty years ago today, British troops were pinned down near a bridge, waiting desperately for help. Suddenly, they heard the sound of bagpipes, and some thought they were dreaming. Well, they weren't. They looked up and saw Bill Millin with his bagpipes, leading the reinforcements and ignoring the smack of bullets into the ground around him.

Lord Lovat was with him—Lord Lovat of Scotland, who calmly announced when he got to the bridge, "Sorry I'm a few minutes late," as if he'd been delayed by a traffic jam, when in truth he'd just come from the bloody fighting on Sword Beach, which he and his men had just taken.

There was the impossible valor of the Poles who threw themselves between the enemy and the rest of Europe as the invasion took hold, and the unsurpassed courage of the Canadians who had already seen the horrors of war on this coast. They knew what awaited them there, but they would not be deterred. And once they hit Juno Beach, they never looked back.

All of these men were part of a roll call of honor with names that spoke of a pride as bright as the colors they bore: The Royal Winnipeg Rifles, Poland's 24th Lancers, the Royal Scots Fusiliers, the Screaming Eagles, the Yeomen of England's armored divisions, the forces of Free France, the Coast Guard's "Matchbox Fleet," and you, the American Rangers.

Forty summers have passed since the battle that you fought here. You were young the day you took these cliffs; some of you were hardly more than boys, with the deepest joys of life before you. Yet, you risked everything here. Why? Why did you do it? What impelled you to put aside the instinct for self-preservation and risk your lives to take these cliffs? What inspired all the men of the armies that met here? We look at you, and somehow we know the answer. It was faith and belief; it was loyalty and love.

The men of Normandy had faith that what they were doing was right, faith that they fought for all humanity, faith that a just God would grant them mercy on this beachhead or on the next. It was the deep knowledge—and pray God we have not lost it—that there is a profound moral difference between the use of force for liberation and the use of force for conquest. You were here to liberate, not to conquer, and so you and those others did not doubt your cause. And you were right not to doubt.

You all knew that some things are worth dying for. One's country is worth dying for, and democracy is worth dying for, because it's the most deeply honorable form of government ever devised by man. All of you loved liberty. All of you were willing to fight tyranny, and you knew the people of your countries were behind you.

The Americans who fought here that morning knew word of the invasion was spreading through the darkness back home. They fought—or felt in their hearts, though they couldn't know in fact, that in Georgia they were filling the churches at four A.M., in Kansas they were kneeling on their porches and praying, and in Philadelphia they were ringing the Liberty Bell.

Something else helped the men of D day: their rock-hard belief that Providence would have a great hand in the events that would unfold here; that God was an ally in this great cause. And so, the night before the invasion, when Colonel Wolverton asked his parachute troops to kneel with him in prayer, he told them: Do not bow your heads, but look up so you can see God and ask His blessing in what we're about to do. Also that night, General Matthew Ridgway on his cot, listening in the darkness for the promise God made to Joshua: "I will not fail thee nor forsake thee."

These are the things that impelled them; these are the things that shaped the unity of the Allies.

When the war was over, there were lives to be rebuilt and governments to be returned to the people. There were nations to be reborn. Above all, there was a new peace to be assured. These were huge and daunting tasks. But the Allies summoned strength from the faith, belief, loyalty, and love of those who fell here. They rebuilt a new Europe together.

There was first a great reconciliation among those who had been enemies, all of whom had suffered so greatly. The United States did its part, creating the Marshall Plan to help rebuild our allies and our former enemies. The Marshall Plan led to the Atlantic alliance—a great alliance that serves to this day as our shield for freedom, for prosperity, and for peace.

In spite of our great efforts and successes, not all that followed the end of the war was happy or planned. Some liberated countries were lost. The great sadness of this loss echoes down to our own time in the streets of Warsaw, Prague, and East Berlin. Soviet troops that came to the center of this continent did not leave when peace came. They're still there, uninvited, unwanted, unyielding, almost forty years after the war. Because of this, allied forces still stand on this continent. Today, as forty years ago, our armies are here for only one purpose—to protect and defend democracy. The only territories we hold are memorials like this one and graveyards where our heroes rest.

We in America have learned bitter lessons from two world wars: It is better to be here ready to protect the peace, than to take blind shelter across the sea, rushing to respond only after freedom is lost. We've learned that isolationism never was and never will be an acceptable response to tyrannical governments with an expansionist intent.

But we try always to be prepared for peace; prepared to deter aggression; prepared to negotiate the reduction of arms; and yes, prepared to reach out again in the spirit of reconciliation. In truth, there is no reconciliation we would welcome more than a reconciliation with the Soviet Union, so, together, we can lessen the risks of war, now and forever.

It's fitting to remember here the great losses also suffered by the Russian people during World War II: 20 million perished, a terrible price that testifies to all the world the necessity of ending war. I tell you from my heart that we in the United States do not want war. We want to wipe from the face of the earth the terrible weapons that man now has in his hands. And I tell you, we are ready to seize that beachhead. We look for some sign from the Soviet Union that they are willing to move forward, that they share our desire and love for peace, and that they will give up the ways of conquest. There must be a changing there that will allow us to turn our hope into action.

We will pray forever that someday that changing will come. But for now, particularly today, it is good and fitting to renew our commitment to each other, to our freedom, and to the alliance that protects it.

We are bound today by what bound us forty years ago, the same loyalties, traditions, and beliefs. We're bound by reality. The strength of America's allies is vital to the United States, and the American security guarantee is essential to the continued freedom of Europe's democracies. We were with you then; we are with you now. Your hopes are our hopes, and your destiny is our destiny.

Here, in this place where the West held together, let us make a vow to our dead. Let us show them by our actions that we understand what they died for. Let our actions say to them the words for which Matthew Ridgway listened: "I will not fail thee nor forsake thee."

Strengthened by their courage, heartened by their valor and borne by their memory, let us continue to stand for the ideals for which they lived and died.

Thank you very much, and God bless you all.

Remarks at the Normandy Invasion Ceremony

OMAHA BEACH, FRANCE
JUNE 6, 1984

Later that same afternoon, I attended a joint U.S.–French ceremony commemorating D day at the Omaha Beach Memorial. A young woman had sent me a beautiful letter about her father, who had participated in the invasion. I had decided to read the letter aloud to the audience because it was so deeply moving and meaningful, but I hadn't expected to fight back the tears. Her words affected me more than I had anticipated as I started reading them. The young woman was right in the front row and I could see her crying. I know she must have been the apple of her father's eye. I know he must have been very proud of this wonderful, loving young woman.

Mr. President,* distinguished guests, we stand today at a place of battle, one that forty years ago saw and felt the worst of war. Men bled and died here for a few feet of—or inches of sand, as bullets and shellfire cut through their ranks. About them, General Omar Bradley later said, "Every man who set foot on Omaha Beach that day was a hero."

No speech can adequately portray their suffering, their sacrifice, their heroism. President Lincoln once reminded us that through their deeds, the dead of battle have spoken more eloquently for themselves than any of the living ever could. But we can only honor them by rededicating ourselves to the cause for which they gave a last full measure of devotion.

Today we do rededicate ourselves to that cause. And at this place of honor, we're humbled by the realization of how much so many gave to the cause of freedom and to their fellow man.

Some who survived the battle of June 6, 1944, are here today. Others who hoped to return never did.

"Someday, Lis, I'll go back," said Private First Class Peter Robert Zanatta, of the 37th Engineer Combat Battalion, and first assault wave to hit Omaha Beach. "I'll go back, and I'll see it all again. I'll see the beach, the barricades, and the graves."

Those words of Private Zanatta come to us from his daughter, Lisa Zanatta Henn, in a heartrending story about the event her father spoke of so often. "In his words, the Normandy invasion would change his life forever," she said. She tells some of his stories of World War II but says of her father, "The story to end all stories was D day.

"He made me feel the fear of being on that boat waiting to land. I can smell the ocean and feel the seasickness. I can see the looks on his fellow soldiers' faces—the fear, the anguish, the uncertainty of what lay ahead. And when they landed, I can feel the strength and courage of the men who took those first

* President François Mitterrand of France.

steps through the tide to what must have surely looked like instant death."

Private Zanatta's daughter wrote to me: "I don't know how or why I can feel this emptiness, this fear, or this determination, but I do. Maybe it's the bond I had with my father. All I know is that it brings tears to my eyes to think about my father as a twenty-year-old boy having to face that beach."

The anniversary of D day was always special for her family. And like all the families of those who went to war, she describes how she came to realize her own father's survival was a miracle: "So many men died. I know that my father watched many of his friends be killed. I know that he must have died inside a little each time. But his explanation to me was, 'You did what you had to do, and you kept on going.' "

When men like Private Zanatta and all our allied forces stormed the beaches of Normandy forty years ago they came not as conquerors, but as liberators. When these troops swept across the French countryside and into the forests of Belgium and Luxembourg they came not to take, but to return what had been wrongly seized. When our forces marched into Germany, they came not to prey on a brave and defeated people, but to nurture the seeds of democracy among those who yearned to be free again.

We salute them today. But Mr. President, we also salute those who, like yourself, were already engaging the enemy inside your beloved country—the French Resistance. Your valiant struggle for France did so much to cripple the enemy and spur the advance of the armies of liberation. The French Forces of the Interior will forever personify courage and national spirit. They will be a timeless inspiration to all who are free and to all who would be free.

Today, in their memory, and for all who fought here, we celebrate the triumph of democracy. We reaffirm the unity of democratic peoples who fought a war and then joined with the vanquished in a firm resolve to keep the peace.

From a terrible war we learned that unity made us invincible; now, in peace, that same unity makes us secure. We sought to bring all freedom-loving nations together in a community dedicated to the defense and preservation of our sacred values. Our alliance, forged in the crucible of war, tempered and shaped by the realities of the postwar world, has succeeded. In Europe, the threat has been contained, the peace has been kept.

Today the living here assembled—officials, veterans, citizens—are a tribute to what was achieved here forty years ago. This land is secure. We are free. These things are worth fighting and dying for.

Lisa Zanatta Henn began her story by quoting her father, who promised that he would return to Normandy. She ended with a promise to her father, who died eight years ago of cancer: "I'm going there, Dad, and I'll see the beaches and the barricades and the monuments. I'll see the graves, and I'll put flowers there just like you wanted to do. I'll feel all the things you made me feel through your stories and your eyes. I'll never forget what you went through, Dad, nor will I let anyone else forget. And Dad, I'll always be proud."

Through the words of his loving daughter, who is here with us today, a D day veteran has shown us the meaning of this day far better than any president can. It is enough for us to say about Private Zanatta and all the men of honor and courage who fought beside him four decades ago: We will always remember. We will always be proud. We will always be prepared, so we may always be free.

Thank you.

Remarks to the Citizens of Ballyporeen

BALLYPOREEN, IRELAND
JUNE 3, 1984

So this was home. This was where my people came from in ages past. That's the great thing about America, we all come from someplace else. We all have roots that reach somewhere far away. Even the Native American Indian apparently came across from Asia when there was a land bridge leading to North America tens of thousands of years ago. We all have another home.

IN THE BUSINESS that I formerly was in, I would have to say this is a very difficult spot—to be introduced to you who have waited so patiently—following this wonderful talent that we've seen here. And I should have gone on first, and then you should have followed—[*Laughter*]—to close the show. But thank you very much.

Nancy and I are most grateful to be with you here today, and I'll take a chance and say, *muintir na hEireann* [people of Ireland]. Did I get it right? [*Applause*] All right. Well, it's difficult to express my appreciation to all of you. I feel like I'm about to drown everyone in a bath of nostalgia. Of all the honors and gifts that have been afforded me as president, this visit is the one that I will cherish dearly. You see, I didn't know much about my family background—not because of a lack of interest, but because my father was orphaned before he was six years old. And now thanks to you and the efforts of good people who have dug into the history of a poor immigrant family, I know at last whence I came. And this has given my soul a new contentment. And it is a joyous feeling. It is like coming home after a long journey.

You see, my father, having been orphaned so young, he knew nothing of his roots also. And, God rest his soul, I told the father, I think he's here, too, today, and very pleased and happy to know that this is whence he came.

Robert Frost, a renowned American poet, once said, "Home is the place where, when you have to go there, they have to take you in." [*Laughter*] Well, it's been so long since my great-grandfather set out that you don't have to take me in. So, I'm certainly thankful for this wonderful homecoming today. I can't think of a place on the planet I would rather claim as my roots more than Ballyporeen, County Tipperary.

My great-grandfather left here in a time of stress, seeking to better himself and his family. From what I'm told, we were a poor family. But my ancestors took with them a treasure, an indomitable spirit that was cultivated in the rich soil of this county.

And today I come back to you as a descendant of people who are buried here in paupers' graves. Perhaps this is God's way of reminding us that we must always treat every individual, no matter what his or her station in life, with dignity and respect. And who knows? Someday that person's child or grandchild might grow up to become the prime minister of Ireland or president of the United States.

Looking around town today, I was struck by the similarity between Ballyporeen and the small town in Illinois where I was born, Tampico. Of course, there's one thing you have that we didn't have in Tampico. We didn't have a Ronald Reagan Lounge in town. [*Laughter*] Well, the spirit is the same, this spirit of warmth, friendliness, and openness in Tampico and Ballyporeen, and you make me feel very much at home.

What unites us is our shared heritage and the common values of our two peoples. So many Irish men and women from every walk of life played a role in creating the dream of America. One was Charles Thompson, Secretary of the Continental Congress, and who designed the first Great Seal of the United States. I'm certainly proud to be part of that great Irish American tradition. From the time of our revolution when Irishmen filled the ranks of the Continental Army, to the building of the railroads, to the cultural contributions of individuals like the magnificent tenor John McCormack and the athletic achievements of the great heavyweight boxing champion John L. Sullivan—all of them are part of a great legacy.

Speaking of sports, I'd like to take this opportunity to congratulate an organization of which all Irish men and women can be proud, an organization that this year is celebrating its one-hundredth anniversary: the Gaelic Athletic Association. I understand it was formed a hundred years ago in Tipperary to foster the culture and games of traditional Ireland. Some of you may be aware that I began my career as a sports announcer—a sports broadcaster—so I had an early appreciation for sporting competition. Well, congratulations to all of you during this GAA centennial celebration.

I also understand that not too far from here is the home of the great Irish novelist Charles Joseph Kickham. The Irish identity flourished in the United States. Irish men and women proud of their heritage can be found in every walk of life. I even have some of them in my cabinet. One of them traces his maternal roots to Mitchellstown, just down the road from Ballyporeen. And he and I have almost the same name. I'm talking about Secretary of the Treasury Don Regan.

He spells it R-e-g-a-n. We're all of the same clan, we're all cousins. I tried to tell the secretary one day that his branch of the family spelled it that way because they just couldn't handle as many letters as ours could. [*Laughter*] And then I received a paper from Ireland that told me that the clan to which we belong, that in it those who said "Regan" and spelled it that way were the professional people and the educators, and only the common laborers called it "Reagan." [*Laughter*] So, meet a common laborer.

The first job I ever got—I was fourteen years old, and they put a pick and a shovel in my hand and my father told me that that was fitting and becoming to one of our name.

The bond between our two countries runs deep and strong, and I'm proud to be here in recognition and celebration of our ties that bind. My roots in Ballyporeen, County Tipperary, are little different from millions of other Americans who find their roots in towns and counties all over the Isle of Erin. I just feel exceptionally lucky to have this chance to visit you.

Last year a member of my staff came through town and recorded some messages from you. It was quite a tape, and I was moved deeply by the sentiments that you expressed. One of your townsmen sang me a bit of a tune about Sean Tracy, and a few lines stuck in my mind. They went like this—not that I'll sing—"And I'll never more roam, from my own native home, in Tipperary so far away."

Well, the Reagans roamed to America, but now we're back. And Nancy and I thank you from the bottom of our hearts for coming out to welcome us, for the warmth of your welcome. God bless you all.

Remarks at the Al Smith Dinner

NEW YORK CITY
OCTOBER 18, 1984

These Al Smith dinners in New York are charity fund-raising dinners that politicians like to attend, especially in election years. I guess you could be cynical and say it's because of the Catholic vote, but it's more than that. The evenings often have a special feeling of warmth. Sometimes you're expected to be funny, sometimes sentimental. This evening in 1984, I decided to talk about my friend Cardinal Cooke, who ministered to me after the assassination attempt on my life. He had recently died and I just wanted to say a few words about him.

T HANK YOU VERY MUCH. I have to catch the shuttle. [*Laughter*]

May it please Your Excellency, Archbishop O'Connor, and members of the reverend clergy, Governor Cuomo, Senators Moynihan and D'Amato, Mayor Koch, and Mr. Toastmaster, Sonny Werblin, and distinguished friends:

I thank you for that welcome.

I must say, I have traveled the banquet circuit for many years. I've never quite understood the logistics of dinners like this, and how the absence of one individual could cause three of us to not have seats. [*Laughter*] But that's enough of that. [*Laughter*]

I'm grateful for your invitation and honored to be here. And I can't help but feel that four great Americans are with us here in spirit tonight: Al Smith, of course, the Happy Warrior, whom time and respect and affectionate memory have elevated beyond partisanship; the beloved Francis Cardinal Spellman, whose remarkable works of charity so notably include his establishment of this Al Smith Dinner thirty-eight years ago; the great Jewish philanthropist Charles Silver. He was enlisted by Cardinal Spellman as chairman of these dinners and raised millions for hospitals serving all faiths; and finally, Terence Cardinal Cooke, that gentle soul whom I, for one, shall never forget.

All of them are gone now, gone to God—Cardinal Cooke and Charlie Silver within a year's passing, as you've been told. And all of them personify the great commandment—to love our fellow man.

Here we are, then, at the height of a season marked by differences of opinion, and yet, all this striving and all these contesting issues fade to insignificance in the clear light of example that these four men set for us, each one in his own unique way: Al Smith, in his lifelong struggles for the working man and woman; Cardinal Spellman, as a prince and builder of the church; Charles Silver, as a friend and colleague in ecumenical service to humanity; and Cardinal Cooke, whom I knew best in circumstances of dire spiritual need.

Nothing could have meant more to me and to Nancy than Cardinal Cooke's visit with us at the White House while I was recovering from young Mr. Hinckley's unwelcome attentions. His Eminence offered prayers and encouragement that maintained us in a time of genuine personal need—a need far more serious, I know now, than we or almost anyone at the time realized.

And so it was only natural that Nancy and I should have been so profoundly grief-stricken upon learning in August of last year that the cardinal was dying. Together, we telephoned our dear friend in New York to tell him of our heartfelt prayers for him and to thank him once again for all he had done to comfort and reassure us in our hour of need. Our prayerful concern for the cardinal, I assured him, was shared by millions of other Americans grateful for all that he had done on behalf of his country.

His letter of September 15th, which followed our call, said our prayers, good wishes, and loving concern "are a source of great comfort to me." But then he wrote, "I want you to know that I'm offering my prayers and my suffering for the gift of God's peace among all the members of His human family."

Nancy and I will always be grateful that we were able to visit him in New York and, as it turned out, only days before his death. We were told that when we arrived that he had been in great pain for the previous forty-eight hours, so much so that they'd feared he wouldn't be able to receive us. But when we arrived, he was so much like his old self, it was hard to believe that he was desperately ill.

Being Terence Cooke, he couldn't resist doing a little lobbying in behalf of a cause that concerned him: "As a nation known for its compassion," he said, "the United States has accomplished so much through the years in advancing the cause of international justice and peace through its programs of economic assistance to the less fortunate peoples of the world." And then he acknowledged the appropriation that I had approved for help to sub-Saharan African nations.

He also talked of my problems, and he said, "When I join the Lord, I'll continue to pray for you." He paused, and then, with something of an abashed or self-deprecatory smile, very simply he added, "Maybe I'm being a little presumptuous in assuming I'll be with the Lord." Well, eleven days later he left us, and none of us have any doubt that he joined the Lord.

I have presumed to share this personal experience with you tonight because it says so much about our gentle friend, Terence Cooke. It says much also about Al Smith and Cardinal Spellman and Charlie Silver, for, linked in charity, linked in service, linked in humanity, they are linked by this occasion.

I think it should make us proud to have known these great Americans and their works of love for their fellow man. I think it should make us just a little bit prouder than ever to be Americans.

Archbishop O'Connor, I know that you're profoundly aware of the great tradition in which you now pursue God's work. And in this you have my every good wish and, I know, those also of a grateful nation. And if you wouldn't think that I was invading your field, could I just say, in addition to a heartfelt thank you to all of you, God bless you.

Remarks at a Rally
in Fairfield, Connecticut

OCTOBER 26, 1984

This speech was typical of the stump speech I delivered out on the hustings. I'd give it or an alternate almost everywhere I went with small variations for the audience and for the local Republican candidates running for office. I don't know why, but during the '84 campaign the audiences seemed to get caught up in the spirit of things and they'd start chanting or yelling things out to me. It was really quite a party, a Republican party as things turned out. The year came to a close with a landslide under our belt and another four-year lease on the White House.

The President. Well, it's great to be here in Fairfield and back in Connecticut again. And I'm proud to be here today with your Congressman Stu McKinney. We need him back in Washington. And that goes for Congresswoman Nancy Johnson, too. She's had a first, great term, and we need her back in Washington.

Today I want to ask everyone in Connecticut to help out this administration by sending Larry Denardis back to the Congress from the third district, electing Herschel Klein in the first district, and Roberta Koontz in the second, and John Rowland in the fifth.

I am always glad to visit again with the good people who

have given America some of its greatest Republicans—John Davis Lodge, Clare Boothe Luce, and yes, a fellow named George Bush. He's a great friend, a strong right arm, and I think the finest vice president this country's ever had.

I would also like to say hello to Donna and Bruce Keith, whose son, Jeff, is undertaking a courageous task to raise money for the American Cancer Society. Jeff, as you probably all know, is running from Boston to Los Angeles, and Nancy and I met him on Monday in Kansas City—where I'd gone for a little fracas of my own. Jeff's run is not only an inspiration, it's a challenge to all of us to go as far as our abilities will take us—and a little bit farther. And I think that all of you probably are well aware of what he's doing and are proud of him, as we all are.

Now, you know that Nathan Hale was from Connecticut. Now, I'm not going to claim he was a Republican; that would be almost as bad as my opponent invoking the name of Harry Truman to defend his defense policies. I hope you've all noticed that my opponent, who back in the primaries sounded like he thought the world was *Mr. Rogers' Neighborhood*—[*Laughter*]—has suddenly discovered that America has some dangerous adversaries out there. The man who, all his years in the Senate, voted against every weapons system except slingshots —[*Laughter*]—is now talking tough about our adversaries and the need for national security.

Audience member. He doesn't know what he's talking about!

The President. You're right. [*Laughter*] He doesn't. For those of you who are too far away to hear, a lady up here said, "He doesn't know what he's talking about." [*Laughter*] She's absolutely right.

And last-minute conversions aren't going to hide the fact that these liberal Democrats don't represent traditional Democrats anymore. You know, national Democrats used to fight for the working families of America, and now all they seem to fight for are the special interests and their own left-wing ideology. We have a tremendous opportunity this year to join with a lot of disaffected Democrats and independents to send a message back to Washington, a message that says the American people want a Congress that won't stalemate or obstruct our agenda for hope and new opportunity for the future.

Abe Lincoln said we must disenthrall ourselves with the past, and then we will save our country. Well, four years ago that's just what we did. We made a great turn. We got out from under the thrall of a government which we had hoped would make our lives better, but which wound up trying to live our lives for us. The power of the federal government, that it had over the decades, created great chaos—economic, social, and international. And our leaders were adrift, rudderless, without compass.

Four years ago we began to navigate by some certain, fixed principles. Our North Star was freedom, and common sense our constellations. We knew that economic freedom meant paying less of the American family's earnings to the government, and so we cut personal tax rates by 25 percent.

We knew that inflation, the quiet thief, was stealing our savings, and the highest interest rates since the Civil War were making it impossible for people to own a home or start an enterprise. And let me interject a news note, in case you've been busy this morning and haven't heard it: Led by Morgan, the bank, two other major banks joined them, and the prime rate came down to 12 percent as of this morning. And I'm sure that the other banks will soon follow.

The Audience. Four more years! Four more years! Four more years!

The President. All right. You'd better let me talk; it looks like it's going to rain.

We knew that our national military defense had been weakened, so we decided to rebuild and be strong again. And this we knew would enhance the chances for peace throughout the world.

It was a second American revolution, and it's only just begun. But America is back, a giant, powerful in its renewed spirit, its growing economy, powerful in its ability to defend itself and secure the peace, and powerful in its ability to build a new future. And you know something? That's not debatable.

Yet four years after our efforts began small voices in the night are sounding the call to go back—back to the days of drift, the days of torpor, timidity, and taxes. My opponent this year is known to you, but perhaps we can gain greater insight into the world he would take us back to if we take a look at his record.

His understanding of economics is well demonstrated by his predictions. Just before we took office, he said our economic program is obviously, murderously, inflationary. That was just before we lowered inflation from 12.4 down to around 4 percent. And just after our tax cuts, he said the most he could see was an anemic recovery. And that was right before the United States economy created more than 6 million new jobs in twenty-one months.

My opponent said our policies would deliver a misery index the likes of which we haven't seen for a long time. Now, there he was partially right. You know you get the misery index by adding the rate of unemployment to the rate of inflation. They invented that in 1976, during the campaign that year. They said that Jerry Ford had no right to ask for reelection because his misery index was 12.6. Now, they didn't mention the misery index in the 1980 election, probably because it had gone up to more than 20. And they aren't talking too much about it in this campaign, because it's down around 11.

He said that decontrol of oil, the oil prices, would cost American consumers more than $36 billion a year. Well, we decontrolled oil prices. It was one of the first things we did. And the price of gas went down eight cents a gallon.

Now, I have something figured out here—that maybe all we have to do to get the economy in absolutely perfect shape is to persuade my opponent to predict absolute disaster. [*Laughter*]

He says he cares about the middle class, but he boasts, "I have consistently supported legislation, time after time, which increases taxes on my own constituents." Doesn't that make you just want to be one of his constituents?

The Audience. No!

The President. He's no doubt proud of the fact that as senator he voted sixteen times to increase taxes on the American people.

The Audience. Boo-o-o!

The President. But this year he's outdone himself. He's already promised, of course, to raise your taxes. But if he's to keep all the promises that he's made in this campaign—we figured it out by computer—he will have to raise your taxes $1,890 for every household in this country.

The Audience. Boo-o-o!

The President. That's better than $150 a month, that's the Mondale mortgage. But his economic plan has two basic parts: raise your taxes, and then raise them again. But I've got news for him: The American people don't want his tax increases, and he isn't going to get them.

If he got them, if he got those tax increases, it would stop the recovery. But I tell you, he did give me an idea: If I can figure out how to dress like his tax program, I'll go out on Halloween and scare the devil out of all the neighbors. [*Laughter*]

If his campaign were a television show, it would be *Let's Make a Deal.* You give up your prosperity to see what surprise he has for you behind the curtain. [*Laughter*] If his plan were a Broadway show, it would be *Promises, Promises.* [*Laughter*] And if the administration that he served in as vice president were a book, you'd have to read it from the back end to the front to get a happy ending.

He sees an America in which every day is tax day, April 15th. But we see an America in which every day is Independence Day, July 4th. We want to lower your tax rates so that your families will be stronger, our economy will be stronger, and America will be stronger.

I'm proud to say that during these last four years, not one square inch of territory in the world has been lost to Communist aggression. And the United States is more secure than it was four years ago.

But my opponent sees a different world. Some time back he said the old days of a Soviet strategy of suppression by force are over. That was just before the Soviets invaded Czechoslovakia. After they invaded Afghanistan, he said, "It just baffles me why the Soviets these last few years have behaved as they have." But then, there's so much that baffles him. [*Laughter*]

One year ago we liberated Grenada from Communist thugs who had taken over that country, and my opponent called what we did a violation of international law that erodes our moral authority to criticize the Soviets.

The Audience. Boo-o-o!

The President. Well, there's nothing immoral about rescuing American students whose lives are in danger. But by the time my opponent decided that action was justified, the students were long since home.

After the Sandinista revolution in Nicaragua, he praised it. He said, "Winds of democratic progress are stirring where they have long been stifled." But we all know that the Sandinistas immediately began to persecute the genuine believers in democracy and export terror. They went on to slaughter the Miskito Indians, abuse and deport church leaders, practice anti-Semitism, slander the Pope, and move to kill free speech. Don't you think it's time my opponent stood up, spoke out, and condemned the Sandinista crimes? [*Applause*]

More recently, he refused, or failed to repudiate the Reverend Jesse Jackson, when he went to Havana and then stood with Fidel Castro and cried: "Long live President Fidel Castro! Long live Che Guevara!"

The Audience. Boo-o-o!

The President. But let me try to put this in perspective. The 1984 election is not truly a partisan contest. I was a Democrat once myself, and for a long time, a large part of my life. But in those days, its leaders didn't belong to the "blame America first" crowd. Its leaders were men like Harry Truman, who understood the challenges of our times. They didn't reserve all their indignation for America. They knew the difference between freedom and tyranny and they stood up for one and damned the other.

To all the good Democrats who respect that tradition, I say —and I hope there are many present—you're not alone. We're asking you to come walk with us down the new path of hope and opportunity, and we'll make it a bipartisan salvation of our country.

This month an American woman walked in space—Kathryn Sullivan—and she made history. And she returned to a space shuttle in which some of the great scientific and medical advances of the future will be made. Cures for diabetes and heart disease may be possible up there; advances in technology and communications. But my opponent led the fight in the United States Senate against the entire shuttle program and called it a horrible waste.

Well, we support the space shuttle, and we've committed America to meet a great challenge—to build a permanently manned space station before this decade is out.

And now, I've probably been going on for too long up here—

The Audience. No!

The President. —but I just want to say the point is we were right when we made a great turn in 1980. Incidentally, I was mistaken when I said there "before this decade is out." I should say within ten years—a decade—we're hoping for that space station.

We were right to take command of the ship, stop its aimless drift, and get moving again. And we were right when we stopped sending out SOS and starting saying U.S.A.!

The Audience. U.S.A.! U.S.A.! U.S.A.!

The President. You are right. The United States was never meant to be a second-best nation. And like our Olympic athletes, this nation should set its sights on the stars and go for the gold.

If America could bring down inflation from, as I said, 12.4 percent to 4, then we can bring inflation from 4 percent down to zero. If lowering your tax rates led to the best expansion in thirty years, then we can lower them again and keep America growing into the twenty-first century.

If we could create 6 million new jobs in twenty-one months, and some 9 million new businesses be incorporated in eighteen months, then we can make it possible for every American—young, old, black, or white—who wants, to find a job.

If our states and municipalities can establish enterprise zones to create economic growth, then we can elect people to Congress who will free our enterprise-zones bill from Tip O'Neill —it's been there for more than two years—so that we can provide hope and opportunity for the most distressed areas of America.

If we can lead a revolution in technology, push back the frontiers of space, then we can provide our workers—in industries old and new—all that they need. I say that American workers provided with the right tools can outproduce, outcompete, and outsell anyone in the world.

Audience member. Give 'em hell!

The President. Someone said, "Give 'em hell." Harry Truman —when they said that to Harry Truman, he said tell them the truth, and they'll think it's hell. Well, if our grassroots drive to restore excellence in education could reverse a twenty-year decline in scholastic aptitude test scores—which it has—then we can keep raising those scores and restoring American academic excellence second to none.

If our crackdown on crime could produce the sharpest drop ever in the crime index, then we can keep cracking down until our families and friends can walk our streets again without being afraid.

And if we could reverse the decline in our military defenses and restore respect for America, then we can make sure this nation remains strong enough to protect freedom and peace for us, for our children, and for our children's children.

And if we make sure that America is strong and prepared for peace, then we can begin to reduce nuclear weapons and one day banish them entirely from the earth. And that is our goal.

If we can strengthen our economy, strengthen our security, and strengthen the values that bind us, then America will become a nation ever greater in art and learning, greater in the love and worship of the God who made us and Who has blessed us as no other people on earth have ever been blessed.

To the young people of our country—and I'm so happy to see so many of them here—let me, if I could, say to you young people: You are what this election is all about—you and your future.

Your generation is something special. Your love of country and idealism are unsurpassed. And it's our highest duty to make certain that you have an America every bit as full of opportunity, hope, confidence, and dreams as we had when we were your age.

You know, last Sunday night I didn't get to finish what I started to say, was going to finish with in that debate, so I can finish it now. I was talking about you young people. And I've seen you all across this country, and you are special. And what I was going to say was that my generation—and a few generations between mine and yours—that we grew up in an America where we took it for granted that you could fly as high and as far as your own strength and ability would take you. And it is our sacred responsibility—those several generations I've just mentioned—to make sure that we hand you an America that is free in a world that is at peace. And we're going to do it.

The Audience. Four more years! Four more years! Four more years!

The President. All right. Thank you. I really hadn't thought about it, but you've talked me into it. You know, if we can, all of us together—we're part of a great revolution, and it's only just begun. America is never going to give up its special mission on this earth—never. There are new worlds on the horizon, and we're not going to stop until we all get there together.

America's best days are yet to come. And I know it may drive my opponents up the wall, but I'm going to say it anyway: You ain't seen nothin' yet.

The Audience. Reagan! Reagan! Reagan!

The President. Thank you very much. Thank you, and God bless you all.

1985

Address to the Nation
on the Upcoming
U.S.–Soviet Summit in Geneva

OVAL OFFICE
NOVEMBER 14, 1985

The U.S.–Soviet summit is the lead for 1985. Who would have guessed it? Here I was, the great anti-Communist, heading off for a meeting with the leader of the evil empire.

Actually, it did not surprise me at all. The only reason I'd never met with General Secretary Gorbachev's predecessors was because they kept dying on me—Brezhnev, Chernenko, Andropov. Then along came Gorbachev. He was different in style, in substance, and, I believe, in intellect from previous Soviet leaders. He is a man who takes chances and that's what you need for progress. He is a remarkable force for change in that country.

We first met in Geneva. My team had set up a guesthouse away from the main meeting area where Gorbachev and I could talk one-on-one. He jumped at the chance when I suggested we sneak away. And there we sat and talked for hours in front of a roaring fire. I opened by telling him that ours was a unique situation—two men who together had the power to bring on World War III. By the same token we had the capability to bring about world peace. I said, "We don't mistrust each other because we're armed. We're armed because we mistrust each other." I asked him how, in addition to eliminating the arms, how could we eliminate the mistrust?

I did not know when I left for that meeting in Geneva, I would eventually call Mikhail Gorbachev a friend. I did not know what to expect. This is the speech I gave to the American people as I prepared to depart for Geneva.

M Y FELLOW AMERICANS:

Good evening. In thirty-six hours I will be leaving for Geneva for the first meeting between an American president and a Soviet leader in six years. I know that you and the people of the world are looking forward to that meeting with great interest, so tonight I want to share with you my hopes and tell you why I am going to Geneva.

My mission, stated simply, is a mission for peace. It is to engage the new Soviet leader in what I hope will be a dialog for peace that endures beyond my presidency. It is to sit down across from Mr. Gorbachev and try to map out, together, a basis for peaceful discourse even though our disagreements on fundamentals will not change. It is my fervent hope that the two of us can begin a process which our successors and our peoples can continue—facing our differences frankly and openly and beginning to narrow and resolve them; communicating effectively so that our actions and intentions are not misunderstood; and eliminating the barriers between us and cooperating wherever possible for the greater good of all.

This meeting can be an historic opportunity to set a steady, more constructive course to the twenty-first century. The history of American-Soviet relations, however, does not augur well for euphoria. Eight of my predecessors—each in his own way in his own time—sought to achieve a more stable and peaceful relationship with the Soviet Union. None fully succeeded; so, I don't underestimate the difficulty of the task ahead. But these sad chapters do not relieve me of the obligation to try to make this a safer, better world. For our children, our grandchildren, for all mankind—I intend to make the effort. And with your prayers and God's help, I hope to succeed. Success at the summit, however, should not be measured by any short-term agreements that may be signed. Only the passage of time will tell us whether we constructed a durable bridge to a safer world. This, then, is why I go to Geneva—to build a foundation for lasting peace.

When we speak of peace, we should not mean just the absence of war. True peace rests on the pillars of individual freedom, human rights, national self-determination, and respect for the rule of law. Building a safer future requires that we address candidly all the issues which divide us and not just focus on one or two issues, important as they may be. When we meet in Geneva, our agenda will seek not just to avoid war, but to strengthen peace, prevent confrontation, and remove the sources of tension. We should seek to reduce the suspicions and mistrust that have led us to acquire mountains of strategic weapons. Since the dawn of the nuclear age, every American president has sought to limit and end the dangerous competition in nuclear arms. I have no higher priority than to finally realize that dream. I've said before, I will say again: A nuclear war cannot be won and must never be fought. We've gone the extra mile in arms control, but our offers have not always been welcome.

In 1977 and again in 1982, the United States proposed to the Soviet Union deep reciprocal cuts in strategic forces. These offers were rejected out-of-hand. In 1981 we proposed the complete elimination of a whole category of intermediate-range nuclear forces. Three years later, we proposed a treaty for a global ban on chemical weapons. In 1983 the Soviet Union got up and walked out of the Geneva nuclear arms control negotiations altogether. They did this in protest because we and our European allies had begun to deploy nuclear weapons as a counter to Soviet SS-20s aimed at our European and other allies. I'm pleased now, however, with the interest expressed in reducing offensive weapons by the new Soviet leadership. Let me repeat tonight what I announced last week. The United States is prepared to reduce comparable nuclear systems by 50 percent. We seek reductions that will result in a stable balance between us with no first-strike capability and verified full compliance. If we both reduce the weapons of war there would be no losers, only winners. And the whole world would benefit if we could both abandon these weapons altogether and move to nonnuclear defensive systems that threaten no one.

But nuclear arms control is not of itself a final answer. I told four Soviet political commentators two weeks ago that nations do not distrust each other because they're armed; they arm themselves because they distrust each other. The use of force, subversion, and terror has made the world a more dangerous place. And thus, today there's no peace in Afghanistan; no peace in Cambodia; no peace in Angola, Ethiopia, or Nicaragua. These wars have claimed hundreds of lives and threaten to spill over national frontiers. That's why in my address to the United Nations, I proposed a way to end these conflicts: a regional peace plan that calls for negotiations among the warring parties—withdrawal of all foreign troops, democratic reconciliation, and economic assistance.

Four times in my lifetime, our soldiers have been sent overseas to fight in foreign lands. Their remains can be found from Flanders Field to the islands of the Pacific. Not once were those young men sent abroad in the cause of conquest. Not once did they come home claiming a single square inch of some other country as a trophy of war. A great danger in the past, however, has been the failure by our enemies to remember that while we Americans detest war, we love freedom and stand ready to sacrifice for it. We love freedom not only because it's practical and beneficial but because it is morally right and just.

In advancing freedom, we Americans carry a special burden —a belief in the dignity of man in the sight of the God who gave birth to this country. This is central to our being. A century and a half ago, Thomas Jefferson told the world, "The mass of mankind has not been born with saddles on their backs. . . ." Freedom is America's core. We must never deny it nor forsake it. Should the day come when we Americans remain silent in the face of armed aggression, then the cause of America, the cause of freedom, will have been lost and the great heart of this country will have been broken. This affirmation of freedom is not only our duty as Americans, it's essential for success at Geneva.

Freedom and democracy are the best guarantors of peace. History has shown that democratic nations do not start wars. The rights of the individual and the rule of law are as fundamental to peace as arms control. A government which does not respect its citizens' rights and its international commitments to protect those rights is not likely to respect its other international undertakings. And that's why we must and will speak in Geneva on behalf of those who cannot speak for themselves. We are not trying to impose our beliefs on others. We have a right to expect, however, that great states will live up to their international obligations.

Despite our deep and abiding differences, we can and must prevent our international competition from spilling over into violence. We can find, as yet undiscovered, avenues where American and Soviet citizens can cooperate fruitfully for the benefit of mankind. And this, too, is why I'm going to Geneva. Enduring peace requires openness, honest communications, and opportunities for our peoples to get to know one another directly. The United States has always stood for openness. Thirty years ago in Geneva, President Eisenhower, preparing for his first meeting with the then Soviet leader, made his Open Skies proposal and an offer of new educational and cultural exchanges with the Soviet Union. He recognized that removing the barriers between people is at the heart of our relationship. He said: "Restrictions on communications of all kinds, including radio and travel, existing in extreme form in some places, have operated as causes of mutual distrust. In America, the fervent belief in freedom of thought, of expression, and of movement is a vital part of our heritage."

Well, I have hopes that we can lessen the distrust between us, reduce the levels of secrecy, and bring forth a more open world. Imagine how much good we could accomplish, how the cause of peace would be served, if more individuals and families from our respective countries could come to know each other in a personal way. For example, if Soviet youth could attend American schools and universities, they could learn firsthand what spirit of freedom rules our land and that we do not wish the Soviet people any harm. If American youth could do likewise, they could talk about their interests and values and hopes for the future with their Soviet friends. They would get firsthand knowledge of life in the U.S.S.R., but most important, they would learn that we're all God's children with much in common. Imagine if people in our nation could see the Bolshoi Ballet again, while Soviet citizens could see American plays and hear groups like the Beach Boys. And how about Soviet children watching *Sesame Street.*

We've had educational and cultural exchanges for twenty-five years and are now close to completing a new agreement. But I feel the time is ripe for us to take bold new steps to open the way for our peoples to participate in an unprecedented way in the building of peace. Why shouldn't I propose to Mr. Gorbachev at Geneva that we exchange many more of our citizens from fraternal, religious, educational, and cultural groups? Why not suggest the exchange of thousands of undergraduates each year, and even younger students who would live with a host family and attend schools or summer camps? We could look to increased scholarship programs, improve language studies, conduct courses in history, culture, and other subjects, develop new sister cities, establish libraries and cultural centers, and yes, increase athletic competition. People of both our nations love sports. If we must compete, let it be on the playing fields and not the battlefields. In science and technology, we could launch new joint space ventures and establish joint medical research projects. In communications, we'd like to see more appearances in the other's mass media by representatives of both our countries. If Soviet spokesmen are free to appear on American television, to be published and read in the American press, shouldn't the Soviet people have the same right to see, hear, and read what we Americans have to say? Such proposals will not bridge our differences, but people-to-people contacts can build genuine constituencies for peace in both countries. After all, people don't start wars, governments do.

Let me summarize, then, the vision and hopes that we carry with us to Geneva. We go with an appreciation, born of experience, of the deep differences between us—between our values, our systems, our beliefs. But we also carry with us the determination not to permit those differences to erupt into confrontation or conflict. We do not threaten the Soviet people and never will. We go without illusion, but with hope, hope that progress can be made on our entire agenda. We believe that progress can be made in resolving the regional conflicts now burning on three continents, including our own hemisphere. The regional plan we proposed at the United Nations will be raised again at Geneva. We're proposing the broadest people-to-people exchanges in the history of American-Soviet relations, exchanges in sports and culture, in the media, education, and the arts. Such exchanges can build in our societies thousands of coalitions for cooperation and peace. Governments can only do so much. Once they get the ball rolling, they should step out of the way and let people get together to share, enjoy, help, listen, and learn from each other, especially young people.

Finally, we go to Geneva with the sober realization that nuclear weapons pose the greatest threat in human history to the survival of the human race, that the arms race must be stopped. We go determined to search out and discover common ground —where we can agree to begin the reduction, looking to the eventual elimination, of nuclear weapons from the face of the earth. It is not an impossible dream that we can begin to reduce nuclear arsenals, reduce the risk of war, and build a solid foundation for peace. It is not an impossible dream that our children and grandchildren can someday travel freely back and forth between America and the Soviet Union; visit each other's homes; work and study together; enjoy and discuss plays, music, television, and root for teams when they compete.

These, then, are the indispensable elements of a true peace: the steady expansion of human rights for all the world's peoples; support for resolving conflicts in Asia, Africa, and Latin

America that carry the seeds of a wider war; a broadening of people-to-people exchanges that can diminish the distrust and suspicion that separate our two peoples; and the steady reduction of these awesome nuclear arsenals until they no longer threaten the world we both must inhabit. This is our agenda for Geneva; this is our policy; this is our plan for peace.

We have cooperated in the past. In both world wars, Americans and Russians fought on separate fronts against a common enemy. Near the city of Murmansk, sons of our own nation are buried, heroes who died of wounds sustained on the treacherous North Atlantic and North Sea convoys that carried to Russia the indispensable tools of survival and victory. While it would be naive to think a single summit can establish a permanent peace, this conference can begin a dialog for peace. So, we look to the future with optimism, and we go to Geneva with confidence.

Both Nancy and I are grateful for the chance you've given us to serve this nation and the trust you've placed in us. I know how deep the hope of peace is in her heart, as it is in the heart of every American and Russian mother. I received a letter and picture from one such mother in Louisiana recently. She wrote, "Mr. President, how could anyone be more blessed than I? These children you see are mine, granted to me by the Lord for a short time. When you go to Geneva, please remember these faces, remember the faces of my children—of Jonathan, my son, and of my twins, Lara and Jessica. Their future depends on your actions. I will pray for guidance for you and the Soviet leaders." Her words "my children" read like a cry of love. And I could only think how that cry has echoed down through the centuries, a cry for all the children of the world, for peace, for love of fellow man. Here is the central truth of our time, of any time, a truth to which I've tried to bear witness in this office.

When I first accepted the nomination of my party, I asked you, the American people, to join with me in prayer for our nation and the world. Six days ago in the Cabinet Room, religious leaders—Ukrainian and Greek Orthodox bishops, Catholic church representatives, including a Lithuanian bishop,

Protestant pastors, a Mormon elder, and Jewish rabbis—made me a similar request. Well, tonight I'm honoring that request. I'm asking you, my fellow Americans, to pray for God's grace and His guidance for all of us at Geneva, so that the cause of true peace among men will be advanced and all of humanity thereby served.

Good night, and God bless you.

Remarks at Bergen-Belsen Concentration Camp

AND

Bitburg Air Base

FEDERAL REPUBLIC OF GERMANY

MAY 5, 1985

I really created quite a controversy when I decided to go to a cemetery in Bitburg, West Germany, where two thousand German war dead were buried. What we didn't know when we said yes was that forty-eight members of the Nazi SS were also buried there. When our advance people had gone over, snow covered the SS graves so our people didn't see them.

The problem was that we couldn't back out without offending our German hosts, who would've taken this as quite a slap.

By the same token, many people in our own country were deeply hurt that I would go where storm troopers were buried because of what those monsters had done. Holocaust survivor Elie Wiesel emotionally pleaded to me at the White House, "Mr. President, that is not your place." Even Nancy thought I should stay away.

I made the decision, however, that we must go. I didn't feel that we could ask new generations of Germans to live with this guilt forever without any hope of redemption. They were not alive during World War II. These young people should not be made to bear the burden. Many of their grandfathers died in that war. These men weren't Nazis; they didn't work in the concentration camps; they were just soldiers doing their job of fighting a war.

Later, I also learned that several of the Nazi storm troopers buried there were buried in prisoner uniforms. They were killed by their fellow SS members for helping concentration camp prisoners. I received letters to this effect from Jewish survivors. I remember one man wrote me that he was in the camp at the age of sixteen. One of the SS kept him from being executed by hiding him.

The following two sets of remarks I've put together because

they are related. A little after noon, I laid a wreath at Bergen-Belsen concentration camp for those who had been murdered there. What an emotional place that is. And the remarkable thing is that every year schoolchildren from all over Germany go there so that they will learn what happened and so that they will not forget. From that ceremony, I went to the cemetery at Bitburg and laid a wreath for the soldiers who are interred there. I actually made my remarks about Bitburg not at the cemetery, but at the air base nearby.

CHANCELLOR KOHL and honored guests, this painful walk into the past has done much more than remind us of the war that consumed the European continent. What we have seen makes unforgettably clear that no one of the rest of us can fully understand the enormity of the feelings carried by the victims of these camps. The survivors carry a memory beyond anything that we can comprehend. The awful evil started by one man, an evil that victimized all the world with its destruction, was uniquely destructive of the millions forced into the grim abyss of these camps.

Here lie people—Jews—whose death was inflicted for no reason other than their very existence. Their pain was borne only because of who they were and because of the God in their prayers. Alongside them lay many Christians—Catholics and Protestants.

For year after year, until that man and his evil were destroyed, hell yawned forth its awful contents. People were brought here for no other purpose but to suffer and die—to go unfed when hungry, uncared for when sick, tortured when the whim struck, and left to have misery consume them when all there was around them was misery.

I'm sure we all share similar first thoughts, and that is: What of the youngsters who died at this dark stalag? All was gone for them forever—not to feel again the warmth of life's sunshine and promise, not the laughter and the splendid ache of growing up, nor the consoling embrace of a family. Try to think of being young and never having a day without searing emotional and physical pain—desolate, unrelieved pain.

Today, we've been grimly reminded why the commandant of this camp was named "the Beast of Belsen." Above all, we're struck by the horror of it all—the monstrous, incomprehensible horror. And that's what we've seen but is what we can never understand as the victims did. Nor with all our compassion can we feel what the survivors feel to this day and what they will feel as long as they live. What we've felt and are expressing with words cannot convey the suffering that they endured. That is why history will forever brand what happened as the Holocaust.

Here, death ruled, but we've learned something as well. Because of what happened, we found that death cannot rule forever, and that's why we're here today. We're here because humanity refuses to accept that freedom of the spirit of man can ever be extinguished. We're here to commemorate that life triumphed over the tragedy and the death of the Holocaust—overcame the suffering, the sickness, the testing, and yes, the gassings. We're here today to confirm that the horror cannot outlast hope, and that even from the worst of all things, the best may come forth. Therefore, even out of this overwhelming sadness, there must be some purpose, and there is. It comes to us through the transforming love of God.

We learn from the Talmud that "it was only through suffering that the children of Israel obtained three priceless and coveted gifts: The Torah, the Land of Israel, and the World to Come." Yes, out of this sickness—as crushing and cruel as it was—there was hope for the world as well as for the world to come. Out of the ashes—hope, and from all the pain—promise.

So much of this is symbolized today by the fact that most of the leadership of free Germany is represented here today. Chancellor Kohl, you and your countrymen have made real the renewal that had to happen. Your nation and the German people have been strong and resolute in your willingness to confront and condemn the acts of a hated regime of the past. This reflects the courage of your people and their devotion to freedom and justice since the war. Think how far we've come from that time when despair made these tragic victims wonder if anything could survive.

As we flew here from Hanover, low over the greening farms and the emerging springtime of the lovely German countryside, I reflected, and there must have been a time when the prisoners at Bergen-Belsen and those of every other camp must have felt the springtime was gone forever from their lives. Surely we can understand that when we see what is around us—all these children of God under bleak and lifeless mounds, the plainness of which does not even hint at the unspeakable acts that created them. Here they lie, never to hope, never to pray, never to love, never to heal, never to laugh, never to cry.

And too many of them knew that this was their fate, but that was not the end. Through it all was their faith and a spirit that moved their faith.

Nothing illustrates this better than the story of a young girl who died here at Bergen-Belsen. For more than two years Anne Frank and her family had hidden from the Nazis in a confined annex in Holland where she kept a remarkably profound diary. Betrayed by an informant, Anne and her family were sent by freight car to Auschwitz and finally here to Bergen-Belsen.

Just three weeks before her capture, young Anne wrote these words: "It's really a wonder that I haven't dropped all my ideals because they seem so absurd and impossible to carry out. Yet I keep them because in spite of everything I still believe that people are good at heart. I simply can't build up my hopes on a foundation consisting of confusion, misery, and death. I see the world gradually being turned into a wilderness. I hear the ever approaching thunder which will destroy us too; I can feel the suffering of millions and yet, if I looked up into the heavens I think that it will all come right, that this cruelty too will end and that peace and tranquility will return again." Eight months later, this sparkling young life ended here at Bergen-Belsen. Somewhere here lies Anne Frank.

Everywhere here are memories—pulling us, touching us, making us understand that they can never be erased. Such memories take us where God intended His children to go—toward learning, toward healing, and above all, toward redemption. They beckon us through the endless stretches of our heart to the knowing commitment that the life of each individual can change the world and make it better.

We're all witnesses; we share the glistening hope that rests in every human soul. Hope leads us, if we're prepared to trust it, toward what our President Lincoln called the better angels of our nature. And then, rising above all this cruelty, out of this tragic and nightmarish time, beyond the anguish, the pain, and the suffering for all time, we can and must pledge: Never again.

THANK YOU VERY MUCH. I have just come from the cemetery where German war dead lay at rest. No one could visit there without deep and conflicting emotions. I felt great sadness that history could be filled with such waste, destruction, and evil, but my heart was also lifted by the knowledge that from the ashes has come hope and that from the terrors of the past we have built forty years of peace, freedom, and reconciliation among our nations.

This visit has stirred many emotions in the American and German people, too. I've received many letters since first deciding to come to Bitburg cemetery; some supportive, others deeply concerned and questioning, and others opposed. Some old wounds have been reopened, and this I regret very much because this should be a time of healing.

To the veterans and families of American servicemen who still carry the scars and feel the painful losses of that war, our gesture of reconciliation with the German people today in no way minimizes our love and honor for those who fought and died for our country. They gave their lives to rescue freedom in its darkest hour. The alliance of democratic nations that guards the freedom of millions in Europe and America today stands as living testimony that their noble sacrifice was not in vain.

No, their sacrifice was not in vain. I have to tell you that nothing will ever fill me with greater hope than the sight of two former war heroes who met today at the Bitburg ceremony; each among the bravest of the brave; each an enemy of the other forty years ago; each a witness to the horrors of war. But today they came together, American and German, General Matthew B. Ridgway and General Johanner Steinhoff, reconciled and united for freedom. They reached over the graves to one another like brothers and grasped their hands in peace.

To the survivors of the Holocaust: Your terrible suffering has made you ever vigilant against evil. Many of you are worried that reconciliation means forgetting. Well, I promise you, we will never forget. I have just come this morning from Bergen-Belsen, where the horror of that terrible crime, the Holocaust, was forever burned upon my memory. No, we will never forget, and we say with the victims of that Holocaust: Never again.

The war against one man's totalitarian dictatorship was not like other wars. The evil war of Nazism turned all values upside down. Nevertheless, we can mourn the German war dead today as human beings crushed by a vicious ideology.

There are over two thousand buried in Bitburg cemetery. Among them are forty-eight members of the SS—the crimes of the SS must rank among the most heinous in human history—but others buried there were simply soldiers in the German Army. How many were fanatical followers of a dictator and willfully carried out his cruel orders? And how many were conscripts, forced into service during the death throes of the Nazi war machine? We do not know. Many, however, we know from the dates on their tombstones, were only teenagers at the time. There is one boy buried there who died a week before his sixteenth birthday.

There were thousands of such soldiers to whom Nazism meant no more than a brutal end to a short life. We do not believe in collective guilt. Only God can look into the human heart, and all these men have now met their supreme judge, and they have been judged by Him as we shall all be judged.

Our duty today is to mourn the human wreckage of totalitarianism, and today in Bitburg cemetery we commemorated the potential good in humanity that was consumed back then, forty years ago. Perhaps if that fifteen-year-old soldier had lived, he would have joined his fellow countrymen in building this new democratic Federal Republic of Germany, devoted to human dignity and the defense of freedom that we celebrate today. Or perhaps his children or his grandchildren might be among you here today at the Bitburg Air Base, where new generations of Germans and Americans join together in friendship and common cause, dedicating their lives to preserving peace and guarding the security of the free world.

Too often in the past each war only planted the seeds of the next. We celebrate today the reconciliation between our two nations that has liberated us from that cycle of destruction. Look at what together we've accomplished. We who were enemies are now friends; we who were bitter adversaries are now the strongest of allies.

In the place of fear we've sown trust, and out of the ruins of war has blossomed an enduring peace. Tens of thousands of Americans have served in this town over the years. As the mayor of Bitburg has said, in that time there have been some six thousand marriages between Germans and Americans, and many thousands of children have come from these unions. This is the real symbol of our future together, a future to be filled with hope, friendship, and freedom.

The hope that we see now could sometimes even be glimpsed in the darkest days of the war. I'm thinking of one special story —that of a mother and her young son living alone in a modest cottage in the middle of the woods. And one night as the Battle of the Bulge exploded not far away, and around them, three young American soldiers arrived at their door—they were standing there in the snow, lost behind enemy lines. All were frostbitten; one was badly wounded. Even though sheltering the enemy was punishable by death, she took them in and made them a supper with some of her last food. Then, they heard another knock at the door. And this time four German soldiers stood there. The woman was afraid, but she quickly said with a firm voice, "There will be no shooting here." She made all the soldiers lay down their weapons, and they all joined in the makeshift meal. Heinz and Willi, it turned out, were only sixteen; the corporal was the oldest at twenty-three. Their natural suspicion dissolved in the warmth and the comfort of the cottage. One of the Germans, a former medical student, tended the wounded American.

But now, listen to the rest of the story through the eyes of one who was there, now a grown man, but that young lad that had been her son. He said: "Then Mother said grace. I noticed that there were tears in her eyes as she said the old, familiar words, 'Komm, Herr Jesus. Be our guest.' And as I looked around the table, I saw tears, too, in the eyes of the battle-weary soldiers, boys again, some from America, some from Germany, all far from home."

That night—as the storm of war tossed the world—they had their own private armistice. And the next morning, the German corporal showed the Americans how to get back behind their own lines. And they all shook hands and went their separate ways. That happened to be Christmas day, forty years ago.

Those boys reconciled briefly in the midst of war. Surely we allies in peacetime should honor the reconciliation of the last forty years.

To the people of Bitburg, our hosts and the hosts of our servicemen, like that generous woman forty years ago, you make us feel very welcome. Vielen dank. [Many thanks.]

And to the men and women of Bitburg Air Base, I just want to say that we know that even with such wonderful hosts, your job is not an easy one. You serve around the clock far from home, always ready to defend freedom. We're grateful, and we're very proud of you.

Four decades ago we waged a great war to lift the darkness of evil from the world, to let men and women in this country and in every country live in the sunshine of liberty. Our victory was great, and the Federal Republic, Italy, and Japan are now in the community of free nations. But the struggle for freedom is not complete, for today much of the world is still cast in totalitarian darkness.

Twenty-two years ago President John F. Kennedy went to the Berlin Wall and proclaimed that he, too, was a Berliner. Well, today freedom-loving people around the world must say: I am a Berliner. I am a Jew in a world still threatened by anti-Semitism. I am an Afghan, and I am a prisoner of the gulag. I am a refugee in a crowded boat foundering off the coast of Vietnam. I am a Laotian, a Cambodian, a Cuban, and a Miskito Indian in Nicaragua. I, too, am a potential victim of totalitarianism.

The one lesson of World War II, the one lesson of Nazism, is that freedom must always be stronger than totalitarianism and that good must always be stronger than evil. The moral measure of our two nations will be found in the resolve we show to preserve liberty, to protect life, and to honor and cherish all God's children.

That is why the free, democratic Federal Republic of Germany is such a profound and hopeful testament to the human spirit. We cannot undo the crimes and wars of yesterday nor call the millions back to life, but we can give meaning to the past by learning its lessons and making a better future. We can let our pain drive us to greater efforts to heal humanity's suffering.

Today I've traveled 220 miles from Bergen-Belsen and, I feel, forty years in time. With the lessons of the past firmly in our minds, we've turned a new, brighter page in history.

One of the many who wrote me about this visit was a young woman who had recently been bas mitzvahed. She urged me to lay the wreath at Bitburg cemetery in honor of the future of Germany. And that is what we've done.

On this fortieth anniversary of World War II, we mark the day when the hate, the evil, and the obscenities ended, and we commemorate the rekindling of the democratic spirit in Germany.

There's much to make us hopeful on this historic anniversary. One of the symbols of that hate—that could have been that hope, a little while ago, when we heard a German band playing the American national anthem and an American band playing the German national anthem. While much of the world still huddles in the darkness of oppression, we can see a new dawn of freedom sweeping the globe. And we can see in the new democracies of Latin America, in the new economic freedoms and prosperity in Asia, in the slow movement toward peace in the Middle East, and in the strengthening alliance of democratic nations in Europe and America that the light from that dawn is growing stronger.

Together, let us gather in that light and walk out of the shadow. Let us live in peace.

Thank you, and God bless you all.

Remarks on Presenting
the Presidential Medal
of Freedom to Mother Teresa

WHITE HOUSE ROSE GARDEN
JUNE 20, 1985

Mother Teresa is a fascinating slip of a woman, so filled with love for every human being. And she is something of a pamphleteer as well. A member of my staff one time reached out to shake her hand and Mother Teresa said, "Love God," and stuck out a pamphlet extolling Jesus instead. That person now has the pamphlet framed. Mother Teresa would sometimes write me when she needed something in particular for her work, and we'd usually find a way to get it to her through a corporation or the government. I believe she is a living saint.

The President. This great house receives many great visitors, but none more special or more revered than our beloved guest today. A month ago, we awarded the Medal of Freedom to thirteen heroes who have done their country proud. Only one of the recipients could not attend because she had work to do —not special work, not unusual work for her, but everyday work which is both special and urgent in its own right. Mother Teresa was busy, as usual, saving the world. And I mean that quite literally. And so we rather appreciated her priorities, and we're very happy, indeed, that she could come to America this week.

Now, a moment ago, I said we'd awarded the Medal of Freedom to heroes who've done our country proud. And I believe Mother Teresa might point out here that she is most certainly not an American but a daughter of Yugoslavia, and she has not spent her adult life in this country but in India. However, it simply occurred to us when we wanted to honor her that the goodness in some hearts transcends all borders and all narrow nationalistic considerations.

Some people, some very few people are, in the truest sense, citizens of the world; Mother Teresa is. And we love her so much we asked her to accept our tribute, and she graciously accepted. And I will now read the citation.

"Most of us talk about kindness and compassion, but Mother Teresa, the saint of the gutters, lives it. As a teenager, she went to India to teach young girls. In time, Mother Teresa began to work among the poor and the dying of Calcutta. Her order of the Missionaries of Charity has spread throughout the world, serving the poorest of the poor.

"Mother Teresa is a heroine of our times. And to the many honors she has received, including the Nobel Peace Prize, we add, with deep affection and endless respect, the Presidential Medal of Freedom."

[*At this point, the President presented the award to Mother Teresa.*]

May I say that this is the first time I've given the Medal of Freedom with the intuition that the recipient might take it home, melt it down, and turn it into something that can be sold to help the poor. [*Laughter*]

And I want to thank you for something, Mother Teresa. Your great work and your life have inspired so many Americans to become personally involved, themselves, in helping the poor. So many men and women in every area of life, in government and the private sector, have been led by the light of your love, and they have given greatly of themselves. And we thank you for your radiant example.

Mother Teresa. I am most unworthy of this generous gift of our president, Mr. Reagan, and his wife and you people of United States. But I accept it for the greater glory of God and in the name of the millions of poor people that this gift, in spirit and in love, will penetrate the hearts of the people. For in giving it to me, you are giving it to them, to my hands, with your great love and concern.

I've never realized that you loved the people so tenderly. I had the experience, I was last time here, a sister from Ethiopia found me and said, "Our people are dying. Our children are dying. Mother, do something." And the only person that came in my mind while she was talking, it was the President. And immediately I wrote to him, and I said, "I don't know, but this is what happened to me." And next day it was that immediately he arranged to bring food to our people. And I can tell you the gift that has come from your people, from your country, has brought life—new life—to our suffering people in Ethiopia.

I also want to thank the families here in United States for their continual and delicate love that they have given, and they have shown, by leaving their children to become sisters and to serve the poor throughout the world. We are now over the world and trying to bring the tenderness and the love of Jesus.

And you, you cannot go where we go. You cannot do what we do. But together, we are doing something beautiful for God. And my gratitude to you, President, and your family and to your people. It's my prayer for you that you may grow in holiness to this tender love for the poorest of the poor. But this love begins at home, in your own family, and it begins by praying together. Prayer gives a clean heart, and a clean heart can see God. And if you see God in each other, you will have love, peace, joy together. And works of love are works of peace. And love begins at home.

So, my sisters, brothers, and fathers, you are going—and all our poor people, thousands and thousands and thousands of people that we deal with, I bring their gratitude to you. And keep the joy of loving. Love them, and begin in your own family first. And that love will penetrate right through the furthest place where no one has ever been—there is that tenderness and love of Christ.

And remember that whatever you do to the least, you do it to Him, Jesus said. You did it to me. What a wonderful opportunity for each one of us to be twenty-four hours with Jesus. And in doing what we are doing, as He said, if you receive a little child in my name, you receive me. If you give a glass of water in my name, you give it to me. What a wonderful and beautiful tenderness and love of Christ for each one of us.

So, once more, I want to thank you for this beautiful gift, which I am sure it will bring great joy to our people by sharing it with them.

God bless you and keep you in His heart.

Remarks at the
Conservative Political Action Conference

WASHINGTON, D.C.
MARCH 1, 1985

You may wonder why I've selected another speech from one of these CPAC gatherings. Well, this is a good representation of what I was trying to accomplish at the start of my second term. These friends were the base of everything that I was trying to do. What I'm saying in this speech to my fellow conservatives could actually serve as the inaugural address for my second term.

T HANK YOU, Vice Chairman Linen,* for those very kind words. I'm grateful to the American Conservative Union, Young Americans for Freedom, *National Review, Human Events,* for organizing this wonderful evening. When you work in the White House, you don't get to see your old friends as much as you'd like. And I always see the CPAC speech as my opportunity to "dance with the one that brung ya."

There's so much I want to talk about tonight. I've been think-

---

* James A. Linen, vice chairman of the American Conservative Union.

ing, in the weeks since the inauguration, that we are at an especially dramatic turning point in American history. And just putting it all together in my mind, I've been reviewing the elements that have led to this moment.

Ever since FDR and the New Deal, the opposition party, and particularly those of a liberal persuasion, have dominated the political debate. Their ideas were new; they had momentum; they captured the imagination of the American people. The left held sway for a good long time. There was a right, but it was, by the forties and fifties, diffuse and scattered, without a unifying voice.

But in 1964 came a voice in the wilderness—Barry Goldwater; the great Barry Goldwater, the first major party candidate of our time who was a true-blue, undiluted conservative. He spoke from principle, and he offered vision. Freedom—he spoke of freedom: freedom from the government's increasing demands on the family purse, freedom from the government's increasing usurpation of individual rights and responsibilities, freedom from the leaders who told us the price of world peace is continued acquiescence to totalitarianism. He was ahead of his time. When he ran for president, he won six states and lost forty-four. But his candidacy worked as a precursor of things to come.

A new movement was stirring. And in the 1960s Young Americans for Freedom is born; *National Review* gains readership and prestige in the intellectual community; *Human Events* becomes a major voice on the cutting edge. In the seventies the antitax movement begins. Actually, it was much more than an antitax movement, just as the Boston Tea Party was much more than antitax initiative. [*Laughter*] In the late seventies Proposition 13 and the Sagebrush Rebellion; in 1980, for the first time in twenty-eight years, a Republican Senate is elected; so, may I say, is a conservative president. In 1984 that conservative administration is reelected in a forty-nine-state sweep. And the day the votes came in, I thought of Walt Whitman: "I hear America singing." [*Laughter*]

This great turn from left to right was not just a case of the pendulum swinging—first, the left holds sway and then the right, and here comes the left again. The truth is, conservative thought is no longer over here on the right; it's the mainstream now.

And the tide of history is moving irresistibly in our direction. Why? Because the other side is virtually bankrupt of ideas. It has nothing more to say, nothing to add to the debate. It has spent its intellectual capital, such as it was—[*Laughter*]—and it has done its deeds.

Now, we're not in power now because they failed to gain electoral support over the past fifty years. They did win support. And the result was chaos, weakness, and drift. Ultimately, though, their failures yielded one great thing—us guys. [*Laughter*] We in this room are not simply profiting from their bankruptcy; we are where we are because we're winning the contest of ideas. In fact, in the past decade, all of a sudden, quietly, mysteriously, the Republican Party has become the party of ideas.

We became the party of the most brilliant and dynamic young minds. I remember them, just a few years ago, running around scrawling Laffer curves on table napkins—[*Laughter*]—going to symposia and talking about how social programs did not eradicate poverty, but entrenched it; writing studies on why the latest weird and unnatural idea from the social engineers is weird and unnatural. [*Laughter*] You were there. They were your ideas, your symposia, your books, and usually somebody else's table napkins. [*Laughter*]

All of a sudden, Republicans were not defenders of the status quo but creators of the future. They were looking at tomorrow with all the single-mindedness of an inventor. In fact, they reminded me of the American inventors of the nineteenth and twentieth centuries who filled the world with light and recorded sound.

The new conservatives made anew the connection between economic justice and economic growth. Growth in the economy would not only create jobs and paychecks, they said; it would enhance familial stability and encourage a healthy optimism about the future. Lower those tax rates, they said, and let the economy become the engine of our dreams. Pull back regulations, and encourage free and open competition. Let the men and women of the marketplace decide what they want.

But along with that, perhaps the greatest triumph of modern conservatism has been to stop allowing the left to put the average American on the moral defensive. By average American I mean the good, decent, rambunctious, and creative people who raise the families, go to church, and help out when the local library holds a fund-raiser; people who have a stake in the community because they are the community.

These people had held true to certain beliefs and principles that for twenty years the intelligentsia were telling us were hopelessly out of date, utterly trite, and reactionary. You want prayer in the schools? How primitive, they said. You oppose abortion? How oppressive, how antimodern. The normal was portrayed as eccentric, and only the abnormal was worthy of emulation. The irreverent was celebrated, but only irreverence about certain things: irreverence toward, say, organized religion, yes; irreverence toward establishment liberalism, not too much of that. They celebrated their courage in taking on safe targets and patted each other on the back for slinging stones at a confused Goliath, who was too demoralized and really too good to fight back.

But now one simply senses it. The American people are no longer on the defensive. I believe the conservative movement deserves some credit for this. You spoke for the permanent against the merely prevalent, and ultimately you prevailed.

I believe we conservatives have captured the moment, captured the imagination of the American people. And what now? What are we to do with our success? Well, right now, with conservative thought accepted as mainstream thought and with the people of our country leading the fight to freedom, now we must move.

You remember your Shakespeare: "There is a tide in the affairs of men which, taken at the flood, leads on to fortune.

Omitted, all the voyage of their life is bound in shallows and in miseries. On such a full sea are we now afloat. And we must take the current when it serves, or lose our ventures." I spoke in the—[*Applause*]. It's typical, isn't it? I just quoted a great writer, but as an actor, I get the bow. [*Laughter*]

I spoke in the State of the Union of a second American revolution, and now is the time to launch that revolution and see that it takes hold. If we move decisively, these years will not be just a passing era of good feeling, not just a few good years, but a true golden age of freedom.

The moment is ours, and we must seize it. There's work to do. We must prolong and protect our growing prosperity so that it doesn't become just a passing phase, a natural adjustment between periods of recession. We must move further to provide incentive and make America the investment capital of the world.

We must institute a fair tax system and turn the current one on its ear. I believe there is natural support in our country for a simplified tax system, with still-lower tax rates but a broader base, with everyone paying their fair share and no more. We must eliminate unproductive tax shelters. Again, there is natural support among Americans, because Americans are a fair-minded people.

We must institute enterprise zones and a lower youth minimum wage so we can revitalize distressed areas and teenagers can get jobs. We're going to take our revolution to the people, all of the people. We're going to go to black Americans and members of all minority groups, and we're going to make our case.

Part of being a revolutionary is knowing that you don't have to acquiesce to the tired, old ideas of the past. One such idea is that the opposition party has black America and minority America locked up, that they own black America. Well, let me tell you, they own nothing but the past. The old alignments are no longer legitimate, if they ever were.

We're going to reach out, and we need your help. Conservatives were brought up to hate deficits, and justifiably so. We've long thought there are two things in Washington that are unbalanced—the budget and the liberals. [*Laughter*]

But we cannot reduce the deficit by raising taxes. And just so that every "i" is dotted and every "t" is crossed, let me repeat tonight for the benefit of those who never seem to get the message: We will not reduce the deficit by raising taxes. We need more taxes like John McLaughlin* needs assertiveness training. [*Laughter*]

Now, whether government borrows or increases taxes, it will be taking the same amount of money from the private economy, and either way, that's too much. We must bring down government spending. We need a constitutional amendment requiring a balanced budget. It's something that forty-nine states already require—no reason the federal government should be any different.

We need the line-item veto, which forty-three governors have —no reason that the president shouldn't. And we have to cut waste. The Grace commission has identified billions of dollars that are wasted and that we can save.

But the domestic side isn't the only area where we need your help. All of us in this room grew up, or came to adulthood, in a time when the doctrine of Marx and Lenin was coming to divide the world. Ultimately, it came to dominate remorselessly whole parts of it. The Soviet attempt to give legitimacy to its tyranny is expressed in the infamous Brezhnev doctrine, which contends that once a country has fallen into Communist darkness, it can never again be allowed to see the light of freedom.

Well, it occurs to me that history has already begun to repeal that doctrine. It started one day in Grenada. We only did our duty, as a responsible neighbor and a lover of peace, the day we went in and returned the government to the people and rescued our own students. We restored that island to liberty. Yes, it's only a small island, but that's what the world is made of—small islands yearning for freedom.

* Washington executive editor, *National Review* magazine.

There's much more to do. Throughout the world the Soviet Union and its agents, client states, and satellites are on the defensive—on the moral defensive, the intellectual defensive, and the political and economic defensive. Freedom movements arise and assert themselves. They're doing so on almost every continent populated by man—in the hills of Afghanistan, in Angola, in Kampuchea, in Central America. In making mention of freedom fighters, all of us are privileged to have in our midst tonight one of the brave commanders who lead the Afghan freedom fighters—Abdul Haq. Abdul Haq, we are with you.

They are our brothers, these freedom fighters, and we owe them our help. I've spoken recently of the freedom fighters of Nicaragua. You know the truth about them. You know who they're fighting and why. They are the moral equal of our Founding Fathers and the brave men and women of the French Resistance. We cannot turn away from them, for the struggle here is not right versus left; it is right versus wrong.

Now, I am against sending troops to Central America. They are simply not needed. Given a chance and the resources, the people of the area can fight their own fight. They have the men and women. They're capable of doing it. They have the people of their country behind them. All they need is our support. All they need is proof that we care as much about the fight for freedom seven hundred miles from our shores as the Soviets care about the fight against freedom five thousand miles from theirs. And they need to know that the U.S. supports them with more than just pretty words and good wishes. We need your help on this, and I mean each of you—involved, active, strong, and vocal. And we need more.

All of you know that we're researching nonnuclear technologies that may enable us to prevent nuclear ballistic missiles from reaching U.S. soil or that of our allies. I happen to believe —logic forces me to believe—that this new defense system, the Strategic Defense Initiative, is the most hopeful possibility of our time. Its primary virtue is clear. If anyone ever attacked us, Strategic Defense would be there to protect us. It could conceivably save millions of lives.

SDI has been criticized on the grounds that it might upset any chance of an arms control agreement with the Soviets. But SDI is arms control. If SDI is, say, 80 percent effective, then it will make any Soviet attack folly. Even partial success in SDI would strengthen deterrence and keep the peace. And if our SDI research is successful, the prospects for real reduction in U.S. and Soviet offensive nuclear forces will be greatly enhanced.

It is said that SDI would deal a blow to the so-called East-West balance of power. Well, let's think about that. The Soviets already are investing roughly as much on strategic defenses as they are on their offensive nuclear forces. This could quickly tip the East-West balance if we had no defense of our own. Would a situation of comparable defenses threaten us? No, for we're not planning on being the first to use force.

As we strive for our goal of eventual elimination of nuclear weapons, each side would retain a certain amount of defensive —or of, I should say, destructive power—a certain number of missiles. But it would not be in our interest, or theirs, to build more and more of them.

Now, one would think our critics on the left would quickly embrace, or at least be open-minded about a system that promises to reduce the size of nuclear missile forces on both sides and to greatly enhance the prospects for real arms reductions. And yet we hear SDI belittled by some with nicknames, or demagogued with charges that it will bring war to the heavens.

They complain that it won't work, which is odd from people who profess to believe in the perfectability of man—machines after all. [*Laughter*] And man—machines are so much easier to manipulate. They say it won't be 100 percent effective, which is odd, since they don't ask for 100 percent effectiveness in their social experiments. [*Laughter*] They say SDI is only in the research stage and won't be realized in time to change things. To which, as I said last month, the only reply is: Then let's get started.

Now, my point here is not to question the motives of others. But it's difficult to understand how critics can object to exploring the possibility of moving away from exclusive reliance upon nuclear weapons. The truth is, I believe that they find it difficult to embrace any idea that breaks with the past, that breaks with consensus thinking and the common establishment wisdom. In short, they find it difficult and frightening to alter the status quo.

And what are we to do when these so-called opinion leaders of an outworn philosophy are out there on television and in the newspapers with their steady drumbeat of doubt and distaste? Well, when all you have to do to win is rely on the good judgment of the American people, then you're in good shape, because the American people have good judgment. I know it isn't becoming of me, but I like to think that maybe forty-nine of our fifty states displayed that judgment just a few months ago. [*Laughter*]

What we have to do, all of us in this room, is get out there and talk about SDI. Explain it, debate it, tell the American people the facts. It may well be the most important work we do in the next few years. And if we try, we'll succeed. So, we have great work ahead of us, big work. But if we do it together and with complete commitment, we can change our country and history forever.

Once during the campaign, I said, "This is a wonderful time to be alive." And I meant that. I meant that we're lucky not to live in pale and timid times. We've been blessed with the opportunity to stand for something—for liberty and freedom and fairness. And these are things worth fighting for, worth devoting our lives to. And we have good reason to be hopeful and optimistic.

We've made much progress already. So, let us go forth with good cheer and stout hearts—happy warriors out to seize back a country and a world to freedom.

Thank you, and God bless you.

Remarks at the Memorial Service for Members of the 101st Airborne Division

FORT CAMPBELL, KENTUCKY

DECEMBER 16, 1985

Why is it so many tragedies seem to occur before Christmas? As you may recall, a plane full of our soldiers was heading home to the U.S. for the holidays. At six forty-five P.M. on December 12, the plane crashed after refueling in Gander, Newfoundland. A few days later I attended a memorial service with family members and friends.

Many people have commented to me about the comfort Nancy and I tried to give the families. My remarks were always designed to give those grieving something to cling to so that they knew their loved ones didn't die in vain. Words do help, but so can simply going from one family to the next and offering personal condolences. So many would just come into your arms sobbing.

I can't remember which memorial service it was—either this one or the ceremony for the crew of the Stark or the one for the astronauts. But Nancy and I were going from person to person trying to help with the grief and I came to a little boy. As I took his small hand, he said to me, "Please bring my daddy home."

I cannot describe to you the anguish.

WE ARE HERE in the name of the American people. The passing of American soldiers killed as they returned from difficult duty abroad is marked by our presence here. At this point the dimensions of the tragedy are known to almost every person in the country. Most of the young men and women we mourn were returning to spend the holidays with their families. They were full of happiness and laughter as they pushed off from Cairo, and those who saw them at their last stop spoke of how they were singing Christmas carols. They were happy; they were returning to kith and kin.

And then the terrible crash, the flags lowered to half-staff, and the muffled sobs, and we wonder: How this could be? How could it have happened, and why? We wonder at the stark tragedy of it all, the enormity of the loss. For lost were not only the 248 but all of the talent, the wisdom, and the idealism that they had accumulated; lost, too, were their experience and their enormous idealism. Who else but an idealist would choose to become a member of the armed forces and put himself or herself in harm's way for the rest of us? Who but the idealist would go to hard duty in one of the most troubled places of the world and go not as a matter of conquest, but as a force that existed to keep the peace?

Some people think of members of the military as only warriors, fierce in their martial expertise. But the men and women we mourn today were peacemakers. They were there to protect life and preserve a peace, to act as a force for stability and hope and trust. Their commitment was as strong as their purpose was pure. And they were proud. They had a rendezvous with destiny and a potential they never failed to meet. Their work was a perfect expression of the best of the Judeo-Christian tradition. They were the ones of whom Christ spoke when He said, "Blessed *are* the peacemakers: for they shall be called the children of God."

Tragedy is nothing new to mankind, but somehow it's always a surprise, never loses its power to astonish. Those of us who did not lose a brother or a son or daughter or friend or father are shaken nonetheless. And we all mourn with you. We cannot fully share the depth of your sadness, but we pray that the special power of this season will make its way into your sad hearts and remind you of some old joys; remind you of the joy it was to know these fine young men and women, the joy it was to witness the things they said and the jokes they played, the kindnesses they did, and how they laughed. You were part of that, and you who mourn were a part of them. And just as you think today of the joy they gave you, think for a moment of the joy you gave them and be glad. For love is never wasted; love is never lost. Love lives on and sees us through sorrow. From the moment love is born, it is always with us, keeping us aloft in the time of flooding and strong in the time of trial.

You do not grieve alone. We grieve as a nation, together, as together we say good-bye to those who died in the service of their country. In life they were our heroes, in death our loved ones, our darlings. They were happy and singing, and they were right: They were going home. And so, we pray: Receive, O Lord, into your heavenly kingdom the men and women of the 101st Airborne, the men and women of the great and fabled Screaming Eagles. They must be singing now, in their joy, flying higher than mere man can fly and as flights of angels take them to their rest.

I know that there are no words that can make your pain less or make your sorrow less painful. How I wish there were. But of one thing we can be sure—as a poet said of other young soldiers in another war: They will never grow old; they will always be young. And we know one thing with every bit of our thinking: They are now in the arms of God.

God bless you.

1986

Address to the Nation
on the U.S. Air Strike Against Libya

OVAL OFFICE

APRIL 14, 1986

I suppose if I had to choose the worst year of my presidency it would be 1986. The Challenger exploded, throwing the nation into shock, grief, and doubt. The Republicans lost control of the Senate, making progress on tough issues even more unlikely with the Democrats now controlling both houses of Congress. My meeting with Gorbachev in Iceland fell apart and ended in disappointment. And what's more, the Iran/contra controversy began to break. On the up side, we passed some historic tax reform legislation and rededicated Lady Liberty in one of the most breathtaking ceremonies I've ever seen.

One of the most newsworthy events of the year was our air raid on Libya. We had irrefutable proof that Colonel Qadhafi was responsible for bombing a disco in West Germany that had killed some U.S. military people. We also had proof Qadhafi's terrorists were responsible for shooting up an airport. The terrorists had used Tunisian passports, passports that Qadhafi had confiscated when he ejected the Tunisian workers from Libya.

We had to show him he couldn't get away with such things. We had absolutely no intention of hitting civilian buildings, including his—although to be honest I wouldn't have shed any tears if that stray bomb that got his tent had gotten him, too. I

have to say that he quieted down after the attack. I guess he's
sane enough to understand that we would retaliate anytime we
had proof linking him to terrorist acts.

M<small>Y FELLOW</small> A<small>MERICANS</small>:

At seven o'clock this evening eastern time, air and naval forces of the United States launched a series of strikes against the headquarters, terrorist facilities, and military assets that support Mu'ammar Qadhafi's subversive activities. The attacks were concentrated and carefully targeted to minimize casualties among the Libyan people, with whom we have no quarrel.

From initial reports, our forces have succeeded in their mission. Several weeks ago in New Orleans I warned Colonel Qadhafi we would hold his regime accountable for any new terrorist attacks launched against American citizens. More recently I made it clear we would respond as soon as we determined conclusively who was responsible for such attacks.

On April 5th in West Berlin a terrorist bomb exploded in a nightclub frequented by American servicemen. Sergeant Kenneth Ford and a young Turkish woman were killed and 230 others were wounded, among them some 50 American military personnel. This monstrous brutality is but the latest act in Colonel Qadhafi's reign of terror. The evidence is now conclusive that the terrorist bombing of La Belle discotheque was planned and executed under the direct orders of the Libyan regime. On March 25th, more than a week before the attack, orders were sent from Tripoli to the Libyan People's Bureau in East Berlin to conduct a terrorist attack against Americans to cause maximum and indiscriminate casualties. Libya's agents then planted the bomb. On April 4th the People's Bureau alerted Tripoli that the attack would be carried out the following morning. The next day they reported back to Tripoli on the great success of their mission.

Our evidence is direct; it is precise; it is irrefutable. We have solid evidence about other attacks Qadhafi has planned against the United States installations and diplomats and even American tourists.

Thanks to close cooperation with our friends, some of these have been prevented. With the help of French authorities, we recently aborted one such attack: a planned massacre, using grenades and small arms, of civilians waiting in line for visas at an American embassy.

Colonel Qadhafi is not only an enemy of the United States. His record of subversion and aggression against the neighboring states in Africa is well documented and well known. He has ordered the murder of fellow Libyans in countless countries. He has sanctioned acts of terror in Africa, Europe, and the Middle East, as well as the Western Hemisphere.

Today we have done what we had to do. If necessary, we shall do it again. It gives me no pleasure to say that, and I wish it were otherwise.

Before Qadhafi seized power in 1969, the people of Libya had been friends of the United States. And I'm sure that today most Libyans are ashamed and disgusted that this man has made their country a synonym for barbarism around the world. The Libyan people are a decent people caught in the grip of a tyrant.

To our friends and allies in Europe who cooperated in today's mission, I would only say you have the permanent gratitude of the American people. Europeans who remember history understand better than most that there is no security, no safety, in the appeasement of evil. It must be the core of Western policy that there be no sanctuary for terror. And to sustain such a policy, free men and free nations must unite and work together.

Sometimes it is said that by imposing sanctions against Colonel Qadhafi or by striking at his terrorist installations we only magnify the man's importance, that the proper way to deal with him is to ignore him. I do not agree. Long before I came into this office, Colonel Qadhafi had engaged in acts of international terror, acts that put him outside the company of civilized men. For years, however, he suffered no economic or political or military sanction; and the atrocities mounted in number, as did the innocent dead and wounded. And for us to ignore by inaction the slaughter of American civilians and American soldiers, whether in nightclubs or airline terminals, is simply not in the American tradition. When our citizens are abused or attacked anywhere in the world on the direct orders of a hostile regime, we will respond so long as I'm in this Oval Office. Self-defense is not only our right, it is our duty. It is the purpose behind the mission undertaken tonight, a mission fully consistent with Article 51 of the United Nations Charter.

We believe that this preemptive action against his terrorist installations will not only diminish Colonel Qadhafi's capacity to export terror, it will provide him with incentives and reasons to alter his criminal behavior. I have no illusion that tonight's action will ring down the curtain on Qadhafi's reign of terror. But this mission, violent though it was, can bring closer a safer and more secure world for decent men and women. We will persevere.

This afternoon we consulted with the leaders of Congress regarding what we were about to do and why. Tonight I salute the skill and professionalism of the men and women of our armed forces who carried out this mission. It's an honor to be your commander in chief.

We Americans are slow to anger. We always seek peaceful avenues before resorting to the use of force—and we did. We tried quiet diplomacy, public condemnation, economic sanctions, and demonstrations of military force. None succeeded. Despite our repeated warnings, Qadhafi continued his reckless policy of intimidation, his relentless pursuit of terror. He counted on America to be passive. He counted wrong.

I warned that there should be no place on earth where terrorists can rest and train and practice their deadly skills. I meant it. I said that we would act with others, if possible, and alone if necessary to ensure that terrorists have no sanctuary anywhere. Tonight, we have.

Thank you, and God bless you.

Address to the Nation
on the *Challenger* Disaster

OVAL OFFICE
JANUARY 28, 1986

The sight of the Challenger *exploding is seared into each of our minds. A few days after the explosion, I attended a memorial service in Houston for the crew. I stood next to Jane Smith, the wife of Michael Smith, one of the crewmen on the* Challenger.

She gave me a most remarkable gift, a three-by-five card that her husband had written before the flight and left on the bedroom dresser. He wrote about the importance of their mission. It was such a personal, generous gift that I didn't feel right keeping it. I made a copy, which is shown here, and gave her back the original. I'll never forget her generosity in offering me that part of her husband's final days.

I delivered the following message to the American people on nationwide radio and television a few hours after the disaster.

LADIES AND GENTLEMEN, I'd planned to speak to you tonight to report on the state of the Union, but the events of earlier today have led me to change those plans. Today is a day for mourning and remembering.

Nancy and I are pained to the core by the tragedy of the shuttle *Challenger*. We know we share this pain with all of the people of our country. This is truly a national loss.

Nineteen years ago, almost to the day, we lost three astronauts in a terrible accident on the ground. But we've never lost an astronaut in flight; we've never had a tragedy like this. And perhaps we've forgotten the courage it took for the crew of the shuttle; but they, the *Challenger* Seven, were aware of the dangers, but overcame them and did their jobs brilliantly. We mourn seven heroes: Michael Smith, Dick Scobee, Judith Resnik, Ronald McNair, Ellison Onizuka, Gregory Jarvis, and Christa McAuliffe. We mourn their loss as a nation together.

For the families of the seven, we cannot bear, as you do, the full impact of this tragedy. But we feel the loss, and we're thinking about you so very much. Your loved ones were daring and brave, and they had that special grace, that special spirit that says, "Give me a challenge and I'll meet it with joy." They had a hunger to explore the universe and discover its truths. They wished to serve, and they did. They served all of us.

We've grown used to wonders in this century. It's hard to dazzle us. But for twenty-five years the United States space

"FOR MAN, THERE IS NO REST AND NO ENDING
HE MUST GO ON -- CONQUEST BEYOND CONQUEST;
THIS LITTLE PLANET, AND ITS WINDS AND
WAYS, AND ALL THE LAWS OF MIND AND
MATTER THAT RESTRAIN HIM. THEN
THE PLANETS ABOUT HIM, AND, AT LAST
OUT ACROSS THE IMMENSITY TO THE
STARS. AND WHEN HE HAS CONQUERED ALL
THE DEEPS OF SPACE AND ALL THE MYSTERIES
OF TIME .. STILL HE WILL BE BUT BEGINNING"

ASTRONAUT MICHAEL SMITH, QUOTING H. G. WELLS.

program has been doing just that. We've grown used to the idea of space, and perhaps we forget that we've only just begun. We're still pioneers. They, the members of the *Challenger* crew, were pioneers.

And I want to say something to the schoolchildren of America who were watching the live coverage of the shuttle's takeoff. I know it is hard to understand, but sometimes painful things like this happen. It's all part of the process of exploration and discovery. It's all part of taking a chance and expanding man's horizons. The future doesn't belong to the fainthearted; it belongs to the brave. The *Challenger* crew was pulling us into the future, and we'll continue to follow them.

I've always had great faith in and respect for our space program, and what happened today does nothing to diminish it. We don't hide our space program. We don't keep secrets and cover things up. We do it all up front and in public. That's the way freedom is, and we wouldn't change it for a minute.

We'll continue our quest in space. There will be more shuttle flights and more shuttle crews and yes, more volunteers, more civilians, more teachers in space. Nothing ends here; our hopes and our journeys continue.

I want to add that I wish I could talk to every man and woman who works for NASA or who worked on this mission and tell them: "Your dedication and professionalism have moved and impressed us for decades. And we know of your anguish. We share it."

There's a coincidence today. On this day 390 years ago, the great explorer Sir Francis Drake died aboard ship off the coast of Panama. In his lifetime the great frontiers were the oceans, and a historian later said, "He lived by the sea, died on it, and was buried in it." Well, today we can say of the *Challenger* crew: Their dedication was, like Drake's, complete.

The crew of the space shuttle *Challenger* honored us by the manner in which they lived their lives. We will never forget them, nor the last time we saw them, this morning, as they prepared for their journey and waved good-bye and "slipped the surly bonds of earth" to "touch the face of God."

Remarks at a Dinner
Honoring Tip O'Neill

WASHINGTON, D.C.
MARCH 17, 1986

Tip O'Neill, the former Speaker of the House of Representatives, is a Democratic politician of the old school. They really don't make them like him anymore, and I'm not saying they should, but he is quite a character.

After I got into office I went to see Tip up on Capitol Hill. And then Nancy and I had Tip and his wife, Millie, down to dinner at the White House. And so I was surprised to see one day in the paper that he was beating my brains out on some issue or another, so I called him up. I said, "Tip, I thought we had something going here?" And Tip said, "Well, old buddy, that's politics. We're friends after six P.M."

Sometimes when he came to see me, I'd set my watch up so that it would be six.

Reverend clergy, Mr. Prime Minister,* Mr. Speaker, ladies and gentlemen, I want to begin tonight by saying how touched I am to know that Tip wanted me here this evening. [*Laughter*] Why, he even called me himself last week and said, "Mr. President, make sure you don't miss the dinner Tuesday night." [*Laughter*]

But to be honest, I've always known that Tip was behind me —[*Laughter*]—even if it was only at the State of the Union Address. As I made each proposal, I could hear Tip whispering to George Bush, "Forget it. No way. Fat chance." [*Laughter*]

I think it was inevitable, though, that there'd be a standoff between us. Imagine one Irishman trying to corner another Irishman in the Oval Office. [*Laughter*] But despite all this, Tip wanted me here. He said that since it was March 17th, it was only fitting that someone drop by who actually had known St. Patrick. [*Laughter*] And that's true, Tip, I did know St. Patrick. In fact, we both changed to the same political party at about the same time. [*Laughter*]

Now, it's true that Tip and I have our political disagreements. Sure, I said some things about Tip, and Tip said some things about me. But that's all history. And anyway, you know how it is, I forget. [*Laughter*] I just follow that old motto "Forgive and forget." Or is it "Forget and forgive." [*Laughter*]

Ladies and gentlemen, I think you know Tip and I've been kidding each other for some time now. And I hope you also know how much I hope this continues for many years to come. A little kidding is, after all, a sign of affection, the sort of things that friends do to each other. And Mr. Speaker, I'm grateful you have permitted me in the past, and I hope in the future, that singular honor, the honor of calling you my friend. I think the fact of our friendship is testimony to the political system

* Prime Minister Garret FitzGerald of Ireland.

that we're part of and the country we live in, a country which permits two not-so-shy and not-so-retiring Irishmen to have it out on the issues, rather than on each other or their countrymen.

But in addition to celebrating a country and a personal friendship, I wanted to come here tonight to join you in saluting Tip O'Neill, to salute him for the years of dedication and devotion to country. Tip's recollections of politics go back, of course, far beyond my own. [*Laughter*] He's seen some who play the game well and others who do not. He's seen some who love politics and some who came to it only out of a sense of duty. But through it all, Tip has been a vital and forceful part of America's political tradition, a tradition that he has truly enriched.

Yet Tip O'Neill represents far more than just this political tradition. Deep within, too, is the memory of places like Back Bay and south Boston, the docks, the piers, those who came off the ships in Boston Harbor seeking a better land, a better way for their children. And they found that something better. They rose above the prejudice and the hardship.

Tip would see one of his contemporaries become president— John F. Kennedy would be sixty-eight today, had he lived. And Tip can remember those golden hours better than most in this room. And then, not too many years later, there was another of immigrant stock who would become Speaker of the House. In so short a time, so much leadership from one city, one place, one people. How fitting that Boston College, a place that became to so many of those new arrivals a symbol of moving upward and onward; how fitting that Boston College, whose towers on the heights have reached to heaven's own blue for so many, should sponsor this salute to Tip O'Neill. Tip, you are a true son of Boston College and our friend. And we salute you.

You are also a leader of the nation, and for that we honor you. But you also embody so much of what this nation is all about, the hope that is America. So, you make us proud as well, my friend, you make us proud.

Thank you. God bless you all.

Remarks at the Statue of Liberty Centennial Ceremonies

GOVERNORS ISLAND
JULY 3, 1986

This was one of the grandest occasions I attended while I was president. What an uplifting experience unveiling the spruced-up lady and relighting her torch. And the thousands and thousands of people who came to celebrate were wonderful. The police told us that even with these great crowds there was never any jostling. Everyone was trying to help make things go smoothly.

We had several events in the area over the course of a couple

*of days, and every time we would come and go, our helicopter
would circle around the top of the statue. I was carried away.
She was so feminine, which I never realized before. I told
Nancy, "This is the other woman in my life."*

THANK YOU. And Lee Iacocca,* thank you on behalf of all
America.

President and Madame Mitterrand, my fellow Americans:

The ironworkers from New York and New Jersey who came
here to begin restoration work were at first puzzled and a bit
put off to see foreign workers, craftsmen from France, arrive.
Jean Wiart, the leader of the French workers, said his countrymen understood. After all, he asked, how would Frenchmen
feel if Americans showed up to help restore the Eiffel Tower?

But as they came to know each other—these Frenchmen and
Americans—affections grew; and so, too, did perspectives. The
Americans were reminded that Miss Liberty, like the many millions she's welcomed to these shores, is of foreign birth, the gift
of workers, farmers, and shopkeepers and children who do-
nated hundreds of thousands of francs to send her here. They
were the ordinary people of France. This statue came from their
pockets and from their hearts.

The French workers, too, made discoveries. Monsieur Wiart,
for example, normally lives in a 150-year-old cottage in a small
French town, but for the last year he's been riding the subway
through Brooklyn. "A study in contrasts," he said—contrasts
indeed. But he has also told the newspapers that he and his
countrymen learned something else at Liberty Island. For the
first time, they worked in proximity with Americans of Jewish,
black, Italian, Irish, Russian, Polish, and Indian backgrounds.

* Lee Iacocca was chairman of the Statue of Liberty and Ellis Island Foundation,
which was responsible for raising funds for the restoration of the statue.

"Fascinating," he said, "to see different ethnic and national types work and live so well together."

Well, it's how we like to think of America. And it's good to know that Miss Liberty is still giving life to the dream of a new world where old antagonisms could be cast aside and people of every nation could live together as one.

It's especially fitting that this lesson should be relived and relearned here by Americans and Frenchmen. President Mitterrand, the French and American people have forged a special friendship over the course of two centuries. Yes, in the 1700s, France was the midwife of our liberty. In two world wars, America stood with France as she fought for her life and for civilization. And today, Mr. President, with infinite gentleness, your countrymen tend the final resting places, marked now by rows of white crosses and stars, of more than 60,000 Americans who remain on French soil, a reminder since the days of Lafayette of our mutual struggles and sacrifices for freedom. So, tonight, as we celebrate the friendship of our two nations, we also pray: May it ever be so. God bless America, and *vive la France.*

And yet, my fellow Americans, it is not only the friendship of two peoples but the friendship of all peoples that brings us here tonight. We celebrate something more than the restoration of this statue's physical grandeur. Another worker here, Scott Aronsen, a marble restorer, has put it well: "I grew up in Brooklyn and never went to the Statue of Liberty. But when I first walked in there to work, I thought about my grandfathers coming through here." And which of us does not think of other grandfathers and grandmothers, from so many places around the globe, for whom this statue was the first glimpse of America.

"She was silhouetted very clear," one of them wrote about standing on deck as their ship entered New York Harbor. "We passed her very slowly. Of course we had to look up. She was beautiful." Another talked of how all the passengers rushed to one side of the boat for a fast look at their new home and at her. "Everybody was crying. The whole boat bent toward her. She was beautiful with the early morning light."

To millions returning home, especially from foreign wars, she was also special. A young World War I captain of artillery described how, on a troopship returning from France, even the most hard-bitten veteran had trouble blinking back the tears. "I've never seen anything that looked so good," that doughboy, Harry Truman, wrote to his fiancée, Bess, back in Independence, Missouri, "as the Liberty Lady in New York Harbor."

And that is why tonight we celebrate this mother of exiles who lifts her light beside the golden door. Many of us have seen the picture of another worker here, a tool belt around his waist, balanced on a narrow metal rod of scaffolding, leaning over to place a kiss on the forehead of Miss Liberty. Tony Soraci, the grandson of immigrant Italians, said it was something he was proud to do, "something to tell my grandchildren."

Robert Kearney feels the same way. At work on the statue after a serious illness, he gave $10,000 worth of commemorative pins to those who visited here. Part of the reason, he says, was an earlier construction job over in Hoboken and his friend named Blackie. They could see the harbor from the building they were working on, and every morning Blackie would look over the water, give a salute, and say, "That's my gal."

Well, the truth is, she's everybody's gal. We sometimes forget that even those who came here first to settle the new land were also strangers. I've spoken before of the tiny *Arabella,* a ship at anchor just off the Massachusetts coast. A little group of Puritans huddled on the deck. And then John Winthrop, who would later become the first governor of Massachusetts, reminded his fellow Puritans there on that tiny deck that they must keep faith with their God, that the eyes of all the world were upon them, and that they must not forsake the mission that God had sent them on, and they must be a light unto the nations of all the world—a shining city upon a hill.

Call it mysticism if you will, I have always believed there was some divine providence that placed this great land here between the two great oceans, to be found by a special kind of people from every corner of the world, who had a special love for freedom and a special courage that enabled them to leave their own land, leave their friends and their countrymen, and come to this new and strange land to build a new world of peace and freedom and hope.

Lincoln spoke about hope as he left the hometown he would never see again to take up the duties of the presidency and bring America through a terrible civil war. At each stop on his long train ride to Washington, the news grew worse: The nation was dividing; his own life was in peril. On he pushed, undaunted. In Philadelphia he spoke in Independence Hall, where eighty-five years earlier the Declaration of Independence had been signed. He noted that much more had been achieved there than just independence from Great Britain. It was, he said, "hope to the world, future for all time."

Well, that is the common thread that binds us to those Quakers on the tiny deck of the *Arabella,* to the beleaguered farmers and landowners signing the Declaration in Philadelphia in that hot Philadelphia hall, to Lincoln on a train ready to guide his people through the conflagration, to all the millions crowded in the steerage who passed this lady and wept at the sight of her, and those who've worked here in the scaffolding with their hands and with their love—Jean Wiart, Scott Aronsen, Tony Soraci, Robert Kearney, and so many others.

We're bound together because, like them, we, too, dare to hope—hope that our children will always find here the land of liberty in a land that is free. We dare to hope, too, that we'll understand our work can never be truly done until every man, woman, and child shares in our gift, in our hope, and stands with us in the light of liberty—the light that, tonight, will shortly cast its glow upon her, as it has upon us for two centuries, keeping faith with a dream of long ago and guiding millions still to a future of peace and freedom.

And now we will unveil that gallant lady. Thank you, and God bless you all.

Remarks on Signing
the Tax Reform Act into Law

WHITE HOUSE SOUTH LAWN
OCTOBER 22, 1986

This legislation really gets to the heart of my conservative economic principles. A nation will prosper if the government will just get out of the way and give the people an incentive to work and produce. This act wouldn't have passed without the active support of the Democratic Congress. This was truly a bipartisan measure.

The act gave the United States the lowest federal income tax rates of any major industrialized nation in the world and one of the fairest systems as well. More than four million lower-

income households were relieved of their federal tax burden entirely.

The top personal tax rate dropped from 70 percent in 1981 to between 28 and 33 percent in 1988, the lowest since 1931. Eighty percent of all Americans now pay a flat 15 percent or owe no income tax at all.

I know that reading about taxes is pretty dull stuff, but I hope you won't skip the following remarks because I think we really accomplished something for the American people.

WELL, THANK YOU, and welcome to the White House. In a moment I'll be sitting at that desk, taking up a pen, and signing the most sweeping overhaul of the Tax Code in our nation's history. To all of you here today who've worked so long and hard to see this day come, my thanks and the thanks of a nation go out to you.

The journey's been long, and many said we'd never make it to the end. But as usual the pessimists left one thing out of their calculations: the American people. They haven't made this the freest country and the mightiest economic force on this planet by shrinking from challenges. They never gave up. And after almost three years of commitment and hard work, one headline in the *Washington Post* told the whole story: "The Impossible Became the Inevitable," and the dream of America's fair-share tax plan became a reality.

When I sign this bill into law, America will have the lowest marginal tax rates and the most modern tax code among major industrialized nations, one that encourages risk-taking, innovation, and that old American spirit of enterprise. We'll be refueling the American growth economy with the kind of incentives that helped create record new businesses and nearly 11.7 million jobs in just forty-six months. Fair and simpler for most Americans, this is a tax code designed to take us into a future of technological invention and economic achievement, one that will keep America competitive and growing into the twenty-first century.

But for all tax reform's economic benefits, I believe that history will record this moment as something more: as the return to the first principles. This country was founded on faith in the individual, not groups or classes, but faith in the resources and bounty of each and every separate human soul. Our Founding Fathers designed a democratic form of government to enlist the individual's energies and fashioned a Bill of Rights to protect its freedoms. And in so doing, they tapped a wellspring of hope and creativity that was to completely transform history.

The history of these United States of America is indeed a history of individual achievement. It was their hard work that built our cities and farmed our prairies; their genius that continually pushed us beyond the boundaries of existing knowledge, reshaping our world with the steam engine, polio vaccine, and the silicon chip. It was their faith in freedom and love of country that sustained us through trials and hardships and through wars, and it was their courage and selflessness that enabled us to always prevail.

But when our Founding Fathers designed this government—of, by, and for the people—they never imagined what we've come to know as the progressive income tax. When the income tax was first levied in 1913, the top rate was only 7 percent on people with incomes over $500,000. Now, that's the equivalent of multimillionaires today. But in our lifetime we've seen marginal tax rates skyrocket as high as 90 percent, and not even the poor have been spared.

As tax rates escalated, the Tax Code grew ever more tangled and complex, a haven for special interests and tax manipulators, but an impossible frustration for everybody else. Blatantly unfair, our Tax Code became a source of bitterness and discouragement for the average taxpayer. It wasn't too much to call it un-American.

Meanwhile, the steeply progressive nature of the tax struck at the heart of the economic life of the individual, punishing that special effort and extra hard work that has always been the driving force of our economy. As government's hunger for ever more revenues expanded, families saw tax cuts—or taxes, I should say—cut deeper and deeper into their paychecks; and taxation fell most cruelly on the poor, making a difficult climb up from poverty even harder.

Throughout history, the oppressive hand of government has fallen most heavily on the economic life of the individuals. And more often than not, it is inflation and taxes that have undermined livelihoods and constrained their freedoms. We should not forget that this nation of ours began in a revolt against oppressive taxation. Our Founding Fathers fought not only for our political rights but also to secure the economic freedoms without which these political freedoms are no more than a shadow.

In the last twenty years we've witnessed an expansion and strengthening of many of our civil liberties, but our economic liberties have too often been neglected and even abused. We protect the freedom of expression of the author, as we should, but what of the freedom of expression of the entrepreneur, whose pen and paper are capital and profits, whose book may be a new invention or small business? What of the creators of our economic life, whose contributions may not only delight the mind but improve the condition of man by feeding the poor with new grains, bringing hope to the sick with new cures, banishing ignorance with wondrous new information technologies?

And what about fairness for families? It's in our families that America's most important work gets done: raising our next generation. But over the last forty years, as inflation has shrunk the personal exemption, families with children have had to shoulder more and more of the tax burden. With inflation and bracket-creep also eroding incomes, many spouses who would rather stay home with their children have been forced to go looking for jobs.

And what of America's promise of hope and opportunity, that with hard work even the poorest among us can gain the security and happiness that is the due of all Americans? You can't put a price tag on the American dream. That dream is the heart and soul of America; it's the promise that keeps our nation forever good and generous, a model and hope to the world.

For all these reasons, this tax bill is less a freedom—or a reform, I should say—than a revolution. Millions of working poor will be dropped from the tax rolls altogether, and families will get a long-overdue break with lower rates and an almost doubled personal exemption. We're going to make it economical to raise children again.

Flatter rates will mean more reward for that extra effort, and banishing loopholes and a minimum tax will mean that everybody and every corporation pay their fair share. And that's why I'm certain that the bill I'm signing today is not only an historic overhaul of our Tax Code and a sweeping victory for fairness, it's also the best antipoverty bill, the best profamily measure, and the best job-creation program ever to come out of the Congress of the United States.

And now that we've come this far, we cannot, and we will not, allow tax reform to be undone with tax rate hikes. We must restore certainty to our Tax Code and our economy. And I'll oppose with all my might any attempt to raise tax rates on the American people, and I hope that all here will join with me to make permanent the historic progress of tax reform.

I think all of us here today know what a Herculean effort it took to get this landmark bill to my desk. That effort didn't start here in Washington, but began with the many thinkers who have struggled to return economics to its classical roots—to an understanding that ultimately the economy is not made up of aggregates like government spending and consumer demand, but of individual men and women, each striving to provide for his family and better his or her lot in life.

But we must also salute those courageous leaders in the Congress who've made this day possible. To Bob Packwood, Dan Rostenkowski, Russell Long, John Duncan, and Majority Leader Bob Dole; to Jack Kemp, Bob Kasten, Bill Bradley, and Dick Gephardt, who pioneered with their own versions of tax reform—I salute all of you and all the other members of the

Senate and House whose efforts paid off and whose votes finally won the day.

And last but not least, the many members of the administration who must often have felt that they were fighting a lonely battle against overwhelming odds—particularly my two incomparable secretaries of the treasury, Don Regan and Jim Baker —and I thank them from the bottom of my heart.

I feel like we just played the World Series of tax reform— [*Laughter*]—and the American people won.

Address to the Nation
on Return from Meeting
with General Secretary Gorbachev

OVAL OFFICE

OCTOBER 13, 1986

I think the television cameras captured very accurately the look of disappointment on my face when I finally left the meeting in Reykjavik, Iceland, with General Secretary Gorbachev.

Mikhail and I had gotten into a discussion of the total elimination of nuclear weapons. Yes, it was breathtaking. The U.S. delegation was supposed to be on our way home, but naturally we stayed through Sunday because we seemed to be making real progress.

Finally after making all this progress, Mikhail said it all hinged on us stopping our Strategic Defense Initiative program, what others call our Star Wars plan to protect ourselves from incoming nuclear missiles. Gorbachev hadn't mentioned this condition before.

Well, I gave him several arguments. I didn't want him to think we were developing this technology only to be better prepared for a fight, so I offered to give it away. He said, "I don't believe you." I said, "Well, maybe you're judging by your own people."

He repeated that none of the progress we discussed was possible unless we dropped SDI. I eventually blew my top and said, "There's no way." And we left.

On returning home, I made the following speech explaining to the American people what had happened to our hopes.

GOOD EVENING.

As most of you know, I've just returned from meetings in Iceland with the leader of the Soviet Union, General Secretary Gorbachev. As I did last year when I returned from the summit conference in Geneva, I want to take a few moments tonight to share with you what took place in these discussions.

The implications of these talks are enormous and only just beginning to be understood. We proposed the most sweeping and generous arms control proposal in history. We offered the complete elimination of all ballistic missiles—Soviet and American—from the face of the earth by 1996. While we parted company with this American offer still on the table, we are closer than ever to agreements that could lead to a safer world without nuclear weapons.

But first, let me tell you that from the start of my meetings with Mr. Gorbachev, I have always regarded you, the American people, as full participants. Believe me, without your support none of these talks could have been held, nor could the ultimate aims of American foreign policy—world peace and freedom—be pursued. And it's for these aims I went the extra mile to Iceland.

Before I report on our talks, though, allow me to set the stage by explaining two things that were very much a part of our talks: one a treaty and the other a defense against nuclear missiles, which we're trying to develop. Now, you've heard their titles a thousand times—the ABM treaty and SDI. Well, those letters stand for: ABM, antiballistic missile; SDI, Strategic Defense Initiative.

Some years ago, the United States and the Soviet Union agreed to limit any defense against nuclear missile attacks to the emplacement in one location in each country of a small number of missiles capable of intercepting and shooting down incoming nuclear missiles, thus leaving our real defense—a policy called mutual assured destruction, meaning if one side launched a nuclear attack, the other side could retaliate. And this mutual threat of destruction was believed to be a deterrent against either side striking first.

So here we sit, with thousands of nuclear warheads targeted on each other and capable of wiping out both our countries. The Soviets deployed the few antiballistic missiles around Moscow as the treaty permitted. Our country didn't bother deploying because the threat of nationwide annihilation made such a limited defense seem useless.

For some years now we've been aware that the Soviets may be developing a nationwide defense. They have installed a large, modern radar at Krasnoyarsk, which we believe is a critical part of a radar system designed to provide radar guidance for antiballistic missiles protecting the entire nation. Now, this is a violation of the ABM treaty.

Believing that a policy of mutual destruction and slaughter of their citizens and ours was uncivilized, I asked our military, a few years ago, to study and see if there was a practical way to destroy nuclear missiles after their launch but before they can reach their targets, rather than to just destroy people. Well, this is the goal for what we call SDI, and our scientists researching such a system are convinced it is practical and that several years down the road we can have such a system ready to deploy. Now incidentally, we are not violating the ABM treaty, which permits such research. If and when we deploy, the treaty also allows withdrawal from the treaty upon six months' notice. SDI, let me make it clear, is a nonnuclear defense.

So, here we are at Iceland for our second such meeting. In the first, and in the months in between, we have discussed ways to reduce and in fact eliminate nuclear weapons entirely. We and the Soviets have had teams of negotiators in Geneva trying to work out a mutual agreement on how we could reduce or eliminate nuclear weapons. And so far, no success.

On Saturday and Sunday, General Secretary Gorbachev and his foreign minister, Shevardnadze, and Secretary of State George Shultz and I met for nearly ten hours. We didn't limit ourselves to just arms reductions. We discussed what we call violation of human rights on the part of the Soviets—refusal to let people emigrate from Russia so they can practice their religion without being persecuted, letting people go to rejoin their families, husbands, and wives—separated by national borders —being allowed to reunite.

In much of this, the Soviet Union is violating another agreement—the Helsinki accords they had signed in 1975. Yuriy Orlov, whose freedom we just obtained, was imprisoned for pointing out to his government its violations of that pact, its refusal to let citizens leave their country or return. We also discussed regional matters such as Afghanistan, Angola, Nicaragua, and Cambodia. But by their choice, the main subject was arms control.

We discussed the emplacement of intermediate-range missiles in Europe and Asia and seemed to be in agreement they could be drastically reduced. Both sides seemed willing to find a way to reduce, even to zero, the strategic ballistic missiles we have aimed at each other. This then brought up the subject of SDI.

I offered a proposal that we continue our present research. And if and when we reached the stage of testing, we would sign, now, a treaty that would permit Soviet observation of such tests. And if the program was practical, we would both eliminate our offensive missiles, and then we would share the benefits of advanced defenses. I explained that even though we would have done away with our offensive ballistic missiles, having the defense would protect against cheating or the possibility of a madman, sometime, deciding to create nuclear missiles. After all, the world now knows how to make them. I likened it to our keeping our gas masks, even though the nations of the world had outlawed poison gas after World War I.

We seemed to be making progress on reducing weaponry, although the General Secretary was registering opposition to SDI and proposing a pledge to observe ABM for a number of years as the day was ending.

Secretary Shultz suggested we turn over the notes our notetakers had been making of everything we'd said to our respective teams and let them work through the night to put them together and find just where we were in agreement and what differences separated us. With respect and gratitude, I can inform you those teams worked through the night till six-thirty A.M.

Yesterday, Sunday morning, Mr. Gorbachev and I, with our foreign ministers, came together again and took up the report of our two teams. It was most promising. The Soviets had asked for a ten-year delay in the deployment of SDI programs.

In an effort to see how we could satisfy their concerns—while protecting our principles and security—we proposed a ten-year period in which we began with the reduction of all strategic nuclear arms, bombers, air-launched cruise missiles, intercontinental ballistic missiles, submarine-launched ballistic missiles, and the weapons they carry. They would be reduced 50 percent in the first five years. During the next five years, we would continue by eliminating all remaining offensive ballistic missiles, of all ranges. And during that time, we would proceed with research, development, and testing of SDI—all done in conformity with ABM provisions. At the ten-year point, with all ballistic missiles eliminated, we could proceed to deploy advanced defenses, at the same time permitting the Soviets to do likewise.

And here the debate began. The General Secretary wanted wording that, in effect, would have kept us from developing the SDI for the entire ten years. In effect, he was killing SDI.

And unless I agreed, all that work toward eliminating nuclear weapons would go down the drain—canceled.

I told him I had pledged to the American people that I would not trade away SDI, there was no way I could tell our people their government would not protect them against nuclear destruction. I went to Reykjavik determined that everything was negotiable except two things: our freedom and our future. I'm still optimistic that a way will be found. The door is open, and the opportunity to begin eliminating the nuclear threat is within reach.

So you can see, we made progress in Iceland. And we will continue to make progress if we pursue a prudent, deliberate, and above all, realistic approach with the Soviets. From the earliest days of our administration this has been our policy. We made it clear we had no illusions about the Soviets or their ultimate intentions. We were publicly candid about the critical moral distinctions between totalitarianism and democracy. We declared the principal objective of American foreign policy to be not just the prevention of war, but the extension of freedom. And we stressed our commitment to the growth of democratic government and democratic institutions around the world.

And that's why we assisted freedom fighters who are resisting the imposition of totalitarian rule in Afghanistan, Nicaragua, Angola, Cambodia, and elsewhere. And finally, we began work on what I believe most spurred the Soviets to negotiate seriously: rebuilding our military strength, reconstructing our strategic deterrence, and above all, beginning to work on the Strategic Defense Initiative.

And yet, at the same time, we set out these foreign policy goals and began working toward them. We pursued another of our major objectives: that of seeking means to lessen tensions with the Soviets and ways to prevent war and keep the peace.

Now, this policy is now paying dividends—one sign of this in Iceland was the progress on the issue of arms control. For the first time in a long while, Soviet-American negotiations in the area of arms reductions are moving, and moving in the right direction—not just toward arms control, but toward arms reduction.

But for all the progress we made on arms reductions, we must remember there were other issues on the table in Iceland, issues that are fundamental. As I mentioned, one such issue is human rights. As President Kennedy once said, "And is not peace, in the last analysis, basically a matter of human rights?"

I made it plain that the United States would not seek to exploit improvement in these matters for purposes of propaganda. But I also made it plain, once again, that an improvement of the human condition within the Soviet Union is indispensable for an improvement in bilateral relations with the United States. For a government that will break faith with its own people cannot be trusted to keep faith with foreign powers. So, I told Mr. Gorbachev—again in Reykjavik, as I had in Geneva—we Americans place far less weight upon the words that are spoken at meetings such as these than upon the deeds that follow. When it comes to human rights and judging Soviet intentions, we're all from Missouri—you got to show us.

Another subject area we took up in Iceland also lies at the heart of the differences between the Soviet Union and America. This is the issue of regional conflicts. Summit meetings cannot make the American people forget what Soviet actions have meant for the peoples of Afghanistan, Central America, Africa, and Southeast Asia. Until Soviet policies change, we will make sure that our friends in these areas—those who fight for freedom and independence—will have the support they need.

Finally, there was a fourth item. And this area was that of bilateral relations, people-to-people contacts. In Geneva last year, we welcomed several cultural exchange accords; in Iceland, we saw indications of more movement in these areas. But let me say now: The United States remains committed to people-to-people programs that could lead to exchanges between not just a few elite, but thousands of everyday citizens from both our countries.

So, I think, then, that you can see that we did make progress in Iceland on a broad range of topics. We reaffirmed our four-point agenda. We discovered major new grounds of agreement. We probed again some old areas of disagreement.

And let me return again to the SDI issue. I realize some Americans may be asking tonight: Why not accept Mr. Gorbachev's demand? Why not give up SDI for this agreement?

Well, the answer, my friends, is simple. SDI is America's insurance policy that the Soviet Union would keep the commitments made at Reykjavik. SDI is America's security guarantee if the Soviets should—as they have done too often in the past—fail to comply with their solemn commitments. SDI is what brought the Soviets back to arms control talks at Geneva and Iceland. SDI is the key to a world without nuclear weapons.

The Soviets understand this. They have devoted far more resources, for a lot longer time than we, to their own SDI. The world's only operational missile defense today surrounds Moscow, the capital of the Sovet Union.

What Mr. Gorbachev was demanding at Reykjavik was that the United States agree to a new version of a fourteen-year-old ABM treaty that the Soviet Union has already violated. I told him we don't make those kinds of deals in the United States.

And the American people should reflect on these critical questions: How does a defense of the United States threaten the Soviet Union or anyone else? Why are the Soviets so adamant that America remain forever vulnerable to Soviet rocket attack? As of today, all free nations are utterly defenseless against Soviet missiles—fired either by accident or design. Why does the Soviet Union insist that we remain so—forever?

So, my fellow Americans, I cannot promise, nor can any president promise, that the talks in Iceland or any future discussions with Mr. Gorbachev will lead inevitably to great breakthroughs or momentous treaty signings. We will not abandon the guiding principle we took to Reykjavik. We prefer no agreement than to bring home a bad agreement to the United States.

And on this point, I know you're also interested in the question of whether there will be another summit. There was no indication by Mr. Gorbachev as to when or whether he plans to travel to the United States, as we agreed he would last year in Geneva. I repeat tonight that our invitation stands, and that we continue to believe additional meetings would be useful. But that's a decision the Soviets must make.

But whatever the immediate prospects, I can tell you that I'm ultimately hopeful about the prospects for progress at the summit and for world peace and freedom. You see, the current summit process is very different from that of previous decades. It's different because the world is different; and the world is different because of the hard work and sacrifice of the American people during the past five and a half years. Your energy has restored and expanded our economic might. Your support has restored our military strength. Your courage and sense of national unity in times of crisis have given pause to our adversaries, heartened our friends, and inspired the world. The Western democracies and the NATO alliance are revitalized; and all across the world, nations are turning to democratic ideas and the principles of the free market. So, because the American people stood guard at the critical hour, freedom has gathered its forces, regained its strength, and is on the march.

So, if there's one impression I carry away with me from these October talks, it is that, unlike the past, we're dealing now from a position of strength. And for that reason, we have it within our grasp to move speedily with the Soviets toward even more breakthroughs. Our ideas are out there on the table. They won't go away. We're ready to pick up where we left off. Our negotiators are heading back to Geneva, and we're prepared to go forward whenever and wherever the Soviets are ready. So, there's reason, good reason, for hope.

I saw evidence of this in the progress we made in the talks with Mr. Gorbachev. And I saw evidence of it when we left Iceland yesterday, and I spoke to our young men and women at our naval installation at Keflavik—a critically important base far closer to Soviet naval bases than to our own coastline.

As always, I was proud to spend a few moments with them and thank them for their sacrifices and devotion to country.

They represent America at her finest: committed to defend not only our own freedom but the freedom of others who would be living in a far more frightening world were it not for the strength and resolve of the United States.

"Whenever the standard of freedom and independence has been . . . unfurled, there will be America's heart, her benedictions, and her prayers," John Quincy Adams once said. He spoke well of our destiny as a nation. My fellow Americans, we're honored by history, entrusted by destiny with the oldest dream of humanity—the dream of lasting peace and human freedom.

Another president, Harry Truman, noted that our century had seen two of the most frightful wars in history and that "the supreme need of our time is for man to learn to live together in peace and harmony." It's in pursuit of that ideal I went to Geneva a year ago and to Iceland last week. And it's in pursuit of that ideal that I thank you now for all the support you've given me, and I again ask for your help and your prayers as we continue our journey toward a world where peace reigns and freedom is enshrined.

Thank you, and
God bless you.

Meeting with Hostage David Jacobsen and Reporters

WHITE HOUSE ROSE GARDEN
NOVEMBER 7, 1986

I found this little episode interesting because it deals more with what presidents can't say than what they can. It also previews one of the biggest controversies of my presidency.

David Jacobsen was the second hostage we had gotten out as a result of our secret negotiations with a group of Iranians who we thought were more moderate. To this day, I don't know what happened to those Iranians after the Iran/contra thing burst into the headlines. I don't know if they're dead or gone underground or just lying low. Anyway, back then they told us that two more hostages would be released in forty-eight hours.

About this same time, a rag of a newspaper in Beirut reported that we had sold arms to Iranians in return for hostages. Well, of course, the press had all sorts of questions at a very delicate time in terms of getting those other two hostages out. I found Mr. Jacobsen's plea to the press so compelling I decided I'd just put it in here. He made his points much more eloquently than I could ever have. We never did get those other two people out.

The President. Ladies and gentlemen, you know who our guest is today, and I know that he has a few words for you. And I think a great many prayers have been answered by his presence here in our country.

Mr. Jacobsen. I certainly have some words, and I would like to read them. I usually like to speak extemporaneously. But we have our people being held prisoners, and I'd like to just preface my remarks by one simple statement.

And what I say today, what you report, what you speculate upon is heard throughout the entire world within twenty-four hours. A simple speculation on your part could cause the death of my dear friend Tom Sutherland, or Terry Anderson, or Joe Cicippio, or any other of the other hostages. And I would ask that you would be responsible and please do not engage in unreasonable and unrealistic speculations. Be intellectually honest. I ask of you, I plead for you: I am worried about what you might say, or someone else, might result in a death of somebody that I love. I don't want that on my conscience, and I don't think you want it on yours.

So, I have a brief statement that I've written, and I'm happy to read it. And it's a thrill to be here.

Mr. President, you can't really imagine—and Mrs. President —can't imagine my joy of being here with you on this very special day. For seventeen long months, I never lost hope of being a free man again. I prayed long and hard. And my dear family—my six wonderful children are here, are with me here today—and my friends—they kept the faith, and they never lost hope despite many, many frustrations. And that knowledge kept me going.

And freedom is a very precious gift, and I really learned it in a very personal manner. Freedom is a very precious gift, and one that we Americans sometimes take for granted. When freedom is taken away, the loss is immense. But that same hope and that faith and that optimism that sustained the founders of our country, of this great land, during the periods of our adversity as a nation also kept my spirits high during my long captivity.

And Mr. President, I know that you and many others in and out of the administration of this government have worked long and hard on my behalf and on the behalf of the other captives and you continue to do so for the others that are still being held hostage. And in particular, there are a number of independent people, religious leaders and others, that deserve special praise for their independent efforts.

Terry Waite, who is one of those great humanitarians, who has given so much of himself so that I may be free—Terry Waite did it as a free man, free of all governments and any type of deals. Terry did it as a humanitarian. The families of Terry Anderson, Tom Sutherland, Joe Cicippio, and the other innocent people still being held hostage should not give up hope.

Contact by you, Mr. President, and others in the administration and especially those very special people in the State Department, who have maintained frequent contact with our families, help our dear ones sustain their hope. And I know, Mr. President, that you have sought our freedom from the day that the first American was taken hostage, and I know that you have not rested, nor will you rest, until every American is home free.

And Mr. President, you really have my eternal gratitude. You're the leader of a truly great country, and I'm proud to be an American. And I really want to thank you very, very much. You're quite a man.

The President. Thank you.

Mr. Jacobsen. Thank you. And please, please, in your comments and evaluations, be responsible. Thank you.

Q. Mr. President, the Iranians are saying that if you'll release some of those weapons, they'll intercede to free the rest of the hostages. Will you?

The President. Bill [Bill Plante, CBS News], I think in view of this statement, this is just exactly what I tried to say last night. There's no way that we can answer questions having anything to do with this without endangering the people we're trying to rescue.

Q. Could you just tell us whether Secretary of State Shultz agrees with your policy or disagrees and has protested as has been reported?

The President. We have all been working together.

Q. And Secretary Shultz supports the policy, and so does Cap Weinberger?

The President. Yes.

Q. Why not dispel the speculation by telling us exactly what happened, sir?

The President. Because it has to happen again and again and again until we have them all back. And anything that we tell about all the things that have been going on in trying to effect his rescue endangers the possibility of further rescue.

Q. Your own party's majority leader says you're rewarding terrorists.

Mr. Jacobsen. Please, you didn't hear what I said at the beginning. Unreasonable speculation on your part can endanger their lives. I would like to take some time now and talk. But this is a day of joy for me. I have my children inside. I want to share it with them. And I want Terry Anderson to share the same joy with his family. And I want Tom Sutherland to share the joy with his family. And in the name of God, would you please just be responsible and back off. Thank you.

Q. Mr. Jacobsen, how are we to know what is responsible and what is not?

1987

Remarks on Signing
the INF Treaty

WHITE HOUSE EAST ROOM
DECEMBER 8, 1987

The country had a good year in 1987. The economic recovery continued and we signed an historic agreement with the Soviet Union eliminating an entire class of nuclear weapons—the intermediate range ones that had been stationed in Europe. Privately, we—and especially Nancy—had a rough year. In October, Nancy had a mastectomy, and before she even had time to recover from the surgery, her mother died. And during the first part of the year, my credibility with the American people according to the polls dropped to an all-time low because of the continuing Iran/contra matter. Although my relationship with the people would soon recover, this was a source of great personal pain to me at the time.

The big news of the year, however, was the INF agreement. We signed it in the East Room of the White House. I believe this proves what progress can be made when we bargain from a position of strength and determination. I don't think the agreement would have been possible without our defense buildup. I also don't think it would have been possible before Gorbachev. He's quite a fellow.

He has a different attitude from previous Soviet leaders regarding not only arms reductions but the need to restructure the Soviet system itself. I've been a little concerned about his safety as a result. Why don't I let you read something I wrote in my diary earlier in 1987 to explain what I mean:

> ... then a fine meeting with XXX. Very interesting—suggested maybe I should go to Moscow instead of Gorbachev coming here. Then XXX dropped the bomb. A top Soviet official [said] Gorbachev might well be killed if he came here. There is so much opposition to what he's trying to do in Russia—they could murder him here and then pin the whole thing on us. I don't find the warning at all outlandish. The KGB is capable of doing just that.

Although I knew that our security people had done everything possible to protect him, when he did come over in December I don't mind telling you I thought about his safety. He's a smart man, so he could have done some handpicking of the Soviet agents he brought with him to the U.S. I don't know. But you can understand why his security and our security people were so jumpy when he got out of his limo on the streets of downtown Washington to shake a few hands.

But his trip here to sign the INF agreement was a big success. He's not above trying to bamboozle you as he tried to do to us in Reykjavik by raising the SDI thing at the last moment, but I believe he is a reasonable man. He is, as Margaret Thatcher once said, a man we can do business with.

And that is exactly what we did that day in December.

The President. Thank you all very much. Welcome to the White House.

This ceremony and the treaty we're signing today are both excellent examples of the rewards of patience. It was over six years ago, November 18, 1981, that I first proposed what would come to be called the zero option. It was a simple proposal—one might say, disarmingly simple. [*Laughter*] Unlike treaties in the past, it didn't simply codify the status quo or a new arms buildup; it didn't simply talk of controlling an arms race. For the first time in history, the language of "arms control" was replaced by "arms reduction"—in this case, the complete elimination of an entire class of U.S. and Soviet nuclear missiles.

Of course, this required a dramatic shift in thinking, and it took conventional wisdom some time to catch up. Reaction, to say the least, was mixed. To some the zero option was impossibly visionary and unrealistic; to others merely a propaganda ploy. Well, with patience, determination, and commitment, we've made this impossible vision a reality.

General Secretary Gorbachev, I'm sure you're familiar with Ivan Krylov's famous tale about the swan, the crawfish, and the pike. It seems that once upon a time these three were trying to move a wagonload together. They hitched and harnessed themselves to the wagon. It wasn't very heavy, but no matter how hard they worked, the wagon just wouldn't move. You see, the swan was flying upward; the crawfish kept crawling backward; the pike kept making for the water. The end result was that they got nowhere, and the wagon is still there to this day. Well, strong and fundamental moral differences continue to exist between our nations. But today, on this vital issue, at least, we've seen what can be accomplished when we pull together.

The numbers alone demonstrate the value of this agreement. On the Soviet side, over 1,500 deployed warheads will be removed, and all ground-launched intermediate-range missiles, including the SS-20s, will be destroyed. On our side, our entire complement of Pershing II and ground-launched cruise missiles, with some 400 deployed warheads, will all be destroyed. Additional backup missiles on both sides will also be destroyed.

But the importance of this treaty transcends numbers. We have listened to the wisdom in an old Russian maxim. And I'm sure you're familiar with it, Mr. General Secretary, though my pronunciation may give you difficulty. The maxim is: *Dovorey no provorey*—trust, but verify.

The General Secretary. You repeat that at every meeting. [*Laughter*]

The President. I like it. [*Laughter*]

This agreement contains the most stringent verification regime in history, including provisions for inspection teams actually residing in each other's territory and several other forms of on-site inspection, as well. This treaty protects the interests of America's friends and allies. It also embodies another important principle: the need for *glasnost,* a greater openness in military programs and forces.

We can only hope that this history-making agreement will not be an end in itself but the beginning of a working relationship that will enable us to tackle the other urgent issues before us: strategic offensive nuclear weapons, the balance of conventional forces in Europe, the destructive and tragic regional conflicts that beset so many parts of our globe, and respect for the human and natural rights God has granted to all men.

To all here who have worked so hard to make this vision a reality: Thank you, and congratulations—above all to Ambassadors Glitman and Obukhov.* To quote another Russian proverb—as you can see, I'm becoming quite an expert—[*Laughter*] —in Russian proverbs: "The harvest comes more from sweat than from the dew."

So, I'm going to propose to General Secretary Gorbachev that we issue one last instruction to you: Get some well-deserved rest. [*Laughter*]

The General Secretary. We're not going to do that. [*Laughter*]

The President. Well, now, Mr. General Secretary, would you like to say a few words before we sign the treaty?

The General Secretary. Mr. President, ladies and gentlemen, comrades:

* Ambassador Maynard W. Glitman, U.S. Negotiator on Intermediate-Range Nuclear Forces, and Ambassador Aleksey Obukhov, Deputy Head of the Soviet Nuclear and Space Arms Delegation.

Succeeding generations will hand down their verdict on the importance of the event which we are about to witness. But I will venture to say that what we are going to do, the signing of the first-ever agreement eliminating nuclear weapons, has a universal significance for mankind, both from the standpoint of world politics and from the standpoint of humanism.

For everyone, and above all, for our two great powers, the treaty whose text is on this table offers a big chance at last to get onto the road leading away from the threat of catastrophe. It is our duty to take full advantage of that chance and move together toward a nuclear-free world, which holds out for our children and grandchildren and for their children and grandchildren the promise of a fulfilling and happy life without fear and without a senseless waste of resources on weapons of destruction.

We can be proud of planting this sapling, which may one day grow into a mighty tree of peace. But it is probably still too early to bestow laurels upon each other. As the great American poet and philosopher Ralph Waldo Emerson said: "The reward of a thing well done is to have done it."

So, let us reward ourselves by getting down to business. We have covered a seven-year-long road, replete with intense work and debate. One last step toward this table, and the treaty will be signed.

May December 8, 1987, become a date that will be inscribed in the history books, a date that will mark the watershed separating the era of a mounting risk of nuclear war from the era of a demilitarization of human life.

Remarks at the Memorial Service
for Malcolm Baldrige

THE NATIONAL CATHEDRAL
WASHINGTON, D.C.
JULY 29, 1987

Mac Baldrige, my secretary of commerce, was a great guy. He told me this story one day when we were horseback riding down at the Marine base in Quantico, Virginia, south of Washington.

His first job was as a cowpuncher when he was fourteen years old. He loved rodeos and riding and roping, but at the age of twenty-eight he was told he could never ride or do anything athletic again because of arthritis of the spine. At one point, he was taking up to fifteen or thirty pills a day—in any event a great many. One day he said to hell with it. He said, "I love to ride and I don't care what the doctors say." So he just started riding again and rodeoing again. Well, it was great therapy. He told me that jumping off a horse and wrestling a calf to the ground was his miracle cure.

In the end, he died when his horse fell on him in a rodeo event, but something tells me that's the way Mac would have wanted to go.

Midge, Megan, Molly,* distinguished ladies and gentlemen:

The day I called Mac Baldrige to ask him to join the cabinet, I was told by Midge I would have to call back later. He was out on his horse roping and couldn't come to the phone. Right then I knew he was the kind of man I wanted.

It's a gift to be simple, we're told. If that means to hold simple, strong, and decent values, Mac had that gift. You could see it in the way he moved around the White House. He seemed to know everyone, not just those in the public eye but the secretaries and assistants, as well. And he treated everyone with the same measure of courtesy and respect, from his driver to the President. He never judged a man or woman by rank or trappings. Despite his many remarkable successes, worldly success was not the way he measured people. No, money was not, position was not, qualities of character were. Honesty, courage, industry, and humility—these were his yardsticks. And if you had these simple qualities, you'd made it in his eyes, whether you were rich or poor, famous or unknown.

Language was one way he decided if you were his kind of person. It's well-known now that he insisted on simple language in memos at the Commerce Department. He banned phrases that were vague or redundant. He once said that the thing he liked about cowboys was that they didn't talk unless they had something to say, and when they said something, they meant it. To him, simple language did not mark a simple mind, but a strong and fearless one. It was a sign of those who didn't hide their meaning behind a cloud of ambiguous words.

Mac, of course, never hid his opinions. Even if the tide was against him, he was forceful and clear and unflinching. I always knew where he stood, and so did the country. I could always count on him for the truth as he saw it, no matter how unpleasant or unpopular. There were times the Cabinet came down on an issue twelve to one, and he was on the short end. But I knew

* Malcolm Baldrige's wife and two daughters.

that if he believed something that others didn't, he wouldn't rein himself in and follow the herd. He would step forward and be clear.

What I'm saying about Mac Baldrige adds up to a simple but extraordinary quality that I would call, more than anything else, American. In his directness, in his honesty, in his independence, in his disregard for rank, in his courage, he embodied the best of the American spirit. I suppose we think of that spirit as living most of all in cowboys. And that's why I've always suspected that it was more than just roping and his place here in Washington that got Mac voted into the Cowboy Hall of Fame. He belonged there. It was in his blood. It was in his heart and soul.

Let me say a word about his many contributions to his country. These were not simple, although they were built on simple principles, principles like his reverence for the independence of the American character, for the freedom that lets independence flourish, and for the opportunities of a free society.

Mac was an architect of American international economic policy during years in which that policy moved to center stage. He also helped shape our policy toward East-West trade in a period in which that was a source of new questions and concerns. And perhaps the least recognized of his major achievements was the securing of trade ties with China. In just four years since his 1983 visit to China, trade has become a pillar of the Sino-American relationship.

To contribute so much required skill and persistence—qualities Mac had in abundance. It also required vision, vision not only for dealing with immediate issues but for the future of the entire world and its economy, as well.

I always prized the quality of Mac's vision. He had the capacity to look up from the dust of the plains to the distant mountains. He never forgot that all the skirmishes and battles over trade policy that we have here in Washington and around the world have one final goal: We're building a world in which our children and grandchildren will live. And we who love freedom and revere the dignity of humanity have a sacred duty to make that an open world of real hope and abundant opportunity, a world in which the spirit of freedom—yes, what you might call that part of the American spirit that lives in all of mankind—in which that spirit can ride across an open range toward the peaks beyond.

I'm told that Mac's staff had orders to interrupt him at whatever time of the day with calls from only two people. I was one, and any cowboy who rang up was the other. Well, I'm honored to have been in that company. Mac, as we know, left us while he was doing what he loved most. And now, whenever any of us wants to ring him up, we'll have to remind ourselves that he's out on a horse somewhere, and we'll just have to wait. Yet in his simplicity, he has entered the company of the men and women who have shaped our nation and its destiny, and he will live in that company forever.

Yes, there is sorrow, but the sorrow is with us and for us. We must believe that door is opened that God promised and he has just gone through that door into another life, where there is no more pain, no more sorrow. And we must believe that we, too, will one day go through that door and join him again.

Thank you. God bless you.

Remarks at a Ceremony
Honoring Residents of Chase, Maryland

OLD EXECUTIVE OFFICE BUILDING
FEBRUARY 3, 1987

I'm quite taken with heroes. And the wonderful thing is that they're all around us in our daily lives. During my presidency, I consistently tried to focus attention on those average Americans who are quietly heroic. And there are so many of them that I think this must just be part of the American character.

In the following ceremony, we honored an entire small community for their response to a terrible train wreck.

IT'S AN HONOR to have you all here at the White House. Now, I know that must sound strange. Most people think of it as an honor to be invited here, and that includes myself. I remember how humble I felt on that day in 1980 when the American people first asked me to come here. But today the tables are turned. For by your deeds, you and the members of your community have honored all America. You've shown us all, once again, the love and courage, the self-sacrifice and eagerness to help and serve those in need—in short, the qualities that for generations have been the heart of American life.

It was an ordinary winter's day at the end of the New Year's weekend. Some of you were hanging out laundry. Some of you were about to watch the football game. And then something happened—investigators are still piecing together just what it was—and your community was face-to-face with the worst accident in Amtrak history. And that's when, on that ordinary day, the people of Chase, Maryland, showed that what we take as ordinary in America is really very wonderful and special, very extraordinary.

Robert Booker and his cousin, Michael Cooper, were among the first on the scene. Robert climbed into a burning car. He couldn't save everyone. And I know that he and all of you've thought a great deal since that day about those whom God took into His arms, but also remember that there are many who are alive today because of your strength and courage. You gave to scores of people the gift of life.

As Michael and Robert worked together helping to pull people out of the train, Eve Booker and Juanita Mattes helped to care for the injured, cleaning their wounds, wrapping them, covering them with blankets from their homes to keep them warm. As one reporter wrote of Eve and Juanita: "They acted quickly, calmly, heroically. But when the night ended, the fifteen-year-olds wept."

Well, those stories of sacrifice and love were repeated hundreds of times that day. All of you and your neighbors helped people escape the wreck, helped care for them, feed them, and gave them shelter. Nancy Tharpe said there were forty-five passengers in her house on that Sunday. As Bob Cooper said later, "Everybody just chipped in and did what they had to do." And as a result, most of the passengers were out of the train even before the emergency crews arrived. In the hours and days that followed, you took into your homes not only the victims of the crash but rescue workers and reporters, too. I don't want to forget the magnificent work of those workers or the people who, within hours, lined up to give blood for the victims. They made us all proud, too.

Some have talked since about how amazing you were, and I know that Cathi Fischer spoke for all of you when she told a reporter, "I don't think it was anything remarkable. I think if it had been another community, they would have done the same thing." But that's just the point; you all did what Americans have done for more than two centuries: When others were in need, you didn't point to the other guys. You just rolled up your sleeves and went to work.

Not long ago a commentator on the network news show said that we Americans had become selfish, only out for ourselves, had lost our dedication to community and country. I know he's paid well to give his wisdom to the country each and every week. But for my money, the true wisdom is in Cathi Fischer's words, and the best answer to him is your example.

Yes, on an ordinary day in January, Americans in an ordinary American community showed extraordinary courage, self-sacrifice, and love for their fellow man. And when it was all over, you didn't brag and shout. You just went back to your daily work. But you left behind a gift not just for crash victims but for all of us. Your strength strengthened all Americans. Your spirit will long inspire and guide us all. And as president, I just asked you here today so I could say thanks.

Thank you all, and God bless you all.

And now I'd like to award the Private Sector Initiatives Commendation to the community of Chase, Maryland. And Robert Booker, will you please step forward and receive this? This is in recognition of the exemplary community service in the finest American tradition.

Thank you all very much. And just for my curiosity, where are the two young ladies sitting that that night cried? I know they're out there with you someplace. There you are. Well, God bless you.

Well, again, I hate to walk away and leave, but they tell me I've still got things to do over there. I haven't told this for a long time, but I got some letters from some young people when I first arrived in Washington. And one of them that always appealed to me was from a little girl and she wrote—and very informed about the things that were facing me and the problems I had to solve and everything. And when she finished she said, "Now, get back to the Oval Office, and get to work." [*Laughter*] So, that's what I'll do. Thank you all.

Address to the Nation
on the Tower Commission Report

OVAL OFFICE
MARCH 4, 1987

The Iran/contra mess got even worse in 1987. I had appointed a commission headed by former senator John Tower to get to the bottom of what had actually happened. The commission's report did not give us a clean bill of health. Something clearly went wrong with our initial plan.

I'm going to cover this more completely in my memoirs, but I get beside myself when I think that people believe I would actually trade arms for hostages. I fully realize that few people buy my argument, but for history's sake I simply feel compelled to make it.

The way I saw it was like this. If your child was kidnapped and someone who wasn't the kidnapper came to you and offered to help you find your child, I think most parents would take that help even if it cost you some money. By the same reasoning, I did not see it as trading arms for hostages because we were dealing with Iranian intermediaries, not the kidnap-

pers themselves. I know it may be a fine line to most people, but it's what I believed then and what I still believe.

I have to say that in looking back I wonder if this whole thing wasn't a setup, a sting operation, by the Iranians. Maybe we were conned into believing these were moderate Iranians seeking to reach out to the West, while in reality they were working directly for the Ayatollah just to get some arms. Who knows? Whatever the real story, the whole thing ended in a mess, but it certainly wasn't the end of the world as some up on Capitol Hill were wailing.

This address is the one I made to the people following the release of the Tower Commission's report.

M Y FELLOW AMERICANS:

I've spoken to you from this historic office on many occasions and about many things. The power of the presidency is often thought to reside within this Oval Office. Yet it doesn't rest here; it rests in you, the American people, and in your trust. Your trust is what gives a president his powers of leadership and his personal strength, and it's what I want to talk to you about this evening.

For the past three months, I've been silent on the revelations about Iran. And you must have been thinking: "Well, why doesn't he tell us what is happening? Why doesn't he just speak to us as he has in the past when we've faced troubles or tragedies?" Others of you, I guess, were thinking: "What's he doing hiding out in the White House?" Well, the reason I haven't spoken to you before now is this: You deserve the truth. And as frustrating as the waiting has been, I felt it was improper to come to you with sketchy reports, or possibly even erroneous statements, which would then have to be corrected, creating even more doubt and confusion. There's been enough of that.

I've paid a price for my silence in terms of your trust and confidence. But I've had to wait, as you have, for the complete story. That's why I appointed Ambassador David Abshire as my special counselor to help get out the thousands of documents to the various investigations. And I appointed a special review board, the Tower Board, which took on the chore of pulling the truth together for me and getting to the bottom of things. It has now issued its findings.

I'm often accused of being an optimist, and it's true I had to hunt pretty hard to find any good news in the Board's report. As you know, it's well stocked with criticisms, which I'll discuss in a moment; but I was very relieved to read this sentence: ". . . the Board is convinced that the President does indeed want the full story to be told." And that will continue to be my pledge to you as the other investigations go forward.

I want to thank the members of the panel: former senator John Tower, former secretary of state Edmund Muskie, and former national security adviser Brent Scowcroft. They have done the nation, as well as me personally, a great service by submitting a report of such integrity and depth. They have my genuine and enduring gratitude.

I've studied the Board's report. Its findings are honest, convincing, and highly critical; and I accept them. And tonight I want to share with you my thoughts on these findings and report to you on the actions I'm taking to implement the Board's recommendations.

First, let me say I take full responsibility for my own actions and for those of my administration. As angry as I may be about activities undertaken without my knowledge, I am still accountable for those activities. As disappointed as I may be in some who served me, I'm still the one who must answer to the American people for this behavior. And as personally distasteful as I find secret bank accounts and diverted funds—well, as the Navy would say, this happened on my watch.

Let's start with the part that is the most controversial. A few months ago I told the American people I did not trade arms for hostages. My heart and my best intentions still tell me that's true, but the facts and the evidence tell me it is not. As the Tower Board reported, what began as a strategic opening to

Iran deteriorated, in its implementation, into trading arms for hostages. This runs counter to my own beliefs, to administration policy, and to the original strategy we had in mind. There are reasons why it happened, but no excuses. It was a mistake.

I undertook the original Iran initiative in order to develop relations with those who might assume leadership in a post-Khomeini government. It's clear from the Board's report, however, that I let my personal concern for the hostages spill over into the geopolitical strategy of reaching out to Iran. I asked so many questions about the hostages' welfare that I didn't ask enough about the specifics of the total Iran plan.

Let me say to the hostage families: We have not given up. We never will. And I promise you we'll use every legitimate means to free your loved ones from captivity. But I must also caution that those Americans who freely remain in such dangerous areas must know that they're responsible for their own safety.

Now, another major aspect of the Board's findings regards the transfer of funds to the Nicaraguan contras. The Tower Board wasn't able to find out what happened to this money, so the facts here will be left to the continuing investigations of the court-appointed Independent Counsel and the two congressional investigating committees. I'm confident the truth will come out about this matter, as well. As I told the Tower Board, I didn't know about any diversion of funds to the contras. But as president, I cannot escape responsibility.

Much has been said about my management style, a style that's worked successfully for me during eight years as governor of California and for most of my presidency. The way I work is to identify the problem, find the right individuals to do the job, and then let them go to it. I've found this invariably brings out the best in people. They seem to rise to their full capability, and in the long run you get more done.

When it came to managing the NSC staff, let's face it, my style didn't match its previous track record. I've already begun correcting this. As a start, yesterday I met with the entire professional staff of the National Security Council. I defined for them the values I want to guide the national security policies of this country. I told them that I wanted a policy that was as justifiable and understandable in public as it was in secret. I wanted a policy that reflected the will of the Congress as well as of the White House. And I told them that there'll be no more free-lancing by individuals when it comes to our national security.

You've heard a lot about the staff of the National Security Council in recent months. Well, I can tell you, they are good and dedicated government employees, who put in long hours for the nation's benefit. They are eager and anxious to serve their country.

One thing still upsetting me, however, is that no one kept proper records of meetings or decisions. This led to my failure to recollect whether I approved an arms shipment before or after the fact. I did approve it; I just can't say specifically when. Well, rest assured, there's plenty of record keeping now going on at 1600 Pennsylvania Avenue.

For nearly a week now, I've been studying the Board's report. I want the American people to know that this wrenching ordeal of recent months has not been in vain. I endorse every one of the Tower Board's recommendations. In fact, I'm going beyond its recommendations so as to put the house in even better order.

I'm taking action in three basic areas: personnel, national security policy, and the process for making sure that the system works. *First,* personnel—I've brought in an accomplished and highly respected new team here at the White House. They bring new blood, new energy, and new credibility and experience.

Former senator Howard Baker, my new chief of staff, possesses a breadth of legislative and foreign affairs skills that's impossible to match. I'm hopeful that his experience as minority and majority leader of the Senate can help us forge a new partnership with the Congress, especially on foreign and national security policies. I'm genuinely honored that he's given up his own presidential aspirations to serve the country as my chief of staff.

Frank Carlucci, my new national security adviser, is respected for his experience in government and trusted for his judgment and counsel. Under him, the NSC staff is being rebuilt with proper management discipline. Already, almost half the NSC professional staff is comprised of new people.

Yesterday I nominated William Webster, a man of sterling reputation, to be director of the Central Intelligence Agency. Mr. Webster has served as director of the FBI and as a U.S. District Court judge. He understands the meaning of "rule of law."

So that his knowledge of national security matters can be available to me on a continuing basis, I will also appoint John Tower to serve as a member of my Foreign Intelligence Advisory Board. I am considering other changes in personnel, and I'll move more furniture, as I see fit, in the weeks and months ahead.

Second, in the area of national security policy, I have ordered the NSC to begin a comprehensive review of all covert operations. I have also directed that any covert activity be in support of clear policy objectives and in compliance with American values. I expect a covert policy that if Americans saw it on the front page of their newspaper, they'd say, "That makes sense." I have had issued a directive prohibiting the NSC staff itself from undertaking covert operations—no ifs, ands, or buts. I have asked Vice President Bush to reconvene his task force on terrorism to review our terrorist policy in light of the events that have occurred.

Third, in terms of the process of reaching national security decisions, I am adopting in total the Tower report's model of how the NSC process and staff should work. I am directing Mr. Carlucci to take the necessary steps to make that happen. He will report back to me on further reforms that might be needed. I've created the post of NSC legal adviser to assure a greater sensitivity to matters of law.

I am also determined to make the congressional oversight process work. Proper procedures for consultation with the Congress will be followed, not only in letter but in spirit. Before the end of March, I will report to the Congress on all the steps I've taken in line with the Tower Board's conclusions.

Now, what should happen when you make a mistake is this: You take your knocks, you learn your lessons, and then you move on. That's the healthiest way to deal with a problem. This in no way diminishes the importance of the other continuing investigations, but the business of our country and our people must proceed. I've gotten this message from Republicans and Democrats in Congress, from allies around the world, and—if we're reading the signals right—even from the Soviets. And of course, I've heard the message from you, the American people.

You know, by the time you reach my age, you've made plenty of mistakes. And if you've lived your life properly—so, you learn. You put things in perspective. You pull your energies together. You change. You go forward.

My fellow Americans, I have a great deal that I want to accomplish with you and for you over the next two years. And the Lord willing, that's exactly what I intend to do.

Good night, and God bless you.

Remarks at the Memorial Service for Crew Members of the USS *Stark*

MAYPORT NAVAL STATION
JACKSONVILLE, FLORIDA
MAY 22, 1987

Another heartbreaking memorial. It was always agony deliver-ing them, but I felt that as commander in chief it was my duty. I felt it was important to be there with the families.

One of the hardest things for a president to do is to send our boys into harm's way. The USS Stark *was mistakenly attacked by an Iraqi fighter jet while patrolling the Persian Gulf. There was a lot of debate at the time about whether we should keep the sea-lanes open. I think it is clear now that this decision helped to bring the war between Iran and Iraq to an end. Some of our seamen paid a price for this with their lives.*

Not too long after the loss, I saw something that caught my eye in the paper. The widow of one of the crewmen had found her husband's Bible, scorched on the outside but otherwise in-tact, amid the warped metal and ashes of his bunk. It was the only thing that survived the attack.

OUR TASK TODAY is simple and sad: to remember, to pay tribute to those we loved.

For some of us here today, our love is the unquenchable, unforgetting love of a wife or child for a fallen father, of a mother or father for a fallen son. For others of us, this love, while more distant, is still anguished and grieving; ours is a love for a fallen countryman who died so that we, a free people, might live and this great nation endure.

Even as we hear these words, we understand again their inadequacy. We appreciate anew Lincoln's humble wisdom at Gettysburg. When brave men die, it is their deeds, not our words, that are remembered. It is their sacrifice, not our brief recollection, that offers everlasting testimony to their love for others, and their love for us.

But we're human, and today we know such great heartache. So, we come to this place to seek the simple assurance of each other and the hope of finding a higher meaning, a greater purpose. And so we ask: Why did this happen? Why to them? Could anything be worth such a sacrifice? And these fallen, whom we knew and loved but rarely thought of as great men or legends, can we now truly say they are heroes? And even if we can, would we not rather have them back, ordinary men again perhaps, but still ours to hold and keep?

The answers are hard. Hard because memory forces some of us to remember other faraway places which Americans have never heard of until their sons and brothers and fathers and friends fell there. Each Memorial Day, and especially with the news of the past week, my own mind has turned many times to the great war of forty-six years ago. Few of us who lived through it can ever forget those opening months of conflict, when our nation and our fighting men were so sorely tested.

In later years, in the South Pacific campaign, American sailors would speak often of the bravery of the marines they put on the beaches to fight and die; but one night, especially, off a place called Guadalcanal, as the shellfire lit the darkness in one of the most violent surface actions ever seen, it was the marines who stood in awe and in silent tribute to the men of the United States Navy. Hopelessly outnumbered and outgunned, a small group of U.S. ships had taken on a powerful enemy fleet. And though five Medals of Honor were won and the enemy was turned back and Guadalcanal was saved, the price was so high and the burden so heavy—nine ships and hundreds of young lives. And none of us who were alive then can forget the special burden of grief borne by Mr. and Mrs. Thomas Sullivan of Waterloo, Iowa. They would remember forever the autumn afternoon they learned that their sons—George, Francis, Joseph, Madison, and Albert—The Five Sullivans as we knew them then, would not be coming home.

But while our sorrow was great in those days, I cannot help but tell you this morning that in some ways it was easier to bear then, because it was easier to understand why we were there and why we were fighting. The burden of our own time is so different. And when young Americans like those of the USS *Stark* die in far-off seas, we learn again how right President Kennedy was when he spoke of the sacrifices asked by a "hard and bitter peace" and our own "long twilight struggle."

Even at moments like these, then, we must address directly the reason the USS *Stark* and her men were there in the Persian Gulf. You're entitled to know the importance of the role that their valor played in keeping our world safe for peace and freedom. There's a reason why since 1949 American ships have patrolled the gulf. Every American president since World War II has understood the strategic importance of this region: It is a region that is a crossroads for three continents and the starting place for the oil that is the lifeblood of much of the world economy, especially those of our allies in Europe. Even more important, this is a region critical to avoiding larger conflict in the tinderbox that is the Middle East, and our role there is essential to building the conditions for peace in that troubled, dangerous part of the world. And it is this objective that has guided us as we've sought to end the brutal war between Iran and Iraq, a war that has gone on for over six and a half terrible years and taken such an awful toll on human life.

Peace is at stake here, and so too is our own nation's security and our freedom. Were a hostile power ever to dominate this strategic region and its resources, it would become a choke-point for freedom—that of our allies and our own. And that's why we maintain a naval presence there. Our aim is to prevent, not to provoke, wider conflict, to save the many lives that further conflict would cost us.

The fallen sailors of the USS *Stark* understood their obligations; they knew the importance of their job. So, too, I believe that most Americans today know the price of freedom in this uneasy world. They know that to retreat or withdraw would only repeat the improvident mistakes of the past and hand final victory to those who seek war, who make war, who know it would only invite further aggression and tragedy. So, it's a simple truth we reaffirm here today: Young Americans of the USS *Stark* gave up their lives so that the terrible moments of the past would not be repeated, so that wider war and greater conflict could be avoided, so that thousands, and perhaps millions, of others might be spared the final sacrifice these men so willingly made.

So, we ask again: Were they heroes? "Heroes are not supermen," Herman Wouk once reminded us, "they're good men, and embodied by the cast of destiny, the virtue of a whole people in a great hour." And writing of the thousands of such heroes in our nation, men and women who wear our country's uniform in this troubled peace of ours, he asked us to never forget "to reassure them that their hard, long training is needed, that love of country is noble, that self-sacrifice is rewarding, that to be ready to fight for freedom fills a man with a sense of worth like nothing else." And he said, "If America is still the great beacon in dense gloom, the promise to hundreds of millions of the oppressed that liberty exists, that it is the shining future, that they can throw off their tyrants, and learn freedom and cease learning war, then we still" need heroes "to stand guard in the night."

The men of the USS *Stark* stood guard in the night. One of our ambassadors paid them this tribute: "They were tough, they were brave, they were great." Well, they were great, and those that died did embody the best of us. Yes, they were ordinary men who did extraordinary things. Yes, they were heroes. And because they were heroes, let us not forget this: That for all the lovely spring and summer days we will never share with them again, for every Thanksgiving and Christmas that will seem empty without them, there will be other moments, too, moments when we see the light of discovery in young eyes, eyes that see for the first time the world around them and know the sweep of history and wonder, "Why is there such a place as America, and how is it that such a precious gift is mine?"

And we can answer them. We can answer them by telling of this day and those that we come to honor here. And it's then we'll see understanding in those young eyes; it is then they will know the same gratitude and pride that we share today, the gratitude and pride Americans feel always for those who suffer and die so that the precious gift of America might always be ours.

The men of the USS *Stark* have protected us; they have done their duty. Now let us do ours. Senior Chief Gary Clinefelter showed us how yesterday. He had volunteered to work at the coordinating center here for the families when he received word that his own son, Seaman Brian Clinefelter, previously listed as missing in action, was among the confirmed dead. "I need to keep working," he said. He stayed at his post; he carried on.

Well, so, too, we must carry on. We must stay at our post. We must keep faith with their sacrifice. In our great hour, we must answer, as did they, the call of history. It's a summons that, as a nation or a people, we did not seek, but it is a call we cannot shirk or refuse—a call to wage war against war, to stand for freedom until freedom can stand alone, to live for liberty until liberty is the blessing and birthright of every man, woman, and child on this earth.

And let us remember a final duty: to understand that these men made themselves immortal by dying for something immortal, that theirs is the best to be asked of any life—a sharing of

the human heart, a sharing in the infinite. In giving themselves for others, they made themselves special, not just to us but to their God. "Greater love than this has no man than to lay down his life for his friends." And because God is love, we know He was there with them when they died and that He is with them still. We know they live again, not just in our hearts but in His arms. And we know they've gone before to prepare a way for us.

So, today we remember them in sorrow and in love. We say good-bye. And as we submit to the will of Him who made us, we pray together the words of scripture: "Lord, now let thy servants go in peace, Thy word has been fulfilled."

May I point out again, so many of you have known long months of separation from your loved ones, from these young men. You were separated by distance, by miles of land and ocean. Now you are separated again, not just by territorial limits but because they have stepped through that door that God has promised all of us. They do live now in a world where there is no sorrow, no pain. And they await us, and we shall all be together again.

God bless you.

Remarks at the Brandenburg Gate

WEST BERLIN
JUNE 12, 1987

The Brandenburg Gate and the Berlin Wall separate Berlin into East and West. In spite of the changes that are going on in Communist countries, especially the Soviet Union, that wall is a reminder of the difference between freedom and totalitarianism. The people of East Berlin are walled in with barbed wire and booby-trapped explosives.

Our advance people had put up speakers aimed at East Berlin, hoping that my speech might be heard on the other side. I could see the East German police keeping people away so that they couldn't hear. They simply don't realize it's going to take more than that to keep out the stirrings of freedom.

There's a couple sentences in this speech about tearing down the wall and opening the gate that I like quite a bit, and it actually makes the speech. I'm told that the State Department and the National Security Council thought the lines were too provocative.

Just because our relationship with the Soviet Union is improving doesn't mean we have to begin denying the truth. That is what got us into such a weak position with the Soviet Union in the first place. The line stayed and got quite a reaction from the crowd.

T HANK YOU VERY MUCH.

Chancellor Kohl, Governing Mayor Diepgen, ladies and gentlemen:

Twenty-four years ago, President John F. Kennedy visited Berlin, speaking to the people of this city and the world at the City Hall. Well, since then two other presidents have come, each in his turn, to Berlin. And today I, myself, make my second visit to your city.

We come to Berlin, we American presidents, because it's our duty to speak, in this place, of freedom. But I must confess, we're drawn here by other things as well: by the feeling of history in this city, more than five hundred years older than our own nation; by the beauty of the Grünewald and the Tiergarten; most of all, by your courage and determination.

Perhaps the composer Paul Lincke understood something about American presidents. You see, like so many presidents before me, I come here today because wherever I go, whatever I do: *Ich hab noch einen Koffer in Berlin.* [I still have a suitcase in Berlin.]

Our gathering today is being broadcast throughout Western Europe and North America. I understand that it is being seen and heard as well in the East. To those listening throughout Eastern Europe, I extend my warmest greetings and the goodwill of the American people. To those listening in East Berlin, a special word: Although I cannot be with you, I address my remarks to you just as surely as to those standing here before me. For I join you, as I join your fellow countrymen in the West, in this firm, this unalterable belief: *Es gibt nur ein Berlin.* [There is only one Berlin.]

Behind me stands a wall that encircles the free sectors of this city, part of a vast system of barriers that divides the entire continent of Europe. From the Baltic, south, those barriers cut across Germany in a gash of barbed wire, concrete, dog runs, and guard towers. Farther south, there may be no visible, no obvious wall. But there remain armed guards and checkpoints all the same—still a restriction on the right to travel, still an instrument to impose upon ordinary men and women the will of a totalitarian state. Yet it is here in Berlin where the wall emerges most clearly; here, cutting across your city, where the news photo and the television screen have imprinted this brutal division of a continent upon the mind of the world. Standing before the Brandenburg Gate, every man is a German, separated from his fellow men. Every man is a Berliner, forced to look upon a scar.

President von Weizsäcker has said, "The German question is open as long as the Brandenburg Gate is closed." Today I say: As long as this gate is closed, as long as this scar of a wall is permitted to stand, it is not the German question alone that remains open, but the question of freedom for all mankind. Yet I do not come here to lament. For I find in Berlin a message of hope, even in the shadow of this wall, a message of triumph.

In this season of spring in 1945, the people of Berlin emerged from their air-raid shelters to find devastation. Thousands of miles away, the people of the United States reached out to help. And in 1947 Secretary of State—as you've been told—George Marshall announced the creation of what would become known as the Marshall Plan. Speaking precisely forty years ago this month, he said: "Our policy is directed not against any country or doctrine, but against hunger, poverty, desperation, and chaos."

In the Reichstag a few moments ago, I saw a display commemorating this fortieth anniversary of the Marshall Plan. I was struck by the sign on a burnt-out, gutted structure that was being rebuilt. I understand that Berliners of my own generation can remember seeing signs like it dotted throughout the western sectors of the city. The sign read simply: "The Marshall Plan is helping here to strengthen the free world." A strong, free world in the West, that dream became real. Japan rose from ruin to become an economic giant. Italy, France, Belgium—virtually every nation in Western Europe saw political and economic rebirth; the European Community was founded.

In West Germany and here in Berlin, there took place an economic miracle, the *Wirtschaftswunder.* Adenauer, Erhard,

Reuter, and other leaders understood the practical importance of liberty—that just as truth can flourish only when the journalist is given freedom of speech, so prosperity can come about only when the farmer and businessman enjoy economic freedom. The German leaders reduced tariffs, expanded free trade, lowered taxes. From 1950 to 1960 alone, the standard of living in West Germany and Berlin doubled.

Where four decades ago there was rubble, today in West Berlin there is the greatest industrial output of any city in Germany—busy office blocks, fine homes and apartments, proud avenues, and the spreading lawns of parkland. Where a city's culture seemed to have been destroyed, today there are two great universities, orchestras and an opera, countless theaters, and museums. Where there was want, today there's abundance —food, clothing, automobiles—the wonderful goods of the Ku'damm. From devastation, from utter ruin, you Berliners have, in freedom, rebuilt a city that once again ranks as one of the greatest on earth. The Soviets may have had other plans. But my friends, there were a few things the Soviets didn't count on—*Berliner Herz, Berliner Humor, ja, und Berliner Schnauze.* [Berliner heart, Berliner humor, yes, and a Berliner *Schnauze.*] [*Laughter*]

In the 1950s, Khrushchev predicted: "We will bury you." But in the West today, we see a free world that has achieved a level of prosperity and well-being unprecedented in all human history. In the Communist world, we see failure, technological backwardness, declining standards of health, even want of the most basic kind—too little food. Even today, the Soviet Union still cannot feed itself. After these four decades, then, there stands before the entire world one great and inescapable conclusion: Freedom leads to prosperity. Freedom replaces the ancient hatreds among the nations with comity and peace. Freedom is the victor.

And now the Soviets themselves may, in a limited way, be coming to understand the importance of freedom. We hear much from Moscow about a new policy of reform and openness. Some political prisoners have been released. Certain foreign news broadcasts are no longer being jammed. Some economic enterprises have been permitted to operate with greater freedom from state control.

Are these the beginnings of profound changes in the Soviet state? Or are they token gestures, intended to raise false hopes in the West, or to strengthen the Soviet system without changing it? We welcome change and openness; for we believe that freedom and security go together, that the advance of human liberty can only strengthen the cause of world peace. There is one sign the Soviets can make that would be unmistakable, that would advance dramatically the cause of freedom and peace.

General Secretary Gorbachev, if you seek peace, if you seek prosperity for the Soviet Union and Eastern Europe, if you seek liberalization: Come here to this gate! Mr. Gorbachev, open this gate! Mr. Gorbachev, tear down this wall!

I understand the fear of war and the pain of division that afflict this continent—and I pledge to you my country's efforts to help overcome these burdens. To be sure, we in the West must resist Soviet expansion. So we must maintain defenses of unassailable strength. Yet we seek peace; so we must strive to reduce arms on both sides.

Beginning ten years ago, the Soviets challenged the Western alliance with a grave new threat, hundreds of new and more deadly SS-20 nuclear missiles, capable of striking every capital in Europe. The Western alliance responded by committing itself to a counterdeployment unless the Soviets agreed to negotiate a better solution; namely, the elimination of such weapons on both sides. For many months, the Soviets refused to bargain in earnestness. As the alliance, in turn, prepared to go forward with its counterdeployment, there were difficult days—days of protests like those during my 1982 visit to this city—and the Soviets later walked away from the table.

But through it all, the alliance held firm. And I invite those who protested then—I invite those who protest today—to mark this fact: Because we remained strong, the Soviets came back to the table. And because we remained strong, today we have within reach the possibility, not merely of limiting the growth of arms, but of eliminating, for the first time, an entire class of nuclear weapons from the face of the earth.

As I speak, NATO ministers are meeting in Iceland to review the progress of our proposals for eliminating these weapons. At the talks in Geneva, we have also proposed deep cuts in strategic offensive weapons. And the Western allies have likewise made far-reaching proposals to reduce the danger of conventional war and to place a total ban on chemical weapons.

While we pursue these arms reductions, I pledge to you that we will maintain the capacity to deter Soviet aggression at any level at which it might occur. And in cooperation with many of our allies, the United States is pursuing the Strategic Defense Initiative—research to base deterrence not on the threat of offensive retaliation, but on defenses that truly defend; on systems, in short, that will not target populations, but shield them. By these means we seek to increase the safety of Europe and all the world. But we must remember a crucial fact: East and West do not mistrust each other because we are armed; we are armed because we mistrust each other. And our differences are not about weapons but about liberty. When President Kennedy spoke at the City Hall those twenty-four years ago, freedom was encircled, Berlin was under siege. And today, despite all the pressures upon this city, Berlin stands secure in its liberty. And freedom itself is transforming the globe.

In the Philippines, in South and Central America, democracy has been given a rebirth. Throughout the Pacific, free markets are working miracle after miracle of economic growth. In the industrialized nations, a technological revolution is taking place —a revolution marked by rapid, dramatic advances in computers and telecommunications.

In Europe, only one nation and those it controls refuse to join the community of freedom. Yet in this age of redoubled economic growth, of information and innovation, the Soviet Union faces a choice: It must make fundamental changes, or it will become obsolete.

Today thus represents a moment of hope. We in the West stand ready to cooperate with the East to promote true openness, to break down barriers that separate people, to create a safer, freer world. And surely there is no better place than Berlin, the meeting place of East and West, to make a start. Free people of Berlin: Today, as in the past, the United States stands for the strict observance and full implementation of all parts of the Four Power Agreement of 1971. Let us use this occasion, the 750th anniversary of this city, to usher in a new era, to seek a still fuller, richer life for the Berlin of the future. Together, let us maintain and develop the ties between the Federal Republic and the Western sectors of Berlin, which is permitted by the 1971 agreement.

And I invite Mr. Gorbachev: Let us work to bring the Eastern and Western parts of the city closer together, so that all the inhabitants of all Berlin can enjoy the benefits that come with life in one of the great cities of the world.

To open Berlin still further to all Europe, East and West, let us expand the vital air access to this city, finding ways of making commercial air service to Berlin more convenient, more comfortable, and more economical. We look to the day when West Berlin can become one of the chief aviation hubs in all central Europe.

With our French and British partners, the United States is prepared to help bring international meetings to Berlin. It would be only fitting for Berlin to serve as the site of United Nations meetings, or world conferences on human rights and arms control or other issues that call for international cooperation.

There is no better way to establish hope for the future than to enlighten young minds, and we would be honored to sponsor summer youth exchanges, cultural events, and other programs for young Berliners from the East. Our French and British friends, I'm certain, will do the same. And it's my hope that an authority can be found in East Berlin to sponsor visits from young people of the Western sectors.

One final proposal, one close to my heart: Sport represents a source of enjoyment and ennoblement, and you may have noted that the Republic of Korea—South Korea—has offered to permit certain events of the 1988 Olympics to take place in the North. International sports competitions of all kinds could take place in both parts of this city. And what better way to demonstrate to the world the openness of this city than to offer in some future year to hold the Olympic games here in Berlin, East and West?

In these four decades, as I have said, you Berliners have built a great city. You've done so in spite of threats—the Soviet attempts to impose the East-mark, the blockade. Today the city thrives in spite of the challenges implicit in the very presence of this wall. What keeps you here? Certainly there's a great deal to be said for your fortitude, for your defiant courage. But I believe there's something deeper, something that involves Berlin's whole look and feel and way of life—not mere sentiment. No one could live long in Berlin without being completely disabused of illusions. Something instead, that has seen the difficulties of life in Berlin but chose to accept them, that continues to build this good and proud city in contrast to a surrounding totalitarian presence that refuses to release human energies or aspirations. Something that speaks with a powerful voice of affirmation, that says yes to this city, yes to the future, yes to freedom. In a word, I would submit that what keeps you in Berlin is love—love both profound and abiding.

Perhaps this gets to the root of the matter, to the most fundamental distinction of all between East and West. The totalitarian world produces backwardness because it does such violence to the spirit, thwarting the human impulse to create, to enjoy, to worship. The totalitarian world finds even symbols of love and of worship an affront. Years ago, before the East Germans began rebuilding their churches, they erected a secular structure: the television tower at Alexander Platz. Virtually ever since, the authorities have been working to correct what they view as the tower's one major flaw, treating the glass sphere at the top with paints and chemicals of every kind. Yet even today when the sun strikes that sphere—that sphere that towers over

355

all Berlin—the light makes the sign of the cross. There in Berlin, like the city itself, symbols of love, symbols of worship, cannot be suppressed.

As I looked out a moment ago from the Reichstag, that embodiment of German unity, I noticed words crudely spray-painted upon the wall, perhaps by a young Berliner: "This wall will fall. Beliefs become reality." Yes, across Europe, this wall will fall. For it cannot withstand faith; it cannot withstand truth. The wall cannot withstand freedom.

And I would like, before I close, to say one word. I have read, and I have been questioned since I've been here about certain demonstrations against my coming. And I would like to say just one thing, and to those who demonstrate so. I wonder if they have ever asked themselves that if they should have the kind of government they apparently seek, no one would ever be able to do what they're doing again.

Thank you and God bless you all.

Remarks at the Memorial Service for Edith Luckett Davis

ST. THOMAS THE APOSTLE
ROMAN CATHOLIC CHURCH
PHOENIX, ARIZONA
OCTOBER 31, 1987

Nancy and her mother were as close to each other as anything I've ever seen. They would talk every night. Even a couple of years after Edie's death, Nancy is still recovering.

I was crazy about my mother-in-law. In fact, after I met her I was never able to tell another mother-in-law joke again, which is something considering how much I like to tell stories. When I became president, Edie would call me whenever she heard a good joke, and she especially enjoyed those that were a little risqué. She was a remarkable woman and I miss her, too.

Father John Doran. We want to welcome all of you to St. Thomas the Apostle Parish. In a sense, it's a home parish for Edie, for though she was not a Catholic, she began coming to this parish in 1951, when we were a little barracks built on the back of the property.

And she, as a matter of fact, became one of the first benefactors of this parish, where she came one Sunday in the old, cold barracks—and we were sitting on folding chairs—and she said, "We've got to do something about this parish." So, she went back up to the Biltmore, and she said, "There's a bunch of you rich Catholics around here, and you've got to do something for that young, little"—years ago—"young, little priest that is trying to build a parish. Now, I'm going to give a bingo game Sunday night, and you're going to come, and you're going to dish out." And thus it happened. When she said something, it happened. And she came down the next day very gleefully with a pocket—or with a bagful of money that she had made for the parish that night.

So, that was her beginning here, and it carried on. As the parish grew, she continued to be a part of it. And one day about eighteen years ago, when Edie wasn't feeling particularly well at that time, Loyal got me aside, and he said, "Father, you've got to make a promise to me." I said, "What?" He said, "When Edie dies, you've got to bury her, and you've got to bury her down in that church, where she's been going all these years."

So, we are fulfilling a promise. And Nancy and I looked at each other the other night, and we said, "We're fulfilling a promise to Edie. We're also fulfilling a promise to Loyal."

So, it is very appropriate that you join with us today, as we say a very happy word of memory to a very happy person. So, we continue now.

The President. How do we say good-bye to someone we've loved for so long, someone of innate tenderness who loved us? Indeed, she loved all humankind. We all have our memories, precious memories. I became acquainted with Deedie by telephone. When Nancy and I were courting, if she were calling her mother or her mother calling her and I was there, she—well, she introduced me to Deedie on the phone. And then she would put me on the phone to visit for a while. And it was quite a time before we met face-to-face, but when we did, we were already close friends.

To paraphrase Winston Churchill, meeting her was "like opening a bottle of champagne." Nancy and I spent our honeymoon with Deedie and Loyal here in Arizona. And after getting to know her and after a period of that kind together, I have to tell you I have never been able to tell a mother-in-law story or joke since.

Somerset Maugham wrote a line that could have been for her: "When you have loved as she has loved, you grow old beautifully."

Many people who only knew about Deedie will remember her as the lady who headed up the great fund-raising charity in Chicago for twenty-five years. Many more will remember her for all that she did here in Phoenix, raising millions of dollars, particularly for children who were disabled or handicapped. But there are countless more individuals who will remember her for what she did for them, personally, when they had a problem or a trouble or something that made them need help.

She didn't just recognize the cop on the corner; they were personal friends. She knew countless other people who just crossed her path—delivery boys, the cleaning woman, Dr. Loyal's patients, and yes, his students in the medical school at Northwestern University.

My first inkling of how well she was known and loved came some years ago when, at that time, my television sponsor had brought me to Chicago to appear at a kind of forum. It ran late, and I came out; it was dark. And I was supposed to meet Deedie and Loyal. They had told me the name of the cafe, and I was to meet them for dinner. And I told the doorman about this and that I needed some instructions as to where was that cafe. And was it far enough away that I needed transportation?

And in doing so, I, without realizing it, I told him who I was meeting. And he just raised his hand when I said that name.

And he left me and went out to the curb, and he started looking, I suppose, for a cab. But the traffic was stopped for the stoplight on the corner, and there was a police car. And he waved the police car over to the curb, and he told them about me and who I was meeting and that I needed to get there. And the next thing I knew, I was a passenger in a police car with two officers who knew Deedie Davis and who drove me right to the door as quickly as they could.

On another occasion, Nancy and I were coming into Chicago on the overnight train from New York, getting in early in the morning in the midst of a blizzard. And there wasn't a redcap in sight. The porters on the cars took the luggage off and sat it down there on the ramp. We were quite a ways from the station.

In that blizzard, and all up and down the train, were all the passengers trying to sort out the luggage and trying to find their own bags. And Nancy and I looked up, and coming down the ramp was Deedie, arm in arm with two redcaps. [*Laughter*] They were having quite a conversation. And as they got closer, I heard she was talking to one about his daughter, and by name. She knew his daughter, also, and how was she getting along in school? And by that time they were close to us. And Deedie said, "Oh, this is my son and daughter. Could you help them with their luggage?" And so the five of us went back up the ramp. And now Edie was arm in arm with both of us, and the two redcaps were carrying our baggage past hundreds of passengers who had no such help.

I remembered one thing that I've never forgotten. She said to her two friends when they caught up with us that I was her son and Nancy her daughter. She didn't say son-in-law.

She gave wit and charm and kindliness throughout all of her life. She also raised a son who was a respected surgeon, an honorable man, caring father and husband. And she gave the world a loving daughter, a woman who has made my life complete.

In the midst of our grief, Dick and Nancy, I hope you'll take

How do we say good-bye to someone we've
loved for so long, because of such sweet tenderness
who loved us. Indeed she loved all humankind.

We all have our memories – precious memories. I
became acquainted with Doris by telephone. When Nancy
& I were ... creating, if I was there when Nancy
was phoning her mother ... Doris could hear she
would put me on the ...
by phone.

It was quite a ...
But when we did ...
paroxysme Winston ...
opening a bottle of P...

Nancy & I spent ...
here in Virginia ...
since that wonderful ...

Somerset Maugham ...
been for Doris's ...
grow old beautifully...

Many people ...
about her, will ...
... among other...
fond of Chi. for ...
resident but a ye...
all she did for Ch...
disabilities & boxes...
in addition to ...
who had ... previous.

But there ...

for what she did for them personally when they had
need for help of whatever kind.

She didn't first recognize the cop on the corner, like
knew him as a personal friend. Just as she knew
countless other people who crossed her path – delivery boys,
the cleaning woman, Dr. Lo; ... nor his medical
... at North Weston

My first inkling of D...
come some years ago.
looked me to partic...
in Chi. Coming out...
behind schedule. I ...
due at a dinner and ...
asked directions – wa...
I need a cab. Some...
was giving the drive...
... & said that's ...
more minutes." He ...
hail a cab. It...
because of the I...
them into the ...
... I was to ...
as a passeng...
knew Doris ...

On a ...
by over ...
blizzardly ...
some dist...
Porters g... grief – Doil...
You were lov...

Yes we w...
Let us be re...
for the loss...
from her ...
but has ...
no pain ...

snow. There wasn't a red-cap in sight. Passengers
the whole length of the train were trying to get their
bags together in the freezing cold, ourselves included –
Suddenly we looked up and saw Doris coming down the
ramp arm in arm with 2 red-caps.
As they got closer it was apparent they were old friends.
Doris was inquiring about their daughter of one of them &
how she was doing in school. As they reached us she said,
"Oh this is my son & daughter – could you give them a
hand with their luggage?"

Back up the ramp we went – the 5 of us & this time
Doris was arm in arm with us and the red-caps
had our bags. We passed the hundreds of passengers still
trying to sort out their luggage. Ours was the only 2 red-caps
in the entire station & she & her son in law.

She gave the world wit & charm & kindliness. She
also raised a son who is a respected surgeon, an
honorable man & a caring father & husband. She
gave the world a loving daughter & husband. And she
made my life ... And in the midst of any
... comfort in this

Where she is... smiling, loving Doris we all
remember. She is there once again
with Lyon – surrounded by other kind in law
... persued son. And yes with she & loving ones who
today looking at us – to be with she – here in this place
the world as to be happy, loving kindness...
all be together again. And I do know Doris will
after life we've been promised we by John Doris, that
because she's been there a while ... better
... our coming

comfort from this: that you were loving children, and you made Deedie happy and very proud.

Yes, all of us who are gathered here feel great sorrow. But let's be sure we know the sorrow is for ourselves, for the loss that we now feel. But let us realize that Deedie has just gone through a door from this life to that other life that God promised us, that life that is eternal, where no one is old, where there's no pain or sorrow, and where she is a smiling and loving Deedie we all remember, now once again hand in hand with Loyal, surrounded by others of her loved ones who have preceded her there.

And she's looking back on us with that loving kindness. Yes, she's here. She's seeing us and hearing us now. She's wanting us to be happy in knowing that one day, we will all be together again. And if I know Deedie, that other life that we've been promised will even be better, because she's been there for a while before we arrived.

1988

Veterans Day Ceremony

VIETNAM VETERANS MEMORIAL
NOVEMBER 11, 1988

I feel very good about the last year of my presidency. Things really came together. I worked hard to elect George Bush as president. The trip to Moscow was a big success. The economy continued to expand with more people at work than ever in our history. And as journalist Lou Cannon has said of my last year in the White House—I was president until the moment I left the place. I like that.

If I had to pick out one speech in 1988 that most represented what I had accomplished over my two terms in office, the following speech might be the one. I feel very good when people say that one of my accomplishments was restoring the spirit and faith of America, because I tried very hard to do that. I think one area where there may be evidence of this is the attitude toward our Vietnam veterans.

A good friend of mine, Dennis LeBlanc, fought in Vietnam. Only three were left alive out of his squadron. When he came back to college, the kids found out he'd been in Vietnam; they called him murderer and shunned him. What kind of welcome home was that for a young man who had risked his life for his country? It hurt when I first heard that story.

One of the best letters I ever received as president was from a Vietnam veteran in Texas who said that I'd helped him hold his head up. If I did have anything to do with that, my entire two terms in office would be worth it.

Well, THANK YOU, JACK WHEELER,* thank you very much. I shall treasure that gift. And to all of you, thanks, and good morning.

Before I begin, let me take a moment to congratulate the Vietnam Veterans Memorial Fund and the other distinguished guests without whom the construction and operation of this memorial would not have been possible. Let me also say that America is grateful to the hundreds of Vietnam veterans who, when I asked them to join my administration, did so, and have and are serving our nation so proudly. For your devotion to America, I salute you.

We're gathered today, just as we have gathered before, to remember those who served, those who fought, those still missing, and those who gave their last full measure of devotion for our country. We're gathered at a monument on which the names of our fallen friends and loved ones are engraved, and with crosses instead of diamonds beside them, the names of those whose fate we do not yet know. One of those who fell wrote, shortly before his death, these words: "Take what they have left and what they have taught you with their dying and keep it with your own. And take one moment to embrace those gentle heroes you left behind."

Well, today, Veterans Day, as we do every year, we take that moment to embrace the gentle heroes of Vietnam and of all our wars. We remember those who were called upon to give all a person can give, and we remember those who were prepared to make that sacrifice if it were demanded of them in the line of duty, though it never was. Most of all, we remember the devotion and gallantry with which all of them ennobled their nation as they became champions of a noble cause.

I'm not speaking provocatively here. Unlike the other wars

* John Wheeler, chairman of the Vietnam Veterans Memorial Fund. He gave the President a bronze replica of the "Three Fighting Men" statue, which is a part of the memorial.

of this century, of course, there were deep divisions about the wisdom and rightness of the Vietnam War. Both sides spoke with honesty and fervor. And what more can we ask in our democracy? And yet after more than a decade of desperate boat people, after the killing fields of Cambodia, after all that has happened in that unhappy part of the world, who can doubt that the cause for which our men fought was just? It was, after all, however imperfectly pursued, the cause of freedom; and they showed uncommon courage in its service. Perhaps at this late date we can all agree that we've learned one lesson: that young Americans must never again be sent to fight and die unless we are prepared to let them win.

But beyond that, we remember today that all our gentle heroes of Vietnam have given us a lesson in something more: a lesson in living love. Yes, for all of them, those who came back and those who did not, their love for their families lives. Their love for their buddies on the battlefields and friends back home lives. Their love of their country lives.

This memorial has become a monument to that living love. The thousands who come to see the names testify to a love that endures. The messages and mementos they leave speak with a whispering voice that passes gently through the surrounding trees and out across the breast of our peaceful nation. A childhood teddy bear, a photograph of the son or daughter born too late to know his or her father, a battle ribbon, a note—there are so many of these, and all are testimony to our living love for them. And our nation itself is testimony to the love our veterans have had for it and for us. Our liberties, our values, all for which America stands is safe today because brave men and women have been ready to face the fire at freedom's front. And we thank God for them.

Yes, gentle heroes and living love and our memories of a time when we faced great divisions here at home. And yet if this place recalls all this, both sweet and sad, it also reminds us of a great and profound truth about our nation: that from all our divisions we have always eventually emerged strengthened. Perhaps we are finding that new strength today, and if so, much of it comes from the forgiveness and healing love that our Vietnam veterans have shown.

For too long a time, they stood in a chill wind, as if on a winter night's watch. And in that night, their deeds spoke to us, but we knew them not. And their voices called to us, but we heard them not. Yet in this land that God has blessed, the dawn always at last follows the dark, and now morning has come. The night is over. We see these men and know them once again —and know how much we owe them, how much they have given us, and how much we can never fully repay. And not just as individuals but as a nation, we say we love you.

These days, we show our love in many ways—some of it through the government. We now fly the POW–MIA flag at this memorial on Memorial Day, Veterans Day, and POW–MIA Recognition Day. This is a small gesture, but a significant one. America also keeps a vigil for those who have not yet returned. We have negotiated with the Vietnamese to bring our nation's sons home, and for the first time, too, have joint teams investigating remote areas of Vietnam that might shed light on the fate of those we list as missing. In Laos, we have also begun a new round of surveys and excavations of crash sites. And we have told Hanoi that it must prove to the American people through its cooperation whether men are still being held against their will in Indochina. Otherwise we will assume some are, and we will do everything we can to find them.

Here, at home, a new Department of Veterans Affairs and extended veterans benefits are merely outward and visible signs of an inward and invisible grace that has come to our land. Vietnam service is once more universally recognized as a badge of pride. Four years ago, I noted that this healing had begun and that I hoped that before my days as commander in chief were over it would be completed. Well, now as I approach the end of my service and I see Vietnam veterans take their rightful place among America's heroes, it appears to me that we have healed. And what can I say to our Vietnam veterans but, Welcome home.

Now before I go, as have so many others, Nancy and I

wanted to leave a note at the wall. And if I may read it to you before doing so, we will put this note here before we leave:

"Our young friends—yes, young friends, for in our hearts you will always be young, full of the love that is youth, love of life, love of joy, love of country—you fought for your country and for its safety and for the freedom of others with strength and courage. We love you for it. We honor you. And we have faith that, as He does all His sacred children, the Lord will bless you and keep you, the Lord will make His face to shine upon you and give you peace, now and forever more."

Thank you all, and God bless you.

Remarks at the White House Correspondents Dinner

WASHINGTON, D.C.

APRIL 21, 1988

One thing I kept wanting to put in this book was a speech from one of the humorous dinners and roasts I frequently attended —the Alfalfa Dinner, the Radio and TV Correspondents Dinner, the Gridiron Dinner, and so forth. I would go every year to these things, and the format calls for you to be funny. The problem is that political humor just doesn't read very funny a few years after the fact.

I thought I would put this one in, however, just to give you a feel for these events.

THANK YOU ALL, and I'm delighted to be here. My, what a crowd. Looks like the index of Larry Speakes's book. [*Laughter*] It's good to see Norm Sandler,* and your incoming president, Jerry O'Leary.

In his book, Larry said that Jerry used to fill his coat pockets with pastry. Jerry denies it. Earlier tonight, just to be safe, I told him, keep his hands off my dinner roll. [*Laughter*] Larry also said that preparing me for a press conference was like reinventing the wheel. It's not true. I was around when the wheel was invented, and it was easier. [*Laughter*] But even Howard Baker's writing a book about me. It's called *Three by Five, the Measure of a Presidency*. [*Laughter*] Mike Deaver, in his book, said that I had a short attention span. Well, I was going to reply to that, but—oh, what the hell, let's move on to something else. [*Laughter*]

Now, I forgot to acknowledge Yakov Smirnov. I've heard him before, and he's a very funny man. And I just have an idea here. Why don't you and I have a little fun? How would you like to go to the summit as my interpreter? [*Laughter*]

But the media has certainly had a lot to report on lately. I thought it was extraordinary that Richard Nixon went on *Meet the Press* and spent an entire hour with Chris Wallace, Tom Brokaw, and John Chancellor. That should put an end to that talk that he's been punished enough. [*Laughter*] And of course, you've been reporting on the New York primary. I'm afraid that Dukakis's foreign policy views are a little too far left for me. He wants no U.S. military presence in Korea anymore, no U.S. military presence in Central America, and no U.S. military presence at the Pentagon. [*Laughter*] Dukakis got great news today, though, about the Jimmy Carter endorsement—he isn't getting it. [*Laughter*]

George Bush is doing well. George has been a wonderful vice president, but nobody's perfect. [*Laughter*] I put him in charge

* The outgoing president of the Association.

of antiterrorism, and the McLaughlin Group is still on the air. [*Laughter*] But with so much focus on the presidential election, I've been feeling a little lonely these days. I'm so desperate for attention I almost considered holding a news conference. [*Laughter*] I've even had time to watch the Oscars. I was a little disappointed in that movie *The Last Emperor.* I thought it was going to be about Don Regan. [*Laughter*]

Of course, I still have lots of work here. There is that Panamanian business going on. One thing I can't figure: If the Congress wants to bring the Panamanian economy to its knees, why doesn't it just go down there and run it? [*Laughter*]

Ladies and gentlemen, this is the last White House Correspondents Dinner that I'll be attending. We've had our disagreements over the years, but the time I've spent with you has been very educational. [*Laughter*] I used to think the fourth estate was one of Walter Annenberg's homes. [*Laughter*]

As my good-bye, I'm not going to stand up here and deliver one of those worn-out sentimental homilies about the press and the presidency. Neither of us would believe it. [*Laughter*] A president may like members of the press personally, and I do— Jerry and Norm and Johanna and Lou and so many others of you—but a president institutionally seeks to wield power to accomplish his goals for the people. The press complicates the wielding of that power by using its own great power, and that makes for friction. Every president will try to use the press to his best advantage and to avoid those situations that aren't to his advantage. To do otherwise results in a diminution of his leadership powers. The press is not a weak sister that needs bracing. It has more freedom, more influence, than ever in our history. The press can take care of itself quite nicely. And a president should be able to take care of himself as well. So, what I hope my epitaph will be with the White House correspondents, what every president's epitaph should be with the press is this: He gave as good as he got. [*Laughter*] And that I think will make for a healthy press and a healthy presidency. And I think all that's left to say is to thank you for inviting me, and thank you for your hospitality.

Remarks and
Question-and-Answer Session
with Students at
Moscow State University

MAY 31, 1988

The trip to Moscow was one of the most intriguing experiences of my years in office. You can understand more about a place by just seeing it. One thing I noticed was that there is such a visible break in the history of the Russian people. It's right there in the architecture.

You see the splendor and glory of the czars, such as I saw at the Kremlin Palace, and Nancy also saw at some of the marvelous palaces in Leningrad. It's no wonder there was a revolution. The wealth of that country was obviously bled from the people for the personal benefit of the czars. And then you see the drab, gray, cold structures of communism. And again you see that the people don't have a lot because the wealth of the country is used to support the state, only this time it is the Communist government and its military that eats up whatever wealth there is.

The architecture of Moscow State University is quite ominous. The university is housed in this threatening, yes, evil-looking, building erected by Stalin. But speaking to these students, I felt I could have been speaking to students any-where. The coldness disappeared.

What a step forward it was just being there in that audito-rium with the big bust of Lenin right behind me. I couldn't speak to the entire student body because the hall wasn't large enough, so the Soviets only let in students who were members of the Young Communist League. I didn't know that at the time, but it didn't seem to make any difference because I could feel that I was still getting a good reaction. I could see the students turn to each other and nod every once in a while, occasionally smile. I came away from there with a very good feeling.

I had complete freedom to explain America to these young Communists. This is how I made our case.

The President. Thank you, Rector Logunov, and I want to thank all of you very much for a warm welcome. It's a great pleasure to be here at Moscow State University, and I want to thank you all for turning out. I know you must be very busy this week, studying and taking your final examinations. So, let me just say *zhelayu vam uspekha* [I wish you success]. Nancy couldn't make it today because she's visiting Leningrad, which she tells me is a very beautiful city, but she, too, says hello and wishes you all good luck.

Let me say it's also a great pleasure to once again have this opportunity to speak directly to the people of the Soviet Union. Before I left Washington, I received many heartfelt letters and telegrams asking me to carry here a simple message, perhaps, but also some of the most important business of this summit: It is a message of peace and goodwill and hope for a growing friendship and closeness between our two peoples.

As you know, I've come to Moscow to meet with one of your most distinguished graduates. In this, our fourth summit, General Secretary Gorbachev and I have spent many hours to-gether, and I feel that we're getting to know each other well. Our discussions, of course, have been focused primarily on many of the important issues of the day, issues I want to touch on with you in a few moments. But first I want to take a little time to talk to you much as I would to any group of university students in the United States. I want to talk not just of the realities of today but of the possibilities of tomorrow.

Standing here before a mural of your revolution, I want to talk about a very different revolution that is taking place right now, quietly sweeping the globe without bloodshed or conflict. Its effects are peaceful, but they will fundamentally alter our world, shatter old assumptions, and reshape our lives. It's easy to underestimate because it's not accompanied by banners or fanfare. It's been called the technological or information revolution, and as its emblem, one might take the tiny silicon chip, no bigger than a fingerprint. One of these chips has more computing power than a roomful of old-style computers.

As part of an exchange program, we now have an exhibition touring your country that shows how information technology is transforming our lives—replacing manual labor with robots, forecasting weather for farmers, or mapping the genetic code of DNA for medical researchers. These microcomputers today aid the design of everything from houses to cars to spacecraft; they even design better and faster computers. They can translate English into Russian or enable the blind to read or help Michael Jackson produce on one synthesizer the sounds of a whole orchestra. Linked by a network of satellites and fiber-optic cables, one individual with a desktop computer and a telephone commands resources unavailable to the largest governments just a few years ago.

Like a chrysalis, we're emerging from the economy of the Industrial Revolution—an economy confined to and limited by the earth's physical resources—into, as one economist titled his book, "the economy in mind," in which there are no bounds on human imagination and the freedom to create is the most precious natural resource. Think of that little computer chip. Its value isn't in the sand from which it is made but in the microscopic architecture designed into it by ingenious human minds. Or take the example of the satellite relaying this broadcast around the world, which replaces thousands of tons of copper mined from the earth and molded into wire. In the new economy, human invention increasingly makes physical resources obsolete. We're breaking through the material conditions of existence to a world where man creates his own destiny. Even as we explore the most advanced reaches of science, we're returning to the age-old wisdom of our culture, a wisdom contained in the book of Genesis in the Bible: In the beginning was the spirit, and it was from this spirit that the material abundance of creation issued forth.

But progress is not foreordained. The key is freedom—freedom of thought, freedom of information, freedom of communication. The renowned scientist, scholar, and founding father of this university, Mikhail Lomonosov, knew that. "It is common knowledge," he said, "that the achievements of science are considerable and rapid, particularly once the yoke of slavery is cast off and replaced by the freedom of philosophy." You know, one of the first contacts between your country and mine took place between Russian and American explorers. The Americans were members of Cook's last voyage on an expedition searching for an Arctic passage; on the island of Unalaska, they came upon the Russians, who took them in, and together, with the native inhabitants, held a prayer service on the ice.

The explorers of the modern era are the entrepreneurs, men with vision, with the courage to take risks and faith enough to brave the unknown. These entrepreneurs and their small enterprises are responsible for almost all the economic growth in the United States. They are the prime movers of the technological revolution. In fact, one of the largest personal computer firms in the United States was started by two college students, no older than you, in the garage behind their home. Some people, even in my own country, look at the riot of experiment that is the free market and see only waste. What of all the entrepreneurs that fail? Well, many do, particularly the successful ones; often several times. And if you ask them the secret of their success, they'll tell you it's all that they learned in their struggles along the way; yes, it's what they learned from failing. Like an athlete in competition or a scholar in pursuit of the truth, experience is the greatest teacher.

And that's why it's so hard for government planners, no matter how sophisticated, to ever substitute for millions of individuals working night and day to make their dreams come true. The fact is, bureaucracies are a problem around the world. There's an old story about a town—it could be anywhere—with a bureaucrat who is known to be a good-for-nothing, but he somehow had always hung on to power. So one day, in a town meeting, an old woman got up and said to him: "There is a folk legend here where I come from that when a baby is born, an angel comes down from heaven and kisses it on one part of its body. If the angel kisses him on his hand, he becomes a handyman. If he kisses him on his forehead, he becomes bright and clever. And I've been trying to figure out where the angel kissed you so that you should sit there for so long and do nothing." [*Laughter*]

We are seeing the power of economic freedom spreading around the world. Places such as the Republic of Korea, Singapore, Taiwan, have vaulted into the technological era, barely pausing in the industrial age along the way. Low-tax agricultural policies in the subcontinent mean that in some years India is now a net exporter of food. Perhaps most exciting are the winds of change that are blowing over the People's Republic of China, where one-quarter of the world's population is now getting its first taste of economic freedom. At the same time, the growth of democracy has become one of the most powerful political movements of our age. In Latin America in the 1970s, only a third of the population lived under democratic government; today over 90 percent does. In the Philippines, in the Republic of Korea, free, contested, democratic elections are the order of the day. Throughout the world, free markets are the model for growth. Democracy is the standard by which governments are measured.

We Americans make no secret of our belief in freedom. In fact, it's something of a national pastime. Every four years the American people choose a new president, and 1988 is one of those years. At one point there were thirteen major candidates running in the two major parties, not to mention all the others, including the Socialist and Libertarian candidates—all trying to get my job. About 1,000 local television stations, 8,500 radio stations, and 1,700 daily newspapers—each one an independent, private enterprise, fiercely independent of the government—report on the candidates, grill them in interviews, and bring them together for debates. In the end, the people vote; they decide who will be the next president.

But freedom doesn't begin or end with elections. Go to any American town, to take just an example, and you'll see dozens of churches, representing many different beliefs—in many places, synagogues and mosques—and you'll see families of every conceivable nationality worshiping together. Go into any schoolroom, and there you will see children being taught the Declaration of Independence, that they are endowed by their Creator with certain unalienable rights—among them life, liberty, and the pursuit of happiness—that no government can justly deny; the guarantees in their Constitution for freedom of speech, freedom of assembly, and freedom of religion.

Go into any courtroom, and there will preside an independent judge, beholden to no government power. There every defendant has the right to a trial by a jury of his peers, usually twelve men and women—common citizens; they are the ones, the only ones, who weigh the evidence and decide on guilt or innocence. In that court, the accused is innocent until proven guilty, and the word of a policeman or any official has no greater legal standing than the word of the accused.

Go to any university campus, and there you'll find an open, sometimes heated discussion of the problems in American society and what can be done to correct them. Turn on the television, and you'll see the legislature conducting the business of government right there before the camera, debating and voting on the legislation that will become the law of the land. March in any demonstration, and there are many of them; the people's right of assembly is guaranteed in the Constitution and protected by the police. Go into any union hall, where the members know their right to strike is protected by law. As a matter of fact, one of the many jobs I had before this one was being president of a union, the Screen Actors Guild. I led my union out on strike, and I'm proud to say we won.

But freedom is more even than this. Freedom is the right to question and change the established way of doing things. It is the continuing revolution of the marketplace. It is the understanding that allows us to recognize shortcomings and seek solutions. It is the right to put forth an idea, scoffed at by the experts, and watch it catch fire among the people. It is the right to dream—to follow your dream or stick to your conscience, even if you're the only one in a sea of doubters. Freedom is the recognition that no single person, no single authority or government has a monopoly on the truth, but that every individual life is infinitely precious, that every one of us put on this world has been put there for a reason and has something to offer.

America is a nation made up of hundreds of nationalities. Our ties to you are more than ones of good feeling; they're ties of kinship. In America, you'll find Russians, Armenians, Ukrainians, peoples from Eastern Europe and Central Asia. They come from every part of this vast continent, from every continent, to live in harmony, seeking a place where each cultural heritage is respected, each is valued for its diverse strengths and beauties and the richness it brings to our lives. Recently, a few individuals and families have been allowed to visit relatives in the West. We can only hope that it won't be long before all are allowed to do so and Ukrainian Americans, Baltic Americans, Armenian Americans, can freely visit their homelands, just as the Irish American visits his.

Freedom, it has been said, makes people selfish and materialistic, but Americans are one of the most religious peoples on earth. Because they know that liberty, just as life itself, is not earned but a gift from God, they seek to share that gift with the world. "Reason and experience," said George Washington in his farewell address, "both forbid us to expect that national morality can prevail in exclusion of religious principle. And it is substantially true, that virtue or morality is a necessary spring of popular government." Democracy is less a system of government than it is a system to keep government limited, unintrusive; a system of constraints on power to keep politics and government secondary to the important things in life, the true sources of value found only in family and faith.

But I hope you know I go on about these things not simply to extol the virtues of my own country but to speak to the true greatness of the heart and soul of your land. Who, after all, needs to tell the land of Dostoevski about the quest for truth, the home of Kandinski and Scriabin about imagination, the rich and noble culture of the Uzbek man of letters Alisher Navoi about beauty and heart? The great culture of your diverse land speaks with a glowing passion to all humanity. Let me cite one of the most eloquent passages on human freedom. It comes, not from the literature of America, but from this country, from one of the greatest writers of the twentieth century, Boris Pasternak, in the novel *Dr. Zhivago.* He writes: "I think that if the beast who sleeps in man could be held down by threats—any kind of threat, whether of jail or of retribution after death—then the highest emblem of humanity would be the lion tamer in the circus with his whip, not the prophet who sacrificed himself. But this is just the point—what has for centuries raised man above the beast is not the cudgel, but an inward music—the irresistible power of unarmed truth."

The irresistible power of unarmed truth. Today the world looks expectantly to signs of change, steps toward greater freedom in the Soviet Union. We watch and we hope as we see positive changes taking place. There are some, I know, in your society who fear that change will bring only disruption and discontinuity, who fear to embrace the hope of the future. Sometimes it takes faith. It's like that scene in the cowboy movie *Butch Cassidy and the Sundance Kid,* which some here in Moscow recently had a chance to see. The posse is closing in on the two outlaws, Butch and Sundance, who find themselves trapped on the edge of a cliff, with a sheer drop of hundreds of feet to the raging rapids below. Butch turns to Sundance and says their only hope is to jump into the river below, but Sundance refuses. He says he'd rather fight it out with the posse, even though they're hopelessly outnumbered. Butch says that's suicide and urges him to jump, but Sundance still refuses and finally admits, "I can't swim." Butch breaks up laughing and says, "You crazy fool, the fall will probably kill you." And, by the way, both Butch and Sundance made it, in case you didn't see the movie. I think what I've just been talking about is *perestroika* and what its goals are.

But change would not mean rejection of the past. Like a tree growing strong through the seasons, rooted in the earth and drawing life from the sun, so, too, positive change must be rooted in traditional values—in the land, in culture, in family and community—and it must take its life from the eternal things, from the source of all life, which is faith. Such change will lead to new understandings, new opportunities, to a broader future in which the tradition is not supplanted but finds its full flowering. That is the future beckoning to your generation.

At the same time, we should remember that reform that is not institutionalized will always be insecure. Such freedom will always be looking over its shoulder. A bird on a tether, no matter how long the rope, can always be pulled back. And that is why, in my conversation with General Secretary Gorbachev, I have spoken of how important it is to institutionalize change —to put guarantees on reform. And we've been talking together about one sad reminder of a divided world: the Berlin Wall. It's time to remove the barriers that keep people apart.

I'm proposing an increased exchange program of high school students between our countries. General Secretary Gorbachev mentioned on Sunday a wonderful phrase you have in Russian for this: "Better to see something once than to hear about it a hundred times." Mr. Gorbachev and I first began working on this in 1985. In our discussion today, we agreed on working up to several thousand exchanges a year from each country in the near future. But not everyone can travel across the continents and oceans. Words travel lighter, and that's why we'd like to make available to this country more of our 11,000 magazines and periodicals and our television and radio shows that can be beamed off a satellite in seconds. Nothing would please us more than for the Soviet people to get to know us better and to understand our way of life.

Just a few years ago, few would have imagined the progress our two nations have made together. The INF treaty, which General Secretary Gorbachev and I signed last December in Washington and whose instruments of ratification we will exchange tomorrow—the first true nuclear arms reduction treaty in history, calling for the elimination of an entire class of U.S. and Soviet nuclear missiles. And just sixteen days ago, we saw the beginning of your withdrawal from Afghanistan, which gives us hope that soon the fighting may end and the healing may begin and that that suffering country may find self-determination, unity, and peace at long last.

It's my fervent hope that our constructive cooperation on these issues will be carried on to address the continuing destruction of conflicts in many regions of the globe and that the serious discussions that led to the Geneva accords on Afghanistan will help lead to solutions in southern Africa, Ethiopia, Cambodia, the Persian Gulf, and Central America.

I have often said: Nations do not distrust each other because they are armed; they are armed because they distrust each other. If this globe is to live in peace and prosper, if it is to embrace all the possibilities of the technological revolution, then nations must renounce, once and for all, the right to an expansionist foreign policy. Peace between nations must be an enduring goal, not a tactical stage in a continuing conflict.

I've been told that there's a popular song in your country—perhaps you know it—whose evocative refrain asks the question, "Do the Russians want a war?" In answer it says: "Go ask that silence lingering in the air, above the birch and poplar there; beneath those trees the soldiers lie. Go ask my mother, ask my wife; then you will have to ask no more, 'Do the Russians want a war?' " But what of your onetime allies? What of those who embraced you on the Elbe? What if we were to ask the watery graves of the Pacific or the European battlefields where America's fallen were buried far from home? What if we were to ask their mothers, sisters, and sons, do Americans want war? Ask us, too, and you'll find the same answer, the same longing in every heart. People do not make wars; governments do. And no mother would ever willingly sacrifice her sons for territorial gain, for economic advantage, for ideology. A people free to choose will always choose peace.

Americans seek always to make friends of old antagonists. After a colonial revolution with Britain, we have cemented for all ages the ties of kinship between our nations. After a terrible civil war between North and South, we healed our wounds and found true unity as a nation. We fought two world wars in my lifetime against Germany and one with Japan, but now the Federal Republic of Germany and Japan are two of our closest allies and friends.

Some people point to the trade disputes between us as a sign of strain, but they're the frictions of all families, and the family of free nations is a big and vital and sometimes boisterous one. I can tell you that nothing would please my heart more than in my lifetime to see American and Soviet diplomats grappling with the problem of trade disputes between America and a growing, exuberant, exporting Soviet Union that had opened up to economic freedom and growth. And as important as these official people-to-people exchanges are, nothing would please me more than for them to become unnecessary, to see travel between East and West become so routine that university students in the Soviet Union could take a month off in the summer and just like students in the West do now, put packs on their backs and travel from country to country in Europe with barely a passport check in between. Nothing would please me more than to see the day that a concert promoter in, say, England could call up a Soviet rock group, without going through any government agency, and have them playing in Liverpool the next night. Is this just a dream? Perhaps. But it is a dream that is our responsibility to have come true.

Your generation is living in one of the most exciting, hopeful times in Soviet history. It is a time when the first breath of freedom stirs the air and the heart beats to the accelerated rhythm of hope, when the accumulated spiritual energies of a long silence yearns to break free. I am reminded of the famous passage near the end of Gogol's *Dead Souls.* Comparing his nation to a speeding troika, Gogol asks what will be its destination. But he writes, "There was no answer save the bell pouring forth marvelous sound."

We do not know what the conclusion will be of this journey, but we're hopeful that the promise of reform will be fulfilled. In this Moscow spring, this May 1988, we may be allowed that hope: that freedom, like the fresh green sapling planted over Tolstoi's grave, will blossom forth at last in the rich fertile soil of your people and culture. We may be allowed to hope that the marvelous sound of a new openness will keep rising through, ringing through, leading to a new world of reconciliation, friendship, and peace.

Thank you all very much, and *da blagoslovit vas gospod*—God bless you.

Mr. Logunov. Dear friends, Mr. President has kindly agreed to answer your questions. But since he doesn't have too much time, only fifteen minutes—so, those who have questions, please ask them.

Q. And this is a student from the history faculty, and he says that he's happy to welcome you on behalf of the students of the university. And the first question is that the improvement in the relations between the two countries has come about during your tenure as president, and in this regard he would like to ask the following question. It is very important to get a handle on the question of arms control and specifically, the limitation of strategic arms. Do you think that it will be possible for you and the General Secretary to get a treaty on the limitation of strategic arms during the time that you are still president?

The President. Well, the arms treaty that is being negotiated now is the so-called START treaty, and it is based on taking the intercontinental ballistic missiles and reducing them by half, down to parity between our two countries. Now, this is a much more complicated treaty than the INF treaty, the intermediate-range treaty, which we have signed and which our two governments have ratified and is now in effect. So, there are many things still to be settled. You and we have had negotiators in Geneva for months working on various points of this treaty. Once we had hoped that maybe, like the INF treaty, we would have been able to sign it here at this summit meeting. It is not completed; there are still some points that are being debated. We are both hopeful that it can be finished before I leave office, which is in the coming January, but I assure you that if it isn't —I assure you that I will have impressed on my successor that we must carry on until it is signed. My dream has always been that once we've started down this road, we can look forward to a day, you can look forward to a day, when there will be no more nuclear weapons in the world at all.

Q. The question is: The universities influence public opinion, and the student wonders how the youths have changed since the days when you were a student up until now?

The President. Well, wait a minute. How you have changed since the era of my own youth?

Q. How just students have changed, the youth have changed. You were a student. [*Laughter*] At your time there were one type. How they have changed?

The President. Well, I know there was a period in our country when there was a very great change for the worst. When I was governor of California, I could start a riot just by going to a campus. But that has all changed, and I could be looking out at an American student body as well as I'm looking out here and would not be able to tell the difference between you.

I think that back in our day—I did happen to go to school, get my college education in a unique time; it was the time of the Great Depression, when, in a country like our own, there was 25 percent unemployment and the bottom seemed to have fallen out of everything. But we had—I think what maybe I should be telling you from my point here, because I graduated in 1932, that I should tell you that when you get to be my age, you're going to be surprised how much you recall the feelings you had in these days here and that how easy it is to understand the young people because of your own having been young once. You know an awful lot more about being young than you do about being old. [*Laughter*]

And I think there is a seriousness, I think there is a sense of responsibility that young people have, and I think that there is an awareness on the part of most of you about what you want your adulthood to be and what the country you live in—you want it to be. And I have a great deal of faith. I said the other day to seventy-six students—they were half American and half Russian. They had held a conference here and in Finland and then in the United States, and I faced them just the other day, and I had to say—I couldn't tell the difference looking at them, which were which, but I said one line to them. I said I believe that if all the young people of the world today could get to know each other, there would never be another war. And I think that of you. I think that of the other students that I've addressed in other places.

And of course, I know also that you're young and therefore there are certain things that at times take precedence. I'll illustrate one myself. Twenty-five years after I graduated, my alma mater brought me back to the school and gave me an honorary degree. And I had to tell them they compounded a sense of guilt I had nursed for twenty-five years because I always felt the first degree they gave me was honorary. [*Laughter*] You're great. Carry on.

Q. Mr. President, you have just mentioned that you welcome the efforts—settlement of the Afghanistan question and the difference of other regional conflicts. What conflicts do you mean? Central America conflicts, Southeast Asian, or South African?

The President. Well, for example, in South Africa, where Namibia has been promised its independence as a nation—another new African nation. But it is impossible because of a civil war going on in another country there, and that civil war is being fought on one side by some 30,000 to 40,000 Cuban troops who have gone from the Americas over there and are fighting on one side with one kind of authoritative government. When that country was freed from being a colony and given its independence, one faction seized power and made itself the government of that nation. And leaders of another—seemingly the majority of the people had wanted simply the people to have the right to choose the government that they wanted, and that is the civil war that is going on. But what we believe is that those foreign soldiers should get out and let them settle it, let the citizens of that nation settle their problems.

And the same is true in Nicaragua. Nicaragua has been— Nicaragua made a promise. They had a dictator. There was a revolution, there was an organization that—and was aided by others in the revolution, and they appealed to the Organization of American States for help in getting the dictator to step down and stop the killing. And he did. But the Organization of American States had asked, what are the goals of the revolution? And they were given in writing, and they were the goals of pluralistic society, of the right of unions and freedom of speech and press and so forth and free elections—a pluralistic society. And then the one group that was the best organized among the revolutionaries seized power, exiled many of the other leaders, and has its own government, which violated every one of the promises that had been made. And here again, we want—we're trying to encourage the getting back those—or making those promises come true and letting the people of that particular country decide their fate.

Q. Esteemed Mr. President, I'm very much anxious and concerned about the destiny of 310 Soviet soldiers being missing in Afghanistan. Are you willing to help in their search and their return to the motherland?

The President. Very much so. We would like nothing better than that.

Q. The reservation of the inalienable rights of citizens guaranteed by the Constitution faces certain problems; for example, the right of people to have arms, or for example, the problem appears, an evil appears whether spread of pornography or narcotics is compatible with these rights. Do you believe that these problems are just unavoidable problems connected with democracy, or they could be avoided?

The President. Well, if I understand you correctly, this is a question about the inalienable rights of the people—does that include the right to do criminal acts—for example, in the use of drugs, and so forth? No. [*Applause*] No, we have a set of laws. I think what is significant and different about our system is that every country has a constitution, and most constitutions or practically all of the constitutions in the world are documents in which the government tells the people what the people can do. Our Constitution is different, and the difference is in three words; it almost escapes everyone. The three words are "We the people." Our Constitution is a document in which we the people tell the government what its powers are. And it can have no powers other than those listed in that document. But very carefully, at the same time, the people give the government the power with regard to those things which they think would be destructive to society, to the family, to the individual and so forth—infringements on their rights. And thus, the government can enforce the laws. But that has all been dictated by the people.

Q. Mr. President, from history I know that people who have been connected with great power, with big posts, say good-bye, leave these posts with great difficulty. Since your term of office is coming to an end, what sentiments do you experience and whether you feel like, if, hypothetically, you can just stay for another term? [*Laughter*]

The President. Well, I'll tell you something. I think it was a kind of revenge against Franklin Delano Roosevelt, who was elected four times—the only president. There had kind of grown a tradition in our country about two terms. That tradition was started by Washington, our first president, only because there was great talk at the formation of our country that we might become a monarchy, and we had just freed ourselves from a monarchy. So, when the second term was over, George Washington stepped down and said he would do it—stepping down—so that there would not get to be the kind of idea of an inherited aristocracy. Well, succeeding presidents—many of them didn't get a chance at a second term; they did one term and were gone. But that tradition kind of remained. But it was just a tradition. And then Roosevelt ran the four times—died very early in his fourth term. And suddenly, in the atmosphere at that time, they added an amendment to the Constitution that presidents could only serve two terms.

When I get out of office—I can't do this while I'm in office, because it will look as if I'm selfishly doing it for myself—when I get out of office, I'm going to travel around, what I call the mashed-potato circuit—that is the after-dinner speaking to luncheon groups and so forth—I'm going to travel around and try to convince the people of our country that they should wipe out that amendment to the Constitution because it was an interference with the democratic rights of the people. The people should be allowed to vote for who they wanted to vote for, for as many times as they want to vote for him; and that it is they who are being denied a right. But you see, I will no longer be president then, so I can do that and talk for that.

There are a few other things I'm going to try to convince the people to impress upon our Congress, the things that should be done. I've always described it that if—in Hollywood, when I was there, if you didn't sing or dance, you wound up as an after-dinner speaker. And I didn't sing or dance. [*Laughter*] So, I have a hunch that I will be out on the speaking circuit, telling about a few things that I didn't get done in government, but urging the people to tell the Congress they wanted them done.

Q. Mr. President, I've heard that a group of American Indians have come here because they couldn't meet you in the United

States of America. If you fail to meet them here, will you be able to correct it and to meet them back in the United States?

The President. I didn't know that they had asked to see me. If they've come here or whether to see them there—[*Laughter*]— I'd be very happy to see them.

Let me tell you just a little something about the American Indian in our land. We have provided millions of acres of land for what are called preservations—or reservations, I should say. They, from the beginning, announced that they wanted to maintain their way of life, as they had always lived there in the desert and the plains and so forth. And we set up these reservations so they could, and have a Bureau of Indian Affairs to help take care of them. At the same time, we provide education for them—schools on the reservations. And they're free also to leave the reservations and be American citizens among the rest of us, and many do. Some still prefer, however, that way—that early way of life. And we've done everything we can to meet their demands as to how they want to live. Maybe we made a mistake. Maybe we should not have humored them in that wanting to stay in that kind of primitive lifestyle. Maybe we should have said, no, come join us; be citizens along with the rest of us. As I say, many have; many have been very successful.

And I'm very pleased to meet with them, talk with them at any time and see what their grievances are or what they feel they might be. And you'd be surprised: Some of them became very wealthy because some of those reservations were overlaying great pools of oil, and you can get very rich pumping oil. And so, I don't know what their complaint might be.

Q. Mr. President, I'm very much tantalized since yesterday evening by the question, why did you receive yesterday—did you receive and when you invite yesterday—refuseniks or dissidents? And for the second part of the question is, just what are your impressions from Soviet people? And among these dissidents, you have invited a former collaborator with a fascist, who was a policeman serving for fascists.

The President. Well, that's one I don't know about, or maybe the information hasn't been all given out on that. But you have to understand that Americans come from every corner of the world. I received a letter from a man that called something to my attention recently. He said, you can go to live in France, but you cannot become a Frenchman; you can go to live in Germany, you cannot become a German—or a Turk or a Greek or whatever. But he said anyone, from any corner of the world, can come to live in America and become an American.

You have to realize that we are a people that are made up of every strain, nationality, and race of the world. And the result is that when people in our country think someone is being mistreated or treated unjustly in another country, these are people who still feel that kinship to that country because that is their heritage. In America, whenever you meet someone new and become friends, one of the first things you tell each other is what your bloodline is. For example, when I'm asked, I have to say Irish, English, and Scotch—English and Scotch on my mother's side, Irish on my father's side. But all of them have that.

Well, when you take on to yourself a wife, you do not stop loving your mother. So, Americans all feel a kind of a kinship to that country that their parents or their grandparents or even some great-grandparents came from; you don't lose that contact. So, what I have come and what I have brought to the General Secretary—and I must say he has been very cooperative about it—I have brought lists of names that have been brought to me from people that are relatives or friends that know that or that believe that this individual is being mistreated here in this country, and they want him to be allowed to emigrate to our country. Some are separated families.

One that I met in this, the other day, was born the same time I was. He was born to Russian parents who had moved to America, oh, way back in the early 1900s, and he was born in 1911. And then sometime later, the family moved back to Russia. Now he's grown, has a son. He's an American citizen. But they wanted to go back to America and being denied on the grounds that, well, they can go back to America, but his son married a Russian young lady, and they want to keep her from going back. Well, the whole family said, no, we're not going to leave her alone here. She's a member of the family now. Well, that kind of a case is brought to me personally, so I bring it to the General Secretary. And as I say, I must say, he has been most helpful and most agreeable about correcting these things.

Now, I'm not blaming you; I'm blaming bureaucracy. We have the same type of thing happen in our own country. And every once in a while, somebody has to get the bureaucracy by the neck and shake it loose and say, Stop doing what you're doing. And this is the type of thing and the names that we have brought. And it is a list of names, all of which have been brought to me personally by either relatives or close friends and associates. [*Applause*] Thank you very much. You're all very kind. I thank you very much. And I hope I answered the questions correctly. Nobody asked me what it was going to feel like to not be president anymore. I have some understanding, because after I'd been governor for eight years and then stepped down, I want to tell you what it's like. We'd only been home a few days, and someone invited us out to dinner. Nancy and I both went out, got in the backseat of the car, and waited for somebody to get in front and drive us. [*Laughter*]

[*At this point, Rector Logunov presented the President with a gift.*]

That is beautiful. Thank you very much.

Remarks at a Campaign Rally for Vice President George Bush

SAN DIEGO, CALIFORNIA
NOVEMBER 7, 1988

I traditionally ended my campaigns in San Diego. I ended my campaign for the election of George Bush as president at the same place. I think it was starting to dawn on me that my days as president were disappearing rapidly. This was the last stop of the last campaign that I would ever be a vital part of again. I felt a little like a boxer hanging up his gloves. I think maybe it shows a little.

The President. Thank you very much and good Duke, thank you very much for that kind introduction. I think some thanks should go also to the Coronado High School Band and the Torrey Pines High School Band. And also I understand that some people that played a helping hand in bringing this all together happened to be my fraternity brothers from San Diego State, my fellow TEKEs. Thank you. I was told back there at Eureka College when I became a member of Tau Kappa Epsilon that it was a fraternity for life. But now let me say hello to Earl Cantos;* to Congressmen Duncan Hunter and Bill Lowery; and to a great future congressman we'll all be proud of, Rob Butterfield; and to one of America's greatest governors, George

* Chairman of the San Diego Republican Party.

Deukmejian; and to one of the finest senators I know, Pete Wilson.

Now, before I start, I have a message from my roommate to every young person here. She told me to say: Please, for your parents, for your friends, for your country, but most of all for yourselves, just say no to drugs and alcohol.

The Audience. Just say no! Just say no! Just say no!

The President. All right. You know, some time ago I told Britain's prime minister, Margaret Thatcher, that if her people had come over this ocean out here instead of the Atlantic the capital of the United States would be in California. But more and more over the last eight years, I've come to realize what a good thing it was for the settling of our continent that the pioneers had to go east to west rather than the other way around. After all, if they'd started out here in our beautiful state with all we have, they'd never have wanted to leave. Instead of "Westward Ho!" their motto would have been what mine has become: "There's no place like home."

Now, please forgive me if from time to time over the next few minutes, there seems to be a lump in my throat and a catch in my voice. This is a special moment for me in a special place and yes, with special people. I closed both of my campaigns for the presidency right here in San Diego. And you see, there was a reason for that. You see, when the parades have ended, the shouting is over, the speeches are done, and the final bell has sounded, a fighter wants to return to his corner and be with family and friends while he waits for the verdict of the judges. And whenever I finish in San Diego, I feel I'm with family, and I know I'm with friends. I love San Diego.

A lot of people have been mighty surprised how far you and I have gone together in our crusade over the years. I remember a story that made the rounds the time I first ran for office. Someone told my old boss Jack Warner that I'd announced for governor. And Jack thought about it for just a second, and then he said, "No, Jimmy Stewart for governor; Ronald Reagan for best friend."

But this year my name is not on the ballot. And it won't appear on a ballot ever again, unless, of course, you—

The Audience. Boo!

The President. No, no—unless you count the one that someone up there casts when your time is done and the moment has arrived for His verdict, which, when all is said and done, is the only election that really counts. But if my name isn't on your ballot tomorrow, something more important is: a principle, a legacy. No, this is not the end of an era; it's a time to refresh and strengthen the new beginning we started eight years ago. At stake are the very things you and I have been working for and fighting for ever since we first joined together almost a quarter of a century ago and set out to restore our state and then our nation. They add up to the difference between candidates who promise that come January "the Reagan era is over" and those who say, "Read my lips: No new taxes." Yes, it's the difference between the liberals and the men and women on the Republican ticket, candidates like this district's next congressman, Rob Butterfield; Senator Pete Wilson; and the next president of the United States of America, George Bush.

And that's why I'm here today: to ask you to turn out to vote tomorrow for our entire federal, state, and local Republican ticket so that our principles survive, our legacy endures, and our truth goes marching on. I've dedicated myself this autumn to making sure that all we've begun these past eight years continues. In the House of Representatives, in the Senate, in the White House, and in the state legislatures—which will redraw congressional district lines after the 1990 census, and through that act profoundly shape the course of the entire nation in the next decade—yes, on every level, the election this year is about what the Vice President called the other day the big issues: freedom; peace; opportunity; respect of government for family and community; the safety of law-abiding citizens; and whether we remain true to our national mission of standing with those who, like our Founding Fathers, would battle against tyranny and for liberty. It's about the values that have made America the greatest, freest nation on earth, as Lincoln said, "the last best hope" of humanity. And we're determined to keep it that way.

I've seen some press reports these last few weeks noting how I've been campaigning so hard for Republican candidates. And they say few other presidents have done what I've done. Well, of course, few other presidents have had the opportunity to be succeeded by a man as good as George Bush or to stump for candidates as good as Pete Wilson and Rob Butterfield. But I'll let you in on a little secret: I'm not doing this just for George Bush or Pete Wilson or our Republican candidates on all levels around the nation. I'm doing it for the country, of course, but for someone else as well—actually for two other people.

He was the best storyteller I've ever heard and the strongest man of principle I've ever known. He believed in honesty and hard work. He was filled with a love of justice and a hatred of bigotry. Once he was out on the road—he was a shoe salesman, traveling around northern Illinois in the winter. And this was in the depths of the Depression. And in a midst of a blizzard, he went into a small-town hotel in the town he was going through. And as he signed his name and the clerk saw the name, which was a very Irish name—"Oh," he said, "you're going to love it here." And then he told him why: Because that hotel would not allow people of a certain faith to stay there. And this man picked up his suitcase and said, "Then I don't stay here." And he spent the night in his car in the snow, caught near-pneumonia, and a short time later had the first heart attack of the several that led to his death.

We called him Jack. And just as he was strong, his wife, Nelle, was filled with goodness and love. In the darkest days of the Depression, when they themselves could barely scrape by, no one ever came to their door in need of a meal who Nelle sent away empty-handed. I'm proud of many things I've done in my life, including more than a few in the last eight years; but nothing has ever given me as much satisfaction as when, after several years in California, I could bring my mother and father out here and give them a home, the first they had ever owned.

So, you see, I'm campaigning this year also for them. A son of Jack and Nelle Reagan never walked away from a battle on principle. This year's election is that kind of fight. And by darn, we're going to win it.

Think of all those who depend on us and the principles we Republicans stand for. Young people just getting out of school, looking for their first job, and able to find it because our recovery has created an average of a quarter of a million new jobs each month for the last seventy-one months. Young couples looking for their first home, who can afford it because we've brought mortgage rates down by a third since we took office. Mothers and fathers trying to keep within the family budget— cutting inflation by two-thirds and bringing the top personal income tax rate that most families pay down to 15 percent has made their lives a lot better.

But these aren't the only people who depend on our success. Tomorrow on the plains of Afghanistan and in jungles around the world, freedom fighters will huddle close to their radios, hoping to catch word that the administration in America will remain their friend. In cells across the globe, political prisoners will await anxiously for assurance that America has chosen strength over weakness, because for many of them, our strength is all that keeps their hope alive.

Just on the plane coming out here I read a letter I had just received. It was a couple thanking me for the fact that they are now in the United States after having spent more than seven years in the prisons and psychiatric wards of the Soviet Union. But all these people—they depend on us, and so help me God, we won't let them down.

And there's some other very special people we won't let down, either. There's no change during our administration of which I'm prouder than that our young men and women once more take pride in wearing the uniform of the United States of America. Thanks to their valor, in the last eight years not one square inch of land anywhere in the world has been lost to communism. And in fact, we've rescued one tiny nation, Grenada, from communism.

This year, we're facing a liberal campaign of unusual deception. First our opponents wanted to conceal their ideology. It took us three months to drag the "L" word out of them. [*Laughter*] And now they're trying to hide what side they're on. They say that they're on your side, but you tell me, yes or no, and shout it loud and clear: When their candidates for president, U.S. senator, and Congress refuse to rule out raising your taxes and have already made their marks as world-class big spenders in state or federal government, are they on your side?

The Audience. No!

The President. When their candidates for president and U.S. senator, as well as for Congress and other posts, have a history of nominating and supporting judges who oppose the death penalty and, all in all, are strictly for the birds—if you know what I mean—[*Laughter*]—are they on your side?

The Audience. No!

The President. I like this audience.

The Audience. Reagan! Reagan! Reagan!

The President. Thank you. Wait a minute, I've got one more. I like this audience, I said, but one last question.

Audience member. We love you!

The President. When their candidates consistently support cutting back on the very weapons—including our Strategic Defense Initiative, SDI—that have forced the Soviets to seek to negotiate serious arms reductions with us, and when they seem to believe that a strong defense is what gets talked about in Right Guard commercials—[*Laughter*]—and that a strong Navy is the color of a suit—[*Laughter*]—when they do all this, are they on your side?

The Audience. No!

The President. Our liberal friends just never seem to learn: You can't be for big government, big taxes, and big bureaucracy and still be for the little guy. In the race for the White House only one guy is for the little guy, and that guy is George Bush. And in the Senate race, that guy is Pete Wilson. In this district, in the House of Representatives, it's Rob Butterfield. And in the state legislature, it's Byron Wear, Steve Baldwin, Carol Bentley, and our other great Republican candidates.

Yes, from top to bottom, the election this year is a referendum on liberalism. Do we want to risk going back to the old, failed liberal policies of the past?

The Audience. No!

The President. Or do we build on the successes of the present—

The Audience. Yes!

The President. —to expand the chances of peace and prosperity in the future?

Consider for a moment the people you'll be sending to Washington tomorrow. Congress and the president are equal branches of government. When you vote for the Senate or for your local congressional seat, you're voting for the direction of the country and the world as much as when you vote for president. And since we have to ride two horses, Congress and the president, across every stream, shouldn't they both be going in the same direction? [*Applause*] Everyone on our ticket—led by George Bush, Pete Wilson and Rob Butterfield—is going the same way. And come to think of it, that's my way, too.

Take our great senator and, I hope, our next great senator as well, Pete Wilson. Pete Wilson, George Bush, and I have been a team: The Three Musketeers—one for all and all for the taxpayers and against the special interests. Now, you know, in Washington, Pete's been named "Watchdog of the Treasury" —five times he's been named that. He's guarding it against liberals like his opponent. He'll work with the new president and not try to cut him off at the knees every chance he gets. Nancy and I cast our absentee ballots last week. And I know I shouldn't tell you this, but we voted, and I hope you will, too, for a great team: Pete Wilson and the entire Republican team.

Last week a major national newspaper ran a story about one of our own liberal California congressmen. In it, he spelled out to the reporter how he tells constituents he's for a strong defense, while voting for less defense, and how he opposed the death penalty amendment to the drug bill, but says he's for the death penalty when he's back home. And then he got down to business. Quoting now, "He wants it understood that a President Bush would get no quarter from him. Any budget proposal will have to include higher taxes, he says, whether a president likes it or not. 'Otherwise, we're going to go after him.' " Well, if you ask me, it's time we went after them, and some of the people to do it are Bill Lowery, Ron Packard, Duncan Hunter, and Rob Butterfield.

We must not forget what we're up against, but we all must never forget what we're for. A poet once wrote: "I have fallen in love with American names," and Americans love no name better than the name of "freedom." Well, in this campaign, and so many others, I've heard America singing, and its song is "freedom." You can hear it in the shipyards near here, as men and women go to work. You can hear it in offices, factories, schools, and stores all over our land. You can hear it when a young man or woman dreams of striking out alone and becoming part of the great boom in entrepreneurship that has created virtually all of the new jobs in America in recent years: 84—or 80.4 million new jobs in these several years. You can hear it in the prayers from every church, synagogue, temple, and mosque in our land. Yes, "one nation, under God, indivisible"—all in the name of glorious freedom.

You know, some years ago two friends of mine were talking with a Cuban refugee who had escaped from Castro. In the midst of the tale of horrible experiences, one friend turned to the other and said, "We don't know how lucky we are." And the Cuban stopped and said, "How lucky you are? I had someplace to escape to." Well, let's keep it that way.

How sacred is our trust—we to whom God has given the

custody of the name and the song of "freedom." America represents something universal in the human spirit. I received a letter not long ago from a man who said, "You can go to Japan to live, but you cannot become Japanese. You can go to France, and you'd live and not become a Frenchman. You can go to live in Germany or Turkey, and you won't become a German or a Turk." But then he added, "Anybody from any corner of the world can come to America to live and become an American."

John Adams once said that "the way to secure liberty is to place it in the people's hands. . . ." And that's what America is: we, the people, holding liberty in our hands. This year I did something I thought that no American president would ever have an opportunity to do. There in the Lenin Hills, at Moscow State University—no TEKE chapter there—[*Laughter*]—I addressed Soviet students, spoke to them, and my speech was about the wonder and glory of human and individual freedom. Now, think of those students. Only if they're very lucky and rise high in the Communist Party will any one of them ever have the influence that each American has just by walking into the voting booth.

So, let me ask you one or two more questions. And I'm asking for a commitment, so if you shout yes, be sure you mean it.

Tomorrow, will you show up at the polls and vote?

The Audience. Yes!

The President. Will you get your friends and neighbors also to vote?

The Audience. Yes!

The President. For the state legislature, will you vote for Byron Wear, Steve Baldwin, Carol Bentley, and the entire Republican team?

The Audience. Yes!

The President. Will you vote to reelect Congressmen Bill Lowery, Ron Packard, and Duncan Hunter and to elect Rob Butterfield?

The Audience. Yes!

The President. And will you vote for Pete Wilson in the United States Senate?

The Audience. Yes!

The President. And will you make George Bush the next president of the United States of America?

The Audience. Yes! Bush! Bush! Bush!

The President. The same thing I'm asking you I've asked our country this year. Eight years ago, America said it's time for a change. Well, we've heard some talk like that in this campaign. Well, we are the change. Won't you stand by the change? We started it eight years ago. Stand by the Republican ticket, and I don't mind if you stand by me.

So, now we come to the end of this last campaign, and I just hope that Nelle and Jack are looking down on us right now and nodding their heads and saying their kid did them proud. And I hope that someday your children and grandchildren will tell of the time that a certain president came to town at the end of a long journey and asked their parents and grandparents to join him in setting America on the course to the new millennium, and that a century of peace, prosperity, opportunity, and hope had followed. So, if I could ask you just one last time. Tomorrow, when mountains greet the dawn, would you go out there and win one for the Gipper?

Thank you, and God bless you all.

Tribute to Mrs. Reagan

REPUBLICAN NATIONAL CONVENTION
NEW ORLEANS, LOUISIANA
AUGUST 15, 1988

At the Republican Convention in 1988, my daughter Maureen organized a lunch in honor of Nancy in order to raise money for Nancy's campaign against drug abuse.

We have a drug crisis in this country that has been building for years. It started with the permissive attitudes toward drugs in the sixties and seventies. I think more than anyone else in this country Nancy helped change the United States's attitude toward drugs. She helped educate an entire nation. She warned of the destructiveness of drugs way back in the early eighties when comedians were still joking about the pleasures of getting high. She foretold the consequences of drugs when many Americans considered drug use a matter of personal choice.

I think history will prove her to be one of the most farsighted first ladies this nation has ever had.

It's a wonderful feeling to be so proud of the person you love. I tried to put a few of these sentiments into words at this tribute.

Mrs. Reagan. Well, wait till I tell my husband about this. [*Laughter*] Maureen, you really did surprise me—everything. I was told that this was going to be a surprise luncheon. I was not to ask any questions, which I didn't, so that I never knew what exactly was going to happen. But really, I do thank you. Thank you. And I want to thank Rich Little, my good friend, and Barbara Cook, who was so wonderful and sang my favorite song, and everybody who spoke up here so nicely about me. I appreciate it so much. And all these wonderful kids—I mean, you were the topping on the cake. And the contribution, of course, was—I never, never expected—the whole thing has been a big, big surprise.

Well, now, if I can come down to earth for a minute here. You know, obviously, this convention is a very warm and nostalgic one for my husband and me. We can't help but think of previous conventions and all the remarkable people that we've met over the years. So many memories come flooding back: Kansas City, Detroit, Dallas. The Republican Party has given Ronnie and me eight of the most wonderful years we ever had. Of course, sometimes they were a little bit frustrating and a little bit frightening, but they were wonderful. So, I'd like to express our thanks to you for giving us those years.

But you know, there are cycles and rhythms to life. There are times to enter, times to stay, and times to leave. And today the curtain begins to close on the Reagan era of the Republican Party. We've had a wonderful run. But the time has come for the Bushes to step into the political leading roles, and for the Reagans to step into the wings. And that's as it should be.

During our two terms together, George and Bar have been totally supportive and helpful and gracious. And they have our gratitude and affection. My husband couldn't have selected a better vice president than George Bush. He's a man of integrity and conscience and loyalty—qualities that aren't always in great abundance in Washington. And I know I couldn't have found a warmer, more considerate, more caring counterpart than Barbara Bush. And I think she'll make a remarkable First Lady.

So, I want to thank George and Bar for that letter that they sent also. And I want to thank all of you here and so many others who aren't here, who have stood by us over these past eight years. I can't tell you how important it is to know that you have friends. So, to my friends, I say a very heartfelt thank you. Thank you very much.

Maureen Reagan. We have one more surprise for you. It wouldn't be complete to pay a tribute to the First Lady of the United States without the real leader of the Republican Party, President Ronald Reagan.

The President. I came over on such short notice that I haven't had a chance to read my remarks yet. [*Laughter*] But the speechwriters usually do a pretty good job, so I'll just begin.

I've known the guest of honor for many years. [*Laughter*] Well, yes, that's true. [*Laughter*] She was once one of the original members of the Reagan inner circle—[*Laughter*]—well, I can't dispute that—[*Laughter*]—who's been involved in some of the most delicate White House matters, such as high-level staff—maybe I better do this by myself. [*Laughter*]

In fact, I've been thinking for several days about what exactly I wanted to say today and how to put Nancy's role in my life in perspective for you. But what do you say about someone who gives your life meaning? What do you say about someone who's always there with support and understanding, someone who makes sacrifices so that your life will be easier and more successful? Well, what you say is that you love that person and treasure her. I simply can't imagine the last eight years without Nancy. The presidency wouldn't have been the joy it's been for me without her there beside me. And that second-floor living quarters in the White House would have seemed a big and lonely spot without her waiting for me every day at the end of the day. You know, she once said that a president has all kinds of advisers and experts who look after his interests when it comes to foreign policy or the economy or whatever, but no one who looks after his needs as a human being. Well, Nancy has done that for me through recuperations and crises. Every president should be so lucky.

I think it's all too common in marriages that, no matter how much partners love each other, they don't thank each other enough. And I suppose I don't thank Nancy enough for all that she does for me. So, Nancy, in front of all your friends here today, let me say, thank you for all you do. Thank you for your love. And thank you for just being you.

Mrs. Reagan. Oh, dear!

The President. You going to puddle up?

Mrs. Reagan. Yes.

1989

Farewell Address to the Nation

OVAL OFFICE
JANUARY 11, 1989

Before I say my formal good-bye, maybe I should tell you what I'm up to now that I'm out of office. Well, I'm still giving speeches, still sounding off about those things I didn't get accomplished while I was president.

High on my agenda are three things. First, I'm out there stumping to help future presidents—Republican or Democrat —get the tools they need to bring the budget under control. And those tools are a line-item veto and a constitutional amendment to balance the budget. Second, I'm out there talking up the need to do something about political gerrymandering. This is the practice of rigging the boundaries of congressional districts. It is the greatest single blot on the integrity of our nation's electoral system, and it's high time we did something about it. And third, I'm talking up the idea of repealing the Twenty-second Amendment to the Constitution, the amendment that prevents a president from serving more than two terms. I believe it's a preemption of the people's right to vote for whomever they want as many times as they want.

So I'm back where I came in—out there on the mashed potato circuit. I have a feeling I'll be giving speeches until I'm called to the great beyond and maybe even after. All it will take is for St. Peter to say, "Ronald Wilson Reagan, what do you have to say for yourself? Speak up."

"Well, sir, unaccustomed as I am . . ."

My FELLOW AMERICANS:

This is the thirty-fourth time I'll speak to you from the Oval Office and the last. We've been together eight years now, and soon it'll be time for me to go. But before I do, I wanted to share some thoughts, some of which I've been saving for a long time.

It's been the honor of my life to be your president. So many of you have written the past few weeks to say thanks, but I could say as much to you. Nancy and I are grateful for the opportunity you gave us to serve.

One of the things about the presidency is that you're always somewhat apart. You spend a lot of time going by too fast in a car someone else is driving, and seeing the people through tinted glass—the parents holding up a child, and the wave you saw too late and couldn't return. And so many times I wanted to stop and reach out from behind the glass, and connect. Well, maybe I can do a little of that tonight.

People ask how I feel about leaving. And the fact is, "parting is such sweet sorrow." The sweet part is California, and the ranch and freedom. The sorrow—the good-byes, of course, and leaving this beautiful place.

You know, down the hall and up the stairs from this office is the part of the White House where the president and his family live. There are a few favorite windows I have up there that I like to stand and look out of early in the morning. The view is over the grounds here to the Washington Monument, and then the Mall and the Jefferson Memorial. But on mornings when the humidity is low, you can see past the Jefferson to the river, the Potomac, and the Virginia shore. Someone said that's the view Lincoln had when he saw the smoke rising from the Battle of Bull Run. I see more prosaic things: the grass on the banks, the morning traffic as people make their way to work, now and then a sailboat on the river.

I've been thinking a bit at that window. I've been reflecting on what the past eight years have meant and mean. And the image that comes to mind like a refrain is a nautical one—a small story about a big ship, and a refugee and a sailor. It was back in the early eighties, at the height of the boat people. And the sailor was hard at work on the carrier *Midway,* which was patrolling the South China Sea. The sailor, like most American servicemen, was young, smart, and fiercely observant. The crew spied on the horizon a leaky little boat. And crammed inside were refugees from Indochina hoping to get to America. The *Midway* sent a small launch to bring them to the ship and safety. As the refugees made their way through the choppy seas, one spied the sailor on deck and stood up and called out to him. He yelled, "Hello, American sailor. Hello, freedom man."

A small moment with a big meaning, a moment the sailor, who wrote it in a letter, couldn't get out of his mind. And when I saw it, neither could I. Because that's what it was to be an American in the 1980s. We stood, again, for freedom. I know we always have, but in the past few years the world again, and in a way, we ourselves—rediscovered it.

It's been quite a journey this decade, and we held together through some stormy seas. And at the end, together, we are reaching our destination.

The fact is, from Grenada to the Washington and Moscow summits, from the recession of '81 to '82, to the expansion that began in late '82 and continues to this day, we've made a difference. The way I see it, there were two great triumphs, two things that I'm proudest of. One is the economic recovery, in which the people of America created—and filled—19 million new jobs. The other is the recovery of our morale. America is respected again in the world and looked to for leadership.

Something that happened to me a few years ago reflects some of this. It was back in 1981, and I was attending my first big economic summit, which was held that year in Canada. The meeting place rotates among the member countries. The opening meeting was a formal dinner for the heads of government of the seven industrialized nations. Now, I sat there like the new kid in school and listened, and it was all François this and

Helmut that. They dropped titles and spoke to one another on a first-name basis. Well, at one point I sort of leaned in and said, "My name's Ron." Well, in that same year, we began the actions we felt would ignite an economic comeback—cut taxes and regulation, started to cut spending. And soon the recovery began.

Two years later another economic summit, with pretty much the same cast. At the big opening meeting we all got together, and all of a sudden, just for a moment, I saw that everyone was just sitting there looking at me. And then one of them broke the silence. "Tell us about the American miracle," he said.

Well, back in 1980, when I was running for president, it was all so different. Some pundits said our programs would result in catastrophe. Our views on foreign affairs would cause war. Our plans for the economy would cause inflation to soar and bring about economic collapse. I even remember one highly respected economist saying, back in 1982, that "the engines of economic growth have shut down here, and they're likely to stay that way for years to come." Well, he and the other opinion leaders were wrong. The fact is, what they called "radical" was really "right." What they called "dangerous" was just "desperately needed."

And in all of that time I won a nickname, "The Great Communicator." But I never thought it was my style or the words I used that made a difference: It was the content. I wasn't a great communicator, but I communicated great things, and they didn't spring full bloom from my brow, they came from the heart of a great nation—from our experience, our wisdom, and our belief in the principles that have guided us for two centuries. They called it the Reagan revolution. Well, I'll accept that, but for me it always seemed more like the great rediscovery, a rediscovery of our values and our common sense.

Common sense told us that when you put a big tax on something, the people will produce less of it. So, we cut the people's tax rates, and the people produced more than ever before. The economy bloomed like a plant that had been cut back and could now grow quicker and stronger. Our economic program brought about the longest peacetime expansion in our history: real family income up, the poverty rate down, entrepreneurship booming, and an explosion in research and new technology. We're exporting more than ever because American industry became more competitive and at the same time, we summoned the national will to knock down protectionist walls abroad instead of erecting them at home. Common sense also told us that to preserve the peace, we'd have to become strong again after years of weakness and confusion. So, we rebuilt our defenses, and this New Year we toasted the new peacefulness around the globe. Not only have the superpowers actually begun to reduce their stockpiles of nuclear weapons—and hope for even more progress is bright—but the regional conflicts that rack the globe are also beginning to cease. The Persian Gulf is no longer a war zone. The Soviets are leaving Afghanistan. The Vietnamese are preparing to pull out of Cambodia, and an American-mediated accord will soon send 50,000 Cuban troops home from Angola.

The lesson of all this was, of course, that because we're a great nation, our challenges seem complex. It will always be this way. But as long as we remember our first principles and believe in ourselves, the future will always be ours. And something else we learned: Once you begin a great movement, there's no telling where it will end. We meant to change a nation, and instead, we changed a world.

Countries across the globe are turning to free markets and free speech and turning away from the ideologies of the past. For them, the great rediscovery of the 1980s has been that, lo and behold, the moral way of government is the practical way of government: Democracy, the profoundly good, is also the profoundly productive.

When you've got to the point when you can celebrate the anniversaries of your thirty-ninth birthday, you can sit back sometimes, review your life, and see it flowing before you. For me there was a fork in the river, and it was right in the middle of my life. I never meant to go into politics. It wasn't my intention when I was young. But I was raised to believe you had to pay your way for the blessings bestowed on you. I was happy with my career in the entertainment world, but I ultimately went into politics because I wanted to protect something precious.

Ours was the first revolution in the history of mankind that truly reversed the course of government, and with three little words: "We the people." "We the people" tell the government what to do, it doesn't tell us. "We the people" are the driver, the government is the car. And we decide where it should go, and by what route, and how fast. Almost all the world's constitutions are documents in which governments tell the people what their privileges are. Our Constitution is a document in which "We the people" tell the government what it is allowed to do. "We the people" are free. This belief has been the underlying basis for everything I've tried to do these past eight years.

But back in the 1960s, when I began, it seemed to me that we'd begun reversing the order of things—that through more and more rules and regulations and confiscatory taxes, the government was taking more of our money, more of our options, and more of our freedom. I went into politics in part to put up my hand and say, "Stop." I was a citizen politician, and it seemed the right thing for a citizen to do.

I think we have stopped a lot of what needed stopping. And I hope we have once again reminded people that man is not free unless government is limited. There's a clear cause and effect here that is as neat and predictable as a law of physics: As government expands, liberty contracts.

Nothing is less free than pure communism, and yet we have, the past few years, forged a satisfying new closeness with the Soviet Union. I've been asked if this isn't a gamble, and my answer is no because we're basing our actions not on words but deeds. The détente of the 1970s was based not on actions but promises. They'd promise to treat their own people and the people of the world better. But the gulag was still the gulag, and the state was still expansionist, and they still waged proxy wars in Africa, Asia, and Latin America.

Well, this time, so far, it's different. President Gorbachev has brought about some internal democratic reforms and begun the withdrawal from Afghanistan. He has also freed prisoners whose names I've given him every time we've met.

But life has a way of reminding you of big things through small incidents. Once, during the heady days of the Moscow summit, Nancy and I decided to break off from the entourage one afternoon to visit the shops on Arbat Street—that's a little street just off Moscow's main shopping area. Even though our visit was a surprise, every Russian there immediately recognized us and called out our names and reached for our hands. We were just about swept away by the warmth. You could almost feel the possibilities in all that joy. But within seconds, a KGB detail pushed their way toward us and began pushing and shoving the people in the crowd. It was an interesting moment. It reminded me that while the man on the street in the Soviet Union yearns for peace, the government is Communist. And those who run it are Communists, and that means we and they view such issues as freedom and human rights very differently.

We must keep up our guard, but we must also continue to work together to lessen and eliminate tension and mistrust. My view is that President Gorbachev is different from previous Soviet leaders. I think he knows some of the things wrong with his society and is trying to fix them. We wish him well. And we'll continue to work to make sure that the Soviet Union that eventually emerges from this process is a less threatening one. What it all boils down to is this. I want the new closeness to continue. And it will, as long as we make it clear that we will continue to act in a certain way as long as they continue to act in a helpful manner. If and when they don't, at first pull your punches. If they persist, pull the plug. It's still trust but verify. It's still play, but cut the cards. It's still watch closely. And don't be afraid to see what you see.

I've been asked if I have any regrets. Well, I do. The deficit is one. I've been talking a great deal about that lately, but tonight isn't for arguments. And I'm going to hold my tongue. But an observation: I've had my share of victories in the Congress, but what few people noticed is that I never won anything you didn't win for me. They never saw my troops, they never saw Reagan's regiments, the American people. You won every battle with every call you made and letter you wrote demanding action. Well, action is still needed. If we're to finish the job, Reagan's regiments will have to become the Bush brigades. Soon he'll be the chief, and he'll need you every bit as much as I did.

Finally, there is a great tradition of warnings in presidential farewells, and I've got one that's been on my mind for some time. But oddly enough it starts with one of the things I'm proudest of in the past eight years: the resurgence of national pride that I called the new patriotism. This national feeling is good, but it won't count for much, and it won't last unless it's grounded in thoughtfulness and knowledge.

An informed patriotism is what we want. And are we doing a good enough job teaching our children what America is and what she represents in the long history of the world? Those of us who are over thirty-five or so years of age grew up in a different America. We were taught, very directly, what it means to be an American. And we absorbed, almost in the air, a love of country and an appreciation of its institutions. If you didn't get these things from your family, you got them from the neighborhood, from the father down the street who fought in Korea or the family who lost someone at Anzio. Or you could get a sense of patriotism from school. And if all else failed, you could get a sense of patriotism from the popular culture. The movies celebrated democratic values and implicitly reinforced the idea that America was special. TV was like that, too, through the midsixties.

But now, we're about to enter the nineties, and some things have changed. Younger parents aren't sure that an unambivalent appreciation of America is the right thing to teach modern children. And as for those who create the popular culture, well-grounded patriotism is no longer the style. Our spirit is back, but we haven't reinstitutionalized it. We've got to do a better job of getting across that America is freedom—freedom of speech, freedom of religion, freedom of enterprise. And freedom is special and rare. It's fragile; it needs production [*protection*].

So, we've got to teach history based not on what's in fashion but what's important: Why the Pilgrims came here, who Jimmy Doolittle was, and what those thirty seconds over Tokyo meant. You know, four years ago on the fortieth anniversary of D day, I read a letter from a young woman writing of her late father, who'd fought on Omaha Beach. Her name was Lisa Zanatta Henn, and she said, "we will always remember, we will never forget what the boys of Normandy did." Well, let's help her keep her word. If we forget what we did, we won't know who we are. I'm warning of an eradication of the American memory that could result, ultimately, in an erosion of the American spirit. Let's start with some basics: more attention to American history and a greater emphasis on civic ritual. And let me offer lesson number one about America: All great change in America begins at the dinner table. So, tomorrow night in the kitchen I hope the talking begins. And children, if your parents haven't been teaching you what it means to be an American, let 'em know and nail 'em on it. That would be a very American thing to do.

And that's about all I have to say tonight. Except for one thing. The past few days when I've been at that window upstairs, I've thought a bit of the "shining city upon a hill." The phrase comes from John Winthrop, who wrote it to describe the America he imagined. What he imagined was important because he was an early Pilgrim, an early freedom man. He journeyed here on what today we'd call a little wooden boat; and like the other Pilgrims, he was looking for a home that would be free.

I've spoken of the shining city all my political life, but I don't know if I ever quite communicated what I saw when I said it. But in my mind it was a tall proud city built on rocks stronger than oceans, wind-swept, God-blessed, and teeming with people of all kinds living in harmony and peace, a city with free ports that hummed with commerce and creativity, and if there had to be city walls, the walls had doors and the doors were open to anyone with the will and the heart to get here. That's how I saw it, and see it still.

And how stands the city on this winter night? More prosperous, more secure, and happier than it was eight years ago. But more than that; after two hundred years, two centuries, she still stands strong and true on the granite ridge, and her glow has held steady no matter what storm. And she's still a beacon, still a magnet for all who must have freedom, for all the pilgrims from all the lost places who are hurtling through the darkness, toward home.

We've done our part. And as I walk off into the city streets, a final word to the men and women of the Reagan revolution, the men and women across America who for eight years did the work that brought America back. My friends: We did it. We weren't just marking time. We made a difference. We made the city stronger. We made the city freer, and we left her in good hands. All in all, not bad, not bad at all.

And so, good-bye, God bless you, and God bless the United States of America.

The Wit and Wisdom of Ronald Reagan

SELECTED BY THE EDITORS

"You know, Senator Kennedy was at a dinner just recently, the ninetieth birthday party for former governor and ambassador Averell Harriman. Teddy Kennedy said that Averell's age was only half as old as Ronald Reagan's ideas. And you know, he's absolutely right. The Constitution is almost two hundred years old, and that's where I get my ideas."

—November 13, 1981

"Since I came to the White House, I've gotten two hearing aids, had a colon operation, a prostate operation, skin cancer, and I've been shot . . . damn thing is, I never felt better."

—March 28, 1987

"Government does not solve problems; it subsidizes them."

—December 11, 1972

"Many governments oppress their people and abuse human rights . . . I have one question for those rulers: If communism is the wave of the future, why do you still need walls to keep people in and armies of secret police to keep them quiet?"

—July 19, 1983

"Well, I know this. I've laid down the law, though, to everyone from now on about anything that happens: no matter what time it is, wake me . . . even if it's in the middle of a cabinet meeting."

—*April 13, 1984*

"And that, in my view, is what the whole controversy comes down to. Are you entitled to the fruits of your own labor or does government have some presumptive right to spend and spend and spend?"

—*July 27, 1981*

"It's true hard work never killed anybody, but I figure, why take the chance?"

—*March 28, 1987*

"And to every person trapped in tyranny . . . our message must be: Your struggle is our struggle, your dream is our dream, and someday, you, too, will be free."

—*July 19, 1983*

"History's no easy subject. Even in my day it wasn't, and we had so much less of it to learn then."

—*September 10, 1987*

"All of these men were different, but they shared this in common: They loved America very much. There was nothing they wouldn't do for her. And they loved with the sureness of the young."

—*Arlington Cemetery, May 25, 1986*

"These last weeks have really been hectic what with Libya, Nicaragua, and the budget and taxes. I don't know about you, but I've been working long hours. I've really been burning the midday oil."

—*April 17, 1986*

"In this two-hundredth anniversary year of our Constitution, you and I stand on the shoulders of giants—men whose words and deeds put wind in the sails of freedom . . . We will be guided tonight by their acts, and we will be guided forever by their words."

—*January 27, 1987*

"I couldn't play baseball because I couldn't see good enough. That's why I turned to football. The ball was bigger, and so were the fellows."

—*June 22, 1981*

"The future belongs to the free."

—*May 6, 1985*

"I heard one presidential candidate say that what this country needed was a president for the nineties. I was set to run again. I thought he said a president *in* his nineties."

—*April 28, 1987*

"Are you better off today than you were four years ago?"

—*1980 campaign*

"Sometimes when I'm faced with an unbeliever, an atheist, I am tempted to invite him to the greatest gourmet dinner that one could ever serve, and when we finished eating that magnificent dinner, to ask him if he believes there's a cook."

—*May 30, 1988*

"If I'm ever in need of any transplants, I've got parts they don't make anymore."

—*February 10, 1986*

"To those who are fainthearted and unsure, I have this message: If you're afraid of the future, then get out of the way, stand aside. The people of this country are ready to move again."

—*September 29, 1982*

"Recession is when your neighbor loses his job. Depression is when you lose yours. And recovery is when Jimmy Carter loses his."

—*1980 campaign*

"We've polished up the American dream."

—*July 8, 1987*

"Sometimes, I can't help but feel the First Amendment is being turned on its head. Because ask yourselves: Can it really be true that the First Amendment can permit Nazis and Ku Klux Klansmen to march on public property, advocate the extermination of people of the Jewish faith and the subjugation of blacks, while the same amendment forbids our children from saying a prayer in school?"

—*February 25, 1984*

"The other day the *Washington Post* ran a story heralding the return of spring, and I thought it was just another one of the reports on the political campaign. The headline said, 'The Sap is Running Again.' "

—*April 13, 1984*

"Nations crumble from within when the citizenry asks of government those things which the citizenry might better provide for itself."

—*April 7, 1975*

"We should end those negotiations on giving away the Panama Canal and tell General Torrijos—we bought it, we paid for it, we built it, and we're going to keep it."

—*1976 Republican primary campaign*

"History will ask and our answer will determine the fate of freedom for a thousand years. Did a nation born of hope lose hope? Did a people forged by courage find courage wanting? Did a generation steeled by hard war and a harsh peace forsake honor at the moment of great climactic struggle for the human spirit?"

—*May 17, 1981*

"With the Iran thing occupying everyone's attention, I was thinking: Do you remember the flap when I said, 'We begin bombing in five minutes'? Remember when I fell asleep during my audience with the Pope? Remember Bitburg? . . . Boy, those were the good old days."

—*March 28, 1987*

"At my age I didn't go to Washington to play politics as usual."

—*October 29, 1982*

"We are with you, Germany; you are not alone."

—*June 9, 1982*

"If the Soviet Union let another political party come into existence, they would still be a one-party state, because everybody would join the other party."

—*June 23, 1983*

"My young friends, history is a river that may take us as it will. But we have the power to navigate, to choose direction, and make our passage together."

—*April 30, 1984*

"Somebody asked me one day why we didn't put a stop to Sam's [correspondent Sam Donaldson] shouting questions at us when we're out on the South Lawn. We can't. If we did, the starlings would come back."

—*May 18, 1983*

"I will not exploit my opponent's youth and inexperience."

—*when asked in the 1984 presidential debate with Walter Mondale about the age issue*

"The federal government has taken too much tax money from the people, too much authority from the states, and too much liberty with the Constitution."

—*February 9, 1982*

"A friend of mine was asked to a costume ball a short time ago. He slapped some egg on his face and went as a liberal economist."

—*February 11, 1988*

"We have to keep in mind we are a nation under God, and if we ever forget that, we'll be just a nation under."

—*May 23, 1983*

"How can the leadership of the other side, as they did last week, open each session of their great convention with an injunction to the Lord, and end each session with a prayer to God, and still insist on denying that right to a child in a public school?"

—*July 26, 1984*

"Seventy-five years ago I was born in Tampico, Illinois, in a little flat above the bank building. We didn't have any other contact with the bank than that."

—*February 6, 1986*

"We were poor when I was young, but the difference then was that the government didn't come around telling you you were poor."

—*July 6, 1986*

"My whole family were Democrats. As a matter of fact, I had an uncle who won a medal once for never having missed voting in an election for fifteen years . . . and he'd been dead for fourteen."

—*August 9, 1973*

"Please tell me you're Republicans."

—*to doctors preparing to operate following the assassination attempt, March 30, 1981*

"I let football and other extracurricular activities eat into my study time with the result that my grade average was closer to the C level required for eligibility than it was to straight A's. And even now I wonder what I might have accomplished if I'd studied harder."

—*May 9, 1982*

"The West won't contain communism, it will transcend communism."

—*May 17, 1981*

"Freedom should be the right to be stupid if you want to be."

—*February 13, 1973*

"The American people weren't put on this earth to become managers of decline."

—*November 16, 1982*

"Heroes may not be braver than anyone else. They're just braver five minutes longer."

—*December 22, 1982*

"And I also remember something that Thomas Jefferson once said: 'We should never judge a president by his age, only by his works.' And ever since he told me that . . .'"

—*February 6, 1984*

"We cannot play innocents abroad in a world that is not innocent."

—*February 6, 1985*

"What our critics really believe is that those in Washington know better how to spend your money than you, the people, do. But we're not going to let them do it, period."

—*June 30, 1982*

"If the federal government had been around when the Creator was putting His hand to this state, Indiana wouldn't be here. It'd still be waiting for an environmental impact statement."

—*February 9, 1982*

"The best view of big government is in the rearview mirror as you're driving away from it."

—*March 24, 1982*

"You know, I keep remembering there would always be a picture of a president standing in the Oval Office looking out the window—usually the picture was from behind. And he's standing there, and then his words are quoted as a tag for the picture about this is the loneliest place and so forth. I don't know about them. I haven't been lonely one minute."

—*farewell to the White House staff, January 18, 1989*

Index